WARRIOR

~ OF ~

MIST

WARRIOR ~ OF ~ MIST

Mists of Redemption ~ Book 1

M. L. REID

To Mom, who has been my creative companion all my life.

*And to Josh, for always supporting me and never complaining
about my odd writing hours.*

This is a work of fiction. Names, characters, places, and incidents are either products of the author's imagination or used fictitiously. Any resemblance to actual events, locales, or persons, living, dead, or undead, is entirely coincidental.

Cover design by Podium Publishing

ISBN: 978-1-0394-3022-8

Published in 2023 by Podium Publishing, ULC
www.podiumaudio.com

WARRIOR

~ OF ~

MIST

CHAPTER 1

I was pretty sure this was how it felt to stand on top of a platform looking down at a tiny river below, knowing that the only thing keeping me alive was a bungee cord tied to my feet. Granted, I wasn't actually bungee jumping, but right now, that might have been less scary. And I wasn't the only one feeling like this, judging by the expressions of all the kids around me.

Yesterday, me and the other seventeen-year-olds graduated from school. Today, we would learn if we were either going on to higher learning with the rest of the humans or joining the ranks of the Hunters on the other side of the Wall.

"Ah, Jynn, I'm so nervous," Marcie said, standing in line ahead of me. She shifted and looked back. "I knew I shouldn't have eaten breakfast. My stomach's all cramped up."

I forced a smile and patted her back. It wasn't like I was much better. "I didn't think you'd be so nervous. You don't have any Hunters in your family. Do you really think you'll be one?"

She moaned and massaged her stomach. "No, but it's not like they can go back over twenty years to check, right?"

It was true; there wasn't a way. When my parents were growing up, magic was a myth. Then, twenty years ago, the Gates to another dimension appeared, and Earth and the humans inhabiting it changed.

I bit my lips and looked to my right, toward the Wall. Red bricked and ten feet high, it stretched out, cutting the city in half. People had been angry when it was first built. Families were torn apart—parents taken from their children, brothers and sisters separated, married couples split apart. But as harsh as it sounded, there was a solid reason. This side of the Wall was Garden City, where normal humans and everyone younger than seventeen lived. On the other side was Eden, where the Hunters—enhanced humans—resided.

Even more importantly, it was where the Gate was.

The Gate's huge black arch loomed over the buildings in the distance. To the naked eye, there was nothing beyond the Gate. It was just a black, seemingly two-dimensional hole. One which spilled out wave upon wave of monsters—*man-eating* monsters that killed (or attacked) everything that moved—if the Hunters didn't keep them under control, coming out and killing everything that moved.

Scientists theorized that humans developed into Hunters because of the Gates; that it was Earth's way to defend itself, to evolve its already most-advanced species. When the Gates first appeared in each major country on Earth, random people across the globe started to Awaken with magical or enhanced powers, regardless of their age. Now, the most common age to Awaken was seventeen, so children have mandatory school until they graduate, then we're all tested.

Ironically, the Wall which surrounded Eden wasn't to keep the Hunters and monsters in. It was actually to keep the crazy humans out.

There were treasures and energy crystals in the Gate, so Hunters were generally pretty rich. The stronger the Hunter, the wealthier they became, but even an E-rank Hunter, the weakest rank available, still had a free ride in life as long as they brought enough energy crystals back. But a normal human with a normal weapon was nothing but dead on the other side of that Wall. Even Hunters had a high mortality rate, which was why they were paid so well.

My dad had lost his life in there ten years ago.

Everyone knew there were hundreds of Hunter deaths a year, but that didn't stop the greed-hungry expressions of the kids around me. They stared at the platform ahead with open desire, dreams of being the next S-rank Hunter written all over their faces. In the entire US, there were only twenty-four of them. S rankers were the gods of the Hunter world; the strongest of the strong, they could level cities with one fire blast or punch. It'd been more than a year since the last one was announced, so the country was ready for another megastar to be added to their roster.

On top of the platform was a giant glass ball, taller than the two Hunters manning it. Every eye—from the students, the family members on portable rafters around the square, and the random watchers in the side crowds—was glued to that ball, waiting to see if it reacted when a boy or girl put their hand on it. If it lit up at all, whether it was red for mage or blue for melee, the person was ushered toward the Wall. The brighter it lit up, the higher the person's rank was. I heard that when the last S rank was found, the ball glowed so bright it made the sun dim. If the ball didn't react at all, the kid was normal. Shoo, go be normal.

Even as I watched, a kid walked up and laid his hand against it. Almost instantly, a glowing red stain appeared in the middle of the glass and spread until it filled the entire orb like a red light bulb.

The people crowded around the edge of the square cheered. Out of the two thousand or so students who had been tested so far, he was the six hundred and thirty-sixth newest Hunter to be found in Garden City. The kid puffed out his chest and strutted to the right side of the platform where a Hunter waited for him.

"Why didn't we get farther back in the line, Jynn?" Marcie muttered her question.

My brows wrinkled as I looked around. "We did line up in the back, remember?" As it was, there were only a couple hundred kids behind us now. It was just that many kids had already been tested.

I couldn't help but glance up into the rafters where the crowd sat. On the right side, my family watched me. I wanted to look at them, but at the same time, I couldn't seem to bring myself to do it. My stomach twisted, and I nervously tapped my fingers on my thigh. If I became a Hunter, I could change their lives, give them a life worth living. But I'd have to leave them to do it. Even with regular visits, it wouldn't be the same as waking up every morning to see my little sister's sweet smile.

In no time, me and Marcie were at the front of the line, staring at the steps ahead. Marcie was shaking so badly she almost missed the step when the man on the stage beckoned her forward.

She looked at me, and I smiled in encouragement, even though I felt like throwing up. She practically ran up the steps and across the stage, slapping her hand on the ball hard enough that I could hear the thump from here.

I stared at the detector so hard that my eyes started to water.

Please, don't change, I thought. *Don't change.*

Her whole family was human, typical dentists—you couldn't get more normal than that. Marcie wasn't Hunter material; she'd never survive on the other side of the Wall.

"Human," the Hunter on the right side of the detector called out.

Marcie's knees bent like they were ready to give out. She sighed and patted her chest, then straightened up. She practically danced as she hurried to leave the stage. Before she disappeared down the stairs on the left, she turned and gave me a thumbs-up, mouthing, "You got this!"

I forced a smile before looking at the top of the platform. Sucking in a deep breath, I stepped up the stairs. It was almost like I was in someone else's body as I walked across the stage on wooden legs. Thousands of eyes were on me like lasers, burning holes into my body.

Jeez, I hated being the center of attention. What did I do with my hands? Were my steps too big or too small? What if my ponytail was crooked?

But the worst part was the giant detector getting closer and closer. I stopped in front of it and looked up as it loomed over me. I wasn't overly tall, but I'd never felt such a crushing weight before. This magical glass ball would completely control the course of my life. I either obeyed what it said or went to jail, so harshly black and white that most kids like me didn't even bother to dream about what they wanted to do with their future until they were tested.

For myself, I just wanted to live. Human or Hunter, my family would collapse without me.

I took a breath and forced my heart to slow down. *No matter what, I've got this.*

I reached out and put my hand on the cold glass. I'd meant to slow down my heart rate, but it seemed to stop altogether as I watched the inside of the detector, just waiting for it to change color. And waited.

Nothing.

Slowly, I let out the air I didn't realize I was holding.

The Hunter next to me opened his mouth. "Hum—" He stopped midword.

I paused just before I lifted my hand from the detector. At the center of the glass, a faint blue mist appeared. It slowly spread out, turning the entire ball a pale robin's-egg blue.

CHAPTER 2

I stared at the pale blue, barely able to breathe. I was a Hunter. The crowd cheered behind me, albeit a softer cheer compared to others.

Instinctively, I turned my head and looked toward the crowd. Surrounded by people pushing in every direction was a fifteen-year-old girl with the same color of honey-brown hair as me and the same hazel eyes as my father. I didn't have to see the tears to know she was crying, even though she was cheering with all her might. Behind her, my aunt, a near carbon copy of my mother, gripped my sister's shoulders as my uncle stood by, both with solemn expressions.

They were the only family I had left in the world. On the other side of that Wall, there was no one waiting for me. Still, I'd be able to give them a better life by being a Hunter, right?

"Go on," the Hunter beside me rumbled.

I nearly jumped out of my skin. "Oh, right."

I forced a smile on my face and walked to the right. At the top of the stairs, I stopped and looked back. On the other side of the stage, head barely within sight, was Marcie. She was staring at me with huge, tear-filled eyes. She waved at me and mouthed, "I love you, Jynn. Bye!"

My forced smile became real as I waved back. "Love you. Bye!"

It wasn't like I would never see them again. Hunters had to live in Eden, but they could visit Garden City whenever they wanted. Sometimes, humans even went to Eden.

At the bottom of the short stairs was a hallway with three doors, and standing next to the farthest one was a smiling man. I couldn't help but pause at the sight of him. He wore a loose pale-blue mage robe over a white button-up shirt and gray slacks. His brown hair was long and tied in a ponytail which hung over his right shoulder.

Twenty years ago, people would have called him a cosplayer, but this was a common look for Hunters nowadays. Earth's advanced technology didn't work inside the Gate. Tanks broke down before they fully crossed the line, and bullets bounced off the weakest E-rank monster, not to mention that guns usually fell into pieces before the second shot.

Nearly half of Earth's population was killed before Hunters realized that only specialized weapons made of materials found inside the Gate, wielded only by Hunters, could kill the monsters. Swords, daggers, bows—that was how they hunted. Even their armor was made from those materials. And since they used that style of weapons, their armor also followed the fantasy-like fashion, so it wasn't uncommon to see the two styles mixed together, like this man's business-casual clothes beneath mage robes.

"Greetings, and congratulations," he said, motioning to the open door. "My name is Jonovan, and I'm going to help you get started as a Hunter." Everything about him was friendly and professional.

I swallowed the nerves bubbling in the back of my throat and nodded. "Thank you." This was the start of my new life. *I am a Hunter now.* My and my family's lives were going to be better than before.

The room I entered looked a lot like a doctor's exam room. There were a couple chairs along the wall and a padded bed in the middle of the space. Two very obvious security cameras hung from the ceiling.

I hated sitting up high on exam tables, so I sank down onto one of the chairs. Even then, my butt was only half on it. It took everything I had to keep my legs from bouncing.

Jonovan walked over to a laptop on a desk and sat down. "First, I'm going to input your information into the Hunter's Association. Then I'm going to give you your Guide, and we'll find out what rank you are, okay?"

In his soothing voice, he started to ask me questions, like my name, date of birth, and SSN. He then went over my weight, height, and physical descriptions. The only thing he didn't ask me for was my zodiac sign. Just as I was about to conclude that the questions would never stop, he smiled at me. "Great, all done."

He walked over to the doctor's table and opened up a drawer at the end, reaching in and pulling out a clear rectangular case. Inside was a small cream-colored pearl. "I'm going to assume you passed your Hunters course in school and know what this is?" He glanced at me.

I nodded while my gaze wandered over to Jonovan's right temple, where a pearl was embedded in his skin. And the one in his hand was going to be implanted in mine.

My heart started to beat faster.

He nodded, satisfied. "I'll just go over it quickly then, as a reminder. This is a Guide. It has all the information available to the Hunter's Association in it, which in turn is available to you as a Hunter. It will help guide you through the Gate, recognize beasts and plants inside, and even keep record of your daily needs and stats." He opened the case and touched the pearl with his long, thin finger. "Sometimes, when first implanted, it can cause dizziness. Would you like to stay seated on the chair or lay down on the table, Miss Devhro?" The pearl began to glow faintly, like a mini moon. When I didn't say anything, he glanced at me expectantly.

"Ah." I blinked out of my thoughts. I could still barely believe all this was happening. "I'll stay here. Thanks." Quickly, I slid back until I felt the backrest.

"Alright." He walked over to me and sat on the chair to my right. "This might hurt. Please bear with me." He lifted one finger up, and the Guide rose into the air with the movement like it was attached to an invisible wire at the end of his finger. He pressed it to my temple.

When he said, "This might hurt," what he really meant was, "This will feel like someone is hammering a stake into your head." My eyes widened, and I sucked in a huge breath, my body freezing. My hands gripped together, and it was all I could do not to shrink away from the pain. I could feel the pearl pressing against my skin until my skin parted.

"You're doing good." Jonovan's voice was right in my ear. "Almost there."

The Guide slid into my skin and stopped just before it touched my skull.

"Done. Sorry that hurt so much." Gently, he rested his fingers against my aching temple. A soft golden light flashed in my periphery, and the pain instantly disappeared. He smiled and patted my shoulder in comfort. "You did well. It's been a long time since someone reacted like that. Honestly, most Hunters don't even feel it because of the numbing magic coating the Guide."

He was all smiles, but I couldn't help but think there was a slight sadness in his eyes.

"What do you think?" He reached into a cabinet and handed me a mirror.

I took it and stared into it. *Jeez.* Under the harsh lights, the bags under my hazel eyes from a sleepless night couldn't be more obvious. But that wasn't what I should be looking at. I turned my head and saw the pearl mostly embedded in my skin. It was a testament of how awesome healing magic was that there was no swelling or anything; it was as if I'd been born with it. Really, he'd put it in a good spot. It sat perfectly in line with the corner of my eye.

"It looks great, thank you." I handed back the mirror.

"Perfect. Now, let's turn it on." His hand began to glow red as he reached out a finger toward the Guide and touched the pearl on my temple.

Instantly, words started to flash in my eyes. It was like I was suddenly wearing a pair of glasses where words appeared and disappeared across the lenses, suspended above real-world items. Transparent blue title bars for everything popped up, labeling the chairs, the desk, the computer, the lights, even the man beside me. I gasped, suddenly dizzy. My mind felt like it was about to overflow.

"Just take a second," Jonovan cautioned. "Right now, it's new and trying to figure out how to work with you. Try focusing on just one thing."

I turned my head and looked at him. All the other names went away until I could just see Jonovan Setter over his head. I blinked a couple of times and glanced to the side. This time, not everything in the room was labeled. I narrowed my eyes and focused my attention on the laptop— only its name popped into my vision. I switched my focus to the chair then over to the table, seeing them named one by one.

"Better?" Jonovan asked.

"Much better."

"Good. In time, you will have more control over it. You can even adjust it so it doesn't identify common items. Now, we're going to look at your stats and see what rank you are. I've been authorized to look at it now and record it. I'll print it out and give it to you, and you can do what you want with it. In the future, you can make your stats known to the people around you, but I would recommend only showing people you trust." He reached out and lightly touched the pearl on my temple with his finger. "Now think, *Open System.*"

What if it didn't work? What if it just said I was a hack?

Open System, I thought hard.

Immediately, a flat transparent blue screen appeared midair, about level to my chest. It looked just like it did in the textbooks I'd read at school. Right now, it was only five inches tall and divided into three buttons. The top one was labeled Stats, under it read Items, and lastly was Guide.

I stared at it with a sinking feeling. Only three options? No Skills or Magic? Granted, most people didn't get those until a couple days after they got the Guide, but there had still been a small hope that I would have one right off the bat. People who did were generally very strong.

Ah, but I shouldn't be surprised there was no Magic button. The detector had turned blue when I touched it, so I was a warrior, not a mage. There was no crossing over.

"Good, good." Jonovan bobbed his head like he could see what I could. Then again, from the warmth I could feel from the pearl in my temple, I was sure he actually could. "These are pretty self-explanatory. On the bottom is the Guide. Everything we know about the Gate and all the how-tos for various things are stored there. There are even basic battle moves, like the ones you learned in your school's Hunters course, which you can view until you join a guild and learn the more advanced techniques.

"The next button is tied to your Items Bag, which I will give you in a minute. If you select it by thinking *Items*, you can see everything inside it. If you have a skill or magic, the option will be above Items."

"Did you start with a skill?" I cut in, trying to not feel so bad about myself.

He nodded and smiled with pride. "As an A-rank healer, I started with Healing and Health Augmenting abilities. It wasn't until several days later that my Null-Elemental abilities appeared."

Yeah, that didn't make me feel better about myself. Jeez, I didn't even notice I was sitting right next to a bigwig A ranker. Then again, it made sense that he would be that strong, considering what he was doing right now.

He must have noticed my disappointment because his expression turned kind. "Give it a couple days, Miss Devhro. Besides, there are plenty of successful Hunters who don't have skills. And if it really matters to a Hunter, they can always save up and buy a Skill Stone to learn one."

I had a feeling they were as expensive as they were rare; it wasn't like you could grab one off the Walmart shelves. They were only found inside the Gate, and most people who found the magical stones that inputted information in your mind kept them for themselves.

I nodded anyway.

"Good. Now, let's look at Stats. This is where you view your statistics such as rank, hit points or HP, magic points or MP, and such. The Guide is tied to your body now. It checks your overall health and converts it into easy-to-read numbers. You don't need to touch the buttons; simply think what you want opened. Please think, *Stats*," he instructed.

Stats, I thought, barely able to breathe. *Please, be at least a C rank.*

The Stats button darkened for a split second before the screen enlarged until it was almost a foot wide. In it, I saw an outline of my body in a standing position. To the right was a table full of numbers.

I stared at them, almost not believing what I was seeing.

Jynn Devhro

Rank E

HP 12/12
MP 5/5

Strength 8   **Agility** 10
Constitution 8   **Perception** 12
                                          Intelligence 8

CHAPTER 3

These were my stats? This . . . this had to be a joke. Seriously, it was a joke. A normal human's stats were eights all the way across; maybe a bodybuilder would have a nine in Strength. But my Constitution, which defined defense and overall health, was an eight. And my Intelligence, which affected magic and skills, was an eight. And my Strength—in other words, how easily I could kill monsters to survive—was also an eight! Eight was average, no better than a normal human.

The remaining stats weren't stellar either. Even my Agility—how fast and nimble I was—and my Perception—hearing and sense of environment—weren't good in the slightest.

I swallowed hard. Then swallowed again.

"Am I . . . really a Hunter? And not just a human in the wrong place?" How much of a joke was I?

Jonovan's face was white as a sheet, his jaw a little unhinged. He cleared his throat. "No, you are definitely a Hunter." His gaze slowly slid over to me. There was a new emotion in his eyes, one I'd seen too many times in my life. Pity.

The day the police came to our front door and informed us that my dad was dead. Every time I walked through the halls to my mom's hospital room, to talk to a woman who would never wake up. When I was at the register, counting pennies to pay for food that day. After all this time, I thought I was immune to the sting it left in my heart.

I thought being a Hunter would make that look go away. I hadn't even been one for an hour, and I was seeing it already.

"Do stats ever change?" I whispered. *Please say yes. Tell me that people wake up all the time to stronger stats. That I'm not stuck with these my whole life.*

Jonovan looked away and stood up. "There have been a handful of cases where a Hunter has Reawakened." His voice was neutral as he forced a kind smile. But he obviously didn't think that would happen to me.

A handful of cases out of millions of Hunters.

I silently watched Jonovan type on the computer. When he finished, he stood up and opened a different drawer under the doctor's table. From inside, he pulled out a small red velvet bag and a short sword in a blue sheath.

Setting the short sword on the table, he walked over to me with the red bag.

"This is your Items Bag. As a standard model, it holds ten items." He reached out and touched the pearl on my temple again; his finger was glowing red when he pulled it back. He then touched the Items Bag with the same glowing digit.

An orange exclamation mark appeared on the corner of my System's interface. Curious, I focused on it, and my Items window opened up to a new message.

[An Items Bag has been attached.]

"Do you see it?" Jonovan asked. When I nodded, he smiled lightly and handed me the bag. "Tie this on your belt, or you can stick it in your pocket. You'll find that most armors and cloaks have special places for Items Bags built into them."

"Thank you." I tied the strings around the belt loop on my shorts and glanced over at the short sword. In theory, that was going into the Items Bag, but how was that going to fit into a piece of red velvet barely four inches tall? Magic was so cool.

I just wished I had some, too.

His smile was a little more natural as he followed my gaze and reached out to pick up the short sword. "Given your strength and size, I thought this might be better suited to you than a longsword." He held out the weapon. "You learned how to use it in your Hunters course?"

I took it and pulled the blade out of the sheath. The office lights gleamed off the pattern weld on the blade as the light-and-dark–colored steel blended together. It was cool looking, but the window that popped up over the blade was a little off-putting.

[Short Sword. A sword for beginners.]

I slid it back into the sheath. "They did teach us some stuff."

At least I knew enough not to cut off my arm, even if I wasn't completely comfortable with it.

. . . No, maybe that wasn't it. The sword itself actually felt good in my hand. The handle seemed to fit perfectly in my palm, and the weight—though enough to get my attention—wasn't too much. The problem was that a short sword didn't have the same reach as a normal sword or inflict the same amount of damage on a large monster. Sure, I could swing it, but every swing would put me closer to danger than most other Hunters.

Jonovan taught me how to equip it through the Stats window, then how to take it in and out of the Items Bag. I spent a couple minutes practicing until I could call out the short sword and have it appear in my hand instantly.

In the end, he nodded and stepped back.

"Alright, that's everything that I have to teach you." He smiled at me and handed me a paper with my stats before he motioned to a door. "On the other side of that door is the way to Eden. I wish you the best of luck." He said that, but his gaze was thick with pity again.

I gripped the paper and smiled as bright as I could. "Thanks for all your help."

His lips wrinkled with . . . guilt? "My pleasure."

I waved and hurried out the door. There were still a lot of things I had to do. First of all, where was I going to sleep tonight? I had a bit of money to pay for food, but two hundred dollars wouldn't last long.

I exited to a hallway formed with room dividers. As I walked down the makeshift corridor, I couldn't resist staring at my stats. Maybe if I stared at them long enough, zeros would appear on the ends. But no matter how hard I did, they stayed the same pathetic numbers.

Something shifted in my periphery, and I glanced up. Ahead of me was a huge iron gate. Several Hunters wearing dark-green police uniforms stood on either side. The entrance to Eden.

I paused and gripped my stupid paper in my hands, staring at the gate.

No, I wasn't going to let my rank get me down. My family needed me to be a successful Hunter. E rank or not, I could do this. Once I joined a guild, buying more powerful equipment and making money would be easier. I wouldn't have to stress about taking out monsters by myself, and there would be a healer around if I got hurt.

Reaching the huge iron gate, it swung open automatically. The Hunter police didn't even acknowledge me as I walked through.

My first thought was that Eden looked more peaceful than I was expecting. There were no cars and no litter on the ground. Green trees lined the sidewalk, and colorful signs hung from red-brick buildings on both sides of the road. One of the most noticeable things was that it was quiet. The only people on the entire road were a crowd of thirty or so Hunters who stood together but eyed each other like they were the enemies.

As soon as I stepped through the gate and onto an Eden sidewalk, every head in the crowd jerked around to focus on me. I froze, clutching my paper tighter. That was when I noticed the symbols on their clothes. It took me a couple seconds to realize these people were guild recruiters.

I took a deep breath and started to walk toward them. I needed to get into a guild. It didn't even have to be a big one, any guild would work for now.

The recruiters looked me over, their sharp eyes cutting through my skin into my shaking bones. None of them made a single move toward me; most even looked away disinterested. The shaking in my stomach formed a pit which grew bigger with every step I took.

One of them nudged another middle-aged man in red. "You lost the bet."

The guy in red scowled at him then sighed and walked over to me.

"Hey there, kid." His square face nearly cracked as he plastered on a smile. "I see that you're an E rank." He motioned over my head.

He could see my rank? For a second, I stared in shock before I remembered how I saw Jonovan's name above his head. Wait, didn't I read once that Hunters could see the ranks of people who were equal to or weaker than them? That meant they could all see my rank, and I couldn't see any of theirs.

"Why don't you show me your stats, and we might be able to work something out, okay?" The man's charity was offered begrudgingly.

I glanced at the symbol on his shirt. The dark red phoenix was familiar—it was the same symbol my dad used to wear. This man was a recruiter for the Fire Bird guild. After my dad died, they did a good job settling his affairs for us quickly and efficiently. It wouldn't be a bad thing to commit to them.

I passed my paper slowly to him.

He took it and glanced at the numbers. Then he choked. "Seriously? What is this?"

I couldn't say that made me feel any better. Any thoughts of joining my dad's old guild vanished with the crude laughter that came from his mouth.

"What? Let me see." The man who egged him on before hurried over and snatched the paper from the Fire Bird recruiter before I could take it back. "Is this even real?" He stared at the paper before looking me up and down. "I've never seen anything like this before." He shoved the paper into my hands. "Look, girly, there's a place for people like you. None of us have the resources to waste on a dead person."

He motioned to the side where a short, old man stood under a tree farther down the road. The old man smiled gently and waved a hand.

My insides froze over as I gripped my wrinkled paper. Before I could finish processing what had just happened, the gate opened up behind me and another new Hunter walked in.

The recruiters looked over. Instantly, all of their faces lit up, and they rushed past me to the young man as if they'd just seen a piece of prime steak. The old man started to walk toward me as I turned and watched them fawn over the beaming young man, promising all sorts of amenities if he joined their guild.

This was my first taste of the discrimination that would color my life. I was a Hunter, but that didn't mean I was equal to everyone else here. Eden was a place where the strong lived and the weak died.

And I was the weakest.

CHAPTER 4

⟶

ONE YEAR LATER

"Ha!"

I lunged forward and stabbed the dog-like monster with everything I had. My short sword pierced its furry chest, and with a sharp yelp, the Vale wolf collapsed to the ground, dead. I still hated that sound, no matter how many times I'd heard it. Since it was one of the weakest monsters in Gate Vale, I heard it nearly every day. Even though the monster had four red eyes, a double-jawed mouth with three-inch fangs, and was longer than I was tall, it still yelped like a normal dog when it was hurt.

Panting heavily and holding the bleeding cut on my arm, I sat back onto my butt and tilted my head, looking around Gate Vale. I knew there was another land on the other side of the Gate, but even I hadn't expected it to be this big. The first time I'd walked in here a year ago, my knees nearly gave out in shock.

For the most part, it looked a lot like Earth. Well, Earth in the pictures from the past. It was a huge valley with huge green forests, a lake with a perpetual rainbow arching over it, a crystal-clear river, a meadow, and even a marshy swamp, all under a blue sky. The mountains that surrounded Gate Vale were always covered in snow. The weather was always perfect, depending on where you were standing, and if you were too hot or cold, you simply moved to a different part in the Vale, and the problem was solved. If it weren't for the "animals"—and sometimes the plants— that wanted to kill you, it would be a paradise.

Never mind the random portals which opened up around the edges of the flat land and spilled out monsters every night.

I'd even heard some high-ranking Hunters say how they wished they could live in Gate Vale. Since Earth's technology didn't work here, there was no pollution. But that didn't change the fact that when night fell, the most dangerous S-ranked monsters came out. For that reason alone, everyone had to leave at the end of the day. It was a given that anyone who stayed would be dead by morning.

As for how amazing those environments were in real life, I wouldn't know. I had never been to most of the Vale. The farther you were from the entrance, the stronger the monsters became, and for someone like me, anything farther than a mile was asking for it.

I frowned at my bleeding arm. It was such a common sight I couldn't even muster the energy to panic. It was a joke, really. I was a joke. My life was a joke. What Hunter got this hurt killing an E-rank monster? Just me. Lucky me.

"Hey, it's dinnertime. Let's head back," a man said somewhere to my right.

He wasn't talking to me but to someone in his party. As a stronger Hunter, I was sure he knew I was here on the other side of the bushes, but that didn't matter to him.

It did to me, though. I didn't know his name or anyone else's in his three-person group—that wasn't important, really. It's just that they were the group I was following today. With them around to take care of the stronger monsters, I could pick off one that was too weak for them to pay attention to and fill my quota for the day. Once they were gone, the odds of me getting seriously injured increased. A lot.

"Crap," I muttered, hurrying over to the dead Vale wolf's side.

I dropped down to my knees beside it and thrust my short sword into its chest. Gritting my teeth, I wedged its rib cage open and stuck my hand into the cold, bloody hole. By now, I knew this breed of monster well enough that my fingers instinctively knew where to search. Once I touched something solid, round, and warm, I grabbed it and pulled out a dime-size energy crystal.

When I'd killed my first monster a year ago, I puked and cried. And proceeded to dry heave again and again as I searched for the energy crystal inside it.

A transparent blue box appeared slightly above my line of sight.

[You have acquired an Energy Crystal.]

I pulled a water bottle out of my Items Bag and cleaned off my hands and the small bright blue crystal.

It was kinda pathetic how these tiny things controlled my life—and the lives of the rest of the humans. Even one as small as this one emitted enough energy to power a house for ten years. The larger crystals found in stronger monsters were infinitely more powerful and worth a lot of money.

I looked at the carcass and scowled. Another Hunter with the time and know-how could skin the hide. The extra money from selling monster parts was always helpful, and those body parts were used to make armor and weapons for other Hunters. But that option wasn't available to me. No one had ever taught me how. I'd tried a couple times before on my own and only managed to gross myself out and make a bloody mess. Literally. And it wasn't like I could ask the guys I was following to do it for me.

They were nice enough to let me trail behind them for protection, and they didn't go out of their way to kill every monster in sight so I could at least get one. Over the long months of learning everything the hard way, I'd figured out which groups didn't mind when I trailed them—but of course, that was as close as it got. Trailing. Any closer, and they shooed me away.

It was the same thing with friends. The few who talked to me were casual friends, the kind you wave and say hi to as you walk by. Maybe stop and have a "Hey, how are you doing?" conversation without putting too much emotion into it. They were afraid I would get too close and start asking for favors. In this dog-eat-dog world, who would choose to let a deadweight join them into a place that was trying to kill them?

I was sure the human world would scream *heartless* and *foul.* But when someone's life was on the line, were they really going to pick someone they knew wasn't strong enough to guard their back? It was as simple as that.

Sometimes, stronger Hunters would let weaker people into their groups to use as bait to ensure an easier getaway if things went bad. With reason, I avoided people like that. I might not be eating great now, but at least I was still alive to eat.

The group started to walk away. I waited a minute, then followed behind in the direction of the giant Gate in the middle of the Vale. I was halfway back when the bright blue sky suddenly flashed red.

I froze, eyes wide. The group I followed gasped in alarm, but I could barely hear them over the stuttering of my heart.

Red. Why did the sky have to turn red while I was here? Of all the times to have a Portal Burst, why did it have to be now?

Desperate, I looked around. *Please be far from me. Please be really, really far from me.*

My horrible luck held true.

Magic pooled in the air only a hundred feet from me, like a rainbow whirlpool. It was gorgeous, the way the colors shimmered in the air. Deadly gorgeous. It ended before I could even take a breath, the colors smooshing together to create a black pit hanging in the air, just like the portals which rimmed the land. This one might be smaller, just the size of a house, but that didn't make it any safer. If anything, it was worse. Portal Bursts had a nasty habit of opening, vomiting out super strong monsters, then disappearing while Hunters were left to deal with the aftermath.

My legs shook as I stood rooted in place. What should I do? The Portal Burst was between me and the Gate. I could either run for it and hope I got past without attracting unwanted attention, or I could run farther into the Vale, where stronger monsters were. Monsters tended to get a dose of adrenaline when a Burst happened. I was SOL no matter what I did.

Before I could make a choice, things went from bad to worse when a huge, earth-shaking roar echoed out of the black pit. I clamped my hands over my ears, and my legs gave out under the tremendous power that pulsed through the ground. From the Portal Burst's depths, a huge black dragon sailed out, the force of the wind under its wings swaying trees and flattening bushes. It tossed its head in the air and roared again, nearly bursting my eardrums. Above its head, a bright red title bar read: [**Dragon, A rank**]. Then its red eyes focused on the closest living thing in the open.

Me.

"Run!" the group of Hunters by me screamed. A second later, three men in armor came hurling through the bushes past me, going faster than I could ever dream of moving. Two of the men vaulted over me and kept running.

One of the guys grabbed my hand and pulled me up after him, but he was moving too fast. I just couldn't keep up. My feet tripped over themselves, and my hand was ripped from his. "Run!" he yelled over his shoulder but didn't come back for me.

The world went dark as the shadow of the dragon settled over me.

I screamed and scrambled to my feet.

The dragon's toothy maw opened, and lightning exploded out of its mouth, hitting the ground where I had been just a second ago.

The ground exploded behind me, sending out a shock wave of power and hot dirt. I think I screamed, but I couldn't really hear anything over the ringing in my ears. All I knew was that I was flipping through the air. I landed flat on my back and rolled across the ground until I came up hard at the bottom of a tree.

I gasped for air, but my lungs hurt too much to hold more than a shallow pant. And it wasn't just my lungs. My back, stomach, and head were screaming in pain, and I had at least a bruised rib on my right side; hopefully, it stopped at that. Broken ribs really sucked.

Red words flashed before my eyes: [**Warning! Your HP has dropped below ten percent. Please seek medical assistance.**]

As if I didn't know how badly I was hurt.

Squinting through my double vision, I watched the dragon as it arched its neck, eyes still locked on me. Apparently, the fact I was alive was simply unacceptable.

With a powerful flap of its wings, it dove at me.

My short sword appeared in my hand. Stupid, I know. I could barely move, and it was a damn dragon. Even an A-rank Hunter would have trouble with this thing. But if I was going to die, I'd die fighting.

A flash of silvery blue streaked across the sky, right in front of the monster, and a huge ring echoed out. The dragon and the blue streak stopped just long enough for me to see a Hunter in silver-and-blue armor suspended in the air, his sword pressed against the dragon's talons. He'd actually stopped the dragon in midair.

My lips parted as I stared at them, that image captured in my memory—something that I would never forget. The beautiful lines of the man's fighting form. The way the bright magi-steel gleamed in the sun, so sharply different from the dragon's solid black talons. The malicious gleam in the dragon's eyes as it focused on a new target, its black body a sharp contrast to the blue sky behind.

The dragon spun in the air, moving almost as fast as its lightning, and whipped at the Hunter with its long tail. The Hunter jumped up using nothing but air, smoothly sailing over the tail that missed him by inches.

I gasped, shocked. Double Jump? I'd heard of the ability, but it was so rare, I never thought I'd see it with my own eyes.

The Hunter landed on the dragon's back. Without hesitation, he sprinted up the spine, his steps as light as if he were dancing across a stage. The dragon roared and arched its back, thrashing around to dislodge him. Nothing seemed to work; it was like the Hunter was glued to the dragon's body. The Hunter reached the monster's long neck, ran the length of it, then halted between the huge arched horns crowning the dragon's head. He raised his sword with both hands, and was it a trick of the light or did his blade start to glow faintly blue? Before I could decide, he stabbed down. As if cutting putty, the sword sank all the way down until the hilt hit the top of the dragon's head.

The dragon immediately plummeted from the sky, its body like a wet noodle, wings flailing lifelessly in the rushing air. The Hunter rode it all the way down, his form as sure as stone. The dead monster slammed into the ground with an earth-shattering bang, so strong that fissures webbed across the ground under the force.

The dust settled, and the Hunter pulled his sword from the dragon's skull before standing up. Neither the dust in the air nor the black blood dripping from his sword could detract from the awe-inspiring way he stood over his kill. He was more than a knight; he was like a god. He had to be, to so easily kill an A-ranked monster. It left only one option.

S rank.

Even though his back was to me, I couldn't help but stare at the Hunter with desire. Yes, I desired that. Strength. To be strong enough that no one would leave me for dead. Or even better: the strength to never need to rely on anyone else.

As much as I desired to be like him, the longer I watched, the more an empty pit opened in my heart which had nothing to do with the pain that still tore at my body. Or maybe it did.

There was such a huge gap between me and that man. Never mind killing a dragon, I couldn't handle the aftermath of its attack. How much longer could I survive in this world?

My family needed me. If I died, what would happen to them? How would my sister handle losing another member of our little family? I wanted to make their lives easier. I'd thought it was something I could do, now that I was a Hunter.

I'm such a joke.

CHAPTER 5

The S-ranked Hunter never once looked in my direction. As an S rank, he had to know I was there, but why should he care? Besides, he was too busy walking around his kill, probably checking on what he could salvage from it.

In the distance, I heard the sounds of Hunters approaching, excited to get a close-up of the dragon.

Slowly, I stood up and hugged my ribs while straightening out my spine as much as I could so I didn't put more pressure on them. I glanced at the dragon slayer one more time. I knew he didn't do it for me. Hunters died weekly, even higher ranked ones. What was one more missing little E?

Still, I found myself glancing at his back. "Thanks," I whispered and wobbled away.

Out of all the times I'd been hurt in Gate Vale, this had to rank in my top ten most painful. Progress was slow, but thankfully, I didn't see any other monsters on my way out. They were probably scared off by the dragon and the S rank's aura. Monsters didn't discriminate, really. They killed anything weaker than them, monsters and Hunters alike. I'd heard that monsters from the same portal could cooperate with each other if they were intelligent enough, but I'd luckily never seen it.

A slight pressure in the air compressed my body as I walked through the Gate. I gritted my teeth. The air around me fizzled as red sparks zipped through the darkness, but the pressure change only lasted a second before my feet landed on the paved ground in Eden and the sounds of the city washed over me.

Since there wasn't a need to make the area around the Gate pretty, everything around it had been cleared for a solid two hundred feet, and the ground was paved with concrete. Not only did it keep maintenance down, it also kept the area open in case a Surge happened and they made it out of the Gate onto Earth. That had only happened twice, luckily before I became a Hunter, but it was enough of a risk no one wanted to build too close to it.

The closest building was a hospital—and the building I was most familiar with, outside of the E Hostel. I limped up to the tall white building and entered through the sliding glass door. My steps echoed off cream-colored tile as I walked to the front desk. Pictures of graceful monsters and green plants decorated the foyer around the off-white walls and maroon plush chairs. In a way, this place didn't feel like a true hospital. Probably because there were very few actual doctors in the building. The staff were mostly healers, so there wasn't a need for most medical equipment.

Such a sharp contrast from when I visited my mom.

An E-rank healer at the front desk looked up and smiled at me. "Oh, good evening, Jynn. Back again?" She shook her graying head, tsking while she smiled.

Why did she have to ask me that every single day? I tried to hide my grimace with a smile. After a year of daily visits, I thought it would be a given by now. After all, who in this entire city had less HP than me? Even an E-rank healer, a class known for its low HP, had more than me.

"Hey, Maria. I'm back." I kept my voice as light as I could.

She tapped away on her computer, not even needing to ask me any of my personal information. By my second month as a Hunter, she—and the other two front desk ladies—had it memorized. "Okay, they know you're here. Why don't you take a seat, and we'll call you back in a bit?" She smiled at me.

I glanced at the maroon chair. I was dying to sink into those fluffy cushions, but if I sat down, I didn't think I'd get back up.

I was saved from having to make a decision when the swinging door to the back opened.

"Jynn Devhro," a familiar voice echoed across the room.

I turned and tried to smile. "Hi, Mr. Jonovan."

The only thing that had changed since the first time I saw him were his clothes. His long brown hair was still tied and falling over his shoulder, and he still sported a mage's robe over his business-casual clothing. He frowned gently at me with a helpless wrinkle on his brow.

"Come on, Miss Jynn." He nodded over his shoulder and held the door open, habit making his movement smooth.

I limped through the door then waited for him to guide me to a room.

This exam room was almost an exact replica of the one where he'd embedded the Guide in my temple. Dark oak cabinetry with a sink, several chairs on the sides of the room, and an exam table on the right wall.

I slipped onto the exam table with a painful grimace, so used to sitting there that it didn't feel awkward anymore.

"What happened to you? God, Miss Jynn, you're a mess." He shook his head and quietly closed the door.

My mouth hooked to the side. "It's always the same thing, right? I was in the Gate."

He sighed and reached out. Golden healing power radiated from his long fingers as he gently touched my shoulder. Instantly, a warm, soothing feeling rippled through my body, washing away all the pain.

I sighed, my muscles relaxing. Out of all the healers, Jonovan was my favorite. It wasn't just that he was the second-highest ranked healer in Eden—only being beaten by the solo S-rank healer in America—but he was also the nicest and most efficient. He didn't get frustrated by my frequent visits like the other healers, who rolled their eyes and complained when they didn't think I could hear. If anything, he seemed to keep an eye out for me.

The only time he wasn't the one who healed me was when he had a day off. I had a feeling it had to do with the guilt hiding in the back of his kind eyes, as if it was his fault that I became a Hunter in the first place.

"Always the same," Jonovan muttered. "You didn't see anything new today?"

As a full-time healer in Eden's hospital, it was a given that Jonovan didn't go into the Gate much. He could very easily join a guild party, but when I'd asked why he didn't, he'd simply smiled and said that he didn't want his skills to be restricted to only a few members. A blessing like his should be shared with everyone. It was easy to see why he'd been voted as the second most-eligible bachelor in Eden. He even had his own fangirl club, not that I ever teased him about it . . . much.

My own ventures into the Gate were pretty average because of the strength restrictions I had. It wasn't safe to go too far from the Gate, so I saw the same things over and over again. But I had to admit, today was different.

"I saw an S-rank Hunter today," I said. Now that my ribs didn't hurt so much, my voice was stronger.

"Hm. Which one?"

I shook my head. "I don't know. His back was to me, so I couldn't see the symbol on his chest plate. But his armor was silver and blue."

Jonovan smiled and shook his head. "Ah, you just described about half of the S-ranked Hunters."

My head cocked to the side. "Have you met a lot of them?"

He nodded. "Quite a few. Most of them have egos as big as their talent, but some are good people."

"I bet. I've met some lower-leveled Hunters with big enough egos as is. I can't imagine what some of those S-ranked gods think of themselves." I looked down and watched the cut on my arm start to close up, as if the skin was being zipped together by an invisible hand.

Out of all the injuries, it was cuts like these which I liked to watch be healed the most. There was something so interesting about watching the skin close over the muscle, as if it had never been torn open to begin with. Although, I had to admit, it was pretty cool watching Jonovan regrow my pinkie last month. And pretty gross.

He hummed in acknowledgement. "Oh, I heard there was a Portal Burst today. Did you know? They said a dragon came out and an S ranker killed it . . . " His voice faded, and he looked at me closely, his brows wrinkled in concern.

I grinned like an idiot and made a peace sign like I didn't almost die an hour ago. "Yep, that happened. Got to see the whole thing up close and personal."

My light words didn't make him laugh like I was hoping. If anything, his face wrinkled more.

Such a waste of a pretty face, even if he was at least double my age. The higher a Hunter's rank was, the slower they aged. Jonovan might look like a very fit man in his early thirties, but he could also easily be over fifty and I wouldn't know the difference. But that was his business, so I never asked.

With all my injuries healed, he turned off his power and leaned back. He looked at me and opened his mouth, paused, then turned to pull a small flashlight from the drawer behind him. "Jynn, have you ever thought about not being a Hunter?"

Only every time I'm lying on the ground, bleeding for a dime-size crystal. Only every night in my hard little bed, listening to my empty stomach. Only . . .

Only it didn't matter.

I smiled and waved a hand. "No one can just stop being a Hunter. Since I tested positive, this is where I belong. I've tried to get a job in a store or something, but they don't pay as much and are in such high demand for

Es like me or people who can't stomach fighting at all, it's impossible to get one without connections."

I couldn't even make a real friend, what connections could I access? And as kind as Jonovan was, I wouldn't call him a close friend either. Simply a shoulder to complain to for a bit, just like for the rest of his patients.

He leaned forward with the flashlight in his hand and shone the light in my eyes, looking closely for who knows what. "No, I mean, apply to go back to the human world."

He must have liked what he saw because he set the light aside and started to test my reflexes.

My smile turned bitter. "Something like that doesn't exist, Jonovan. We both know that."

He stopped and looked at me. "But it could. In a case like yours, it should."

Why, because I was so pathetic? I didn't belong in the human world since I'd tested as a Hunter, but I was too damn weak to survive in the Hunter world as well.

Unfortunately, it all came down to money. There wasn't a job in the human world that I could get which would pay as good as a Hunter job. Even the scrap crystals I picked up daily were enough to pay for my mother's hospital stay. And as a Hunter, I was guaranteed three meals a day and a bed in the E Hostel as long as I brought back something every day. The quality of the meal depended on what I brought back, but it was still considered free room and board. And it was one less mouth my aunt had to worry about feeding. In fact, me being a Hunter was one of the reasons my family could eat at all.

But no one needed to know that.

I smiled. "Thanks for the concern, but it's okay. Really."

His mouth wrinkled into a frown. He shook his head and continued my quick physical check in silence. In the end, he stood up and gave me a gentle smile. "All better. Try to keep it that way tomorrow, alright?"

I smiled and hopped off the table. There was no way I was going to promise something like that, so I simply said, "Thank you for your help, Healer Jonovan."

He smiled and held the door open for me.

"Miss Jynn, if you change your mind about leaving Eden, let me know. I'll see what I can do."

I waved and walked away.

CHAPTER 6

It was dark when I left the hospital, and now that I wasn't hurt, my stomach woke up to complain with a vengeance.

It was easy enough to figure out which direction I needed to walk to get to the E Hostel. It was in the opposite direction of all the fancy lights and buildings. Really, the *land of the free and equal* didn't apply in Eden, the city of the strong. When the strong could make the weak pass out with their sheer presence, who was brave enough to fight for equal rights?

Eden was pretty much shaped like a pie chart, with the Gate in the middle. The right side of the city was mostly taken up by the guilds, each with their own campuses with a main building and housing. The rest of Eden was divided loosely but efficiently by ranks of the people who didn't belong to a guild or chose to own a home. The higher the rank, the better their living conditions were, such as apartments and eateries.

Even though there was a high turnover rate in Eden, housing was packed. Only A ranks and higher could actually afford to live in a single house, since they weren't free through the government. Sometimes, when I had time to kill, I'd walk around their neighborhood, awed by the green lawns and beautiful homes. Such a sharp difference to my own tiny room. It was fun to look at the pretty clothes in shop windows and imagine what the treats in bakeries tasted like. Of course, all I could do was look. Someone like me wasn't allowed in places like that.

No, my place was in the northwest corner of Eden, where lighting was scarce, and all apartments were the sizes of closets. The trees and shrubs that lined the streets in E District, and which were laid when Eden was first built, were only managed once a year. Since that time wasn't for another month or so, *ragged* was a good description of the streets right now.

Most of the streets were empty as I walked. Well, at least the side streets where I walked, even if it took longer to get home. By now, I'd learned where to avoid. The Hunter's Association tried to keep peace and safety for everyone, but even they wouldn't stop a person from drowning in alcohol after a long day in the Gate. Or prevent intoxicated, superpowered individuals from acting up.

I was almost to the hostel when I heard something. Pausing, I frowned and looked around the dark street corners. What was that sound? It didn't sound like a drunk scuttling around, and my sense of danger wasn't going off. Was it ahead? No, it was coming from my right.

Instinct summoned my short sword from my Items Bag to my hand. In theory, I shouldn't ever need to use it in Eden—it was actually illegal to use weapons outside of official duels here—but if I walked into every situation empty-handed, I'd be dead by now.

Carefully, I leaned around the corner of the building and looked down the alley.

There was a girl sitting on the ground in the middle of the walkway, trying to stifle her sobs with her knees. I scanned the rest of the alley in case there was someone else there. The sensor in the System didn't show anything, and I couldn't see any movement. Survival instincts urged me to turn around and leave, but I found myself stepping closer.

"Hey," I said softly.

The girl screamed and jumped to her feet. She stumbled back and nearly fell over.

Her reaction was so extreme, I jumped myself. "Oh, hey. Calm down." My short sword disappeared as I put my hands up. "Sorry I scared you."

I could tell she was younger than me, but it couldn't be by too much. For a person younger than seventeen to enter Eden was near impossible. She stared at me with huge, wet dark eyes, her long brown hair swaying across her back as she panted in fright. Her hands shook as she pressed them against her chest.

"Who . . . who are you?"

"I'm Jynn." I smiled, trying to show I wasn't a threat. Like, seriously. This girl might look like a startled bird, but she'd beat me in an arm wrestle any day regardless of her rank. Which had to be a lot higher than mine based on how fast she'd moved just then. "I heard you crying. Are you okay?"

She wiped at her cheeks and swallowed a sob.

"I . . . " She bit her lip. "No. I'm not. I don't know where I am. I got separated from Mr. Smith, then there were these guys, so I ran. And now

I'm even more lost," her frantic yet barely audible words rushed out. She must have found the wrong streets by accident. Poor thing. Unfortunately, *Mr. Smith* was too vague for me to guess where she needed to be right now.

"Okay." I took a couple steps closer. She didn't jump this time; if anything, she relaxed more.

Jeez, she had a lot to learn. She had no idea if I was a threat yet or not. Luckily for her, I wasn't. Still, there was something about her eyes which reminded me of my sister. A naive gleam that life hadn't tarnished yet. It was refreshing. "What's your name?"

"Emma." She took a deep breath and stopped crying.

"Hi, Emma." I smiled at her. "So, who is Mr. Smith, and where was he taking you?" If she followed just anyone, she wasn't going to survive very long.

Still, it was weird to find someone so clueless. Couldn't she tell she was in E District? And if she was lost, all she had to do was walk toward the Gate and start all over again from there, since every district branched out from it. I looked at her normal street clothes, her cute tee, shorts, and sandals. Other than the Items Bag attached to her hip, she didn't have any Hunter attire at all. But it was the wrong time for a new batch of Hunters to come to Eden.

"Mr. Smith is the recruiter for the Stone Mace guild. I met him today, and he was showing me around Eden when we got separated." She gripped the hem of her shirt.

I couldn't help but be impressed. Stone Mace wasn't the strongest guild, but it was one of the top fifteen, and they weren't afraid to throw their weight around. They were also picky on who they let in. If Emma met them today . . .

"Did you just get tested?" I asked.

She nodded. "Yeah. My Hunter abilities woke up early, so I was tested today. I'm a C-rank melee."

I nodded slowly. A good, solid rank. High enough to be useful without threatening someone else's position. Still, it had to be tough being thrown into this place alone. It was something I was familiar with. "Do you have any family here?"

Emma shook her head. "I'm the first Hunter in my family." A small smile touched her cute face. "They were so proud."

"Yes, they usually are," I muttered under my breath. Especially when they didn't know what it was really like. At least she wouldn't deal with the same crap I did, since she was already part of a guild. Hopefully, they could keep the naive light in her eyes strong.

I jerked my head over my shoulder. "Come on, I'll take you to the Stone Mace guild."

My stomach was so empty it hurt, but it wasn't the first time, and Emma was probably just as hungry.

Her face lit up, and she fell into step with me. "Thank you! Are we close to it?"

I gave a little laugh. "If you count being on the other side of the city close, sure."

"Oh." She sighed. "Are we going to walk?"

"There aren't many cars in Eden. Only the richest of the rich own one," I muttered, noticing she was slightly limping. It wasn't until we passed under a streetlamp that I noticed the blister rubbing on the back of her right heel. Seriously, was it too hard to ask for shoes that were cute and comfortable at the same time? It was like asking for jeans with pockets—a one-in-a-million shot.

My lips pulled to the side, thinking. "There's a tram a couple blocks from here we could take. Trams are free throughout the city."

Without further ado, I took her in that direction.

All the way, Emma babbled about her life before today. How she'd always been good with a bow, then last week, a stupid boy in her Hunters course class made her so mad that she shot his bow out of his hand. Not only that, but his bow was snapped in half, and her arrow embedded itself almost all the way through the wall. That's when they figured out she'd Awakened; her Hunter power had come early.

I couldn't help but laugh, even though I felt bad for her.

It was a big deal when the new group of freshly graduated kids came in. People took special care for the first couple weeks, helping the new Hunters adapt. But that didn't exist for the unfortunate kids who Awoke early.

As for the possibility of someone becoming a Hunter later than seventeen, that didn't happen. The huge glass ball each person touched wasn't just a tester: it also forced hidden Hunter talent to Awaken right then and there.

We climbed onto the tram and rode to Gate Square. As we went, I pointed out places and talked about things she might not have learned yet. It was fun. Really, it was. It had been so long since I talked with someone my age, but more importantly, someone who didn't look at me like I was a cockroach.

When we got off the tram, I took a second to point out the hospital to her. As a C rank and a member of a guild, she wouldn't be there as often as I was, but it was still a good thing to know. Then I took her through the Guild District as I pointed out the different guilds.

I came to a stop at the bottom of a set of wide curved stairs. With a sigh, I looked up at the heavy double doors of the white marble building. "And here we are."

"Oh." Emma's jaw dropped as she looked up at the stately building. "This is the Stone Mace guild? I thought this was like a city building or something." She turned her head, looking at the stone spires highlighted beautifully with lights so they glowed against the night sky. "Whoa."

I smiled and nodded to the side. "Yep, this is it."

If she thought this was gaudy, she might faint when she saw some of the bigger guild buildings. One of them was literally a castle.

I glanced at Emma to say goodbye but stopped at the apprehensive look on her face. "Hey, it's okay. I'm sure they've been looking for you. Just tell the front desk your name, and it will all work out."

She pressed her lips together. "Will you come with me?" Her voice was small and hard to hear.

Me? Go in there? I couldn't even laugh at the absurd thought. My smile felt strained, but I managed to keep it in place. "You'll be fine, really."

She gripped the hem of her shirt and looked down at her toes. "The truth is, I got separated from Mr. Smith while we were in the Gate. I was supposed to kill a monster and get its energy crystal. It was just an E rank, but I was scared and ran away. When I couldn't find him in the Gate, I went outside to wait in the square. But he didn't show up, so I thought I'd go to the guild. Then I went the wrong way, and well . . . "

Her head drooped even lower. "I'm supposed to bring an energy crystal back with me. That's part of the contract with the guild, you know. What should I do, Jynn?" She looked in the direction of the Gate, her face wrinkling in fear.

That was a problem. The Gate was the most dangerous during the night hours. No Hunter had ever survived a night in there.

I tapped a finger on my lips in thought. I knew exactly what it was like to come back without a crystal, and how it affected the way Hunters looked at you. She had it rough already. Did she really need to know about the dark side of Hunters on her first night? Guilds didn't keep weak or useless people. If she went in there without an energy crystal, it was possible they could say it was a breach of contract and throw her out.

A solution to her problem popped into my head. It was an easy solution, but it hurt my heart anyway. With a silent sigh, I held out my hand to her. The energy crystal in my Items Bag appeared in my palm. "Why don't you give them this one? Just tell them it's yours."

She blinked at the faintly glowing stone in my hand then gaped at me. "Are you sure? I mean, you've already helped me so much."

I shrugged. What was one more night of just rice and a few veggies? Honestly, my body was so used to it by now, it wouldn't matter. Even as I thought that, my stomach twisted into a painful, empty knot.

"It's nothing." I stuffed the crystal into her hand before I could change my mind and stepped back. "Well, see you later, Emma." I waved at her and turned around.

"Ah, bye, Jynn!" Emma called to my back. "Thank you!"

I waved a hand and ran off.

CHAPTER 7

——

I felt like a thief, sneaking into the E Hostel so late at night. I might be at the tail end of the rebellious teenage years, but I'd never had the chance to be one. Even so, I didn't want to disappoint Henry. I mean, he was the closest thing I'd ever had to a grandpa. If I could sneak in and get to my room without him noticing, I could play it off like I was taking a nap in my room the whole time.

Carefully, I eased the front door open. Or at least, I meant to do it carefully. What I didn't plan on was how the door squealed high and horrible the whole way. I didn't even have time to wince and step inside before Henry's head popped out from the kitchen at the end of the hall.

"Jynn girl, is that you? What took you so long?" The short man came down the hall, wiping down a glass with a kitchen towel. A decade-old injury caused him to limp but didn't affect the way his eyes turned into upside-down crescent moons behind his thick glasses when he smiled.

"Hey, Henry," I greeted sheepishly. *Man up, Jynn,* I mentally kicked myself. I wasn't a child anymore; I shouldn't feel this guilty about coming home late. Yet here I was, trying not to turn into a tomato with shame. "I'm back."

I closed the door behind me and stepped to the left around the stairs to meet Henry in the hall.

"I can see that," he said slowly. "Everything okay?" He looked at me closely; it was a look I was used to. One of his hobbies was called *making sure Jynn is okay.*

"Yep." *I almost died again today. Fun, huh?* "I ran into"—*a dragon, then a tree*—"a girl who needed help. That's all." Of course, if I said what I was really thinking, Henry might just have a heart attack. Personally, I wanted him to hang around a lot longer.

He bobbed his head and started to walk back to the kitchen. "I saved you a plate."

"Food," I practically sang as I floated down the hall.

The hall opened up to a U-shaped kitchen with dark oak cabinets, white counters, and a tiled floor. To the left was a huge dining area which could fit all twenty-five inhabitants in the building when we actually ate together, which was once in every third or fourth blue moon. Not that anyone regretted it.

Right now, there were a couple guys sitting apart from each other with headphones on, playing on their phones, and a girl sitting at the corner of one of the two tables, fidgeting on her laptop. No one bothered to look up when we entered.

Henry pulled a plate out of the fridge and put it in the microwave. He touched a couple buttons, and it turned on with a loud hum. "Do you even remember how microwaves were before the energy crystals?" He glanced over at me.

The corner of my mouth hooked up, and I shook my head. "I thought old people hated dating themselves."

My favorite adopted grandpa tried to scowl at me, but the smile he attempted to hold back ruined the effect. "Young people nowadays have no respect."

He lifted his nose into the air.

I opened my eyes wide and covered my mouth with my hand. "I'm sorry. How could I call you old?" I clapped my hands together and gave a cheesy smile. "You're the youngest, most handsome man in the entire world!" And the one who controlled the food at the hostel.

He snorted flat out and pulled my food from the microwave. "Old, short, and fat, you mean. And don't you say otherwise." He handed me the warm plate and shook his finger under my nose.

The smile died on my face when I looked down at the chicken, mashed potatoes, gravy, and green beans. My mouth watered, and my stomach twisted painfully hard. Still, I handed the plate back. "I don't have an energy crystal." Without one, all I could eat was white rice and some vegetables.

Henry's heavy lids lowered until his eyes were barely more than lines. He sighed and was silent for a second before he scowled at me. "I already heated it up now. Don't waste food. I'll lend you a crystal today, but don't make it a daily habit." His familiar words were harsh, but his eyes were kind.

I nodded, trying not to feel guilty. I heard that speech probably four times a month, mostly when he noticed I'd only eaten rice for a couple days in a row. Eating a good meal was important. Without the right amount of calories, it was hard to have enough energy the next day to stay safe in the Gate. It was a vicious cycle between getting enough to eat and getting enough crystals. Once one side broke, it was hard to fix.

Henry was like Jonovan. Instead of going in the Gate, he worked full time as the property manager of the E Hostel, and that paid for his housing and food and very little else. It was also probably one of the reasons why he was still alive. At sixty with a lame leg, it was a guarantee that he'd die in the Gate. He'd told me before it didn't matter if he died. At least he'd finally get to see his family again.

It made me feel guilty because I had extra crystals in my room upstairs; I just couldn't use them to buy myself food. There were more important things I needed them for than to fill my stomach.

Yet Henry was using his own money on me.

Feeling touched and torn, I thanked him and sat down at the corner of the table to eat. Henry wasn't an A-ranked chef, but every bite filled me with tender emotion. Even when my small stomach was full, I still forced myself to finish all the food on the plate until the last crumb was gone. When Henry returned to take it, I dodged around him and washed it myself. Smiling, I waved goodnight and hurried up the stairs.

The second floor of the hostel was nothing but a long hall with a dozen doors lining it. Since I wasn't male, I turned the corner and went up to the third floor. Halfway up the stairs, I felt a cool tingle from the barrier which prevented any man but Henry from entering the women's living quarters.

The third floor was just like the second floor: a long, tan-colored hallway with doors to the sides. Unlike downstairs, however, some of the entries were decorated with things like sparkling stars or hearts. Some had slogans of guilds the girl wished she could join. Unfortunately, like the second floor, there were only two bathrooms for all twelve girls to share. Needless to say, my showers were usually pretty cold.

I walked to the bare door at the end of the row. After the long day I'd had, I couldn't wait to lie on my bed and just sleep it off. Tomorrow was already promising to be a busy day. I needed all the rest I could get.

Unlocking the door, I stepped inside the tiny room. Really, it was barely big enough for the twin-size bed, a small desk, and a small dresser next to the small closet. Aside from the two star-shaped pillows on the plain blue comforter and a couple family pictures on the dresser, there weren't any more decorations. After all, decorations cost money.

Absentmindedly, I pushed the door shut.

The last thing I expected was for it to bounce back open.

The corner of the door hit the back of my head, and I staggered forward. I could already feel the goose egg growing as I rubbed at it. Scowling, I looked over my shoulder. I didn't even have time to get a good look at the young woman before she walked into my room, but I knew exactly who it was by the sickly sweet perfume and the sounds of her heeled boots clicking on the ground.

Leticia walked right up to my bed, reached out, and grabbed the comforter. With a flip of her hand, she ripped it off, spilling the pillows all over the floor.

"What are you doing?" I demanded.

She looked at me nonchalantly, her purple-and-brown hair swinging behind her with the simple turn of her head. "It's getting cold at night. I need another blanket."

Cold my butt. She just couldn't let her favorite victim go twenty-four hours without a show of strength. My fingers in my hair curled into a fist. The tingle of pain helped remind me not to do something stupid. "There are plenty of blankets in the linen closet downstairs. Go get one of those."

"I could. But I don't want to." Her glossy lips curled as her chin lifted up, her very air asking what I was going to do about it.

What could I do about it? The answer was a big fat nothing.

Leticia was an E, like me. The difference was that she was at the top of the spectrum. Honestly, she was good enough that she could join a small guild and move out of here if she wanted to, but why would she? She was the strongest E in the hostel and knew it. As pathetic as this little building was, she was a queen here. Why give it up to be the bottom dog in someone else's guild?

I glared at her. Really, the blanket didn't actually belong to me. The only things I owned were the pillows, the pictures, and the handful of odds and ends in the closet with my clothes. The furniture and bedding were provided by the government, but that didn't mean I was just going to go belly up and hand over everything to her.

I reached out to take the blanket back.

She grabbed my wrist and swung me around, pulling me completely off the ground. I skidded across the twin bed before my back hit the wall with a thud. I swallowed a groan as pain radiated from my tailbone to my head. By the time I opened my eyes, she was at the door.

She sneered. "Thanks for the blanket." Her two-tone hair whipped through the air as she turned. Gradually, the clicking of her boots faded until I heard laughter and the sound of a door closing.

Frustrated, I scrubbed my hands over my face.

Seriously, I gave today an *F*, a complete failure. No, an *F* wasn't bad enough. It was a huge *Z*. What more could go wrong? How much more shit was going to be piled on? Letting out a low snarl helped, but it wouldn't get me a blanket.

Ignoring my aching back, I rolled off the bed and trekked all the way down to the first floor, stalking over to the linen closet under the stairs.

Henry paused in the act of turning off the lights in the kitchen. "Everything alright, Jynn girl?"

I took a breath to smooth out my features before I turned and gave him a lopsided smile. "Yeah, everything is great. I'm just a little cold, that's all."

I could tell him about Leticia, but what would be the use? Nothing would change. I was weak, meant to kneel to the strong. And what if she turned her sights on Henry if he reported her? What if she staged an accident or worse? For all he'd done for me, that was hardly the payback I wanted to give him.

Henry blinked his narrow eyes at me and scowled. "Cold? In the middle of June? I thought you girls were always complaining that the AC didn't work good enough on the top floor." He paused and reached out. "You're not getting sick, are you?" His cool fingers touched my skin. "No? That's good."

I waved away his concern.

"No, it's all good. I just want an extra blanket, that's all. Thanks anyway, Henry." I retrieved a random blanket and bundled it into my arms. Since it was just a spare, it wasn't the same quality as my original blanket—as if they were that great to begin with—but it worked. "See you in the morning."

I hurried up the stairs before any more crap happened.

CHAPTER 8

The next morning, I got up early. Most of the other girls were still asleep, so I didn't have to wait long for the bathroom and even had a warm shower. Not a bad way to start the day after the disaster of yesterday.

When I was clean and dressed, I went to the small safe in the back of my closet. Since I hadn't been able to get a better Items Bag, I could only carry ten things in it at a time. All the rest of my stuff had to be kept here, with only a door between Leticia and it. Luckily, she actually cared about the surveillance cameras in the halls for now and hadn't broken into my room yet. I didn't know what I'd do if she or anyone else stole my safe.

I glanced over my shoulder to make sure the door was shut and locked. It always was, but I couldn't be too careful. Satisfied, I opened the safe. Inside were ten E-ranked energy crystals, glowing different shades of blue in the dim closet light. I picked one out and fingered the smooth, cool surface. Just holding it, I could feel the energy pulsing from it like a heart.

I emptied everything out of my Items Bag and filled all the slots with the crystals. It wasn't safe to walk around with these on hand; it was just asking to get mugged, even with crystals as puny as these.

When I finished, I pulled out a brown satchel purse and filled it with my wallet and the other things I'd just taken out. With the convenience of Items Bags, purses were more of a fashion statement than a necessity. As for me, I only wore one on the last day of the month.

I locked the safe and left the hostel before that she-devil woke up, taking the tram to the other side of the city where the south exit of Eden was. A year ago, I'd walked through that opening naively thinking how great my life would be as a Hunter.

Well, I'd learned a lot since then.

I stood in line with all the Hunters exiting the city, waiting for my turn. Once I finally got to the window, I smiled at the guard. "Hi. Jynn Devhro."

On the other side of the thick glass, he clicked on a computer, checking for my leave request. After a moment, he nodded. "Have a good trip." The energy crystal–infused gate swung open, revealing the city I grew up in.

I waved at the guard and stepped out into Garden City.

It was funny. This might be my hometown, but it didn't feel like home anymore, as if the seventeen years I'd spent on these streets were a movie I used to watch. And it was all for one simple reason: I didn't belong here anymore. I was a Hunter; I belonged in Eden. Although I couldn't say anywhere in there felt like home, either.

With a sigh, I looked at the soft clouds floating in the pretty blue sky. Someday, maybe I'd find a home. But right now, there were more important things I needed to do.

Years of habit directed my feet through the bends and twists of the city, past stores and shops, most still closed in the early morning hours. Cars and buses filled the streets as people hurried to their nine-to-five jobs. Runners trekked across the cement with lazy steps, as if they'd never known what it was like to run for their lives.

All the while, I watched the safe world around me. I liked these trips to Garden City. They were a reminder that my life sucked for a reason. If Hunters didn't beat back the monsters continually regenerating in the Gate, this city would be overrun and killed off like when the Gate first appeared twenty years ago. Hunters reclaimed the city, and it was because of us that these humans could rebuild and have the relaxed life they did.

Eventually, I stopped on the top floor of a small apartment complex and knocked. Barely a second went by before the door was wrenched open, and I was tackled around the waist by a young teen in pink Hello Kitty pajamas.

"Jynn!" Aliya and I went down hard in the hall. My sister sat up, her full weight on my stomach. "Oh my gosh, Jynn, I'm so sorry!" She blinked down at me with the same green hazel eyes we'd inherited from our father.

As if my back wasn't still aching from last night. By the new burning sensation where my shirt had slid up, I was sure I'd just added a giant scrape to the sore muscles. But she didn't need to know that.

"Hey, Aliya." I reached out, smooshed her head to my chest, and kissed her hair like she was a little kid. "I missed you, too."

She squealed and wiggled, trying to get out of my hold. Laughing, I held her tighter and rubbed her head with my hand. In seconds, her long, smooth hair was a mess.

"Jynn! I'm not a baby anymore!" She planted her hands on my chest and pushed as hard as she could.

"You will always be my little baby sister," I cooed and patted her head while she tried to get away. No matter how she wailed, I needed this. After all the shit I'd gone through lately, I needed a reminder of why I was even dragging myself to and from the Gate. I needed to look at her face and remember I was keeping her safe and fed. I'd break without it.

"Jynn? It's so early," Aunt Mina's sleepy voice drifted out of the open door.

"Morning!" I let go of Aliya and straightened up.

My sister scowled and shoved me down as she stood up. After brushing herself off, she held out her hand to help me. I grinned at her. With a prissy snort, she looked away. But her hand was still steady when I grabbed it, and her lips curled into a small smile.

We went inside and closed the door. Aliya thumped me on the shoulder before disappearing down the hall.

Aunt Mina finally stepped into the main room, wrapped in a purple robe. If it weren't for her graying hair and the worry lines on her face, it would have been easy to mistake her for my mom. But that wasn't possible. Mom was in the same hospital room she'd been in for the last six years. Still, Aunt Mina had done her best to fill the hole that losing a mother left behind, and I was grateful. For both me and Aliya.

Aunt Mina hugged me tight. "Welcome home."

"Thanks." I glanced around the front room, which was a living room and kitchen combo. It took up half of the eight-hundred-square-foot, two-bedroom apartment. If there was anywhere I considered home, it was this aged but clean place. The very reason why I still breathed was the people in this house. Well, here and the hospital.

Aliya returned, pulling a brush through her hair.

Aunt Mina smiled at her and looked back at me. "How about some breakfast?"

I waved a hand. "Ah, no. I've already eaten." Honestly, I could eat more, but they were just as tight on money as I was. "It's just a quick trip this time." Just enough to fill the battered void that was growing in my heart. "I need to drop these off here since I don't have time to visit Mom today."

I held out my hand over the table. The ten crystals in my Items Bag appeared on the surface, shining and glittering from their internal energy. These ten crystals would cover my mom's medical expenses for the month, and they were due today.

When the Gates first appeared, half of the Earth's population died before the monsters were contained. Of the remaining humans, a third became Hunters. Then suddenly, another fourth of the population slipped into a coma for no apparent reason. Dreamers, is what they were dubbed. Without medical help, they died—*expensive* medical help. Most of the Dreamers had died already, whether their bodies finally gave out or their plugs were pulled. But some of us were still hoping for a cure.

When my dad died, he actually left behind a lot of money. But the six years of medical expenses for my mom had pretty much eaten it all up. The only reason we could afford to keep her alive now was because the price had been negotiated down since I was now a Hunter. Without my contract through the Hunter's Association, we would have had to pull her plug ten months ago.

And I wasn't ready to bury another parent. Even if it meant that I had to forgo a decent dinner ten out of the thirty days in the month, it was worth it to me.

"Is that Jynn?" Uncle Carl stepped out of the hall, wearing a blue robe over his thin frame. "Hey, kid, how are you doing?" He gave me a short side hug.

"Hey, I'm good." I hugged him back, swallowing the questions on the tip of my tongue. What was he doing here? Why wasn't he at work?

He patted the back of my head. "That's good." He opened his mouth but must have changed his mind because he sighed and stepped back. With that, he turned and shuffled back down the hall.

I blinked after him. What was that about? Where was the energy he normally had? I waited until I heard the click of the bedroom door then glanced at Aunt Mina.

Aliya looked away, frowning, and walked into the kitchen. She pulled a black lunch box from under the kitchen sink, the kind you would think had a cake inside for someone, and started to carefully stack the crystals in it.

Aunt Mina sighed then motioned her head toward the front door.

I glanced at Aliya before following my aunt out the door. Even though she was in her bathrobe, she was still taking me out of the house to talk. There was no such thing as privacy in such a small apartment sometimes.

Aunt Mina checked to make sure the windows were closed before she sighed again and leaned on the rail. "Your uncle . . . "

I knew just by her expression. "He lost his job again, didn't he?" My voice was just as soft as hers.

She nodded, tears in her eyes.

My aunt and uncle were great people. Despite suffering from infertility, they never once took out their frustration on my family. And when Mom became a Dreamer, they stepped up and became the supportive substitute parents that Aliya and I needed.

But just because they were good, it didn't mean good people could keep steady jobs. Neither of them completed high school—that's when the Gates opened, so staying alive was more important than education at the time—so the high-paying jobs were limited. Things were fine when they both worked, but a work-related neck injury put Aunt Mina out of a job permanently. With two to three debilitating migraines a week, who would hire her? As if things weren't hard enough, the business Uncle Carl worked for went under a couple months later. Since then, he'd bounced around from job to job as he slowly slipped into depression. Most of the time, he was good at hiding it. But . . .

Aunt Mina moaned and covered her face. "I don't know how I'm going to pay the rent next month."

My hands fisted at my side, but I didn't let my frustration show on my face. My sheer hopelessness.

A part of me wanted to demand, *Haven't I done enough? Haven't I bled enough to keep Mom alive? I'm just an eighteen-year-old girl, how much more do I have to shoulder?*

But I couldn't say that. And I couldn't let my family end up on the streets.

I would need twelve crystals on top of the ten that Mom's hospital bills required to get enough money for rent. That didn't include food and energy costs.

How would I ever get enough?

My knees wobbled from the emotional weight that settled on my shoulders. Even so, I smiled. "It'll be okay. I'll come up with something."

My aunt's lips quivered as tears popped in her eyes. "I'm so sorry, Jynn. I know it's a lot to ask of you." She pulled me into a hug. It was like she was trying to squeeze out all her worries into me.

I held her back and let her vent.

After a while, she straightened and wiped the tears from her lashes. "Are you sure you don't want to stay for breakfast?"

I shook my head. If I stayed any longer, I might miss the groups of Hunters who were safe to trail behind. Now that I absolutely had to get two or three crystals a day—something I'd never done before—I couldn't let that happen.

I opened the door and went in to find Aliya eating a bowl of cereal. "I'm going to head out. But I'll be back soon, okay?"

She dropped her spoon into the bowl and looked up with big eyes. "Really? Already? But you just got here."

I shrugged. "It was just a quick trip, remember?"

Aunt Mina glanced at me, guilt plucking her eyebrows together. She patted my shoulder then went into the kitchen to make coffee.

Aliya looked from Aunt Mina to me. It was obvious she'd guessed what was going on. Suddenly, her face brightened into a smile. She stood up and threw her arms around me. "Just one more year, and I'll graduate. I'm so excited. Twelve more months, and we get to be the Devhro Sisters, taking on the world! We'll be the strongest team ever!"

Her worshiping words were just as sweet as her loving arms around my neck, but I felt like I was just gut-punched by a rock ogre.

No, I didn't want that. I didn't want my baby sister within ten miles of the Gate and the hell inside. I didn't want to see the naive gleam in her eyes dull as she faced the blood and violence every day.

But most of all, I didn't want to see the adoration in her gaze change to disdain like all the other Hunters who looked at me. I didn't want her to find out what a disappointment her older sister was. Right now, my family had no idea. They knew I was an E, but not that I was the weakest Hunter in recorded history. Aliya, my aunt, and my uncle lived with the romanticized ideals which normal humans had of Hunters. Like they just walked into the Gate, and crystals rained down from the sky for the taking. My family was already beaten down enough. They didn't need to know how I was living in Eden, too.

I hugged her tightly, burying my face in her slim shoulders. "You make it sound like you're going to be a Hunter for sure." Since she couldn't see my face, it was easier to bluff the teasing behind my words. Easier to hide the fear which nearly crippled me.

"Of course!" she boasted and patted my head like she was the older sister. "My odds of being a Hunter are high, remember? After you and dad?"

Finally able to control my expression, I leaned back and poked her babyish cheek. "Genetics have nothing to do with it, silly. No matter who your parents are, it's still only a thirty-percent chance." The smell of coffee filled the room, and I used that as my cue to leave. I gave Aliya another quick hug and waved at my aunt. "See you later!" After they called their goodbyes, I shut the door.

For a moment, I stayed standing outside. If I took up Jonovan's suggestion and quit being a Hunter, I wouldn't have to leave. I could wake up every morning in the same room as my sister and make breakfast with my aunt. But we wouldn't be living here because we wouldn't be able to afford it. And I'd be visiting my mom in the cemetery, not the hospital.

In the end, it wouldn't be worth it.

I took a deep breath and pushed off the door. I didn't have time to mope. There was work to be done.

CHAPTER 9

After a quick stop at the E Hostel to put on my leather gear, I hurried to the Gate. It was late enough in the morning, I had probably already missed the teams I normally followed. Still, I loitered at the entrance for a bit, hoping I was wrong. I wasn't. After another half an hour without seeing any of the members of the "safe" groups, it became clear I was out of luck.

With a deep breath, I crossed into the Gate. On the other side, I looked around before heading toward the wooded area up north. Every night, the portals around Gate Vale opened up, spilling out millions of new monsters, so needless to say, it was the most dangerous to hunt in the mornings until higher-ranked Hunters killed off the stronger ones.

That being said, it was also easier to find a monster I could actually handle in the mornings, since the other Hunters hadn't cleared them out yet. And since weaker monsters tended to hang out in this little forest— Glenn Holt—maybe I could pick off one around the entrance without actually going in and risking running into anything stronger deeper in the woods.

At the edge of Glenn Holt, I pulled out my short sword and listened hard for sounds of movement. When I couldn't hear anything, I took a few cautious steps down the dirt path until the shade of the trees fell over my head. The hairs on the back of my neck suddenly rose; a monster must be close, but I couldn't see it.

A sound between a squeak and a growl exploded to my right. I twisted to the side, staggering back. A dire rat the size of a medium dog sailed past my arm, so close that its gray fur brushed against my skin. My heart tightened with a cold shot of adrenaline. That was close. I whirled to face it, not trembling like I used to. Instead, I was grateful that this was a monster I could handle without getting too hurt. Finally, something was going my way.

I lunged at the dire rat and lashed out with my short sword. It ducked, sword sailing over its head. Rearing back on its hind legs, it hissed, revealing dagger-like front teeth. I relaxed into a fighting stance, the one I learned from the basic guide in the System's tutorial book, ready to lunge. If I took it down fast enough, I might not get hurt at all, and that would save time from having to walk back and forth between here and the hospital.

Just as I was about to attack, a sharp whistle echoed through the air. I leaned to the side as a dagger sailed over my shoulder. The blade stabbed the dire rat hard enough that it flew back three feet.

My eyes widened, staring where the monster used to be. *What? That was my kill!* Stealing someone else's kill without being asked for help was against the Hunter's Code. Unfortunately, it was only punishable if I could prove it.

The sound of crunching dirt beneath rushing boots reached my ears. I spun and glared at a group of eight Hunters.

"Hey, good shot, Blake!" A woman dressed in a revealing purple dress under a matching mage robe laughed. She patted the leading man on the shoulder. "Right over her shoulder and all. It was like a trick shot!"

Blake's mouth hooked up on the side, and he leaned his head back, pleased with himself. "Told you I could do it." His steel shoulder pads gleamed in the sun as he strutted forward.

It was like I wasn't even there, even though we were only ten feet apart. My hand fisted at my side. "That was my kill." I lifted my chin in the air, trying to act like I wasn't nervous by the sight of their flashy, superior equipment.

They finally acknowledged me, but their expressions weren't any better. Derision, disdain, mockery. It was all there, like always.

Blake rested a hand on his chest and had the gall to look taken aback. "I just saved your life. Shouldn't you be saying *thank you* instead?" Then he glanced over his shoulder to get the approval of his comrades.

Even though he looked more than five years older than me, I guess some people never grew out of needing to have their egos stroked.

"I didn't ask for help. That kill should be mine." I needed the crystal from the carcass. Did this Blake even know how hard it was for Es to find weak monsters because of Hunters like him? If he did, he obviously didn't care.

He snorted and opened his mouth. Before he could answer, a voice from behind him cut him short.

"I know you!" A girl stepped around the group and hurried to me.

I blinked at her. Emma.

I knew she got into a good guild, but I didn't think Emma would get attached to a group like this. At least it looked like they were taking care of her. Instead of the basic equipment that everyone got when they started as a Hunter—the kind I still used—she wore light armor and had a nice-looking bow over her shoulder. The armor was obviously borrowed, since it wasn't tailored to her shape, but it was still much better than what I had.

I smiled at her. "Hey—"

"Emma, you know this girl?" Blake cut in.

She smiled over her shoulder at him. "Yeah. It's the girl I told you about. The one who brought me to the guild last night." She beamed at me. "Good morning, Jynn!"

"Good mor—" I was cut off again.

"Ah, I get it," the female mage from earlier spoke up. "You should stay away from her. She's a leech."

A twinge of fresh anger washed over me. "I am not!"

Emma's face wrinkled. "That doesn't sound very nice." She turned and looked at the group of older people.

Blake motioned to a guy next to him. Without a word, he walked over to the dire rat, cut out the energy crystal, then began skinning the carcass.

My eyes narrowed. It was mine, but what could I do against someone so much stronger than me?

"A leech is exactly what it sounds like," Blake's voice broke through my thoughts and drew back my attention. "Someone who sponges off another Hunter for a free ride. They think that being friends with stronger Hunters means free energy crystals. Most E insects are leeches." His chin lifted as he stared down at me. There was a light, a gleam in his dark eyes, which sent a chill down my spine.

I couldn't deny what he said because, for the most part, it was true. A lot of Es did attempt to leech off of other Hunters. But that didn't mean *I* did. Every crystal I got was by my own hand; none were given to me. Only, what was the use of arguing with narrow-minded people? It never worked. I might as well save my energy so I could find another monster.

"That's not true," Emma insisted. Her voice shook as she glanced at me, waiting for me to speak up. "Jynn's not like that. She even gave me a crystal last night when she saw I didn't have one."

There was an instant change in the group. Their barely tolerant gazes sharpened at the comment. Obviously, they didn't take kindly to her siding with an E.

Blake snorted. "She only did that to get your sympathy so she can take advantage of you later."

I glanced at her and paused. It was there in her stubborn gaze—a small gleam of doubt, a slight wrinkle in her brow as a question formed.

I sighed. Whatever. It was always the same thing. Why should I think it would ever be different? Why did I always feel the same prick of disappointment when I already knew how it was going to end? Besides, at this rate, Emma was going to get in trouble with her group—which could be fatal within the Gate.

I glanced back at the mostly skinned dire rat. Someday . . . someday, I wasn't going to get kicked while I was down. And then the world would end.

I smirked at my own bitter thoughts.

When I turned to Emma, my smile turned genuine. "It was good seeing you again. I'm glad you found a strong group." Even if they were pricks. Hopefully, she'd learn something from them, then find better companions before they rubbed off on her.

But that wasn't any of my business. I needed to find another monster as soon as possible. It was better to move to a different area, in case this group started to target me out of spite.

Emma looked at me with a torn expression. Her gaze flicked between me and her team, then focused over my shoulder. Her eyes widened in horror, and she screamed shrilly.

What? I whipped around and gasped as the man skinning the dire rat slumped to the ground. Only . . . he was missing his head.

The loose head rolled to a stop just inches from my boot, staining the ground red.

The shadows beneath the forest canopy shifted and moved.

My eyes narrowed. Stealth. Whatever had done this was using Stealth. There were several levels to this skill, the first being the ability to walk silently, but I could only think of a couple Hunters who were strong enough to use the highest level and become completely invisible. Each one of them was ranked A or higher.

This was bad. Really, really bad. From the looks of the dead Hunter, one of the concealed monsters had to be mere feet from me.

My hand tightened on my short sword, and I lifted it into a defensive position, my stance alert.

The shadows in the forest shifted and moved again, this time thinning until I could make out humanoid figures—eight-foot-tall humanoid figures.

Emma screamed in my ear and stepped behind me. Stupid, if you asked me. She was how much stronger than me? Still, it was easy to see she'd never seen anything die before. Even for me, seeing a dead human was startling. It could have been me if Blake hadn't taken my kill.

"Hunters," Blake commanded, "ready!"

The Stealth fell away from the monsters, and I gasped and froze when one appeared just ten inches away from me. With wide eyes, I stared up into its red face. It was an orc, but not like any I'd read about in the *Monster Manual*. Its build was leaner than the pictures, but its bare chest and arms were still more muscular than any I'd ever seen. Its skin was the color of red clay, the thick black hair on its head tied in messy braids and beading. The scariest part was the vicious intelligence in its dark red eyes. It stared down at me like it was thinking how to dissect me, and not quickly.

Heavy power radiated from it and washed over me. My muscles seized as terror filled my mind. Even if I could think straight, I doubted I could do anything but shiver with fear. Oh my god. When did this giant monster get so close to me? How could I not sense it?

Emma whimpered and grabbed onto my shoulder.

The group behind me yelled attacks with gusto, but their cries quickly changed to screams of pain.

Emma was shaking so hard she was moving my own body. I wanted to look behind, but I was just as scared to take my eyes off the red orc staring down at me. Slowly, my head shifted until I could glance at the group behind. My eyes widened, and I gasped in horror.

The Hunters who were so strong had been disarmed. One lay dead, two were on the ground bleeding, and the rest—even the arrogant Blake—were obviously defeated. Around them stood twenty or so red orcs, red and tall like the one by me. They were in the process of tying up the remaining Hunters.

Something cold, wet, and sharp touched my neck just under my chin. A frigid chill stabbed through my heart as I recognized the feeling of a blade. Without turning my head, I glanced at the red orc with wide eyes.

He looked down at me with derision. His cruelly jagged sword, covered in blood, rested at my throat. A smile stretched across his lips, revealing pointed fangs. Then his mouth opened, and he said something in a rough, clipped language.

I didn't think I could get any more horrified. These orcs had a language? I'd never, not in any book or lesson or experience, ever heard of a monster with its own language. Most were more animal than anything else, growling and such. But this red orc was obviously speaking.

Then I was shocked out of my mind when the universal translator in my Guide System activated, and a message appeared in front of my eyes.

[**This will work perfectly.**]

Suddenly, I felt dizzy and couldn't seem to get enough oxygen in my lungs.

It spoke, and my translator knew what it said. How was that possible? How could my translator know the language of a monster?

"I-It spoke," a shaky voice whispered behind me. The defeated team was just as shocked as I was.

The red orc jerked his sword away from me, leaving a stinging cut on my chin. He looked over my head and spoke again. [**Take them all.**]

CHAPTER 10

The words had barely processed before I was grabbed from behind by huge, strong hands. In seconds, I was disarmed, just like the rest of the Hunters. The red orcs even removed all magical items, including Items Bags. The monsters kept the weapons but tossed away the bags. We were then hog-tied and dragged across the ground behind two red orcs. They didn't bother with the dead Hunter.

What was going on? Were we being kidnapped? No monster had ever kidnapped Hunters. What did they want from us?

Under their oppressive aura, I could barely move or make a sound, and I wasn't the only one. The others looked just as paralyzed, which meant that these monsters were stronger than all of us.

They dragged us deeper into the forest, then I noticed the sounds of the footsteps ahead of me disappearing. I glanced over and gasped. There was a small portal tucked between two trees. The portals around the rim of Gate Vale were the size of a large house, and the Gate was as big as a skyscraper. This portal was small enough that the red orcs had to duck to go through, one after another, dragging us behind them.

I wiggled, trying to resist. *Don't take me in there. Please, don't take me in there.* Only one Hunter—an S—had ever dared to go into a portal. He never came back out.

My resistance was pointless. The red orc holding me didn't even pause as it stepped into the portal and jerked me through.

My surroundings changed, and I gasped as I looked around. I thought it would be like a fiery hell on the other side; I didn't expect a city like Ancient Rome. We stood in the middle of a plaza under a cloudy sky, stone pillars and buildings stretched out around us. After my initial shock,

I noticed there were broken statues scattered across the ground, and some of the buildings were crumbling.

Ahead of me, Blake cleared his throat and spoke in a strong voice like he wasn't bound and cowering. "Where are we?"

The red orc holding Blake hit him on the side of the head, leaving a bloody scratch. The first orc I saw—the leader, judging by the way the other orcs treated him—turned and sneered at Blake. [**We're not there yet.**]

Wait, did that mean he could understand us, too? Goose bumps spread down my back.

We were dragged through dusty streets until the buildings opened up to a Roman-like palace, two stories tall with a triangular, tiled roof. Well, Roman-like with a sadistic flare. Huge vats of oil were placed between the columns, and green flames ten feet tall blazed from the vats, casting a freakish light on everything.

I gaped up at the palace, trying to grasp what I was looking at. It was a legit civilization—a crumbling one, by the state of everything, but one nonetheless. Was this how it was on the other side of every portal? I always thought they were just random dimensions with monsters roaming around that were dumped into Gate Vale every night. I never thought there could be structured societies within the portals. Why hadn't we learned more about them? Were they all this unfriendly?

Me and the rest of the Hunters were dragged around to the side of the palace. It wasn't until we were closer that I saw a row of doors lining the walls. A red orc opened one of them, and we were thrown into a room. Half of us landed headfirst on the pale-yellow dirt floor, then the iron door swung shut.

The leader stared at us through the bars with his blood-red eyes.

[**Make yourself comfortable for now. We'll be back soon enough.**] The side of his wide mouth curled into a toothy sneer, then he turned and walked away.

I sat up and rubbed my aching chin on my shoulder, trying to get the dirt off my face. Everything inside my mind was screaming in fear, but I couldn't let myself fall apart now. There was too much I had to live for to give up now.

Emma huddled in a ball, her breath a gasping sob she was trying to control.

"Emma," I whispered, shifting over to her. "Hey, Emma, are you hurt?"

She looked at me with wide, wet eyes. Slowly, she shook her head.

"What does it matter if she's hurt?" Blake snarled from the other side of the room. "We're all going to die." He stood up, chin high in the air like he wasn't tied up. "At least, the people who don't listen to me will." Apparently, now that the red orc's oppressive aura was gone, he was back to his normal *charming* self.

A shiver went down my back, almost as strong as the one that red orc gave me. Did he seriously think he could do something about this situation?

No one else seemed to share my thoughts. A collective sigh of relief sounded, as if they felt better now that Blake was acting like a king again. Even Emma looked a little less scared.

That's testosterone for you, I thought as I stood up. "What are you thinking?"

It was like I hadn't even said anything. Blake looked at a guy dressed in light armor on his right. "Mark, do you have any weapons on you?"

Mark nodded his shabby head. "They didn't take the one on my back, but I can't get it with my arms tied like this." He jerked his chin over his shoulder, motioning to his hands tied behind his back like the rest of us. "Someone get it." He knelt on the ground.

Another man walked behind him then turned around and lowered himself until his hand disappeared beneath Mark's collar.

Mark's mouth wrinkled. "Damn, dude. Cut your nails sometime. No wonder you can't get a girl, if you leave her bleeding like this."

"Shut up." The guy straightened, grasping a small dagger in his hand. He turned and shoved Mark to the ground with his boot before he returned to Blake. Back-to-back, the guy started to saw at Blake's bindings.

I sat there, listening to the sounds of the knife against the rope. He could have chosen anyone, even himself, to free first, but he chose Blake. It was very telling of just how high Blake was in the hierarchy here. And I wasn't even on that totem pole at all.

The ropes around Blake's wrists fell to the ground, and he stretched his arms. "That's better." He took the knife from the guy and cut his ropes off with a vicious swipe. With that done, Blake tossed the knife back to him, who then went around freeing everyone.

He paused when he got to me, but still squatted down and cut my ropes off.

"Thanks," I muttered, rubbing at the burns on my arms.

The healer walked around, touching members of the group with his golden fingers, but he skipped right over me. Emma's eyes widened, and she looked from the healer to me. When she opened her mouth to complain, I waved at her.

Frankly, I was just glad they actually untied me. I wasn't part of their group, so what obligation did they have to take care of me? Sheer humanity wasn't a good enough excuse. We were Hunters. If I didn't want to die, I had to be strong enough not to.

I watched Blake frown at the metal door. The walls of the room were made of thick pale bricks, and the only opening and source of light came from that door. It didn't look like much, but no matter how Blake pulled at it with his bulging muscles, he couldn't pull it open or even bend the bars to make a wider opening. Surprisingly, no one came to check on us even with all the racket he was making.

With a frustrated growl, Blake turned and glared at a girl leaning against the side of the wall. "Penny, get over here."

The cute young woman walked over, the soles of her soft, thigh-high boots noiseless against the packed yellow dirt. "Sup, boss?" she asked, her voice thick with an accent. She tilted her head, brown hair tied up high and spilling over her shoulders.

He jerked his shoulder at the door. "Open it."

Her lips curled up, and she slid past him. "Sure thing, boss." It wasn't until she pulled several thin metal picks out of her hair that I understood what was about to happen.

I may not have lived in the best neighborhood the last eight years of my life, but this was a skill I'd never picked up, even though some of my childhood friends had. Given her skill set, I couldn't help but wonder where this Penny had learned it from. Or how many people she'd inconvenienced with her talent.

One of her picks broke, and she let out a soft curse.

"Come on, I thought you were better than this." Mark rolled his eyes.

"Shut up." Penny glared at him and pulled another lockpick from somewhere I couldn't see. It couldn't be from an Items Bag because the red orcs had taken all of them. She started fidgeting with the lock again. A couple minutes later, she muttered, "Open, says me."

A latch clicked.

My lips pursed to the side. Why did Blake even tug at the door? Why not have Penny open the door right off the bat? Did he really have to be so much of a hero? But I wasn't dumb enough to ask the question out loud.

Blake patted Penny's shoulder like he was rewarding a dog, then he slowly leaned his head out. "It's clear," he whispered. "Let's go."

"It can't seriously be this easy," another member of the group said exactly what I was thinking.

"Where do you think they took our stuff?" another guy asked. "I just bought that sword. I don't wanna lose it now."

"Do you really think that's important right now?" I couldn't help but ask. The words were barely out of my mouth before Blake cut me off—yet again.

"I ain't waiting around." Blake tossed a look at the guy over his shoulder. "If you wanna loot, then go ahead. I'd rather lose my shit than my head." At least he could be reasonable at a time like this. I thought he'd be all for brainlessly looting these dangerous creatures.

Emma reached out and gripped my sleeve, her hands trembling. The rest of the group remained quiet, silently agreeing with Blake.

He nodded at the door. "Let's go. Keep your guard up and be quiet." His eyes flicked over me and Emma, a frown marring his face.

I didn't have to be told what to do. My very survival depended on silently following groups every day. It had gotten to the point that it shocked me when I *could* hear my own footsteps, but I had a feeling it was a skill Emma hadn't learned yet.

I glanced at the fingers clutching my sleeve. Man, she really was hanging onto the wrong person. If she wanted to raise favorability in her group, she was failing miserably.

Blake jerked his head at a silent guy in the back of the group. Without a word, he hunched over and crept out of the door. He obviously had some sort of Stealth skill because his black cap should have stood out against the pale yellow ground and the white stone buildings, but he was like a shadow, slipping across the ground and slinking smoothly along the building. A moment later, a soft whistle sounded in the air.

Blake waved his hand to the rest of the group.

Shouldn't there be a guard or something? I couldn't help but look around suspiciously, not seeing any. My luck was never this good. Everything just felt wrong. Maybe that was why this guild was so well known? They weren't just strong; they were also blessed with godly levels of sheer dumb luck?

We pressed against the white stone walls of the palace and slid across the building, under the open windows. Voices—a lot of loud, harsh voices—were coming from inside. What were they doing in there?

When we reached the corner, we stopped. Every building looked the same. They were all made of white stone with cream tiled roofs. Five streets plowed through them, all leading toward the palace entrance. Now that I actually looked at them, I couldn't help but notice the curves and designs carved into the crumbling structures. Funny, I would have never guessed that the red orcs had an artistic side to them. Just picturing their brutal mannerisms, I couldn't help but think they didn't belong in a place like this.

"This place all looks the same," Mark muttered, looking around the roads that spread out from our location. At least he was smart enough not to talk too loud.

I flicked a glance at him before pointing to our left. "We came from that direction—"

"The portal is this way," Blake cut me off. He motioned with his hand in the direction I'd just pointed, and the group obeyed. Our collective pace was quick yet silent.

I took a deep breath as I followed at the rear. *Don't get mad*, I chided myself. *Don't get mad*. I already knew what they thought of me. Of course they wouldn't care about anything I said.

Emma glanced at me and fell into step beside me.

I looked at her and jerked my head, indicating that she should join the rest of the group ahead of us.

She scowled and kept my pace. It was obvious from her expression alone that she'd been disillusioned about her team. Granted, I couldn't say I wanted her to stay with them, but right now was a bad time to split from stronger Hunters. Especially over a puke E-ranked one.

A guttural roar echoed behind me, and goose bumps erupted up and down my body as I looked over my shoulder.

A red orc stood just outside our empty cell, his head tilted back and his mouth open. I didn't need a translator to know he was announcing our escape.

Red orcs spilled from the palace front doors.

"Run!" Blake yelled.

I didn't need him to tell me that. Since they already knew we were gone, there was no point in trying to sneak away. I launched into a full sprint along with the rest of the Hunters. The problem was, there was a significant difference in our abilities. One by one, the other humans grew smaller in my sight, and the red orcs were quickly getting louder behind me.

Even so, Emma didn't leave my side.

"Go!" I yelled.

"No!" Her face had paled with fear and her breath was hitching, barely suppressed tears hanging on her lashes. Still, she kept pace with me.

I opened my mouth to argue with her. I knew since the day I became a Hunter that I was going to die—it was only a matter of time. But that didn't mean I wanted to drag someone down with me. Especially a good girl like Emma.

She never gave me the chance. Instead, she grabbed my left arm and half-hoisted me onto her shoulder. With most of my weight on her, she took off running faster than I ever could. She didn't have the best hold and I was a little taller than her, so every once in a while, I had to skip my feet when they were about to touch the ground, but at least it sounded like the red orcs weren't getting closer anymore.

But they didn't go away, either. In fact, I think there were more following us than before. I didn't dare look back.

"Turn left," I yelled in her ear over the rushing air. She was running faster than some motorbikes I'd ridden.

She veered left, the bottom of her boots skimming across the pale yellow dirt as she followed my directions. For a second, our balance tipped to the side. I kicked my foot out and tapped the ground, pushing us back upright. She corrected our position and kept running through the empty street. Well, empty except for the sounds of dozens of red orcs charging behind us.

"There!" I pointed ahead.

On the right side of the street, next to a mostly crumbled building, was a black portal. Blake and Mark stood next to it, watching as me, Emma, and the red orcs neared. I'd assumed they'd be long gone. Who would have thought that Blake was a legit leader after all?

"Let's get out of here!" Mark inched toward the portal.

"The signing bonus, you shithead," Blake hissed at him.

My eyes widened as I understood. Most groups got a bonus—usually money or some other significant reward—when they took on new Hunters and trained them for a period of time. It was a method guilds used to mix old and new Hunters together so their new recruits weren't killed right off the bat in the Gate. Apparently, Emma had a good enough signing bonus that Blake wanted to keep her alive. No wonder he was so tolerant of her.

Once we reached them, Blake gripped my shoulder painfully, and with a jerk, he ripped me off Emma. My knees gave out, and the only thing keeping me up was his hold. If he didn't let go soon, my shoulder bone might crack.

Emma lost her balance and tipped to the side.

Mark grabbed her midfall and threw her toward the portal. "One at a time! Hurry!"

"Wait!" Emma twisted in the air and looked at me with big, worried eyes. She fell through the black hole and vanished.

She'd barely disappeared when Mark lunged in after her.

The whole time, Blake stared down at me with cold eyes. A shiver went down my spine, but I ignored him and tried to jump into the portal. His fingers tightened on my shoulder, holding me in place. Suddenly, his grip changed, and his other hand grabbed my thigh. He hoisted me into the air.

I gasped and wiggled over his head, staring at the red orcs closing in on us. Each one of them held a weapon, but none of them attacked.

"Annoying insects are only good for one thing." Blake's words were as cold as steel.

He threw me at the red orcs.

CHAPTER 11

I gasped, suddenly airborne. As I spun through the air, I saw Blake jump through the portal, and a second later, I crashed into several hard bodies.

Air whooshed from my lungs, sending me into a panic. Pain pierced my skull, and I cried out as my vision darkened. I dropped to the ground at the red orcs' feet and blinked up. They hadn't even flinched when I hit them.

The leader yelled something above me, his voice a snarl.

Gasping, I turned my head in time to see a handful of red orcs race to the portal. One shoved his hand out, but instead of passing through, it slapped against the black circle like it was made of solid stone.

He growled and looked back. [**Shut, again.**]

My eyes widened. *Shut? But I just saw three people leave through it! It can't be shut!*

I was still dizzy, but I clawed at the ground, trying to get to the portal. "No. No!"

I barely moved when a foot landed on my back, pinning me into place without actually crushing me. No matter how I wiggled, I couldn't get out from under it. I clawed at the air as if sheer will would get me to the portal. It didn't.

I was so close. Just ten more feet, and I'd be safe. I didn't know why the red orcs couldn't go through, but I fully believed that humans could. I had to believe it, or I would break.

They left me.

They actually left me. And it wasn't just that my own kind left me, Blake literally threw me away. Threw me like a piece of trash, nothing but a small diversion to the monsters chasing us. He didn't even have to. It was something he consciously decided to do.

I was still trying to process everything when the foot let up and rolled me over onto my back. The red orc leader stared down at me, his eyes burning with anger. Several others joined him, just as big and imposing. He tilted his head up and looked at the portal before his red eyes landed back on me.

Every muscle in my body froze under his oppressive glare.

In a blur of movement, he spun around, and the orc to his right screamed out. The leader's grizzly sword protruded from the unsuspecting red orc's stomach. The one to his left flinched, his features tightening, but he didn't say anything. Was something like this typical for them?

The leader pulled the sword out and turned back to me, his expression without a care, as though one of his people wasn't slumping to the ground, dead by his hand. Thick black blood splattered the floor, barely missing me.

The leader glanced at a red orc behind him. [**My guards are lacking. But only one of you will do for now.**] He jerked his head toward me.

The red orc stepped forward and reached for me.

Without the pressure of the leader, my body finally started to move again. I tried to jump to my feet, but I was barely up before I was seized by his huge hand. I tried to jerk away, but that only caused him to dig his sharp nails into my skin. The red orc jerked me forward, almost all the way off my feet.

[**It won't do to have it damaged.**] The leader started to walk away, and the group fell in step behind him, leaving the dead orc on the ground like it was nothing.

The guard dragged me back through the city, headed once again toward the palace. There was nothing I could do to stop him; he was twice my height and a hundred times stronger. When I planted my feet on the ground, he simply kept walking, and the soles of my shoes slid across the dirt. Even so, I still resisted. They were going to kill me; I knew they were. But that didn't mean I had to meekly follow.

The group of orcs branched off at the bottom of the palace stairs, leaving just the leader, the guard, and me. I was dragged up the stairs and past the pillars to two huge wooden doors. A mural carved onto their surface showed a woman floating in the clouds. It would have been pretty if it weren't for the hundreds of scratches all over it. Her face was completely gone, and it was hard to make out anything else about the carving.

The leader pushed open the doors.

Rough laughter, low-pitched screams, and indiscernible noise polluted the air. I couldn't understand any of it, but one thing was clear: every creature in here was bigger than me. The leader looked over his shoulder in my direction. The green light from the fires that flanked the doors cast an eerie shade on his red face, as if his eyes were nothing but demonic black pits. He sneered and walked in.

On the other side of the door was a huge room, the size of a football field at least. Pillars lined two sides of the space, with green flames flickering from the sconces. And as if that weren't creepy enough, the room was filled with hundreds of red orcs. Some were male, broad shouldered and bare armed, and some appeared to be female—super muscular females, with only slightly more defined chests and clothed in colorful, Roman-like dresses. Honestly, if it weren't for the clothes, I wouldn't be able to tell them apart at first glance. They all filled the space, swarming around the pillars with their loud noises and drinking from bronze cups.

The room quieted when we entered, and every single menacing eye focused on me. Whispers rose up like a wave of noise washing over me. What was worse was that my translator tried to keep up with the thousands of words, flooding my vision with so many text boxes I could barely see in front of me.

[**Look at it!**]

[**So small and ugly! So weak!**]

[**This is the current intelligent species? So disappointing!**]

[**Ooh, I hope I get a turn to play with one!**]

On and on, their rough words filled my ears and eyes until I almost collapsed. And it wasn't just their words but the heavy, powerful air in the room which settled on my pathetic E-ranked shoulders and made it hard to even breathe.

A loud, feral growl echoed from the back of the room. Instantly, all the noise stopped. Red orcs parted, and I was marched down the aisle they created. Occasionally, an orc leaned from the crowd to get a closer look at me—one even smelled my hair—but after the leader started to kick the brazen monsters away, they stopped trying to get closer.

On the other side of the room was a low platform. Centered in the middle was a tall golden chair with the biggest red orc I'd seen yet dressed in a black robe which revealed his huge red chest. A thick black braid hung from both temples, and the rest of his hair lay loose against his massive shoulders. He acted aloof to the handful of females at his feet who massaged his legs and filled his golden cup. His blood-red gaze was focused on me.

The red orc holding my arm threw me forward, and I stumbled to the bottom of the stairs, barely able to keep upright. I was physically free, but the look in the king's eyes held me more captive than any restraint.

[**Welcome, creature of the current intelligent species.**] His low voice rumbled.

All the hair rose on the back of my neck, and I stopped breathing as his aura washed over me.

He motioned to the red orcs behind me. [**Are you enjoying the party?**]

Did he actually want to talk with me?

I had to swallow twice before my dry throat was moist enough to speak. "Why did you bring me here?"

[**As the great current intelligent species, it only seemed right to invite one to a celebration.**] He laughed as if he were actually funny.

Low snickers filled the air.

Current intelligent species? Why did he keep calling me that? Would he even tell me if I asked?

Before I could decide, he spoke again. [**Now that you're here, let the entertainment begin!**] He roared and smashed his cup against the ground. The metal warped and cracked beneath his strength like it was made of glass.

Instantly, a female offered him another cup.

The red orcs in the room roared in response, so loud that I had a moment of vertigo. Something landed on the ground next to my feet. Looking down, I noticed a longsword with a red, thick blade. Wide eyed, I looked up to see the red orc leader staring down at me with a malicious sneer. A smile stretched over his face as he held up a sword of his own. At least, that's what it would be called from the shape of it, except that it was as long as I was tall.

It was then that I realized *I* was the entertainment at this party.

The leader motioned to the sword at my feet with his own blade. [**Show me the strength of the current intelligent species.**]

What strength? Still, I reached down and grasped the handle. It was heavy—so much heavier than the short sword I was used to carrying—and poorly balanced, so the blade felt overweight. My shaking arms could barely hoist it up into position. My brows pulled together as I glared at him, trying to hide how scared I actually was. How suddenly desperate I felt.

I was going to die. There was nothing I could do about it.

Why . . . ?

My teeth gritted together, and I lunged forward, my form bad. It wasn't just the weight of the weapon; I didn't know how to use a longsword. I'd never been taught, and it required a different hold from the one-handed stance that my short sword needed. But even if I had my normal weapon, the result would be the same.

With a casual flick of his wrist, the leader knocked me to the ground. But he didn't leave it at that. He made sure to leave a cut on my left arm in the process, just deep enough to bleed but not to prohibit my movement.

I glanced at the fat drop of blood that rolled off my arm and seeped to the ground. He could have killed me right then. But he didn't. He was toying with me.

And he couldn't look more pleased with himself.

The red orcs around us cheered as the king howled with laughter.

Why . . . ?

I grabbed the sword and stood up. I couldn't even get within six feet of him. The leader didn't knock me down again, but each time I took the offense, he left me with another cut that shaved a fraction off my HP. Soon enough, I wasn't even on the offense anymore but making a pathetic attempt at defense. Really, the red orc had free rein over our exchange. Ten cuts turned into a hundred cuts, a hundred quickly turned into two hundred.

Why couldn't I . . . ?

My whole body dripped blood; each cut ached with every move I made. Blood loss was starting to get to me. My body shook, and I could barely lift the heavy sword. My vision distorted—not just because of the System warning me of my low HP but also from the graying clouds around the edges.

It was torture, plain and simple. He was going to cut me to death for fun in front of these loud, laughing orcs. I always knew I would die early— being so weak and all, it was a given. But I never thought I would die in such a humiliating way.

Why couldn't I be stronger?

My knees gave out, and I collapsed to the ground. No matter how much I filled my lungs, I couldn't seem to get enough air.

A red System box appeared in my vision, flashing with urgency. [**HP has reached a critical level! Seek medical assistance immediately!**]

If only I were stronger, it wouldn't be like this. I wouldn't have been flung behind by Blake. Maybe I could have gotten away before I was even taken into this portal. If I were stronger, I wouldn't have even been in that blasted forest. I would have been somewhere else, like the Marsh, somewhere where I could actually get enough energy crystals so me and my family could live properly.

I thought I could persevere. Having the tenacity of a human cockroach, I thought I'd make the best of what life dealt me. All I had to do was hang on and keep going.

Why . . . couldn't I have been stronger?

The darkness that edged my vision thickened and began to fill in. Even the red System box disappeared. Finally, finally, the thundering noise of the red orcs began to dim until all I could hear was my heart beating. It was slow, sometimes with a pause between each beat.

I want to be stronger. Aliya, I'm sorry . . .

Dimly, I felt tears pool in my burning eyes.

Then I will make you stronger, a crystal-clear female voice spoke in my mind. Her voice was soothing and calm, like a balm to my aching heart.

My eyes widened with shock.

The red orc leader walked up to me and used his foot to flip me onto my back. All I could do was stare up at him with blurry vision, barely able to make out his cruel face.

Suddenly, a teal System window opened in my vision, clear and clean.

[You have fulfilled the requirements for the Becoming Stronger Quest. Do you accept? Y/N?]

Beneath the words were numbers counting down.

[5 . . .]

The leader grasped his sword with both hands.

[4 . . .]

He raised the sword over his head.

[3 . . .]

"Yes," the word escaped my cracked lips.

The sword plunged down.

A bright light flashed, filling my vision until it was all I could see.

Then, nothing.

CHAPTER 12

Slowly, my eyes cracked open. Weird. I should be dead, so why did that ceiling look so familiar? And the cream shade of paint on the walls. I knew the solid feeling under my fingers, a durable cloth that was neither soft nor rough. How many times had I been wrapped in one of these blankets while Jonovan healed me?

But how did I get to Eden's hospital?

My shaking hands covered my face as the memory of that red orc thrusting his sword down on me flooded my mind. I'd been on my last couple HP at that point—there was no way I should've survived that.

Yet here I was, lying in a hospital bed with an IV in my hand and listening to the heart monitor. The beeping glitched sporadically as I remembered everything that happened leading up to the bright flash of light. I didn't die and go to heaven, right? There was no way I was going to believe heaven was a hospital. That was just too much of a rip-off.

A strange bell-like sound chimed softly in my ear.

Huh? Did someone come in? I lifted my hands and glanced toward the wooden door. It remained shut, just like the blue curtains over the window. Then I noticed a pale teal System screen hanging in the air in front of me.

[You have four new notifications. Would you like to read them? Y/N?]

"What?" I whispered, sitting up.

Since when did the System window change color? It had always been blue; there were no other options. But that wasn't the only strange thing. The System was passive; it never announced any changes until I opened the window first. The only exception was when a teammate passed messages to other teammates, a feature I'd never used.

. . . No, that was a lie. My eyes widened as those horrible memories, so fresh I could still feel the pain on my smooth skin, flashed through my mind. I wrapped my arms around my stomach and worked on slowing the rate of the beeps on the heart monitor. *The System did pop open its own window one other time.*

Right before . . . and I said yes. But what did I say yes to?

It seemed so harmless, really. I was used to the System, looking at it daily. But that was when I could control when the window opened and closed. Did the reason why it was different have to do with the new notifications? Did I have to say my response out loud, or could I just think them like normal?

Was this a dream? Something my mind thought up to deal with the trauma I just went through? I reached over and pinched my arm, hard. The pain made me flinch as another pain came to mind. Jeez, how long was it going to take before I forgot that feeling?

I frowned at the window and thought, *Yes.*

The teal screen opened up to my main menu, a message flashing across.

[Welcome to the Becoming Stronger Quest.]

"Becoming Stronger Quest?" I whispered. A quest? Since when did the System hand out quests? That sounded completely different from a monster bounty, and there was no way I'd ever accept one of those. Those were things higher-ranking Hunters dealt with.

Still, I couldn't deny that *Becoming Stronger* was attractive to me.

The door to my room opened, and a nurse stepped inside. She paused, half through the door, and gaped at me. "Jynn! You're finally awake." Melea, a sweet, plump woman in pink scrubs, hurried to my bedside.

Now I knew this was real. As much as I liked Melea, I'd never put her in my dreams.

I glanced at the System window, but Melea didn't seem to see it. Weird. Hunters could usually see the windows of other Hunters, though they were just a blank screen to them. But by the way she immediately started to check me over, it was clear it was invisible to her.

"Goodness' sake, you gave us a scare," Melea chided gently. She pushed a button at the side of my bed, and the bed shifted under me until I was raised to a sitting position.

I gave them a scare? "What do you mean?"

"You've been unconscious for four days." She looked me in the eye.

"Four days?" My eyes widened. "Does . . . my family know?"

"Of course they do," Jonovan's soothing voice came from the door.

I jumped and looked over as he walked into the room. Melea flushed as pink as her scrubs and stepped to the side while Jonovan pulled up a chair beside my bed.

"Good morning, Miss Jynn. Or should I say, good evening, given what time of day it is?" He sat down and gave me a soft smile. "We always contact the family members when something major happens to a Hunter. Especially when one slips into a coma for no apparent reason." He reached out and took my hand. His fingers began to glow gold as he used his power to check my condition. "Some of the other healers were starting to wonder if it was Dreamer's disease, but that should be impossible for a Hunter, given the nature of the disease."

A chill went down my back. Oh no, what was my family thinking right now? It was bad enough that my mom was stuck in a hospital. I groaned and scrubbed my hands over my face. The IV tugged at my skin, but I ignored it. "How did I get here?"

What happened after I said yes?

"A friend of mine found you on the ground in Gate Vale, perfectly whole and healthy but unconscious, so he brought you to me. From what I understand, that's the second time he's saved you in a week. Maybe I should take you to thank him. You two obviously should meet each other."

I dropped my hands and stared at him with a confused expression. Who on earth was he talking about?

A small smile tugged on his lips, then his expression grew serious. "But that's for another time. As for what happened before you passed out, I hoped that you could tell me, Miss Jynn." His hands stopped glowing, and he looked at me with expecting eyes.

I bit my lips, playing over everything that happened from the time Blake and his crew showed up to when I woke up here. A lot did, but what should I say about it? I didn't have to be psychic to know Blake was going to cover up what he did. Besides, taking my kill was the worst thing that could be proven with witnesses. It was against the code, but not against the law. And his whole group saw him help me escape from the cell with them, but no one saw him throw me at the red orcs.

In the end, it was my word against his. With his backing, who would believe me over him? Especially when I was completely healthy now. If I did accuse him of trying to kill me, what lengths would he go to to keep me quiet?

And who would believe me if I told them how the red orcs tortured me to death but a white flash of light appeared and saved me? That woman also spoke to me, but I didn't recognize her voice. Really, the whole thing was like a nightmare I wanted to forget. Only, I could still feel the tip of the red orc's sword digging into my skin when I closed my eyes.

I bowed my head and stared at the white blanket over my legs. I forced my hands to stay loose at my side. "I don't remember what happened."

Since I didn't know if the authorities even knew about me and the other Hunters getting kidnapped through the portal, it was better not to say anything about it at all. I just hoped that Emma stayed quiet about it, too.

"Nothing?" Jonovan mulled over the word. "Nothing at all? Do you even remember going into the Gate that morning?"

I slowly nodded. "Yes. But after that, it gets a little . . ." *scary*. "Blurry," I said slowly. "I remember a white light and waking up here." That should be enough. Start with the truth, end with the truth, and gloss over everything in between.

"Are you sure?" Jonovan looked at me with a serious expression.

I looked at the System screen still floating in front of me and nodded. "Yeah."

He sighed and ran a hand through his hair, slightly messing up his ponytail. "Okay, if you need to talk about anything, I'm always here."

I bit my lip. As if I could talk to anybody about this. Who would believe me, anyway? Technically, Jonovan should be able to see the screen, but he obviously didn't notice my oddly colored window because he hadn't asked about it yet.

I mean, I didn't even know why it changed. And I still hadn't even had time to open the windows and see what the notifications were about. To see what the *Becoming Stronger Quest* was even about. I wasn't going to lie—it kind of sounded like a hack. Or a name someone would spout if they had no idea what else to call it. I was dying to open it and see, but there was something else I had to do first.

I looked up at Jonovan. "Do you have a phone? I'd like to call my family."

He stared at me for another couple seconds before he stood up. "Yes. I'll have Melea bring you the phone." He paused while turning and looked at me again. "Are you sure you don't remember anything?"

I shook my head. "No, nothing."

I guess he finally accepted my lie, because he said, "I'm going to keep you in the hospital till tomorrow morning just to make sure that everything is okay. Rest well, Miss Jynn. I'll be back later today to check on you again." He paused at the door. "Oh, when you were found, your Items Bag was missing, so I gave you another one, but I don't know where your original items are. You can go to the Hunter's Association and get a new sword and armor tomorrow." With that, he left.

A moment later, Melea walked back into the room holding a phone. She told me how to use it and then handed it over.

Taking it, I stared at the numbers for a couple seconds. Jeez, what had my family thought of these last four days? Guilt tore at me. Was it even fair for me to call and say, JK, you were worried over nothing?

My fingers felt stiff as I dialed the number to my aunt's apartment and put the phone to my ear, listening to it ring. I almost didn't want them to pick up. Would it be easier just to leave a message? No, that would be a jerk move.

I didn't have to worry about it for long. All too soon, my sister's voice came over the phone. "Hello?"

I closed my eyes and let the sound of her voice wash over me. I didn't know how badly I needed to hear her voice until that moment. For the first time, I finally felt like I was alive. "Aliya," I whispered. "It's me."

She let out something between a gasp and a scream. "Jynn! Oh my god, Jynn, is that you?" Her voice broke as she started to cry.

My stomach twisted like a pretzel. I knew what an emotional toll it would take on my family, that's why I never told them about what happened in the Gate. But since I wasn't even awake, there was no way I could have prevented the Hunter's Association from telling them about my condition. "Yeah, it's me—"

"They told us you got hurt," she cut me off, wailing so loud that my ears started to ring. "And that you wouldn't wake up. I thought you were . . ." She dissolved into tears. " . . . like Mom . . . "

Tears pooled in my eyes, and I glanced up at the ceiling, trying to blink them dry. I knew that's what they would think. Even after all this time, my mom being in that hospital bed was an open, festering wound which couldn't close. There was still hope that someday they would find the cure, but it didn't mean my family could handle having a second Dreamer in the family—emotionally or financially.

Listening to her cry, I felt like I let her down. My weakness almost left Aliya alone, without a father, mother, or sister. Even with our aunt and uncle, I knew she was like me. Losing another family member might just break her.

But now, there was more to that. What was going to happen when Blake found out I was still alive? It was a pure miracle I survived once. At this point in time, I wouldn't survive a second attempt on my life.

I focused on the System screen and read the words *Becoming Stronger* over and over. All the raging emotions, the anxiety, the doubt, the disappointment in myself, calmed. For the first time since I stepped into Eden, I felt like I could breathe. For the first time, I knew what to do, and I wasn't scared to do it.

I talked to her for a couple minutes longer, listening to her tell me about the places my aunt and uncle had applied for, how she was doing in school and whatnot until she calmed down a bit. All the while, I never took my eyes off the System screen.

"Hey," I said, "I'm sorry, but I can't come see you right now."

Aliya paused. "What?"

"There's something I have to do. I can come and see you in a couple days, okay? I promise I'm okay. Healthy as an ox." And weak as a duckling. But not for long.

I didn't know what this Becoming Stronger program was about, but I was going to milk it for all it was worth.

CHAPTER 13

Alone in my room, I stared at the System window and took a deep breath. I couldn't resist glancing at the door again. I'd locked it after Melea left, but my nerves were tingling so much that paranoia was kicking in. I didn't even know why I felt like this. My mind was calm, I knew what I was going to do, but my heart began beating like a clock on steroids. It was like I suddenly knew a secret, and if it got out, my whole world would crash.

I read the line again.

[Welcome to the Becoming Stronger Quest.]

Mentally, I selected the window. It vanished, replaced with the main menu of my normal System—only, it looked different. The color remained teal, and I was starting to get the impression that it would stay that way from now on.

A red exclamation point marked the corners of the Stats, Items, and Guide buttons. In other words, something happened to all of them while I was asleep. But there were more important alterations to my main menu. There was a new button above Guide and below Items—*Tasks*.

Where should I even start? Obviously, something big happened, but I felt normal. Pathetically normal.

"I'll just start at the top and work my way down," I muttered, opening my Stats window.

Jynn Devhro

Rank E   **Level** 1

		EXP to Next Level	8
HP	12/12	**Stat Points**	0
MP	5/5		
Strength	8	**Agility**	10
Magic	8	**Perception**	12
Constitution	8	**Intelligence**	8

My lips parted, and my eyes popped wide open. "Wha . . . ?"

I could hardly process what I was looking at. What did *Level 1* mean? I mean, I got what it meant—if I were in a video game. I'd played a few of them at friends' houses, and I'd heard that before the Gates opened, people spent trillions of dollars on just entertainment. But that was when society didn't have to worry about how to survive or rebuild itself. Right now, that kind of technology was so expensive and excessive that most people didn't even bother with it.

Even though Hunter stats were formatted in a game-like manner, it was mostly for efficient readability—not because they wanted us to treat our lives like a game. But I'd never heard of anyone being given a level.

It made sense that I would begin at level one. Even that was generous. Really, I should be starting at level zero. But what blew my mind even more was the next line.

"'EXP to Next Level: Eight,'" I whispered. In a gaming sense, this meant I could actually level up. That I could get stronger. The name of the quest popped into my head again.

My heart was beating so hard that the monitors at my bedside started to wail.

The doorknob rattled and jerked. "Jynn?" Melea yelled and started to pound on the door.

I jumped so badly that I almost fell off the bed. "Ah, yes, Melea?" With a flick of my hand, my System window disappeared.

A half second later, the door flung open, and Melea leapt in, looking ready for battle. Her half-manic eyes examined me with laser-like precision, looking for something out of place.

I stiffened and clutched my blanket, feeling like a thief caught with a billion-dollar-size energy stone. "Uh, hi?"

She frowned and entered, checking the heart monitor. It continued beeping like crazy, but I bet it had more to do with my guilty conscience now.

"Is everything okay?" Melea pressed a button then touched my forehead. "Why did you lock the door?" She took my wrist and looked at her watch.

I took a breath and forced my pulse to slow down. As much as I appreciated Melea for being a supernurse, I wouldn't get anything done if she kept interrupting me. That's why I locked the door, but I wasn't going to tell her that. "I'm okay, really. I was just thinking about something that stressed me out."

"Hmm," she hummed slowly, letting go of my wrist. "Do you want to talk about it?"

I shook my head. "No. It's fine, really." I glanced at the machine. "But can we unplug that?" I had a feeling I was going to see a few more shocking things in the next couple minutes.

Melea frowned. "Absolutely not. Not until Healer Jonovan says so."

"Okay . . ." I tried to smile, but even I could tell it was wobbly. I guess the monitor had to stay; I was sure if I unplugged it by myself, Melea would rip the door apart. I'd just have to be careful not to let my heart spike. "But what about the IV?"

She relented and pulled out the IV, but it took another couple minutes before I could convince her that I was really okay. Once Melea left, I didn't even think to lock the door; I just made a mental note to be quieter.

I opened the window again, and this time, I focused on my stats, looking them over. The numbers were still pathetically low, but there was a huge difference from before. For the first time, I had a Magic stat—albeit still really low. But the fact that I had one was huge. Hunters were divided into mages and melee. Mages were much weaker physically, but they made up for it with their magic. A melee Hunter didn't have magic at all; they fought with their enhanced, superhuman strength and abilities. None of which I had . . .

I was a melee Hunter, so why had I also been given a Magic stat? I went back to the main menu and checked again. Sure enough, there wasn't a Spells option. But could I learn magic? I had to admit, I was petty enough to fantasize how great it would be to light Leticia's hair on fire the next time she barged into my room.

Since there was no clear answer about my sudden stat, I finally looked at the Tasks button. The beeping on the monitor increased a bit as my heart sped up with anticipation. What crazy thing did this System want a level one puke to do?

I took a deep breath and forced my emotions to calm before opening the Tasks. For a moment, I stared at the screen, my brows furrowed. It was completely blank, except for the words [**No new tasks.**] across the top of the window.

"That was anticlimactic," I muttered, closing out of it.

Next was Items. Since the red orcs took my Items Bag and Jonovan gave me a new one, there shouldn't be anything inside yet. So why was there an exclamation point on the button?

Curious, I opened it. Two of the ten slots were filled, but it wasn't with items I was familiar with. I frowned and held out my hand. Instantly, the number-one slot emptied as a short sword appeared in my hand. "Where did this come from?"

A window appeared above it.

[**Her Will (Kindjal) +10 Attack. A blade whose might is greater than its reach. Cannot be dropped, sold, or stolen.**]

"Her Will? That's its name?" Kind of an odd name for a sword. I mean, it wasn't like it was a horse or something. Wouldn't a name like *Slasher* be better?

Name aside, I couldn't describe the sudden rush of rightness I felt holding the blade.

The handle fit my grip like it was made just for me. I couldn't resist rubbing my thumb over the dark metal. It was steel, but somehow, it held the warmth of wood; I'd never felt anything like it. As a Hunter, I'd seen my fair share of weapons, so this wasn't my first time seeing a Russian kindjal, but it was my first time seeing one with a cross guard. Normally, they just had a stub—usually metal—on the knuckle side of the grip. But this one had a small platinum-colored guard which protected my hand.

My lips curled into a smile as I moved the kindjal around, watching the light gleam across the seventeen-inch blade. All Hunter swords were made by forging different monster byproducts together with steel, since the only thing which could hurt a monster was parts of other monsters. There were swords made with dragon scales, wolf's fangs, and other items. S-ranked Hunters were so strong that only swords made with powdered energy crystals could withstand their moves. This meant that Hunter swords were never a solid color; the metal developed multiple tones and patterns blended into the blade.

But this kindjal's curved blade was different from anything I'd ever seen. Instead of having multiple shades of steel, it was eighty percent steel and twenty percent crystal, which swirled and blended together. Absolutely stunning. Any Hunter would look at this and snort, since the clear stone was obviously not an energy crystal. This short sword was nothing but a pretty pencil sharpener.

Only the description made me pause. It said it was stronger than my last short sword. In fact, my old weapon didn't have any boosts. I didn't even know weapons *could* have boosts; I thought that just applied to talismans and mage robes, and even those were minimal. Was it something I could see now because of my new System, or was the kindjal just that unique?

Humming to myself, I put the weapon away then pulled out the other item in my Items Bag.

A fitted, black leather breastplate dropped onto my lap. It was obviously well made and obviously my size, but there was nothing special about it. After the pretty weapon, the new armor was a bit of a letdown. Then a window blinked into sight.

[Her Resistance (Leather Armor) +10 Defense. It might be just a breastplate, but the defense applies to the whole body. Cannot be dropped, sold, or stolen.]

"Her Will, Her Resistance, Becoming Stronger Quest," I muttered. "These are the weirdest names. At least it's easy to understand what they mean, I guess."

I picked up the armor and paused. It was light as a feather and flexible as cotton. I mean, I'd seen Hunters do flips and somersaults while clothed in lorica segmentata armor, but I could be folded into a pretzel in this armor. How was it supposed to protect me? And how was it supposed to protect my legs when it was just a breastplate?

I frowned and retrieved the kindjal again. I glanced from the pretty blade to the useless armor. What if I ruined one? Then again, if they were a piece of junk, it was better to know now than when I was face-to-face with a monster.

I took a breath and stabbed the armor. The point of the kindjal stopped dead on contact; I couldn't even feel the pressure on the other side of the breastplate.

"Cool," I whispered.

So the armor wasn't worthless after all? Or was the blade dull? It didn't look like it. Curious, I poked at the bed by my hip. The kindjal sank down two inches, cutting the mattress like soft butter.

"Gah!" I gasped and pulled the kindjal out. "Whoops," I whispered, shifting over until the hole was hidden beneath my hip.

That was enough playing around, I decided, putting them away. If this continued, I was going to get myself in real trouble.

Opening the main menu back up, there was only one option with a notice symbol left—the Guide.

I selected it and instantly saw what was new. Amidst the usual options—monster info, fighting movements, Hunter laws and common knowledge, maps of Gate Vale and Eden—was the option Becoming Stronger Quest. I clicked the button, and instantly, a screen appeared.

[Welcome to the Becoming Stronger Quest, a program specially designed for the host to gain Experience Points (EXP) through appointed tasks and the elimination of monsters. The EXP will enable the host to grow stronger and unlock abilities. Further explanations will be given when the host is ready. The contract has already been agreed upon and cannot be revoked. Please note that the host is not permitted to talk about this program or its contents with anyone.]

I stared at the screen with mixed feelings. It was exciting—amazing, even—that I could actually level up—whatever that meant. But the fact that I couldn't take back whatever contract I made was alarming. I didn't even fully know what I'd signed up for.

And maybe I shouldn't feel so relieved that I couldn't tell anyone about it, but knowing I didn't have to make that decision was like a weight I hadn't noticed till now was lifted from my shoulders.

It all didn't seem real, but I couldn't deny that it was. I was alive, and somehow, this quest had attached itself to me. I didn't know why, and honestly, right now, I didn't care. As long as I could get stronger, as long as I could finally give my family the life I always wanted to, I'd pay the price when the creditor came.

CHAPTER 14

After a very long, sleepless night—I'd just woken up after sleeping for four days; who slept that long?—I was finally released from the hospital.

Stepping out the front doors in a borrowed pair of pants and T-shirt, I took a deep breath of nonmedically sterile air. With my horrible track record, I might be used to being in the hospital, but that didn't mean I liked staying in it for a long time. And Melea was determined to make sure I didn't move an inch from my bed.

Before I could even release my breath, a System screen popped up.

[Congratulations on being released from the hospital.]

I choked on the air stuck in my chest. Coughing and blinking away tears, I stared at the screen. Was . . . was the System *interacting* with me? *What?*

I didn't have time to fully accept or reject the idea before a soft, bell-like *ping* chimed, and another window popped up.

[Daily Task: Kill two Vale Wolves.]

"Are you shitting me?!" I screeched like a banshee.

The few people passing by the hospital entrance turned and looked at me. A mix of emotions were displayed, from amusement and concern to derision. So uncomfortable. My face went red, and I hurried away from the onlookers. It wasn't until I was a whole street away and free from curious eyes that I loosened up and my mind started to work again.

I opened my main menu and saw there was something in Tasks.

[Daily Task: Kill two Vale Wolves before nightfall. Failure to do so will result in punishment.]

That was it. There was nothing else to it.

In the brief explanation of the Becoming Stronger Quest, it said that I would get EXP for completing tasks, but not how much. Would I get different points for different tasks based on their difficulty? That would make sense. Then again, it's not like killing two Vale wolves was easy for me right now, anyway. I usually lost at least half of my HP just by killing one.

Granted, a week ago, I came to the realization I was going to have to kill two a day to help my aunt pay for rent, so this wasn't a new idea. But it was different when I was doing it for my family versus when a faceless System told me to. And if I didn't kill the wolves, I'd get punished. Somehow. It could be a slap on the hand or something major; I wouldn't know what it was until it happened, but after the last week, I wasn't going to openly look for crap dropping on my head out of sheer curiosity.

Still, it was a win-win case for me. I'd get two energy crystals, which I desperately needed since I should have had eight by now, and I'd get EXP to level up. It just wasn't going to be easy—at first. And if killing Vale wolves didn't get easier after leveling up a little, I was going to find a way to return this Becoming Stronger Quest to whoever put it on me.

But before I could complete the task, I needed to change. The clothing I'd been wearing when I was taken to the hospital had been so trashed— who'd have thought after my experience with the red orcs?—that Melea had lent me a set of clothes. The plain blue T-shirt and cotton pants were fine enough to walk around in; it wasn't like I had anyone to impress, anyway. But they just wouldn't cut it for fighting inside the Gate Vale.

Quickly, I returned to the E Hostel. I'd barely taken two steps inside when Henry came out of the front office.

The pages he held slid from his fingers and fluttered to the ground as he jumped forward.

"Jynn!" He hugged me and started to thump me on the back hard enough to knock the wind out of me. "Ah, this girl, you scared me! I haven't had a good night's rest in four nights!"

I arched my aching back and slid out of his hold. Jeez, I should get EXP for surviving that.

"Hey, Henry. Sorry I worried you." I smiled at him, grateful for his concern. I bent down and started to pick up the papers he was stepping on. Hopefully, he wouldn't get in trouble for the footprints on their backs.

"I got that," he said and started to pick them up as well. "It's still break- fast time. Have you eaten yet?" He looked me up and down then sighed. "What are they doing in that hospital? You look skinnier than ever."

I laughed, remembering all the food Melea had shoveled into my mouth. "Yes, I've eaten. Thanks." After reassuring Henry several more times I was just fine, he let me go up the stairs.

I unlocked my bedroom door, pausing after turning the key. There was no resistance when I turned it. The door was already unlocked, but I knew for a fact I'd locked it when I left. Cautiously, I pushed it open and peeked inside. The knob slid from my hand as I stared in shock at Leticia, who was crouching in front of my closet.

"What are you doing?" I yelled. That was when I noticed she was kneeling in front of the safe. And it was open. And her hand was inside.

Leticia scowled at me like I was in her way, never mind that she had broken into my room and was stealing my stuff. She pulled her hand back and stood up. "Nothing." She kicked the safe closed with her toe as if it wasn't a big deal that she'd busted it open.

I lunged forward. Leticia skipped around me and walked out the door, not even bothering to shut it behind her. Her hands were empty, but that didn't mean anything. She could have put something—or everything— inside her Items Bag. I didn't bother with her just yet. I didn't own a lot of stuff, but what I did have was priceless.

I dropped to my knees hard enough that I would have winced if I wasn't so desperate. My stomach tightened painfully at the sight of the bent handle. I almost didn't want to touch the safe, like it had been violated. I grabbed the handle, feeling the unfamiliar shape in my hand, and jerked it back. It swung open easily.

"Damn her," I muttered under my breath. "Is she ever going to give me a break?" Never mind the fact that I'd just spent five days in the hospital.

It wasn't empty like I thought it would be, but it only took me a couple seconds to realize what was missing. Ten years ago, when my dad was still alive and we weren't scrounging for money, he gave my mom a charm bracelet for their tenth anniversary. There were five charms on it, four flat hearts engraved with mine, Aliya's, and my parents' initials, and a small ruby rose charm. As money got tighter and things started to get pawned off, Aliya took the necklace with Mom and Dad's wedding rings on it, and I kept this. It was the only thing I had left which belonged to both of them.

My hands started to shake as my mind went blank. I didn't even remember what happened next, but suddenly, I was at Leticia's closed door.

I grabbed the handle; it was locked. Furious, I started to pound on the door.

"Leticia, get your cheap ass out here!" I screamed at the top of my lungs. "Give it back, you piece of shit!"

Doors clicked open up and down the hall as heads peeked out, the women shocked yet curious at the commotion I was making. For the first time, I didn't care that I was the center of attention; if anything, I pounded a little harder and screamed abuse even louder. Twelve months of pent-up anger bubbled up and exploded in waves of fury which I directed at the door.

With my strength, the door stood up well, aside from a few shallow dents. My hands, on the other side, were turning black and blue from hitting the door. I knew she was in there; I could hear pacing on the other side of the door and cold hisses to every insult I screamed.

I wouldn't leave until I had my bracelet back.

Most of the women were in the hall now, watching me with flabbergasted expressions. They didn't seem to care that they were in various states of nighttime dress, a few even bold enough to stand there in only a cami and panties.

"Hey, what's going on?" one of the girls asked.

I completely ignored her and pulled the kindjal from my Items Bag. Without pausing, I stabbed the door. The blade sank through the wood grain until the guard thudded against it.

Screams of shock sounded around me and also from inside Leticia's room.

I pulled the kindjal out and prepared to attack again. I was going to get my bracelet back, even if I had to hack the door to pieces.

"What the devil is going on up here!" Henry's loud voice broke through my mindless state.

I blinked and looked over to see him standing at the top of the stairs, staring at me like I was insane.

I didn't really care, though. I felt a little insane. So much crap had built up up to now that I just couldn't handle any more. I wasn't so crazy that I'd hurt anyone, I promised, but I did want to break apart Leticia's door. Let her know how it felt to have her stuff defiled.

The door swung open, and Leticia appeared. "Henry, this bitch is trying to kill me! She's gone insane!"

My gaze snapped back to her. With a deadly calm I'd never felt before, I leveled my kindjal at her. "Give it back." My words were like a bucket of cold water dousing her fiery explosion. "Give my bracelet back!"

Henry hurried up to me and grabbed my wrist. He pushed down on my arm, trying to move the weapon away from Leticia. "Put your weapon away, and we'll figure this out."

I resisted. "Not until I get my bracelet back."

"Jynn!" Henry barked. "You know the rules!"

"So does she!" I finally let him lower my arm and put the kindjal away. "I might get in trouble for fighting, but theft is against the law!"

Everyone looked at Leticia, no one acting surprised at all. Even Henry looked disapproving but not shocked.

"I didn't steal anything!" Leticia slapped a hand against her chest and had the gall to look offended. "What could that poor slut own that I would even want?"

"As if you have ever left me alone since the minute I stepped into this building!" I yelled back. "Is it that you just can't breathe unless you're stepping on someone? Blankets and pillows, who the hell cares? Just give my bracelet back!"

Henry put a hand on my shoulder. He looked between us. "Yelling won't solve the problem. Jynn, tell me your side first. Then Leticia will get her turn." He glanced around the hall, his sight skipping fast over some of the lesser-dressed young women. "The rest of you, I think it's time you returned to your rooms. There's nothing to see here."

As if that would work. Still, Henry was in charge of the food here. Some muttered under their breaths and cast looks at me and Leticia, but soon enough, the hall cleared out; though I bet every single one of them had their ears pressed to their doors.

Henry sighed before turning back to me and Leticia. He crossed his arms. "Now, Jynn, what happened?"

I took a breath and motioned to her. "When I opened my bedroom door, Leticia was inside, rummaging through my safe."

"I was not!" she wailed.

"Quiet!" Henry barked. "You will have your turn to talk."

She still looked ready to yell, but I kept going.

"When I checked inside, I found that my mother's bracelet was missing. It has four heart charms and a red rose on it. I want it back." I glared at her.

She snorted and tossed her two-toned hair over her shoulder. "She's lying. I didn't take anything. I don't know where she lost it, but I didn't take it."

"Yes, you did. I know for a fact it was in my safe the last time I was in my room. The only one who's opened my safe in the last five days is you. You even bent the handle getting it open. It's back there." I waved toward my open door. "Anyone can go check it. I don't know where you put my bracelet, whether it's in your Items Bag or you stashed it somewhere, but you took it."

Henry scowled at Leticia. "Did you forget about the security cameras, girl? You like to prance about like a princess, but even you can't escape the law. Do you really want me to get the authorities involved?"

Leticia's eyes widened. For the first time, the smug look on her face started to slip.

"Yes!" I yelled before she could respond. "I want it back, even if I have to press charges."

That could be a double-edged sword, really. If they couldn't find proof that she stole it, I would get in trouble for slander. But I wasn't worried about that, since I knew for a fact she took it.

Leticia's expression slid through emotions like the ticking of a clock. Shock, fury, then loathing. She glared at me before her gaze slid to Henry. "It's just a damn piece of trash. The hell are you getting so worked up for?" She swung her hand out.

A flash of silver flew through the air. It struck the wall at the other side of the hall and clattered to the ground.

I gasped and ran over. My heart was pounding in my ears as I stared down at the bracelet. The ruby rose had broken off, and a couple links were bent. My hands shook as I scooped it off the floor, my thumb smoothing over Mom's and Dad's initials as I checked it for any more damage. Finally, I let out a sigh. All the pent-up emotion drained from my body, and my shoulders sagged. I didn't even realize I was that tense until now. It was damaged, but it could be fixed.

Henry was still glaring at Leticia. "Since you gave it back, I won't contact the authorities. But I have to record this incident."

Even if she gave it back, something like this could prevent her from a number of things in the future, especially if she wanted to move up in the Hunter world. Theft wasn't unheard of—hell, neither was murder. All was fair in the Gate Vale as long as you weren't caught. But inside Eden, Hunters had to abide by the laws. As long as there was proof, it became a black mark on your record.

I couldn't get revenge on Blake, but it felt good to finally get back at Leticia, even if it was only a little.

Leticia reacted like a furious cat. "What the hell! It's just a damn bracelet. I gave it back; there's no reason to write it down."

Henry shook his head as if he couldn't believe her. "Why did you take it to begin with? You knew you'd get in trouble if you were caught."

She snorted and planted her hands on her hips. "That waste was gone for days. Normally, it means they are dead and their stuff is fair game. How was I supposed to know she was going to randomly show up again? Someone like her should just stay dead." She glared at me.

My heart jumped and accelerated as the image of watching my skin get sliced off piece by piece and feeling my blood dripping off my body drop by drop came back so vividly that I could almost feel it again. My knees almost gave out. I reached out and planted a hand against the wall.

Henry was scolding her, completely oblivious to my reaction. "No, Leticia. When a Hunter dies, their possessions go to their family. It's not a free-for-all. No matter what, taking something that doesn't belong to you is theft. If I catch you at it again, I'll kick you out."

I could barely hear him over the ringing in my head. *No*, I thought, trying to banish the image of the red orc's gleeful face as he flung another piece of my flesh to the ground. That would never happen again. I would never be a victim again.

Starting today.

I glanced at Henry still yelling at Leticia and went into my room to change.

I got my bracelet back. That's all that mattered. Henry could handle the rest.

I had a task to complete.

CHAPTER 15

Even with the early start I had on the day, it was still almost noon before I reached the Gate. That left me eight hours to find two Vale wolves and kill them—including any healing I might need if I had to visit the hospital in between. The typical safe groups I usually tailed had already entered the Gate and were long gone, so it would be just me and my pretty kindjal in there.

Since it didn't break when I stabbed Leticia's door this morning, I felt optimistic it wouldn't crumble in battle. And if the blade broke, I could just chuck the handle at the monster and hope that distracted it enough to get away. It always worked against Superman.

I took a deep breath, feeling my new leather armor shifting and expanding as I moved. The fact that it was so light and flexible still threw me off. I almost felt like I was naked, even though I was covered from head to toe. I sighed and tapped my leather helm with the kindjal in my hand. With my new vest and old brown leather pants, my armor didn't match anymore, but I'd never been a fashionista. I just hoped that the System's description of the breastplate was true, and it protected my entire body, even the parts it didn't cover.

I was going to need it.

"Here goes nothing," I muttered to myself and walked into the Gate.

Gate Vale spread out before me. For a second, my stomach twisted nauseously just looking at the beautiful valley, so colorful and vivid compared to the monochromatic city I'd just come from.

My gaze automatically wandered to Glenn Holt. A chill started at the back of my head and seeped down my spine just looking at the cheerfully green leaves swaying beneath the warm sun. The Portal Burst had closed, right? I never really asked about it, but honestly, I didn't want to know. And if there was a problem, I'd have heard about a red orc issue by now. It was safe to assume that S-rank Hunters had already taken care of the problem.

Luckily, my task didn't say I had to return to Glenn Holt or kill dire rats.

I turned and ran south toward the Edmond Woods. Within a hundred feet of the Gate entrance, the flat grass changed into thick brush which quickly gave way to thick trees two stories tall.

Funny how the last time I'd been in this forest, I nearly died from a dragon. But there wasn't a single trace of the fight between the S-rank Hunter and the monster left. So much stuff had happened since then, it felt like a lifetime ago.

Instead of trekking through the untamed underbrush, I crept down a trail which cut through the middle of the forest before branching out in several directions. Since I was looking for a Vale wolf, there wasn't a need to go too far in. I just hoped that stronger Hunters hadn't already cleaned the forest out. Granted, more Vale wolves—and every other monster found in Gate Vale—would reappear every night, but that wouldn't do any good for my task today.

It was nerve-wracking when the only sound I could hear was my own loudly beating heart. What if there were no more wolves? What if they had all been defeated for the day? Were there only stronger monsters left?

A hundred feet down the path, I stopped and looked around. *Please, just let me find two. I only need two.* According to the clock in my main menu, I'd been in Gate Vale for almost an hour already. This wasn't looking good. The longer it took, the more likely it was that I wouldn't be able to find one, never mind two.

Ten more minutes ticked by before I decided to leave the trail and head into the brush. Low-hanging tree branches obscured my visibility, and every time a bush brushed against my leg, my heart leapt. When I'd follow other groups, I could always use them to take the brunt of the attacks. And when they alerted each other about an approaching monster, I always knew about it too. Right now, I didn't have that buffer, and my nerves were starting to fray.

Forget the daily task. It wasn't like it would matter if I wasn't even alive.

A low growling rumbled from behind me.

My heart jumped into my throat as I whipped around and leaned to the side just as something huge lunged at me. It sailed past, the corner of its claw catching my left arm at the edge of the leather breastplate. I expected to see a thick red gash, but all that was there was a bruise as my HP dropped a point. So the armor did affect my whole body. But I didn't have time to think about it more.

I turned and faced the monster again, feeling both relieved and worried. I'd finally found the right creature. The Vale wolf's shoulder was almost as tall as my chest, and it was easily longer than I was tall. Beams of sunlight streamed through the gaps in the tree canopy and highlighted the monster's gray pelt with glints of silver. Four red eyes narrowed as its lips pulled away from its red gums, revealing huge fangs. Above its head, a window read: [**Vale Wolf Lv2**].

So my new System showed me the levels of monsters, not just their ranks. Convenient.

A level two Vale wolf, and I was only a level one puke. Then again, I doubted there were any monsters as weak as me. Level two might just be the lowest I could find. Maybe I should be grateful, but right now, my heart was pounding too much. My hand was shaking so much that I couldn't even keep my kindjal steady. In my mind, the wolf in front of me kept morphing into a sneering red orc, then back again.

The wolf lunged at me. I whimpered and dodged to the side as it landed and kicked out with its hind legs. I grunted and stumbled away, almost losing my balance while a few more hit points dwindled from my bar.

Come on, Jynn! I mentally screamed, but my muscles threatened to lock up. This wasn't my first time against a Vale wolf. *I've killed hundreds of them. What's wrong with me?*

The wolf swung a paw at me, sharp claws bright white against its gray fur. Instantly, its image distorted until all I could see was the red orc thrusting a huge sword. Desperately, I raised the kindjal and blocked the attack with the blade.

A heavy pressure hit the weapon and stopped as I successfully caught the attack.

It stopped. That painful, punishing assault that wouldn't let go of my mind stopped. And I wasn't hurt. My eyes widened as the mirage of the red orc shattered, leaving just the Vale wolf behind.

I twisted my wrist and deflected the rest of the wolf's energy. The monster was forced left, but its feet barely tapped the ground before it lunged back, snarling mouth aiming for my neck. I crosscut its snout with all my might, the blade slashing through and snapping its head to the side. The monster yelped and fell back, snarling at me with its bleeding lip.

I stood there breathing hard, but my hands weren't shaking anymore. Adrenaline pumped through my veins, but my heart wasn't a chaotic mess like a second ago. Because this wasn't the red orc that almost killed me. And a Vale wolf would never be as scary as that red orc. Ever.

As long as I never forgot that, I had nothing to fear.

"Ha!" I slashed at the monster. It leaped to the side and snapped back while I flourished the kindjal, taking the offense. The wolf lunged with a snap of its jaws just inches from my sleeve. I spun the kindjal and reversed its grip in my hand, stabbing back at the Vale wolf with everything I had.

My blade sank into its neck. *Shit.* I missed the vitals.

The wolf opened its mouth and clamped down on my chest, taking nearly half my ribs into its maw. I gasped in pain as half my hit points were wiped out. Without my new vest, this attack would have killed me. My teeth gritted together, and I reached up with my free hand. Gripping the protruding handle with both hands, I forced the kindjal forward, severing everything I could as I pulled the blade to the front of the monster's neck.

The monster collapsed to the ground in a pool of blood.

Air burst from my lips as I staggered back, relief robbing all the strength from my body. I slumped to the ground and rested a hand on my aching ribs while I stared at the wolf's carcass. A chime rang in the air. Above the body, a window flashed. [**+4 EXP**]

Then another. [**Daily Task: Kill two Vale Wolves. (1/2)**]

Curious, I opened my stats. Sure enough, where it used to say eight points to my next level, it had gone down by four points.

I leaned my head back and stared up at the trees above. "Only four more points, and things will get a little easier. I just have to kill one more Vale wolf, and I'll be at level two."

Was each task designed to make me level up each time? I mean, the first task was pretty much forcing me to get enough EXP for level two. Jeez, how many monsters would I have to kill a day once I got up to level twenty? Or even higher?

Just thinking about being that strong was like a dream.

I paused as a random thought came to me. What level was a C-rank Hunter? Or an S-rank? If the System had a level for the Vale wolf, something that was normally just labeled as an E-rank monster, then it would only make sense that Hunters had levels, too.

Ah, but I didn't have time to think about that. I glanced at the Stats window which still hung in the air above me and frowned at my HP bar.

[3/12 HP] I definitely needed to visit the hospital before I looked for another wolf.

But first, I needed to carve out the energy crystal and get out of here before another monster found me.

Every single move sent a sharp pain through my chest, but I climbed to my feet anyway.

"Stupid mutt," I muttered, kneeling down by the carcass. Scowling, I made a very practiced cut along the wolf's sternum. However, just before my hand reached inside to retrieve the energy crystal, a red window flashed in front of my face.

But it wasn't just one screen. Another one appeared, then another. In seconds, over twenty flashing red windows filled my vision until they were all I could see, all with the same message.

[Don't touch the Energy Crystal!]

CHAPTER 16

I gasped and stumbled back. As soon as my hand moved away from the wolf's carcass, the notifications disappeared. Still in shock, I looked around, half expecting them to pop back open and give me another heart attack.

"What is that supposed to mean?" I demanded to the open air like a crazy person. "It's the Hunter's job to collect energy crystals from monsters."

I'd spent the last twelve-plus months slaving away just to dig these tiny crystals out of monsters. It was how I ate and how my family could stay off the streets and how Mom got medical attention. Now this new System was telling me to leave it alone? After I just nearly killed myself for it?

Nothing happened around me; no dings, no random screens with an answer to my question. Maybe I'd been wrong when I thought the System was interacting with me.

I scowled at the body. Like hell was I going to just walk away from an energy crystal and leave it for someone else to stroll in and take. I knelt down and reached out again. Instantly, my vision filled with red windows telling me not to touch the energy crystal. There were so many that it was like the sky suddenly turned red—a scary thought in and of itself. I'd certainly had enough of Portal Bursts lately.

With a frustrated growl, I stepped back until the messages disappeared. "Then what am I supposed to do? How can I survive without collecting energy crystals? I can't get stronger if I starve to death!"

A white glowing orb appeared on the ground in front of the Vale wolf. A teal title window labeled it: [**Drop Item**].

"What is that? Did you do this?" I muttered, then slapped a hand on my forehead.

Maybe I really was going crazy, talking to the System like it was a person. If this was only the first day, I was scared to think of how I was going to be in a week or even a month from now. There was a special place where deranged and dangerous Hunters were kept. If I couldn't survive in Eden, well, there was no way I could survive there.

I sighed and reached out for the glowing orb. Hunter 101 said to never touch unknown items—especially ones which glowed. But it's not like I could touch the energy crystal, so I could only assume this was the next best thing. The System seemed to want to help me, so it should give me something to compensate for it. Well, in theory.

The instant my fingers skimmed the orb, it vanished, and a message appeared.

[You have obtained a Vale Wolf Pelt.]

The message disappeared, and the Vale wolf's body exploded into tiny light fragments. The lights scattered in the air and faded to nothing in less than two seconds. In the end, it was like the carcass was never there. Even the wolf's blood on my body faded away.

In awe, I opened my Items screen and stared at the new addition in there. "Cool," I whispered. This was just like a drop item in a game. The System could go this far, even manipulating the monsters I killed?

One crystal from a Vale wolf counted for about a hundred dollars. As long as I made at least that much by selling drop items, I wouldn't actually need to collect them. Not to mention, the rarer the item, the more money it would be worth.

My greedy thoughts jerked to a halt when a message appeared.

[Destroy the Energy Crystal.]

"What?" I blinked and looked down. Sure enough, on the ground where the wolf used to be was a dime-size glowing light.

I stared at it. I knew what the System had said, but just twelve of those could cover nearly all of my family's living expenses for a month. And one just lay there on the ground, glowing like a pale blue star.

I reached for it but paused, my fingers just inches away. This time, the red warnings didn't flash in my eyes—but I couldn't get them out of my mind. Why would the System prevent me from touching the crystals? They were literally the energy source for the entire human population.

I drew back and summoned the kindjal to my hand. For a moment, I stayed there crouching, watching as it glowed in the dirt. I glanced up at the message still hanging in the air and frowned.

"I must be crazy," I muttered. Then I lifted the kindjal in the air and thrust down, hard.

The energy crystal exploded in bright blue sparks. Was it my imagination, or did a sound come from it when it broke? Before I could decide one way or the other, it dissolved into powder then sank into the dirt and disappeared.

I stared at the spot a second longer. "That was so much money . . ."

I still didn't understand what had just happened or why, but I did know that my heart ached seeing the crystal disappear. I almost hated the hand that held the kindjal.

It'll be fine, I told myself. If I got enough drop items, the crystals wouldn't matter. Although, it would be amazing to have drop items *and* crystals at the same time, the devil on my shoulder whispered.

With a sigh big enough to fill a sail, I stood and winced. I was so distracted that I'd actually forgotten about how much my ribs hurt and the state of my HP. Without waiting another second, I hurried back to Eden.

The look on Jonovan's face when he saw me sitting on the exam table could only be described as *spitting mad*. For the first time, he glared at me. His face turned red, and his hands fisted at his side. "Miss Jynn, what the devil do you think you're doing?" His voice shook in an effort to keep it calm. "Do you think that I spent so much effort on you the last five days so you could just turn around and nearly die in the Gate again?"

I smiled at him, finding his words funnier than I should. "Isn't this how it always is? I nearly die in there, get healed by you, then wake up and do the same thing all over again? It's nothing new."

He swore under his breath and tugged on his ponytail hard enough it almost displaced the tie. He approached me with quick movements and put his hand on my shoulder. A second later, his warm power coursed through my body, soothing away all pain.

"Has anything happened to you since last night?" Just like that, his anger disappeared as his brows wrinkled in concern.

Happened? How big is your imagination? I thought.

As soon as the thought crossed my mind, a warning flashed for just a second before it was gone. [**Talking about the Becoming Stronger Quest and anything related to it is prohibited.**]

I sighed. It wasn't like I was really going to tell him. I just wanted to know what kind of face he'd make if I did. You know, before I laughed it off as a joke.

Still, I cocked my head to the side and gave Jonovan a clueless expression. "No? Why?"

He frowned and slowly pulled his hand back. "You almost feel . . . a little different but not, at the same time. I can't put my finger on it." He stared at me like he was trying to dissect my brain.

I couldn't help but fidget under his gaze. I mean, it didn't matter how much he stared; I couldn't tell him about it, anyway. "Okay," I said slowly, starting to slide off the table. "Since there's nothing else—"

"Hold it," Jonovan cut me off.

I froze midmotion and looked back at him. Was he still going to talk about how I'd changed?

"Stay right there," he said while he stood up. "I'll be right back." Without explanation, he left the room.

I shifted back onto the table. With nothing else to do, I opened my main menu and checked the time. It was already almost four o'clock. I only had four hours left to track down and kill another Vale wolf, then get out of Gate Vale before dark. Frowning, I glanced at the door, hoping Jonovan would hurry up.

The thought barely left my mind before the door swung open and Jonovan came back in. He handed me a stack of papers and stared at me expectantly.

"Ah." I glanced at the papers but didn't really read them. "Thanks?"

"I want you to quit being a Hunter," he announced.

A jolt went through my body. All I could do was stare at him with wide eyes.

He motioned to the papers in my hands. "I pulled some strings and found a way to recall your Hunter status. You don't have to keep getting hurt anymore. You can go to college like the rest of the normal kids your age and have a long, peaceful life away from the monsters and violence. You don't have to be a Hunter anymore; you can be anything you want."

Slowly, I looked down at the papers and leafed through them. It was like holding a key to a locked door, one I'd been staring at for so long I didn't comprehend there was a handle. I could wake up in the morning and eat breakfast with people who actually cared that I was alive. Go to sleep with Aliya's sweet *good night* in my ear. I could go to school with Marcie, whom I hadn't seen in months, and actually choose what career path I wanted to follow.

I could be anything I wanted. I could be . . .

I gripped the papers hard enough to wrinkle them. A million things popped into my head that I could be. A sales associate, a teacher, a businesswoman—there were hundreds of options. But there was only one word which struck a chord in my soul. A desperate desire I wanted so badly, my chest ached.

Stronger. I want to be stronger.

I couldn't gain that if I signed these papers and walked away. Who knew, maybe the System wouldn't even let me sign them? Regardless of what it did, I personally didn't want to give up now. After struggling for so long, I finally had a chance to get what I truly wanted.

It wasn't going to be easy; I knew that. But nothing could be worse than being powerlessly thrown into a group of red orcs. The next time I faced a monster, it would be on my terms. And if I ever got to meet that red orc leader again, he was going to be the one bleeding on the ground. As for Blake, I'd figure out his fate later.

All I knew was that these papers weren't needed. I smiled softly at Jonovan.

"Thank you. Really, thank you for always doing your best for me. It means a lot. But I'm not going to sign them." I held them out to him.

His eyes widened. "Jynn, what are you talking about? Can you honestly say that you like your life right now? You always hide behind a small smile and sarcasm, but truthfully, are you actually happy?"

That was an easy answer. "No," I whispered. "I'm not happy." I was so powerless to control my life, how could I be? My chin tilted up until I could meet his level gaze. "But I will be. I will be happy. I can't get that if I sign these."

He didn't move. It was like he'd turned into a statue from how he just stared at me. Finally, he sighed and jerked on his ponytail again. "Fine. Fine! Do whatever you want. I don't care anymore!" He stepped back and dropped onto his chair, still scowling. "But I don't want those papers back. You keep them. That way, when you finally get sick of this life, you can sign them and be done."

In the end, I thanked Jonovan and left. I still needed to find another Vale wolf, and I was running out of time.

It was nearly five o'clock by the time I made it back to Edmond Woods. My stomach reminded me it was dinnertime, so I took out the rest of the sandwich I'd had for lunch and inhaled it as fast as I could. It wasn't a lot, but it would be enough to hold off my hunger for at least a couple more hours.

All set, I slowly walked down the trail again. It was getting later in the day, and the odds of finding another wolf were getting slimmer by the second. After walking up and down the path for a while, I bit the bullet and started to creep through the brush once again. I returned to where I'd found the first Vale wolf and wasn't too surprised when I didn't come across another one. Undaunted, I kept going, fully aware I was getting farther and farther from the edge of the forest. Finally, I couldn't take my nerves anymore and turned around.

I'd barely taken a step when a low growl echoed behind me. I spun around, swinging my kindjal out at the same time. A yelp sounded as my blade smashed into the jaws of a Vale wolf midjump. It fell to its side, bleeding, while I stumbled back and quickly regained my balance. Adrenaline surged through my body, yet my mind remained clear as I stared at the monster, waiting for its next move.

I couldn't get hurt as badly this time. Jonovan knew I'd already killed a wolf today, so I technically didn't need to go back into Gate Vale. If I returned to be healed a second time on the same day, I doubted he'd let me leave until I gave him a good reason why I was hurt again. I didn't want to lie to him, but I couldn't tell him the truth. So it was better to just not get hurt at all.

Wish I could have done that from day one.

The wolf jumped at me, so I sidestepped and slashed at its Achilles tendon as it passed by. The monster yelped and rolled to the ground while I spun and lunged at it, trying to take advantage of its position.

It retaliated just as fast as I surged forward. Mouth open, the monster angled for my throat. I pulled back, lifting my left arm, and the wolf clamped down on my forearm, its fangs piercing my skin. My new armor's effect prevented a fatal wound; somehow, its boost kept the wolf from biting my arm off. I cried out as my HP bar dropped four points, then with all my strength, I gripped the kindjal in my right hand and stabbed it down as hard as I could into the monster's skull. There was a dull crack, then my blade sank deeper until the bloody tip exited its throat. The wolf released my arm and collapsed at my feet.

Breathing hard, I hugged my arm to my chest. God, I really needed to stop using my body as a shield just to get the kill shot. First, it was my chest. Now, it was my arm. What was next, my hand? Jonovan would be pissed if he had to grow back my pinky again.

The puncture wounds burned like the devil, but the wound wasn't the end of the world; I'd only lost four HP from the attack. If I didn't get the punctures treated, they'd leave scars, but it could have been worse.

A teal screen appeared over the wolf. [+4 EXP]

A loud chime sounded in my ears, and a second window appeared.

[You have Leveled Up! Please assign available Stat Points.]

I barely had time to read that before yet another screen appeared.

[Daily Task: (Kill two Vale Wolves) Completed. +5 EXP]

[Would you like to accept your reward? Y/N?]

CHAPTER 17

Did I want to accept a reward? Who wouldn't? "Yes!"

A pool of light flashed from the ground, expanding until it was a foot wide. With one last bright pulse, the light disappeared, leaving behind two black leather arm bracers, an obvious matching set to the leather breastplate I wore.

"Wahoo!" Like a kid at Christmas, I threw my hands in the air—and instantly wailed in pain. Breathing hard, I hugged my arm and applied pressure to the now freshly bleeding wounds. I glanced at the arm bracers on the ground. "Too bad I didn't have those five minutes ago," I muttered. Reaching out, I put them in my Items Bag.

That done, I looked at the next order of operations—the notice that there was something new to my stats. I opened the screen and gasped. *My HP went up!* But that wasn't the only thing. All of my stats had increased by one. In addition to that, there was also something new.

[Stat Points +3]

There was a *ping* sound, and a new window popped open.

[Please assign your new Stat Points.]

"So all my stats go up by one every level and then I get three extra points to do whatever I want with them?" I whispered to myself. "So if I want to add one to Strength . . . " The words were barely out of my mouth when it increased by one point. I blinked at my new number, shocked. "Oh, well, I guess that works. I better put some thought into this a little more, though."

I didn't want to put myself at a disadvantage by stockpiling all my points in just one area—I *did* want to improve my strength, however. In the end, I added another point to Strength and the remaining point to Constitution.

Jynn Devhro

Rank E		**Level** 2	
		EXP to Next Level 9	
HP 15/22		**Stat Points** 0	
MP 10/10			
Strength 11 (+10)		**Agility** 11	
Magic 9		**Perception** 13	
Constitution 10 (+10)		**Intelligence** 9	

After living with and viewing such horrible stats for so long, I felt like crying. My total HP had practically doubled, so each tiny little hit wasn't going to kill me. On top of that, most of my stats were in the double digits. Granted, they were just barely there, but it still felt like a miracle.

For the first time, I felt hopeful for the future. I still couldn't feel the differences in my stats, but seeing the changes was enough for now.

I closed out of the window then paused—two new buttons had appeared on the main menu. The first read Abilities, right beneath the Stats button. I clicked on it. It opened, showing only one thing titled [???]. That was it. The pale gray question marks just sat there on the screen, mocking my curiosity. I couldn't even look it up in the *Hunter's Guide*.

Humming with slight annoyance, I went to the next new button, labeled Skills, only to face another [???] mystery.

"What?" I moaned. "It's my body! Why can't you give me more of a hint?"

I closed out and looked at the glowing orb lying on the ground beside the wolf's carcass. I reached out and added another wolf pelt to my Items Bag. The body vanished, leaving its energy crystal on the ground. I couldn't stop myself from looking at it, wishing I could pick it up. With a frustrated sigh, I swung my kindjal, and the crystal dissolved into dust.

It's okay, I thought to myself. *I can still sell the drop items*. I didn't know a thing about sales, but if there was a day to learn something new, it was today.

* * *

I stood outside the door for a minute, staring at the sign that read Armorer Gil's Shop and Trade. The reviews gave this place a good evaluation, so that counted for something, and it sounded like he didn't ask as many questions as other shops did about where items for hock had originated from. Since I had no idea how much this pelt was worth, I figured he would.

I took a deep breath and walked inside, the smell of animals hitting me like a nine-pound hammer. The small storefront was clean enough inside. Shelves behind glass cases were organized and full of cool things, like the dragon claws arranged in a rainbow pattern, from purple to yellow gold and all the colors in between. I didn't even know dragons came in that many colors.

The pelt of something huge, furry, and acid green hung on the wall. I had no idea what it was, but I could tell from the look of the hide that it was once a very strong monster. Arranged on the countertops were other smaller items, like scales and eggs, and something which looked like steel turds.

No matter where I looked, everything screamed expensive and high quality. Was my plain little Vale wolf pelt really going to cut it here? The owner wouldn't look at it and laugh, would he? I mean, it could still make armor and whatnot, right?

A bell jangled as the door closed behind me, and a gruff voice called from the open door to the left of the shop's counter. "Be there in a bit."

I thumped my fist on my thigh nervously and walked to the counter. A handful of glittering energy crystals were displayed under the glass. They were so much bigger and brighter than the two I'd shattered today, perfect for smelting together with metal to make a weapon for a Hunter.

A burly man entered the room from the back door. It was obvious that he dealt in rare items and armor from his clothes alone. Two magic pendants dangled from his neck, and the belt buckle peeking out from his rounded belly was also laced with magic. He wore custom arm shields on both arms, a chest protector I was sure was more than it looked, and studded armored pants. The quality of his equipment alone was very high. He looked me up and down, his gaze lingering on my armor, then smiled, friendly.

"Evening, miss. I'm Gil. What can I help you with?"

I shifted my injured left arm slightly behind me as I pulled out the two wolf pelts and set them on the table. "I want to sell these."

The rolls of fur looked so pathetically average compared to the dragon claws and huge . . . whatever that green thing was. Especially compared to all the refined products Gil wore.

"Let's see what you got." Gil picked up one of the pelts and started examining it. He ran his hand over the top and bottom and stretched it out across the counter, measuring the size. He leaned in close, obviously seeing more than I could with a glance.

The door dinged behind me, and someone with a powerful presence walked in, but I was too focused on the trader to see who entered.

"I'll be with you in a minute," Gil said to the customer. He took one last look at the pelt, then his eyes focused on me. "Well, I can give you thirty-five dollars for each pelt."

I froze, shocked. Thirty-five for each? Seriously? That was only seventy dollars; nowhere near enough money. One small E-rank energy crystal was worth a hundred dollars alone.

I bit my lips, thinking of how the System warned me not to touch the crystal. I didn't even know why. I mean, the main reason why Hunters hunted was for them. If this was all I would get for two pelts, could I really afford not to collect them?

Gil waved his hand, and a blue screen appeared in front of me asking if I accepted the trade of my two wolf pelts for thirty-five dollars each.

I stared at it, my finger hovering over the accept button. Sure, I didn't have to skin the wolf myself, but how was this any better than what I had before? Struggling to stay fed?

"Thirty-five?" a man spoke up behind me. "If the pelt was in bad shape, it might be worth that. But it's in pristine condition. They should be worth at least sixty apiece." His subdued voice was thick with disapproval.

My eyes popped open as a chill went from the base of my skull to my toes. I almost sold them for half their value? Jeez, how stupid was I? I was so ashamed I couldn't even turn around to face the man behind me.

Gil's squared features scrunched up, looking flustered. "Ah, sir . . . " He stalled, as lost for words as I was.

The man's presence receded from me, and the door dinged again.

The trader jumped. He reached out, eyes still on the door. "Wait, where are you going? This won't take much longer."

My fists clenched at my side. Of course not. I was such an easy target, after all.

"I don't deal with dishonest scum," the man said.

I peeked a glance over my shoulder just as the door slammed shut. All I could make out through the store light reflecting from the small window was neatly trimmed bleach-blond hair. A second later, the man was gone.

The trader growled low in his throat as he turned his furious face to me. "You just cost me my best customer."

I glared back and drew the wolf pelts back into my Items Bag. "You just cost yourself two customers." Ignoring the foul words he spewed, I hurried out the door.

By the time I made it outside, the blond man had vanished into the darkening night. *Crud.* I'd wanted to thank him for helping me and ask where I could go that wouldn't rip me off. I guess I'd have to gamble on reviews again. At least now I knew roughly what the pelts were worth.

Almost an hour later, I found myself in an armorer shop in the hazy area between the C and B Districts. The previous shop had felt overwhelming with all the high-end items that filled the shelves. This new one, Maveric Armory, also displayed amazing items, but it was done in such a tasteful way that I felt quite comfortable. The room was designed in whites and cool grays, and there was a set of shining armor in the corner, a scaly pattern weld crisscrossing the steel, making it look like dragon hide. Green and blue magic stones gleamed from the gauntlets and shone around the waist. The design was simple yet elegant.

A man dressed in a simple red tunic over jeans looked up from polishing an energy stone. His pale brown hair was cut short and spiked lazily. He smiled at me, his plain but neat features friendly. "Good evening, miss. I'm Maveric. Can I help you?"

I was a bit disappointed that there wasn't a bleach-blond man in the room. Throwing him completely out of my head, I walked up to the counter.

If I'd learned something from the last shop, it was that I'd been naive. Even though I wasn't inside Gate Vale, there was still a hierarchy. If I acted weak, then I was weak and fair game to anyone stronger. Even if I was weaker—and inexperienced in trade—I couldn't show that. I had to act strong.

I took a breath and gave him a small smile. "Evening. I wanted to sell these." I reached out and laid the two wolf pelts on the counter.

"Let's take a look, then." The energy stone and rag disappeared from Maveric's hand, obviously put into his Items Bag. He smoothed out one of the pelts and ran his heavily scarred hand over it, his movements slow and careful. "You did a nice job, miss," he said.

I wasn't the one who actually did it, but I nodded anyway. "Thanks."

"These are Vale wolves from Edmond Woods, correct?" He looked up at me, his expression nothing more than polite professional indifference.

There was no use trying to deny that they were the weakest of the weak or that I was still a level two, E-rank puke. Since he was higher ranked than me, he could view where I stood.

I nodded. "Yes."

He bobbed his head and ran his hand over the pelt again. "As it is, I've already started collecting wolf pelts to get ready for the new Hunters next year. I'll give you sixty dollars for each."

Sixty bucks—just like what that strong Hunter had said. Still, looking at the chill Maveric, I couldn't help but wonder if I could press for more. I'd heard before that some armorers negotiated. Maybe Maveric would?

I wouldn't know unless I tried.

I swallowed and tried to look like my insides weren't wiggling like worms. "How about seventy?" It was only a small increase, but right now, I needed every penny I could get.

Maveric tilted his head to the side, thinking. "How about we meet in the middle and say sixty-five?" He waved his hand, and a trade transaction screen appeared in front of me, asking to confirm the sale.

"Deal." I smiled at him and gladly accepted the trade. Instantly, my System dinged, letting me know that money had been transferred into my account. The fact that there was money in my account at all was a novel idea.

I couldn't have been happier at how smooth everything had just gone. As uncomfortable as it was to exit E territory and venture into districts I wasn't welcome in, I had a feeling I'd see Maveric often. If every transaction went like this, I was pretty sure that every drop item I sold would go to him.

Just before I left, Maveric called out, "Ah, miss?"

I froze, worried that he'd ask me more questions. "Yes?" I looked back.

"I'm curious about your breastplate. It's very well done, but I can't figure out whose handiwork it is, and there is no branding. Who made it for you?" He paused. "And . . . what type of leather is it made out of?"

What type of leather? I glanced down at it. The type? Black. It was black leather; that's all I knew. What surprised me was that Maveric knew his trade, so I thought for sure he would know more about my armor than I did. I mean, I just wore it and hoped it worked.

"Um." I tried not to fidget under his gaze. What should I say? "I don't actually know. It was a gift and . . . the one who gave it to me isn't here anymore."

I didn't feel that bad about lying to him because it was only a little lie. The armor *was* a gift; he didn't need to know more than that. It's not like I could tell him the System had given it to me.

My brief explanation could be taken several ways. Luckily, Maveric interpreted it how I hoped.

He nodded slowly. "Ah, I see. I'm sorry to pry." After all, who hadn't lost someone inside the Gate? It was just one of those things no one talked about. "Well, have a good evening. I look forward to future dealings, miss."

I smiled and waved. "Bye."

That night, I lay in my bed, dead tired. My arm, cinched by a bundle of medical gauze, still hurt, but I felt at peace in my little hard bed.

There was a new safe in my closet, a new lock on my new, thicker door, and I was now at level two.

CHAPTER 18

Unfortunately, the sense of peace didn't last forever.

I'd barely opened my eyes in the morning when a System window popped up in my face, telling me there was a new daily task. It startled me so badly that I nearly jumped out of my skin, and all my sleepiness vanished just like that.

"Right, that." I moaned, scrubbing my hands over my face.

I paused and looked at my left arm. It didn't hurt. Last night, even with the heavy dose of Tylenol, it'd still hurt when I moved it around. But now . . .

Frowning, I moved my arm in circles. When I still didn't feel anything, I poked at it. At first gently, then a little harder. Still nothing.

"Huh." I pinched the edge of the medical gauze and tugged, pulling it apart until the last inch slipped off my arm. My mouth parted as I gaped at my smooth skin. Eyes wide, I twisted my arm around as I tried to see every inch of my perfectly intact flesh. There wasn't even a slight skin variation. "What is going on?"

I mean, it was amazing, but how did it happen?

Confused, I opened my main menu and found that Tasks wasn't the only button with a notification sign. There was one by Abilities, too.

Excited now, I opened it. The three question marks were gone, replaced with [**Regen (Limited)**]. When I clicked on it, it read: [**While resting, your health will heal at the rate of one percent per minute. The effect is doubled while sleeping. Limitations: Cannot regrow severed appendages or heal poisons. Seek medical assistance in such cases.**]

"Wow." All I could do was gape at the screen. Only the strongest of the strong had an ability like this. Not even all the S-rank Hunters had

Regeneration—only half of the ones in America did. I didn't know about the rest of the world.

Still, it was amazing. It meant that a fifty-minute nap would completely heal me. Or if I couldn't shut my eyes, I could simply rest, and the problem would be fixed in about an hour and a half. I also couldn't help but wonder if there was a next step to the ability. If I could level myself up, did that mean I could level up my abilities, too?

I guess only time would tell.

I checked the daily task and read it out loud. "Destroy three energy crystals."

It didn't even say what kind of monster it wanted them from; it simply said *three energy crystals.* In theory, I didn't even have to kill a monster to get them. If I were faster and stronger, I could steal them from other Hunters and destroy them, but I wasn't faster and stronger—I still had a long way to go to get there. But even if I were capable enough to steal, I wouldn't. I'd never get stronger that way.

I jumped out of bed. Unlike yesterday, now I could actually feel the difference in my body when I moved. I felt lighter, as if gravity didn't have the same hold it had on me yesterday. Was that because of my increased Strength? Was this how all Hunters felt? Man, just a small taste was heady stuff. I couldn't wait till I was stronger.

I quickly dressed and pulled out my armor to suit up. That was when I found out that it regenerated overnight, too. It looked brand new; any scuffs or marks from yesterday were just gone.

It was still early when I stepped out of my room. I froze with my hand hovering over the doorknob as a chill went down my spine. I felt like I was being watched.

Looking down the hall, I saw I was alone, all other doors closed. Moving to the stairs, there wasn't a single sound outside of my boots' soft shuffle on the hall runner, even when I passed by Leticia's new door, but I still couldn't shake the creepy feeling that lifted the hairs on the back of my neck. It wasn't until I was halfway down the stairs that the feeling finally went away.

Henry bustled around downstairs, preparing oatmeal and fruit for breakfast on one side of the U-shaped kitchen. On the other side, the counter was covered in lunch prep, some already full paper bags sitting on the counter next to the kitchen door. Henry passed me a bowl of food and motioned to the table. "Go eat."

I smiled at him and turned. It wasn't until then that I noticed that the dozen or so other Hunters at the tables were all staring at me. Some of their faces looked at me like I was insane, while others were curious. A couple even looked me up and down with incredulous expressions.

My hands tightened on my bowl, and I took a deep breath, trying not to squirm under their gazes. *Don't show weakness*, I reminded myself. *Don't let them get to you.*

I sat down at one end of the table and focused on eating my oatmeal while keeping my expression as unaffected as possible.

"Hey," a guy sitting a couple chairs over put his elbow on the table and openly stared at me. "Did you really go crazy and stab Leticia's door yesterday?"

Ah, that's what the gawking was about. Well, I guess it was out of the ordinary for the weakest Hunter to attack one of the strongest here. God, I hoped none of them caused trouble for me just to get closer to Leticia. I looked at him like it was no big deal and simply answered, "Yes."

His brows shot upward, nearly touching the brown fringe of his hairline. The Hunter beside him snickered under his breath while the brown-haired one snorted and shook his head. "You're insane, provoking that woman. Watch your back, that's all I can say. She doesn't work alone."

Henry cleared his throat loudly from the kitchen. "If you're done eating, be sure to bring your dishes over." He stared pointedly at the brown-haired guy.

The younger man's mouth wrinkled, and he shoved his last few bites in his mouth. He picked up his stuff and brought it to the sink without complaint, then grabbed a lunch bag off the counter and left.

Most of the other Hunters went back to their meals, but others still continued to stare at me as if they wanted to see if I was going to freak out. Determined to let them down, I calmly ate my breakfast and put my bowl away.

"I've already talked to her," Henry muttered under his breath. "Don't stress over it."

As if talking to Leticia would fix the problem. No, my little blowup yesterday just blew things out of proportion and, according to the warning I'd been given while walking down the hall upstairs, I was going to suffer some consequences. Would something happen in Gate Vale?

I picked up my lunch and smiled at Henry. "I won't."

There were more important things to do than stress—like complete the daily task and work on getting stronger. I just hoped I would be strong enough to handle whatever Leticia might be planning by the time it happened.

With a quick goodbye, I left the kitchen.

As I trudged down the hall to the front door, steps on the stairs caused me to look up. Two older girls stared at me like jungle cats, ready to pounce. At a glance, I recognized them as Leticia's posse. Just like their leader, their armor was covered in rhinestones and sparkling stitches. It was a look popular with young women, and it looked good when it was done right. But as Es, the two obviously didn't have the income to pull off the look. They just looked tacky.

Tacky or not, their stares sent a chill—like the one I'd felt in the hall—sweeping through my body. I lengthened my stride and walked out the door, slamming it behind me.

They were going to come after me; I knew it.

I hurried to the tram, catching it as it left the station.

All was fair in the Gate, but that was only if Leticia and her posse could find me. If I could put distance between us, then the odds of them getting to me later would be lower. Luckily, it didn't look like anyone was following me yet. If Leticia did anything to me the day after we'd had a row, it would be pretty damning, even if there wasn't a lot of evidence.

For once, I didn't look for a group to follow but entered the Gate all by myself. I was still weak enough that I could use the protection, but how would I explain myself if someone saw the carcass of a monster disappear? Or how would I handle the reaction of the other Hunters if someone saw me destroy an energy crystal? If I thought my reputation was bad now, I didn't even want to think of what it would be like if I was labeled a crystal breaker. After all, the entire world was powered by those shiny stones.

My task was simply to destroy three energy crystals. I could choose wherever I wanted to go—I chose to return to Edmond Woods. It was so early in the morning that most of the monsters wouldn't have been cleared out yet. The timing was good and bad at the same time.

I found a Vale wolf pretty fast. Unfortunately, a much stronger steel tiger came by before I could finish the kill, and in the end, I had to run away. Monsters instinctively attacked the weakest creature around them, so the steel tiger stayed to eat the Vale wolf while I escaped.

The System flashed a message at me. [**Your kill was stolen. +0 EXP**]

Was it mocking me?

I slowed down and leaned against a tree, puffing for air.

"Gee, thanks," I muttered and leaned back, tipping my head against the trunk. Now I had to find another Vale wolf. At least I'd only lost a couple HP in that encounter; my new arm bracers made a world of difference.

I took a deep breath and got ready to move.

"Are you sure she went this way?"

I froze. The female voice was undeniably familiar. I'd never learned her name, but I'd seen her face at the hostel for the last year.

"That's what those guys said," another girl spoke, also from the hostel.

Carefully, I leaned around the tree and peeked. Sure enough, they were the girls from the stairs this morning—Leticia's posse. So they weren't going to let me go, after all. At least they didn't seem like they knew where I was, just what location I was in.

The girls looked around then huffed and started walking in the opposite direction.

I waited until they were gone before I ran the other way. It was time to change locations. I didn't want to be seen by other Hunters, but maybe the tall grass in the Golden Meadows would give me enough cover.

Just before exiting the woods, I ran into another Vale wolf. Determined, I put everything I had into a quick kill. Since I knew I was being hunted by more than just monsters, I really needed to get out of there.

I was breathing heavily by the time the wolf dropped to the ground, and as quickly as I could, I collected the wolf pelt into my Items Bag and shattered the crystal. There was a giant bruise on my leg, and I couldn't keep from limping as I walked away, but I was otherwise okay.

I'd barely gone a couple feet when I felt something to my right. As I turned, acid-green liquid flew at me. I moved out of the way, and it landed on the ground where I was standing. Instantly, the puddle started to smoke and boil as the liquid sank into the dirt.

"What the?" I looked up and froze.

A thick, short snake hung from a tree branch. Its pink mouth still gaped open, showing off long fangs. Above its head read: [**Acid Spitter Lv3. Warning: Poisonous.**]

Sometimes, the names of these monsters were just a little too literal. I didn't even have to guess what was going on when a fleshy tube in the back of the snake's throat contorted and another stream of green liquid gushed out.

I dodged to the side and heard the ground sizzle behind me. I was in a hurry, but that didn't mean I was going to run away now. I might not be ready to take on the girls hunting me, but I wanted to see how I would fare against a level three snake.

I gripped my kindjal and lunged at it.

Five minutes later, the snake dropped to the ground, and a joyful *ding* echoed in my ears.

[You have Leveled Up!]

At the same time, three orbs appeared next to the carcass. I gaped at them, shocked. I never thought I'd get so much from one little—albeit pain-in-the-ass—snake. But it also raised a problem. My Items Bag only held ten items. When I added those, it would be more than half full. If the next monster I killed dropped three items, I'd have to carry things in my arms. That just screamed *rob me!* I needed to get another Items Bag soon.

Quickly, I assigned my status points then collected a snake fang, a snakeskin, and a drop of poison. With a quick slash, the energy crystal exploded, and the carcass faded away. Breathing heavily, I limped away, sporting a burn on my arm and hip. The bruise on my leg was aching more than ever.

There was a patch of grass next to the Gate that I could sit down on and rest for a while to eat an early lunch. With my newfound Regen ability, a lunch break would give me enough time to heal before going after my last monster. And since I was in the open, if those girls did find me, they wouldn't be able to do anything to me. A smile pulled at my lips as I hobbled along.

I've got this.

Jynn Devhro

Rank E		**Level** 3
		EXP to Next Level 23
HP 13/32		**Stat Points** 0
MP 15/15		
Strength 13 (+10)		**Agility** 13
Magic 10		**Perception** 14
Constitution 12 (+10)		**Intelligence** 10
Skills		**Abilities**
[???]		Regen (Limited)
[???]		

CHAPTER 19

[**You have Leveled Up!**]

I shifted back. Breathing heavily, I looked at the message. The kindjal vanished from my hand as I focused on the Stats page and distributed the bonus points.

In the week since my row with Leticia, life had become pretty monotonous. I'd get up in the morning, sneak out of the hostel before the other girls could find me, then wander around the Gate looking for monsters. Unfortunately, Leticia's posse was getting harder and harder to avoid, especially since Leticia got out of detention yesterday. I thought it was odd that she hadn't come for me yet. Well, now I knew why.

The good thing was that I made it to level five while she was gone. With each level I gained, I got less and less injured, and my moves became faster and stronger. I found that the daily tasks didn't always give me prizes, but yesterday, it surprised me with a Quick Hit skill.

After I gained Quick Hit, I thought it was the mystery skill in my page, but I was wrong. The original [**???**] still remained. Even more confusing, another mystery skill had appeared beneath it after I'd picked up the drop of snake venom from a week ago. The odd thing about that was, I knew I'd picked up the venom, but it wasn't in my Items Bag when I went to sell it. It had vanished, leaving a killer question in its place. Where did it go?

Still thinking about it, I collected the drop items—a wolf fang and pelt—and watched the wolf disappear. If only I could find another acid spitter, maybe I could clear up the mystery, but I'd been all over Edmond Woods and hadn't found one yet.

My train of thought crashed when a System message popped up in my face.

[Daily Task: Defeat three Preta-Squirrels by the end of the day.]

"Preta-squirrels?" I'd never even heard of them before.

Frowning, I opened up the *Monster Manual* and scanned the list. Once I found the name, I opened up the page.

I hissed out a curse that would have made my aunt scowl. "Seriously? I have to kill three of these?"

It wasn't until I saw their nickname that I figured out what they were. Their common name was ghost biters, which was a lot more literal. They were corporeal flying squirrels, hell-bent on making anything that moved suffer their tiny wrath. The monsters themselves weren't such a problem—I was sure I could handle them at my level. The problem was where they lived.

The Fogmire was famous for the treants that lived there. The living monster trees were nearly impossible to detect, since they blended in with actual trees, and the continual heavy fog made it all the harder to see them. With an attack range of almost twenty feet, even C-ranked Hunters came out of that bog with injuries.

My stomach tightened painfully, but I took a deep breath and forced my body to relax.

It's fine. The System wasn't asking me to take on a treant. If I could avoid them, killing the preta-squirrels wouldn't be a problem. *Heh, right. Avoid the creepy monster trees I can't see.*

I slapped my cheeks, not letting my thoughts drop down that black hole. Pulling up the Gate Vale map, I started to jog out of Edmond Woods. I just needed to take the trail through Golden Meadows straight to Fogmire.

Of course, nothing ever happened that easily for me. Halfway through the Golden Meadows, I slowed to a walk so I didn't use all my energy. The tall yellow grass whispered in the light breeze, each stalk flashing gold in the bright light. Charmed, I couldn't resist reaching out to touch the soft bristles on the top of a stalk.

"There she is!" The shrill yell was faint behind me, but loud enough that it reached my ears.

I jumped and looked over my shoulder.

Leticia and her two followers were running down the path, their scowls focused on me.

"Shit!" I took off running as fast as I could.

The golden grass was nearly four feet tall. If they dragged me in, no one would see anything. It would be all too easy for them to leave me injured enough to fall under the next monster which came along. Unfortunately, I just didn't think I was strong enough to take on all three girls at the same time.

Come on, I thought. I just needed another Hunter to pop out of the tall grass. As long as there was a witness, Leticia would have to leave.

Of course, it never happened.

My Agility and Strength stats had gone up, but the other girls were still faster than me. Even running as fast as I could, they still gained ground. But the Fogmire was getting closer.

The golden tall grass opened up and thinned out. On the other side loomed a forest shrouded in mist. The barely visible trees were thick and twisted in odd shapes, some almost looking like humans in the middle of a torture session. Dull leaves hung half-heartedly on the tops of the branches, looking like they'd fall at the slightest touch. Thick tree roots webbed across the ground, obstructing anything which might remotely resemble a path.

I just needed to get there. As long as I could get into the Fogmire, I could hide in the mist and lose Leticia. Then I could return to my task.

"Run all you want!" Leticia yelled behind me. They were close enough that I could hear the sounds of her friends panting. "You're going to pay for defying me!"

Seriously, I must have had a sign on my forehead reading "Delusional person, please pick on me!"

"As if it's my fault you broke into my room, you kleptomaniac!" I yelled over my shoulder.

Ten feet! I was almost there. The fog leaked out of the trees and swirled around my feet like a lover, trying to pull me into its depths. I didn't resist, simply ran faster.

Suddenly, heat warmed my back, growing hotter and hotter. I dodged to the side just as a small fireball shot past me, close enough that it singed my sleeve black.

Stepping unevenly on a raised root, I gasped as I pitched to the side. My hand shot out and grabbed a branch, using my momentum to swing around forty degrees before taking off running at a new angle, zigzagging between mist-covered trees.

Instantly, my field of vision was cut down to about five feet in front of me because of the fog. The musky smell of earth and water was so thick I could almost taste it. After a minute, I realized the only thing I could hear was my own muffled steps over damp soil. Pausing, I looked around, straining to hear or see something, anything. How was I supposed to find a preta-squirrel?

My brittle sleeve pulled tight over my arm, and I glanced at the black spot. It was a good thing that Posse One was only an E. Any stronger and I would have been in big trouble. I bet her magic was limited in range and size, which was why I didn't have to dodge fireballs the whole way through the field. Even so, if I got too close to her in the forest, I would still be at risk from her ranged spells—even if visibility was low here.

Still thinking about it, I brushed my hand over the charred spot. I paused and touched my sleeve again. It wasn't wet.

Frowning, I patted my armor, my legs, then held my hands out to the thick fog around me. Dewy particles sifted through my fingers, cool and damp, but my skin felt completely dry. If anything, the mist almost seemed a little lighter around my hand.

"Odd," I whispered, taking a step closer to the tree next to me to check if its bark was damp like the ground.

"Where did she go?" The words drifted through the air to my right.

I jumped, shocked to hear Leticia so close. They couldn't be more than fifteen feet away. The bottom of my boot stubbed against a gnarled root, and I pitched to the side with a gasp. As I fell, something flashed in my periphery. Instead of correcting my balance, I dove to the side just as something slammed into the ground hard enough to shake the earth.

Gaping, I stared at the huge tree branch that had missed my feet by inches. It was at least a foot and a half thick, with five long, sharp twigs at the end. It almost looked like—a hand? My eyes widened, and I followed the branch up to the tree it was connected to.

The tree stared back at me. A huge, deformed face took up almost one-third of the twisted trunk. Its eyes were sharp triangles a shade paler than the dark bark covering the rest of the tree. A stubby nose jutted out over a wide, uneven mouth which nearly split the trunk in half. That mouth gaped open, and a low rumble barely more than a whisper rippled through the air. Above its face was a System box which read in red letters: [**Treant Lv15**].

Goose bumps rose on my arms. I scrambled to my feet.

The treant let out another rumble and jabbed another branch at me. I grabbed the tree next to me and swung around it, completely ignoring the bark burn on my hands. Just before I could finish the move, the treant's twig hand scraped my back and continued on until it thudded against the ground. I swallowed a moan of pain and crouched down, hugging the bark.

I expected it to attack the tree I was hiding behind, maybe even pull it out of the ground. Seconds ticked by, but nothing happened. Suddenly, the twig hand on the ground just inches from my feet lifted. My eyes widened. What was it doing?

I peeked around the tree trunk and watched as the treant shifted back into a neutral position, its arms rising like they were actual branches. Its eyes closed, and just like that, it looked like a normal—albeit ugly—tree. In the mist, I could barely tell it had a face at all.

Why? It had to know where I was. Why wasn't it still attacking me?

"Did you hear that?" Leticia said, still so close. "I think it came from this way."

I held my breath and shifted while keeping the tree between me and the treant. Leticia and the two other girls appeared through the mist, walking slowly, obviously as jumpy as I felt.

Posse Two looked around and whispered. "This is—"

The treant's eyes opened and focused on them.

"—like, the creepiest—"

Its arms started to shift, completely unseen by the girls.

"—forest ever."

They then shot toward the girls like battering rams.

Leticia and Posse Two jumped out of the way in time. The other girl was a step too slow, the twig hand hitting her shoulder with a crack as she screamed. Posse Two grabbed her and pulled her out of the way. If not, then the thick arm would have pinned her to the ground. There was no question she would have died.

"What is that?" Leticia gasped, finally seeing the monster.

"Treant!" the injured girl sobbed, tears streaming down her face. "It tracks by sounds."

"Let's move." They dodged another attack and ran away, disappearing into the fog. Faintly, I could hear them threatening to do all sorts of things to me once they found me.

When I couldn't hear them anymore, I let out a silent breath and watched the treant move back into a tree position. I still needed to find three preta-squirrels. I glanced at the monster. There could be thousands of those hiding in the forest, but as long as I didn't make any noise, I wouldn't have trouble with them. In theory.

I was just about to move when a window popped open.

[Sit down and cultivate for five minutes.]

I blinked at the message, completely confused. Sit down? Like, sit down right now, right here, with a treant looming on the other side of my hiding place? And what the heck did *cultivate* mean?

As if answering my thoughts, a new window replaced the original message. It showed a diagram of a person sitting cross-legged with their hands resting in their lap, fingertips pressed against each other and thumbs touching. But what threw me the most were the words beside the diagram. They talked about how there was energy in the world, and how that energy, if compatible, could be stored in a body.

It sounded bogus to me, but if it helped me level up faster, then what the heck? It was just five minutes. I sat down on the cold ground and arranged my body like the picture. A System timer screen appeared in front of me, ready to count down. I closed my eyes, cleared my mind as much as I could, and tried to *open up my senses*—whatever that meant.

There was no noise, and all I could feel around me was a cool mist.

I had no idea what the System wanted, but I was pretty sure I failed. The timer went off with nothing happening from beginning to end, but at least the bruise across my back had a little time to heal.

I stood up and patted my butt clean. I really needed to find the ghost squirrels. Leaning around my hiding place, I glanced at the treant tree. It was just as still as before.

Okay, all I had to do was sneak away in the opposite direction as quietly as I could.

I took a slow step back, keeping the monster in sight. The toe of my boot noiselessly landed on the moist ground, and I shifted my weight back onto it.

Something moved on the treant.

A jolt went through my body, as if all my nerves were electrified and ready to run. Then my mouth dropped open in a silent gasp.

A small creature moved around the branches of the tree monster. It was pale gray with a fat, bushy tail and so light on its feet as it jumped from branch to branch that it almost looked incorporeal.

Without a doubt, it was a preta-squirrel. Hiding in the treant.

And I needed to kill it.

Damn.

CHAPTER 20

I pursed my lips and looked around, trying to think of something to do. If I were fifteen levels higher, I might be able to take on the treant and get the preta-squirrel after, but that wasn't going to happen today. The treant attacked sound, so if I was really quiet, I could sneak up close. But that didn't change the fact that the little monster was on its branches. So how would I get up there without getting squished by them?

I reached down and pulled out a couple gray rocks from the moist ground. Carefully, I stepped out from my hiding place, being sure to move as quietly as possible. My heart was pounding in my ears so loudly, it wouldn't surprise me if the treant could hear it, but my feet didn't make a sound. I gripped the stone and shifted, ready to dive to the side at any time.

I bit my lip and threw the first rock at the preta-squirrel. The rock hit the bark just below the tiny monster, who looked at me and let out an ear-piercing, stuttering sound, flashing its needle-point teeth.

I flinched in surprise but didn't move.

Because the treant didn't move. Its eyes opened and it slightly shifted, obviously looking around, but it was like I was invisible to it. Seconds ticked by, and then it shifted the bark under the preta-squirrel and closed its eyes.

I couldn't tell if throwing the rock was a fail or not. I didn't get attacked, but the squirrel monster didn't run away like I hoped it would. Frustrated, I threw another rock at it, just to repeat the same process. How close could I get without making a sound?

I'd have to be absolutely stupid, like, brain-dead crazy, to consider nearing the tree.

I stepped forward, my feet silent over the ground.

The preta-squirrel watched me, chittering like an evil, broken music box, but the treant remained still.

I took another step closer. When nothing else happened, I picked a couple more rocks off the ground. What would happen if . . . ?

I threw one of the rocks ten feet to my right. The rock hit the ground with a dull thud, and the treant's eyes opened and focused on that spot. But it didn't attack. I waited until it closed its eyes again, then I threw another rock at the same place. Its branch arms moved before its eyes even opened all the way. They rammed down on the exact location where the rocks landed, sending a soft ripple through the damp ground.

It took everything I had not to jump.

Don't move, I thought. *Don't move, don't make a sound, and it won't know I'm here.*

The treant's face screwed up in frustration once it realized there was nothing beneath its attack. After another quiet minute—aside from the preta-squirrel's awful chittering—the monster shifted back into a neutral position.

I blew out a silent breath and picked up a couple more rocks. Slowly, I walked closer. With each step I took, it was a little bit easier to approach silently. The treant never moved.

The preta-squirrel finally stopped screeching. It stared down at me, bared its teeth, and growled, high and long, as I stopped beside the treant, eye level to its open mouth. My nose wrinkled when I caught a whiff of decay and rotten flesh.

I couldn't just throw my kindjal at the preta-squirrel. Even if I killed it, I wasn't sure I'd get it back if the blade became embedded in the bark. I looked up at the tiny monster and narrowed my eyes. The things I'd do just because a teal-colored screen promised me the heavens.

I crouched and jumped as high as I could, swinging the kindjal up. With my improved strength, my body felt lighter than ever—this little white girl got off the ground! But my stats couldn't help the fact that the little monster climbed higher in the tree before I could reach it.

Oh shit! My kindjal missed completely and sliced into the treant. Panic broke my form, and I tipped in the air until my hands and knees skidded against the damp, rough bark. The tip of my kindjal slid all the way down the bark as I fell, right between its eyes, and nearly sliced its nose in half.

The treant's eyes popped open as it let out a rumbled howl right in my face. The stench was enough to roll my already knotted gut. Its branches thrust down at me, a little slower than normal since I was so close. That little bit of time saved my life and enabled me to get out of the way while the branches continued to thunder after me, missing me by millimeters as I ran for cover.

Counterproductive or not, I still tried to keep my movements as silent as possible. If the treant lost track of me midflight, that would be all the better. Pulling the wolf fang out of my Items Bag, I threw it to the side, purposefully skipping it across the ground so it made as much noise as possible. Instantly, the tree's two arms shot out and slammed against the ground where the fang lay.

I froze. My heart was pounding like crazy, but my labored breaths were quiet.

Everything went still. The treant, me, the preta-squirrel. Even the fog in the air seemed to stop moving for an eternal minute. I was still out in the open, only fifteen feet from the monster, but slowly, it pulled back its arms and shifted back into a tree, eyes closed. The wolf fang was nothing but dust at the bottom of the hole the treant pounded into the ground. It sucked losing an item, but not as much as losing an arm—or even worse, my life—would.

That was another failure, but it also helped me realize I wasn't going to be able to get up to the preta-squirrel with leg strength alone. And it wasn't like the treant was going to hold still while I rested a ladder against it and climbed up.

Another crazy idea came to my mind; I silently sighed and tapped my forehead. If this one didn't work, I really was going to turn into a bloody pancake.

No, I thought as I forced myself to calm down. *This is going to work. I can do this.*

As scary as the treant was, it would never be as scary as that red orc and his huge sword.

I scooped up two handfuls of rocks and held them in my hand. I bent my legs, getting ready, then tossed a handful just a foot to my side. Just as the pebbles hit the ground and the treant twitched, I tossed the second handful at the same place. The second pile of rocks clattered on top of the first one, and the treant's arms shot out, aiming at that spot. At the same time, I jumped into the air, focusing on my intended landing place with all I had.

Its limbs smashed into the ground, and a second later, I landed on the thick branch. I didn't even pause for a second before I sprinted up the arm as fast as I could, each toe digging in and thrusting me upward. The treant froze, as if confused at the feeling of something running on it. That pause was all I needed to make it nearly all the way up the arm, my hands reaching out for the screeching preta-squirrel before the shock spell broke and the treant started to violently shake, lifting its arms in the air.

My teeth gritted together, and I jumped off the limb, aiming at the ghostly squirrel. It turned to climb higher, but it was too late. I grabbed it in one hand and used the other to help scramble between the gaps in the branches. They thrashed and squeezed together, but I slipped through and jumped with all I had to the tree behind it.

The preta-squirrel might look semitransparent, but it was surprisingly solid as it thrashed in my hand and bit viciously into my skin. I didn't let go. If anything, I gripped it tighter while it scratched at my fingers and let out a shrill, chittery scream. *Damn thing!* I thought, but I was too busy trying to get away from the treant to bother with it just yet.

The treant smashed at the tree I was in, clearly responding to the noise the preta-squirrel was making. Leaves and wood splinters rained down on me as I slid around the trunk to put something between me and the monster; a second later, it started to tip to the side. I ran down the slowly tilting main branch and jumped to the next tree just before it crashed to the ground.

With one arm out to help keep my balance, I tiptoed across my new tree, but my left foot slid off and I started to fall. In desperation, I spun around and threw myself back into the trunk. All the air was knocked out of me, my butt landing hard on the branch as one of my legs wrapped around it while I reached out to steady myself with my free hand. I was able to salvage my balance, but I looked up just in time to see the two blunt ends of the treant's branch-arms coming at me.

My eyes widened; there was no way I'd escape this time.

Two feet from my chest, the branches stopped. My mouth dropped open. *What happened?* The twig-like fingers wiggled as the limbs thrashed through the air. One even smashed into the branch I sat on and snapped a huge chunk off, but they never got any closer. It wasn't until I followed the limbs back to the treant that I realized why: it couldn't go any farther. It had bent to its limit, nearly at a ninety-degree angle, but it couldn't move any closer because it was rooted to the ground. And yet, it still wouldn't give up as long as this damn alarm clock kept shrieking.

I glared down at the preta-squirrel. My hand was so wet with my own blood that it was getting harder and harder to hold. Without another moment of hesitation, my kindjal appeared in my hand, and I skewered the creature. Instantly, the noise stopped, and the treant froze.

I let out a silent sigh of relief.

A teal box popped up. [**+9 EXP**]

I stared at the box, feeling more than a little bitter. All that work for just nine experience points? But now, I only had fifteen points left until I was level six. That was a good thing, right? When I killed the third preta-squirrel and achieved the daily task points, I should just barely make it to the next level. I was stewing over that thought when another System box popped up.

[Daily Task: Defeat three Preta-Squirrels. (1/3)]

Two drop orbs appeared in my lap and were instantly absorbed into my Items Bag. The tiny monster disappeared from my hand, leaving only my own bloody flesh. An energy crystal dropped onto the branch between my legs, and with a scowl, I destroyed it. Wincing in pain, I took some bandages from my Items Bag, and while I wrapped my hand, I opened my Items screen and checked what they were. My eyebrows rose in surprise.

One of them was called a Ghost Pearl, a cool name for a pale white pearl. It didn't look important, but hopefully, it had a high price tag. The other caught my attention. The whole box was pale white, as if someone had taken a worn-out marker and tried to fill in the square. It was called Essence of Nothing.

I stared at it, trying to think of what it could be used for, but the longer I stared at it, the more it changed. No, not changed. The white color was disappearing. A second later, the Essence of Nothing disappeared from my Items Bag.

"What?!" I mouthed the word and gaped at the empty box. I worked hard for that! How dare it disappear.

A notification dinged in my ear, and I was prompted to open my Abilities. There was another mystery [**???**] added to the list.

I let out a silent breath. Okay, I could handle losing the money if I got an ability out of it. The only question was when I would actually get it. Hopefully soon.

My attention was pulled away when the treant suddenly shifted back. I watched as it turned back into a "normal" tree, completely uncaring about the wreckage it'd left in its wake. There were holes in the ground and splinters of wood littered everywhere, never mind the whole tree that had collapsed in broken angles on the damp earth.

The whole exchange had probably scared off anything I wanted to find—like another preta-squirrel.

Just before I stood up, another window popped up.

[Cultivate for ten minutes.]

CHAPTER 21

This again? Seriously, what did it want?

I must have really messed up last time because the instructions on how to cultivate popped up again. I couldn't help but notice that a couple sentences were bolded.

[Use your awareness. Absorb the compatible essence into your body.]

My head tilted to the side as I reread the instructions several times. Still slightly confused, I folded my legs on the branch and put my hands together. What did I miss last time? If the System was instructing me to cultivate again, there must be something around me that I was compatible with. What was it?

I closed my eyes. What did it mean by *awareness*? Was that like my senses? Or was it referring to magic? According to my stats, I had magic now, but I still didn't have any magical abilities. Well, outside of those mystery question marks. Was my magic different from other people who just suddenly got Fire or something? Was it something I needed to earn then level up like everything else?

I took a deep breath and tried to clear the spinning thoughts from my mind. Slowly, I became aware of the noise—or lack thereof—around me. I felt the cool mist as it drifted around me, the cold bark under and behind me. The smell of damp earth and the thick, stale air. But what kept coming back to me was the *feeling* of the fog.

My eyes cracked open. For once, I didn't notice the shape of the trees in the distance but the pale air that swirled and shifted around them. It was everywhere, thick and heavy. The first time I ever saw mist was in the Gate Vale, but this was the first time I'd ever been in it. And I wasn't scared. Sure, I was nervous that I couldn't see very well, but I wasn't as discomfited as I thought I'd be.

I raised my hands and watched the pale fog drift through my fingers, cool but not wet. That's right. The mist dampened everything—the trees, the monsters, the ground, even Leticia and her group showed signs of being affected by the moist air—but not me.

An essence I was compatible with.

I repositioned my hands and closed my eyes. This time, I didn't just listen to what was around me. I built an image of my surroundings in my mind, then I imagined the fog and really focused on it. I pictured drawing it into me as I breathed.

A cool sensation pressed into my chest and swirled around until it warmed and disappeared. But it didn't really disappear; it was more like it . . . acclimated to my body and became a part of me. I could feel it but couldn't pinpoint where the feeling was coming from.

Shock nearly fried my nerves, and I almost slipped off the tree, but I suppressed the feeling before it ruined everything I'd worked to get. I calmed my thoughts and continued to pull the mist into my body. With each breath I took and every passing minute, my body felt lighter, as if I could just float away. And yet, there was a small flare of power inside. Not strength—this was different. It had nothing to do with my muscles but everything to do with my soul. It was heady stuff. The more I felt it, the more I wanted it.

A ding chimed in my mind, and I blinked out of my focus. It took me a second to realize that the System's timer was going off. I was tempted to continue cultivating, but a new window popped up.

[Gained Ability: Feather Step.]

Shocked, I opened my menu and looked it up.

[Feather Step: The ability to make your body light as air. MP Cost: 5 MP + 1 MP for every consecutive minute.]

"Cool," I whispered.

Just then, something moved to my right.

I glanced over. Through the thick fog, a pale gray shape crawled around a dark tree trunk.

Is that what I think it is? I slowly stood up and leaned closer. It didn't see me, which was good because that meant it didn't run away. But I also couldn't see what it was properly either. The tree it was on was a good ten feet away; I couldn't jump that far.

Or I couldn't jump that far until a moment ago. Right? I glanced at my previously unused MP. I had enough to activate Feather Step then keep it for twenty additional minutes. I hoped that monster was a preta-squirrel; if I had to keep reactivating Feather Step, it was going to blow through my MP fast.

Here goes nothing. I took a deep breath and thought, *Feather Step.*

My body turned buoyant, as though gravity had no effect on me. I remained standing on the tree trunk, and the slight breeze in the air didn't blow me over, but I finally knew what a balloon felt like. Focusing on the tree with the pale gray monster crawling around its base, I jumped.

I shot through the air, the strength behind my jump launching me like a rocket to the next tree. Halfway through my leap, I could see that my gamble paid off.

A preta-squirrel stopped midstep to look at me. Its mouth dropped open, and it gave a hair-raising shriek.

Oh no! I glanced down at the tree it was on, expecting to see an ugly treant face on the trunk. For once, luck was on my side; it was just a normal tree. At least, I was lucky until the little monster turned and jumped to the next one over.

I landed and leapt after it, my moves just as light and quick as the ghostly squirrel. On and on, we jumped from one tree to another, pushing over branches and sliding around trunks. At first, my movements were awkward, but the longer I used Feather Step and worked my way around bare, damp trees, the smoother my movements became. But no matter what, the squirrel stayed three feet ahead of me, screaming as I pursued it.

The tiny monster leapt through the air, missing the main branch that was its target and falling until it clung to the thick trunk. Now was my chance. I launched myself at the preta-squirrel, blade first. My weapon was just inches from the creature when I felt the mist move around me. Something was coming at me. Fast.

Looking up, I gasped as a treant's limb aimed right for me. I twisted in the air and kicked off its side, vaulting myself out of harm's way. I slammed against the ground, my lungs seizing as I lost my breath, but I continued to roll because the other limb was targeting me now. The tree monster's branch crushed an indent into the earth just as I rolled to my feet. The preta-squirrel was already skittering up the treant's face, up into the branches at its back.

Damn. My MP was already half empty at this point; I couldn't keep Feather Step engaged for much longer. I still had to find another preta-squirrel after this one.

Speed was key now.

The treant retracted its limbs and shifted back into a neutral position. I scooped up some rocks then sprinted across the ground and leaped. I kicked off a half-raised branch and launched myself at the preta-squirrel.

It screamed, jumping away as I clambered over the treant and soared after it. The treant swung its limbs after me, smashing everything I stepped on just a half a second after my foot left that spot. I aimed a rock and threw it just in front of the squirrel. A second later, the treant aimed for that same location. The tiny monster skidded to a stop and scrambled in the other direction.

My kindjal appeared in my hand, and I swung it, aiming at the trapped monster. I stabbed the preta-squirrel at the same moment the treant's limb came down and broke the branch clean off with its attack. I pinned the dead monster to the remaining half as I threw the rest of my rocks away, directing the treant away from me. It smashed at the ground for a minute before slowly settling back into a creepy tree.

I took a second to catch my breath. I might have been weightless for that chase, but I'd moved faster than I ever had in my life, and it was exhausting. After a moment, I collected the drop items, put them in my Items Bag, then destroyed the energy crystal. Just before closing my inventory, the Essence of Nothing disappeared. Again. Seriously, what was up with that? What did it mean?

I glanced back at the treant before slipping down to the ground. I didn't relax until I was another ten feet away and I was sure the tree monster wasn't going to move.

"Teresa? Is that you?"

I froze when I heard the hatefully familiar voice. I stepped back and pressed against a thick, damp tree, controlling my breathing to be as quiet as possible, then leaned around.

A second later, Leticia stepped out of the fog. Her damp hair was a mess, half flattened to her head and half scrunched in funny places with a leaf stuck in it. Her eyes were wide and a little manic as she turned this way and that, jumping at every little sound. Dirt smudged her clothes, and her left sleeve was torn. It was nice to know I wasn't the only one who'd had a tough time here.

She stopped and looked around. "Teresa? Judy?" she whispered.

She was so close; just five feet away.

My hands fisted so tight that my fingers hurt. This bitch had made my life hell for the last year. From the moment I stepped into the hostel, she never let up; she was even hunting me right now. Since she took it all the way into Gate Vale, it was obvious she wasn't after a simple blanket anymore.

I didn't remember pulling my kindjal out, but suddenly, I felt the cool, comfortable handle in my hand. Leticia didn't know I was watching her; it would be so easy to get the sneak attack. Just one move, and I would be free of her endless torment. I could even push her another ten feet to the left and trigger a treant to react. It would have the same consequence.

She took another step closer. My muscles tightened, and I shifted my kindjal in my grip, getting ready.

A breeze kicked up and rustled the leaves overhead. Leticia jumped and looked up, exposing her throat.

I . . . froze.

Go, a devil whispered in my mind. *Get rid of her, and you'll be one step closer to a carefree life.*

Just like I'd always wanted. God knew I'd been thrown to a group of red orcs for a lot less than what she'd done.

I wanted respite, wanted peace. Wanted it so badly I was willing to sell myself to a mysterious System which had taken over my life. But I didn't want it enough to lose my humanity. There were a lot of Hunters who were no different from monsters. Anything that was weaker than them didn't deserve to live, whether or not it was human.

I wouldn't be like them. I would get stronger. I would be the strongest—but I wouldn't do it soaked in the blood of another human being.

Leticia walked right by me, completely oblivious, and disappeared in the mist.

My hand tightened on the kindjal's handle as I closed my eyes and pulled in a breath. I held it and counted. *One. Two. Three.* Slowly, I let it out, releasing all the tension in my body. The kindjal disappeared, and my hand slackened to my side. My eyes opened and I looked in the direction Leticia had gone.

Funny. I thought it would be harder to let go of the anger in my heart. I didn't forgive her, but I also wouldn't allow her to affect my emotions like this anymore. I didn't know how freeing it would be, as if a weight I'd been carrying around for so long suddenly disappeared. Why had I spent so much time and effort lugging it around with me? What a waste of energy.

My lips curled in a mocking smile, and I walked in the opposite direction. It was time to find the last preta-squirrel.

A System window popped up. [**Cultivate for fifteen minutes.**]

I wasn't going to turn that down. I still didn't know why it wanted me to do all this cultivating, but the sensation was so cool that I couldn't wait to do it again.

I picked a tree with a good sitting place and climbed up. When I was comfy, I got into position and began drawing the mist in. In no time at all, the System's alarm chimed, and I opened my eyes. What would happen if I kept going even after the alarm went off?

I was tempted to continue cultivating when a notification popped up.

[Gained Ability: Mist.]

I threw my hands up in the air in victory but held in a yell. Then I paused. What was this Mist ability, anyway? I'd never heard of it. I could guess what it meant, but it wasn't listed in the *Hunter's Guide*.

Still, it was an ability I got from cultivating, just like Feather Step. Did that mean that every time I cultivated, I'd get a new ability? Should I do it some more?

Like always, the System seemed to know what I was thinking.

[At your current level, cultivating too much would be detrimental to—]

Suddenly, my vision was filled with a huge, red message overlapping the teal.

[GET OUT OF THE DIMENSION NOW!]

Before I could do more than gasp, the ground started quaking. I leaped from the tree and stumbled while I tried to steady myself. It wasn't just a small rumble like when treants smashed the ground but a full, staggering ripple.

"What's happening?" I yelled, but I couldn't even hear my own voice.

A deafening roar rose into the air as if every single monster in Gate Vale was howling with all their might.

Freaked out to the extreme, I ran as fast as I could. The ground split and moved so much that I kept tripping with each new vibration. Trees tilted around me, slanting in my way or crashing right to the ground. Desperate, I activated Feather Step and put my all into sprinting through the chaos. I rushed over falling trees and touched off the top of the rolling ground. After what felt like forever and also no time at all, I broke out of the Fogmire trees as the mist faded away from me. Even though I was in the open and the Gate was in view, I still didn't cancel Feather Step. Instead, I used it to speed through the Golden Meadows.

Another message appeared in my vision, and it took me aback for a second. I'd gotten so used to the teal System boxes I'd almost forgotten they used to be blue.

[Alert! The Gate has destabilized. All Hunters return to Eden immediately. Prepare for a Gate Surge.]

CHAPTER 22

I didn't have time to wonder why the message boxes were different colors because the ground started rumbling again, but for a whole new reason.

Looking up, thousands of Hunters came into view, a chaotic stampede to exit the Gate. But not only Hunters were present; monsters were mixed into the crowd, fleeing in the same direction. They didn't even seem to care who they were running next to; they appeared just as driven to get through the Gate to Earth on the other side. Hunters swung their weapons as they ran, taking down monsters. Some were killed; others were simply wounded and left in the Hunter's dust.

[**HURRY!**] Another teal message prompted me.

A crowd of monsters surged around the Gate, trying to exit the portal, but they couldn't pass through the flat black surface. Hunters crashed into the mass, slicing, forcing paths through. There was no way I could fight my way across, so I jumped as high as I could, landing on a monster's back, then leaped to the next monster's head, skipping over every creature in my way with feather-light steps.

I neared the Gate threshold and launched off the last monster just as a pulse went through the air. It washed over me, sending all of my nerves stinging. What the hell was that? I twisted in the air and my eyes locked onto something impossible.

In the distance, one of the portals that ringed Gate Vale was swelling, growing bigger and bigger, like a black hole, disintegrating everything it touched. As I looked, it exploded in a flash then collapsed onto itself, leaving a huge hole where it had been. It wasn't black on the other side like I thought it would be. It was a pale, topaz blue, shining like a star.

As monsters howled so loud that my ears rang, I soared through the Gate, gasping as familiar tingles spread over my body, like walking under a veil of cold air. I could no longer hear the howls but the wail of sirens and cries of people yelling.

I landed on the concrete and staggered to a stop, falling right at the feet of a Hunter. Stunned, I just stopped there, trying to catch my breath, before the presence of this unknown Hunter's strength surrounded me. My eyes widened and I jerked up, staring right into the helm of the person towering over me in full steel armor.

It wasn't just his presence that smothered a reaction from me but his intimidating stature, which exuded a colossal strength. His red-and-silver armor was so handsome, and it complimented his deep brown eyes. The pattern of a sword made out of red magic stones decorated the right side of his chest, the emblem so iconic I knew exactly who I was looking at.

He was, without a doubt, S-rank Blood Sword.

But the pressure I felt wasn't just coming from Blood Sword's strength alone; I could also feel the pressure mounting behind me. I looked around and was shocked to see that eleven other S-rank Hunters circled me—every single one who lived in Eden. I knew who they were based on their armor, even though I couldn't name a single one of them because they only ever publicized their nicknames. Of course, none of them acknowledged me, focused on their conversation. It was like they couldn't even tell that hundreds of Hunters like me were spilling frantically out of the Gate.

I blinked as I caught sight of Jonovan on the outside of the S-rank Hunters, talking with a woman dressed in a violet mage robe. From the symbol on her chest, she was probably the only S-ranked healer in America.

"Es are in the back." Blood Sword drew my attention back to him. His tone was civil, neither condescending nor encouraging. His words cut through the blaring siren which rang in the air, announcing the threat. He jerked his head to the back of the crowd forming around the Gate. "We'll take care of the big stuff. You're responsible for catching the ones that slip through."

As if the sirens weren't enough, the Gate's smooth surface suddenly rippled and pulsed. I'd never seen it do that before, but I knew from history books that it was a sign it was getting ready to let monsters out.

I snuck a glance at Blood Sword and jerked my head in a small nod before running as fast as I could, sliding between Hunters. I was starting to get stronger, but even I wasn't stupid enough to think I belonged on the front line yet.

One of the first things every Hunter learned was how to handle a Gate Surge. The S ranks were responsible for the front line and taking out the biggest threats that came out. The next line of defense was the major guilds, followed by smaller guilds. The last line of defense was the unattached Hunters, like me, who would take out the little monsters that slipped through the cracks.

If any monster got through all of us, the only thing holding them back from the humans in Garden City was a flimsy red brick wall. In the last Gate Surge five years ago, a flock of rocs actually managed to get out of Eden. They decimated three Garden City blocks and killed nearly a hundred humans before they were finally brought down.

I didn't stop running until I was in the very back of the crowd. Not too far from me stood a thin healer wearing a green cape. He cupped his hands and shouted over the noise of the crowd, "If you need healing, come to me!"

My HP wasn't awful since I was resting as I cultivated, but it had been a long day, and I didn't know what was going to come. I walked over to the healer and extended my hand as if for a handshake. "I can use some healing."

He looked me up and down, obviously taking in my dirty clothes and lopsided ponytail. "Of course." There wasn't any doubt in his voice; he reached out and gripped my hand. His fingers started to glow gold—not as pure or clear as Jonovan's, but that didn't surprise me. Since this healer was in the back with me, it was a given he wasn't strong, but I appreciated the seriousness in his face as he worked.

Snippets of conversation from the people next to me caught my attention over the siren, and I glanced over.

"Are you for real?" a woman gasped, staring at the man beside her in rapt attention.

The man nodded. "I heard it right from Blood Sword's mouth when I walked by. An S went into a portal, wiped out every monster inside, and then the portal started to collapse!"

My eyes widened. Something like that could actually happen? A person could cause a portal to collapse? I didn't even know a portal that wasn't a Portal Burst could collapse at all.

But of course it could. I watched it collapse with my own eyes. Was that why the monsters were going crazy?

The healer next to me paused and glanced over, obviously just as shocked. I mean, the portals and the Gate were like the sun, an existence that would just always be.

The woman covered her mouth in shock. "Oh my god!" She went up on her tiptoes, trying to see over the crowd. "That's just—wow."

The man bobbed his head again. "I know. Only, right after it happened, the monsters went crazy. At least it's the end of the day and not the beginning, so a lot of them have already been taken care of, but still . . . " He rolled his shoulders and shifted side to side, his features tight.

The healer released my hand. "There you go." He gave me a soft smile.

I bobbed my head. "Thank you." He didn't heal me all the way—I was at 49/54 HP—but I was grateful, anyway. I turned and focused on the gossiping man a couple feet away. "Which S Hunter was it?" I asked.

The guy jolted and looked at me, surprised by my interruption. "I don't know. It's one who hasn't published his information."

I nodded. S Hunters were superstars. Most of them were millionaires, with adoring fans scrambling to snatch up every magazine and poster they graced. S Hunters were the faces of hope, the backbone which kept all the worst nightmares at bay. Even though they used nicknames, everyone knew who they were. But that didn't mean that all twenty-four of the country's S Hunters enjoyed the spotlight. A handful of them refused to join stardom, preferring to hide in plain sight.

The ground started to rumble, and the noise of the crowd shut off like someone threw a switch as every single eye focused on the pulsing Gate. Tension hung in the air, so thick it was hard to breathe.

Even though I was on my tiptoes, I still couldn't see more than a couple people ahead of me. Glancing around, I spotted a lamppost on the other side of the healer, so I stepped around him and jumped up, gripping the post with my left hand and supporting my weight on a small lip a third of the way up the pole. It wasn't the most comfortable thing, but at least I could see.

The whole of Eden's population spread out before me, tens of thousands of Hunters all in a giant ring surrounding the Gate, filling up the flat concert area of Gate Square; some even spilled out into the streets that led here. Melee Hunters gripped their weapons, and mages began summoning their magic, causing bright flashes of color to spark above the crowd. It was truly awe-inspiring. Eden was a dog-eat-dog world, but right now, every single Hunter was ready to throw down their lives to stop the monsters that would come out of the Gate. This wasn't just about the

Hunter's duty—nearly everyone here had someone they wanted to protect in Garden City.

I couldn't help but glance in the direction of the city. Sirens were going off there, too. According to protocol, my family would be hiding in the bathroom right now. I could still remember five years ago, hugging Aliya in the bathtub while my aunt and uncle stood in front of us, holding plain swords and staring at the locked door. Since they were normal humans, they couldn't do anything against a monster, but that didn't stop their determination. Luckily, the rocs never got close to us. And I wouldn't let anything get close to my family this time either.

A pulse of power ripped through the air, blowing hair around and causing loose clothes to flap in its wake. I gripped the pole tighter and pulled my attention back to the middle of the square. The huge two-dimensional black arch loomed hundreds of feet over our heads, pulsing like a ticking time bomb. Its edges rippled like disturbed water.

All at once, it became completely still.

"Get ready!" an S-ranked Hunter yelled from the front line.

A figure fell out of the portal—a Hunter. He flopped onto the ground, gasping for air. He was bloody from head to toe, his right arm barely more than a stump. When he raised his head, his left eye was nothing but a bloody, empty socket.

A chill froze my heart and spread to the rest of my body.

"Run!" he screamed with all his might.

A huge, bare foot as long as I was tall tipped with yellowed toenails pushed through the black Gate. It stepped down, right on the Hunter.

I looked away, knowing I'd never unhear the *splat* which echoed throughout the square.

Half a second later, the rest of the monster's body emerged from the Gate, dragging a battered tree trunk behind. The thirty-foot-tall cyclops raised its head. Its howl shook the heavens.

CHAPTER 23

The dam broke, and hundreds of monsters spilled out from both sides of the two-dimensional Gate. In the wake of the first cyclops, ten more followed, with monsters of all shapes and sizes filling up every gap between them. The Hunters responded with their own deafening war cry as the groups collided, with the S ranks in the lead taking on the cyclops.

From my post, the fight drew closer like a ripple in the water, ever-expanding toward the edge of the crowd. Some guilds worked together in flawless teamwork with beautiful strategies and coordinated moves between the melee and mage Hunters, taking out groups of monsters at once. Some guilds broke into smaller groups which worked together to take on larger monsters; most had good teamwork, while others were obviously just working together. Other guilds didn't band together at all but let each individual Hunter fight alone with a random helping hand for aid.

Monsters continued to spill out of the Gate. If they could be killed with a single blow, the stronger Hunters took out weaker monsters while fighting their targets. If they couldn't, they didn't even bother with the small fries. They just left them to the next Hunter down the line and concentrated on the one they were dealing with.

The air filled with sounds of battle. Monsters roared and howled. The screech of claws on metal grew louder than the city sirens. Men and women yelled in fury or pain, and the names of spells echoed in a deafening swell. Flashes of brightly colored magic snapped overhead—some as fast as strobe lights, others slower and beautiful against the horror of death.

"Here it comes!" I called out to anyone who'd listen as the monsters breached the E-rank line. I pulled out my kindjal and focused on a goblin weaving between Hunters, its short legs pumping as it giggled evilly. I pushed off the light post and launched myself at it.

I lost track of time. All I knew was the fight. Dodge attack, counter with weapon, repeat. As soon as one monster fell, I turned around and came face-to-face with another. Unlike normal, I purposely didn't destroy the energy crystals or drop orbs. There were too many eyes around, and I couldn't answer questions if someone asked later why my kills disappeared. My Items Bag was full anyway, so I wouldn't be able to keep the drop items that would have appeared. I might have agonized over it more if I hadn't been so busy trying to stay alive.

[You have Leveled Up!]

[You have Leveled Up!]

That was how I kept track of things. With each level, I could feel myself getting stronger, even though there wasn't time to assign my bonus points; that would just have to be taken care of when the madness ended. And even if I got a boost of health when my HP went up with each level, I was still losing points, and fatigue began setting in.

With a yell, I stabbed a giant spider between its eyes. My kindjal nicked one of the eyeballs, and it popped like a cherry. I grimaced and recoiled, pulling my short sword out. Breathing hard, I glanced at the window flashing in the corner of my vision.

[HP is low. Please seek medical assistance.]

Another monster came at me. Instead of taking it on, I dodged around a healthy-looking Hunter behind me. He scowled but attacked the monster anyway while I turned and ran to the clear space where healers were on standby. I pushed through the line of Hunters keeping them safe and approached the strongest healer who wasn't busy.

"Holding up?" The healer took my hand and started to channel golden magic into my body.

I nodded, breathless. The fatigue which had been building inside me smoothed away as my HP started to fill up.

"This is something, isn't it?" he muttered, looking around at the chaos on the other side of his protective circle. "But, god, look at the S Hunters!"

I turned toward the huge explosions and flashing lights on the other side of the crowd. For good reason, the Ss were given the most space; the cyclops lay dead, replaced with a handful of hydra. As I watched, a familiar Hunter in a shining blue-and-steel armor leapt into the air and sliced a hydra in half. So strong.

A gruesome scream of pain rang out beside me, and I turned just in time to see a D-ranked drake throw a Hunter into the air. The Hunter landed hard on the ground and didn't move. The reptilian monster was twice the size of a horse and covered in dark blue scales, its square head topped with huge, scaly antlers which dripped with blood. Roaring, it charged forward. With a toss of its head, another Hunter was thrown in the air, and the drake disappeared down the street.

"No!" I bolted after it.

It turned through the streets, somehow finding its way toward the entrance to Garden City—it was like it was drawn to the smell of humans. I couldn't let it leave Eden.

It was a D-ranked monster, true, but my System labeled it as level thirteen. It was five levels above me, but that didn't matter right now. It could be a level one monster, and humans would still be helpless against it.

I activated Feather Step and sped up, coming up to its right side. The drake noticed me and spun its antlers as it turned; I dropped and slid under, barely dodging the attack, as the bottom of the antlers grazed the stray hairs on my ponytail. I whipped out my kindjal and slashed at the drake's ankles then rolled to my feet.

It roared and lashed out with its thick tail. I gasped and raised my arm bracers to protect myself as the tail smashed into me, my arms taking most of the hit. For a second, they were just numb. Then the pain set in. I didn't even have time to cry out before I was thrown back from the force of the hit.

I slammed against the wall behind me, losing half of my HP. My mouth opened in a breathless scream as all the air was knocked out of me. The back of my head hurt just as badly as my arms, and my vision blurred; I slid down the wall until my feet touched the ground. Blinking furiously, trying to get rid of the gray dots in my vision, I looked up just in time to see the drake charging.

Instincts taking over, I leaped with all my might. The drake's antlers smashed into the wall beneath me, brick crumbling to pieces. I landed on the drake's head, and using my fall as momentum, I thrust my kindjal down as hard as I could. The blade glanced off the top of its head, plunging into the monster's neck. The drake howled and threw its head back.

I careened through the air but maintained enough control to land on my feet, stumbling back and resisting putting a hand to my aching head. The drake turned to me and bared its huge teeth, hissing low.

I glared back and brandished my kindjal at it. The monster bled from its neck and left ankle, but that barely seemed to matter—the damn thing was just too strong and fast. If I could dodge faster, gaining the upper hand would be easier. If only it couldn't . . .

A thought came to my mind. Right as it lowered its head to charge, I thrust out my hand and cast Mist; a two-foot diameter cloud of thick fog formed around the drake's head. I hadn't read the instructions yet, so I didn't really know how Mist was supposed to work. I was probably using it wrong, but it was exactly what I needed.

The drake roared and charged blindly, the mist remaining attached to its head. I dodged to the side, and the monster charged past. Unlike before when it missed me by inches, my actions were now completely calm and controlled. I twisted and stabbed its stomach. My kindjal caught inside, and I was dragged with its momentum. Grimacing as the motion wrenched my shoulder, I skipped my feet to keep up with its speed.

The drake smashed into the opposite wall head-on, leaving another hole. It twisted its body and tried to pin me, but I jumped and landed on its back, releasing my kindjal to avoid crushing my hand. The hilt of the sword hit the wall with the force of the drake's attack and jammed itself deeper into its flesh.

Effective, I guess, but now I didn't have a weapon, and the monster still had half its HP left. *What do I do now?*

Its thick tail whipped up at me. I jerked out of the way and slipped off its smooth, scaly back. The drake's hind leg kicked out and caught me in the chest, sending me flying back five feet before I landed in a crouch.

Huffing for air, I stood up.

Jeez, every time it hit me, it took out a huge chunk of my HP. Since I wasn't even at full health before, I was down to twenty percent now. Another hit would kill me.

The drake turned toward me, its mist-covered head weaving in the air.

Suddenly, my kindjal appeared in my right hand. I was so shocked I almost dropped it—the bloody hilt slipped in my grasp. My eyes widened as I remembered the description. *Cannot be dropped, sold, or stolen.* So it would keep coming back?

The monster roared, bowed its head, and charged. I activated Feather Step, leaving only 4 MP left, and jumped, stepping one foot on top of its head. The moment I touched it, it jerked; my foot slipped and I fell, but I managed to twist in midair and ended up straddling its neck. The drake howled and flailed, trying to throw me off.

The last thing I wanted to do was to fall and take another hit, so I reversed the grip on my kindjal, putting the blade against the base of the right antler, then locked my other arm at a ninety-degree angle with my bracer on the blade. I clamped my legs around its thick neck.

It was a desperate move, but it anchored me to the monster as it tried to throw me off.

The fog around its head encircled mine, but for some reason, my vision wasn't obstructed by it. I could even see perfectly when the drake turned and charged another wall.

"Shit!" I gasped. I needed to stop it. Now.

I pulled back on the antler with everything I had, trying to make it change directions, but the drake just growled and tossed its head, resisting my actions.

The pressure on my hand and arm locked on the kindjal was nearly unbearable. My hand wanted to give out, and I could feel my skin starting to split under my bracer, but I gritted my teeth together and pulled back with all my strength.

There was a crack, and suddenly, the antler was cut right off. It fell with a thud to the ground as the monster howled loud enough to make my ears ring, skidding to a halt just feet from the wall.

With my anchor gone, I wobbled on its neck. Grabbing the other antler with my left arm as the monster flailed around in obvious pain, my upper body landed on its head, my eyes just inches from the bloody socket where the antler had been.

I gasped. It was hollow inside; a direct hole to a spongy tissue. Wasting no time, I whipped my kindjal around, aimed, and stabbed through. I felt the blade hit something hard which resisted for a second, then the kindjal cut through it.

The drake exploded into little balls of light right from under me. I dropped to the ground, disoriented and confused as to where it went.

Several teal messages popped up simultaneously.

[**+105 EXP**]

[**You have Leveled Up!**]

[**You have Leveled Up!**]

[**Gained Skill: Throw.**]

[**Gained Skill: Critical Hit.**]

I lay there on the ground, breathing hard. Now that my battle had ended, I could hear the sounds of the Gate Surge still going on, but I didn't care. I was too tired and sore. But I was alive.

I punched my fist in the air in a pathetic victory. "Yay!" I breathed. "Go me! I killed a level thirteen monster." And my whole body hurt like hell because of it. Man, the System really needed to add a fanfare when I defeated hard monsters.

After my short celebration, I focused on the messages. *So that thing I hit in the drake's skull was an energy crystal?* Even though I'd killed a lot of monsters during the Gate Surge, I was too busy to destroy any of the energy crystals, and I wasn't interested in finding out what the punishment for not getting the daily quota was.

But the most important thing was that I survived and leveled up while I worked. Level ten. I never thought it would happen.

Now that there was a moment of quiet, I opened my stats and received another shock.

I was a D rank.

I stared at the letter with my mouth open. Slowly, I reached out. It wasn't until my finger passed through the screen that I snapped out of my stupor. I wasn't an E rank anymore! This time when I threw my fists in the air, there was more energy behind it.

"I'm a D!" I yelled to the open air, my voice echoing off the alley's battered brick walls. "I'm a D rank now!"

A screen popped up. [**Please note, as part of the confidential nature of the Leveling Up System, other Hunters will continue to see your rank as E.**]

Even that didn't kill the excitement. It didn't matter what the other Hunters saw, as long as I was getting stronger.

[**Becoming Stronger Quest has Leveled Up! Congratulations.**]

"What?" I gasped and sat up. My heart was pumping a million miles per hour as I opened up my menu. I didn't even see the term Becoming Stronger Quest anymore. It had been replaced with . . .

"Warrior of Mist?" I read aloud.

What was that? I opened it up, but the description was the exact same as the Becoming Stronger Quest.

I flopped back onto the ground. So this whole getting stronger thing was turning me into a Warrior of Mist? What was that?

"System, are there other Warriors of Mist?" Was I supposed to find them and become a disciple there or something?

[**There are no others.**]

Which meant I had to rely on the System to teach me everything. I guessed it was no different from right now.

I took a second to distribute my bonus Stat Points and rolled to my feet. There were other notifications on my menu, but I needed to get back to where the fighting was. Not only to get healed but to keep getting stronger.

Jynn Devhro

Rank D		**Level** 10	
		EXP to Next Level 138	

HP 24/119		**Stat Points** 0	
MP 4/57			

Strength 25 (+10)		**Agility** 24	
Magic 20		**Perception** 24	
Constitution 22 (+10)		**Intelligence** 20	

Skills	**Abilities**
Throw	Mist
Critical Hit	Feather Step
Quick Hit	Regen (Limited)

CHAPTER 24

The battle was hard fought. Thousands of monsters were killed. Over two hundred and fifty Hunters died. Four buildings surrounding Gate Square collapsed, and innumerable smaller structures were damaged by monsters rampaging through Eden streets. The victory was that the Gate Surge had been contained to Eden for the first time in history. That was considered a success.

Amidst the rubble, the crowd's deafening cheers died out. Then came the hard part—cleaning up. Medics removed bodies while healers walked around and helped the injured Hunters who were still breathing. Guilds staked their claim to the monster carcasses that were in their given area. Solo Hunters hurried to mark which monsters they'd killed—whether or not they'd actually killed them. I found some of the monsters I'd brought down, but in the end, I couldn't locate more than half of them.

I'd gotten so used to how the System cleaned up so perfectly that it was odd to pile my kills together and wait for the government official to come over to record them and how much money I'd get from the parts. Most of the other Hunters dug out the energy crystals and simply sold them without caring about the rest. Those were also the Hunters who got to bed before 2:00 a.m. While the government cleaned up and the armorers had a field day collecting dead monsters, the rest of the Hunters threw in the towel.

I didn't wake up until the next afternoon; no surprise there. No daily task awaited me, just a simple message.

[Due to unforeseen events, there is no punishment for failing yesterday's Daily Task. Daily Tasks will be suspended until the other dimension stabilizes. Enjoy the vacation.]

That was great and all because after last night, I needed a break. But what I needed more was to know what a Warrior of Mist was. However, no matter how many times I asked, the System never responded. I'd gotten so used to it randomly answering me that its sudden silence threw me off. The System had warned me it would give me information when I was ready for it, but I didn't want to follow the System's timeline. I wanted to know *now* what I was becoming.

With nothing else to do, I did the old-fashioned thing and left for the library on my own legs to do some research with my own mind. Since I didn't have a laptop or cell phone, I had to go to the Eden Library in A District.

The smell of blood was still thick in the air as I headed to the tram. Since Gate Square was still being cleaned up, the tram took the roundabout way instead of going straight through the middle of Eden. It was still faster than if I walked, since A District couldn't be farther away from the E Hostel. The streets were quiet, which made sense. Being lazy in bed sounded great after last night.

Only, I couldn't let go of my desire to know what was going on. I trusted the System—I mean, it had done nothing but help me, and it was the very reason why I was still alive—but that didn't mean I was going to wait for answers. What if instead of telling me, the System was waiting for me to find out what a Warrior of Mist was on my own?

A District couldn't be more different from E District; there was nothing ghetto or run-down there. The red-brick buildings were as vibrant as the day they'd been laid. Green gardens and full trees bloomed everywhere, perfectly accenting shops and buildings in a soothing, sophisticated way. The sidewalks were clean and clearly defined from the street. There were even several cars parked on the side of the road, just as clean and expensive looking as the rest of the district.

I stopped and looked at the cars. Jeez, how much did those cost? I couldn't imagine having enough disposable income to afford something like that.

Shaking my head, I moved on and came to a stop not a hundred feet later at a pretty little park spread out to the left of the road. It wasn't big, and there wasn't a playground in it because kids weren't allowed in Eden, but the roses blooming—in reds, pinks, yellows, and whites—were gorgeous. I couldn't resist walking across the green grass to them and reaching out. The petals were so soft, so smooth. So innocent.

Being constantly surrounded by plants in the Gate, it was common knowledge that the prettier they were, the more likely it was that they would kill you. Nearly every flower in Gate Vale was poisonous, and half of them were actually monsters that moved and ate people. Or there were plants like the treants which I'd become so familiar with—ugly and scary. Between that and the constant violence of fighting for my life, it was easy to forget there was something so simple as a harmless rose in a gorgeous garden. It was like a balm to my tired soul; something I didn't even know I needed until I touched it.

I closed my eyes and took a deep breath of the sweet scent. Surrounded by flowers, the scent of the bloody battle disappeared. A small smile pulled at my lips. I should get to the library as soon as possible. Instead, I sat down on the grass in front of the roses and tipped my face toward the warm sun.

There weren't a lot of people walking around, but there were enough that I could hear them coming and going. As carefree as I felt, I couldn't keep my eyes closed forever—it was instinct to pay attention to the threats around me. Granted, I didn't expect the Hunters here to hurt me; I probably wasn't even on their radar of possible threats. Still, I opened my eyes and watched the few people as they strolled by.

Since last night, when my Becoming Stronger Quest changed to Warrior of Mist, I'd noticed a change in my scanner. Normally, a Hunter couldn't see what rank another Hunter was unless they were stronger than them. But now, I could see the ranks of everyone around me, even those who ranked higher. It was odd, and I couldn't wait to see what else would change about me.

A tingle went down my spine, breaking me out of my thoughts. My sixth sense went off, signaling there was a very strong threat to my left.

That couldn't be right. The Gate was a good mile away from me, and even from here, I could see it wasn't acting up. It wasn't possible for a monster to be here in the middle of A District. If there were, how many Hunters would have found it by now? It couldn't be left over from last night.

Alarmed, I stood up and tried to locate where the feeling was coming from. All I could see was a couple walking hand in hand and another guy walking with his hands in his pockets. All three of them were A-rank Hunters and perfectly at ease. There was no monster.

My brows wrinkled. Maybe I should have stayed in bed a little longer?

Then another man walked by, his movements just as relaxed as anyone else's. But the title bar above his head was red. Just like a monster's.

Name: ???

Katharian

Lv: ???

I gasped. What did that mean?

I'd never heard that word before. "Katharian?" I sounded it out under my breath.

The man froze as if I'd screamed the word at the top of my lungs. Several people walking behind stepped around him as he slowly turned and looked at me. He was in his early twenties, tall and slender. Even from here, I was struck by the icy blue of his piercing eyes. Even though his hair was pale blond, his lashes were black as night; the contrast against his pale skin made him even more striking.

His eyes narrowed, and he started to walk toward me.

A wave of power washed over me, making the hair on my body stand up. Just . . . just how powerful was he?

As if I needed more of a hint, a System message started to blink under his title bar.

[DO NOT PROVOKE!]

It flashed over and over, as if the way his power was a heavy blanket smothering me wasn't a big enough clue. *Thanks for nothing, you useless System.*

He stopped with a comfortable distance between us. His head tilted to the side. "You're . . . " His low and smooth voice trailed off, then he asked, "What did you just say?"

"Ah . . . haha . . . " I shuffled back a couple steps. It was hard to focus on his face when a warning flashed so insistently in my vision. "I . . . ah . . . I don't think . . . I said anything? Erm . . . " My hand waved through the air. "I need to . . . I have something . . . hahaha."

Wow, I sounded so lame, but my nerves were shot.

His eyes narrowed, and he took a step closer. "You said—"

"Kesstel!" a female voice let out a singsong shout. "There you are!"

The man turned just as a beautiful young woman ran into the park toward him. Her blonde curls and ample bust bounced with every step she took.

While he was distracted, I activated Feather Step and jumped to the other side of the rose bushes. Without sparing a glance, I ran as fast as I could. The only thing that mattered right now was getting away.

I didn't know who he was, but it was clear I needed to stay away from him.

What surprised me was that no one chased after me. I stopped in front of a pastry shop and looked around, but I couldn't catch sight of the monster inside a man's body at all. I patted my chest and slowed my pounding heart. Talk about a sudden heart attack. I took one last deep breath . . . and was instantly seduced by the smell coming from the pastry shop.

I looked at the storefront window, my mouth watering. How long had it been since I'd tasted a gourmet dessert? God, way too long. I stepped from one foot to the other. A flaky pastry would be divine, but a life of frugality won over, and I walked away.

There was actual money in my account for once, and I was making more money than last month, but with all my debts and then paying back Henry, I was still in the red—and would be for a while longer. At least I was eating full meals every day. That had to be enough for now.

I pulled out my map, found my location, and started to work my way to the library. Before I'd run from the park, I'd only been a block away. Now, it would take me nearly twenty minutes to get there. I wasn't complaining, though. Twenty minutes should be enough time for that scary Kesstel guy to leave the area.

At least, I hoped so.

I kept my eyes peeled as I crept back but saw neither hide nor hair of him. Still, I didn't relax until I was inside the library.

"My list of people I want to avoid grows daily, I swear," I muttered to myself as I looked around.

Whoever had designed the library went for an old-fashioned feel. Like, a hundred-years-ago old fashioned. The floor was white marble with a wide red rug leading to a huge circular room. The ceiling arched up several stories high, the white marble carved and stacked in an impressive and eye-catching way. Dark wood shelves were placed in the middle of the room, highlighted by the bright lights from the countless windows and the soft glow from the chandelier hanging from the ceiling. Padded mustard-colored chairs and couches were placed against round walls beside bright green plants, encouraging someone to sit and stay for hours.

I followed the red carpet around to the other side of the books and saw a cluster of sectioned-off desks in the back. I slid behind a computer, logged on with my Hunter information, and looked up *Warriors of Mist* on the internet. It was a long shot because a lot of data was lost when the Gates appeared and the world fell apart. In fact, there were thousands of abandoned servers all over the world, just waiting for power to boot them up, but that required manpower and resources which most countries didn't have. Still, given how limited my options were, I gave the internet a shot.

Waiting for the results seemed to take forever, and as soon as they popped up, I let out the breath I'd been holding. Nothing. There were several references to fictional books written before the Gates opened, but there was nothing more recent than that. Still, I wasn't ready to give up just yet.

I didn't know how long I spent browsing, but I couldn't find anything. With nothing to show for my time, all I could do was swallow my disappointment and log out. However, I wasn't beaten just yet. I walked up to the librarian sitting behind the front desk.

"Hi, I'm looking for information on the—" My voice cut out. My eyes widened, and I froze.

The librarian smiled at me politely, waiting for me to finish.

Ah, right. I wasn't allowed to talk about my new System. I swallowed and tried again, going for the roundabout method. "A guild or title which has something to do with mist or fog? Like a Hunter of . . . fog or something? Have you ever heard of that? Is it like, a rank or term for something?"

The man's face pulled into a thoughtful frown. "Hm, I don't know that I've heard that term before." He turned and tapped on his computer's keyboard for a minute. He must have seen the same thing I did because he smiled at me. "It looks like it was part of a fictional work by Norman Ghere twenty-three years ago called *Fog Master*. I can order the books in for you if you'd like. It'll take a couple weeks, since they'll have to come from the west coast."

I bit my lips and shook my head. "That's okay. Thanks."

As unrealistic as my System seemed, I instinctively knew that fictional books wouldn't hold any clues to what I was looking for.

I turned to leave but paused before looking back at the librarian. "What about a Katharian?"

I slowly spelled it out for him. He tapped on his computer a couple times then shook his head in the negative.

Today was a bust. With nothing left to do, I went back to the tram station and headed for the hostel. At least there was still enough time left in the day to practice my new abilities. I guessed that counted for something.

CHAPTER 25

There was a gym behind the hostel. Well, once upon a time, it *was* a gym. After so many years of abuse without proper repair, it looked more like an overly large shed. Most of the local tenants trekked to the city gym over in C District, so this one was usually empty.

Henry must have just been here because the air was still thick with the smell of cleaner, though no amount of bleach and elbow grease would help the faded blue paint on the walls or the dents in the laminate floor. On the right side were a couple sets of free weights, a bench, and several weight machines. There was even a treadmill and a stair climber, but there wasn't much else; ninety percent of the gym was just open space. In fact, there was so much room that someone hung up a basketball hoop on the right wall.

Walking to the middle of the room, I stretched a bit before opening my menu. After a second thought, I closed it and pulled out my kindjal. Just how far could I go before this thing came back to me?

Curious, I set it on the ground and took a step away. Nothing happened, so I took another one. Then another. I kept backing up until the short sword vanished from the ground and reappeared in my hand.

"Four feet," I muttered. At least that was the range when it wasn't in motion; it didn't make sense to be limited to four feet when I had a Throw skill. I considered that for a moment then went to the closet behind the weights and rummaged through it.

"Ah-ha!" I cried out, pulling out a thick rectangle with a bull's-eye on it. "This should do. Well, as long as I can actually hit it."

I hurried over and set it against the wall. When I was satisfied, I stepped back and pulled out my kindjal. That was when I paused. I'd never actually thrown a weapon before, and swords weren't normally used for throwing, but it was the only weapon the System had given me. Maybe there were instructions? I quickly opened my menu and looked at it. The description for Throw didn't give anything extra, so I went to the Guide and looked up moves. And received a shock.

There was now a thorough tutorial on throwing knives and short swords. It had to be new because I couldn't remember seeing it before. But that wasn't the only thing; there were now over a dozen different techniques I'd never seen before, most of them stealth moves and quick hits which involved using the attacker's force and movements against them. From the descriptions, all of them were tied to the Warrior of Mist Quest.

The System really did want me to become this mysterious Warrior of Mist.

I slowly nodded and opened up the tutorial on throwing. According to the instructions, I could throw my kindjal in either a straight line or curved like a boomerang.

First things first, I thought, and read the instructions two more times.

"Here goes nothing," I muttered once I was ready, getting into position twenty feet away from the target. I arched my arm like it showed and threw my kindjal with all my might. It shot through the air like a bullet . . . and sank into the wall a good foot from the target.

"Gah!" I hurried over and pulled it out of the wall. "Crud," I whispered, leaning down. I couldn't resist poking the clean hole in the wall, trying to block the stream of sunlight with my fingers. That was not what I wanted to do.

I cringed and walked fifteen feet back. It was cool I could throw that far, but maybe I should start a little closer and work on accuracy first?

I shook out my arms and focused on the target again. "I can do this," I chanted over and over. It took another three tries before I actually hit the rectangular pad. After a quick celebration, I held my hand out; I was getting used to how the kindjal came back every time. It also saved a lot of running back and forth.

Smiling big, I focused on the target again and arched my arm back.

Then I paused.

What would happen if I coupled Throw with Critical Hit? My eyes widened. *Oh, that might be cool.* Without waiting another second, I activated Critical Hit and threw the kindjal. It soared like a shooting star and sank into the bag, exactly in the middle of the bull's-eye.

"Whoa!" I cried out before holding out my hand.

Curling my fingers around the newly appeared weapon, I looked down at it. Even with all the abuse I'd put it through, even with the Gate Surge and going straight through a wall just now, the steel-and-crystal blade remained sharp as ever. I hoped it always stayed that way.

As cool as it was to combine Throw with Critical Hit, it was a crutch I couldn't lean on. It was good to know I could do it, but I continued practicing with just Throw. I didn't know how much time passed, but it felt like no time at all before I began hitting the target every time. It wasn't always at the center, but that would come with more practice.

I changed to the curved throw after that. That one gave me more grief. The only time I ever hit the target was when I paired it with Critical Hit, so after struggling with it for nearly an hour, I pulled up another move and worked on that one. Most of the moves involved a lot of footwork, so careful to follow the instructions, I stepped around the gym floor, repeating the motions over and over again until it felt natural to move my body like that. I twisted this way, stabbed that way, and swept my leg out while pretending I was in actual battle.

Sweat dripped down my back and I was breathing hard when I finally stopped. I stood up and put my kindjal away. Mentally, I felt good, but my muscles were complaining about being used in a new way, so I took a minute to stretch before moving back to the middle of the gym. Now that I'd practiced my new melee moves, I wanted to work on my Mist ability.

Just before I activated it, the door to the gym opened, casting a bright glare on the floor.

I jumped.

Two women entered, Leticia at the front. For a relaxing day, she was sure dressed for battle. There were scuff marks and a couple blood spots which weren't completely washed off on her armor. Her hair was pulled up and her makeup done light enough it didn't quite hide the black bags beneath her eyes.

Posse One stood a step behind Leticia, her brown hair a lot shorter than last night. Her battered gear also said she was ready for a fight, but her eyes were puffy, and her nose was red.

I frowned at them. Where was the other girl, Posse Two? Then I remembered. I'd heard a couple of the Hunters who died in the surge were from our hostel. Posse Two must have been one of them. It was unfortunate she'd died and I didn't even remember her name.

My head tilted to the side as I stared at the duo. "I'm done here, if you want to work out." I stepped forward like it was nothing.

"Oh, we're going to work out." Leticia reached behind her and flicked the lock on the door. "And you're going to help." She lifted her chin in the air.

I stopped and narrowed my eyes.

"It's your fault Judy died," Posse One snarled low in her throat.

Oh, right. The names Leticia called out in Fogmire were Teresa and Judy. If Judy was dead, then this girl had to be Teresa.

I folded my arms. "How does that work? I don't even know how she died."

The enraged girl pointed at me. "If we hadn't been looking for you in Fogmire, we never would have gotten caught behind that crowd of monsters around the Gate." Teresa's hand started to shake, and her voice broke. "We got separated and she . . . she . . . "

I frowned at her. "Look, it's sad that she's gone, but it had nothing to do with me. You are the ones who keep tailing me. And I want you to stop it."

"Shut up!" A sword appeared in Teresa's hand, and she brandished it at me. "If you didn't exist, Judy would be alive today!"

That hurt. A lot of people didn't care much for me from my rank alone—really, in this violent world, most people were too busy staying alive to care about others' lives. But I'd never been told I shouldn't even exist before. *She's just a grief-stricken voice.* What she had to say was nothing compared to how much my family needed me. And I wasn't going to apologize for Leticia and her friend's actions.

"If you weren't so bent on making my life hell, she would be alive. Her blood is on your hands, not mine." I scowled at Leticia. "Why me? What did I ever do to you?"

"You're weak." Leticia stepped forward and flicked her hand out. A rapier appeared in her hand, just as gaudy as her studded leather armor. "Weak insects are meant to be stepped on." Her heavy-lidded eyes narrowed as she sneered. "It's time to remind you where your place is."

I lifted my chin. I wasn't weak anymore. The window over Leticia's head showed she was a level nine and Teresa was level eight. Who was the weak one now? It didn't feel right to beat on them just because I was stronger, but I'd be damned if I let them walk all over me anymore.

I was a Warrior of Mist now, whatever that meant, and I was a force to be reckoned with.

I pulled my kindjal out and flipped it around my hand, a fun move I'd just learned. Then I shifted into a fighting stance. "I'll give you one last chance. Leave. Or do you not care about the security cameras?"

Leticia sneered. "Security cameras only work when they're turned on."

Cool. That was perfectly fine with me. Now I'd get to actually test out the new moves I'd just learned.

My lips curled up as my eyes narrowed.

Something on my face must have pissed Leticia off because she glared at me. "Bitch!" She launched at me like a dart, her rapier leading the way.

Teresa was right behind her, aiming at my other side, trying to trap me in the middle. They were fast, but not as fast as the drake last night. I sidestepped the rapier directly into the path of Teresa's sword. Midstep, I twisted and deflected Teresa's blow to the side. She lost her balance and tipped to the right as I whipped around and kicked her back, sending her crashing into Leticia.

Leticia dodged out of the way and thrust her sword at me. I blocked it, and our weapons slid against each other until her cross guard and mine collided.

She glanced at my sword and sneered. "You really think this fake sword can hold up against me?"

"Where there's a will, there's a way." I smiled at my inside joke. For the first time, the name Her Will didn't seem so bad.

Teresa jumped to her feet and stabbed at me. I pushed off Leticia and jumped back, Teresa's blade going right between us. I skipped back a couple steps and thought hard. What moves could I use on them? I'd already decided I wasn't going to kill them, but everything I'd learned so far was to do just that. I just wanted them to go away.

I dodged around Teresa and lunged at Leticia, who thrust her rapier at me. I lifted my bracer and used it to direct her flexible blade over my left shoulder, then I twisted my right hand and jabbed the pummel of my short sword into her unguarded chest, hard. She gasped and fell back.

Teresa turned and swung out. I stepped to the side but wasn't quite fast enough—the tip of her blade caught me under the ribs. Hissing in pain, I lunged forward, and with a flick of my wrist, I knocked her weapon out of the way before throwing my elbow into her jaw. She yelled and fell back right on top of Leticia, knocking her back to the ground.

I walked up to them and stepped on Teresa's back, pushing down. "Stay down. And leave me the hell alone."

Leticia glared up at me, but there was another emotion in her gaze which overshadowed the anger. *Fear.* We both knew how much easier it would have been for me to use the point of my sword instead of the pummel when I hit her. The only reason she wasn't dead now was because I chose not to kill her.

Her mouth opened. "Dam—"

I pressed down harder on the girls with my foot. Teresa squawked and Leticia gasped, obviously out of breath. "Think about what you want to say. Are you going to leave me alone now? Or are we going to fight for real?" It was a bluff, but she didn't need to know that. I really was a lot more tired than I was acting.

Leticia's face warped into something almost inhuman as she tried to swallow the bitter pill of defeat. Then her chin jerked in a short nod.

"Okay. Be sure to remember what you promised." I stepped back and calmly walked to the door. Inside my head, I was cheering with the victory, but there was no way I was going to show that to Leticia—I would just be asking for more. I'd shown her I wasn't a pushover anymore. I needed to maintain that if I wanted peace.

Behind me, Teresa whispered with a wobbly voice, "I thought she was the weakest Hunter. What just happened? Are we that weak too?"

"Shut up!" Leticia hissed.

My lips curled into a grin as I left the gym. I would live to fight another day for my family.

And another, and another.

CHAPTER 26

The next week felt like a vacation. Leticia and Teresa avoided me like the plague, and I couldn't be happier. The other tenants were confused, but every time those girls ran away when our eyes met, it made me smile. It was nice not being on the bottom for once. I didn't have to walk around with my head down any longer.

The biggest problem I'd run into was in the Gate. I wasn't an E anymore, so it wasn't fair to keep killing E-ranked monsters. I mean, I knew more than anyone the frustration of being left without a kill I could handle. But more than that, E-ranked monsters gave so little EXP that it would really just be a waste of my time and take me longer to level up. Sure, I'd accomplish my daily task of destroying three energy crystals easily, but it would take me over a week to advance to my next level. I didn't have the patience for that.

I couldn't make the System tell me what a Warrior of Mist was, but I could control leveling up.

As a result, after I did my daily task of cultivating for thirty minutes in Fogmire, I ventured out farther into Gate Vale than I ever did before, looking around the beautiful valley.

Huh. This place wasn't so bad after all.

I took out the monsters I could and evaded the stronger ones using Feather Step. In my week of peace, I advanced to level thirteen and was making enough money daily to cover my debts. There wasn't a lot left over—I still counted pennies—but I slept easier at night.

Life would have been great if it could have continued like that forever. But my luck just didn't work like that.

* * *

I crouched low against a tree and gripped my kindjal. Four feet away was a level fourteen basan. If it weren't for the title over its head, I would have thought it was a sickly rooster; there was nothing plump about its red, feathered body. The green plume on the top of its head drooped as badly as its tail feathers, which nearly touched the ground. I might have felt bad about killing this knee-high bird monster if it weren't for the little blast of blue fire which shot out of its mouth when it clucked as it scratched at the ground with its pale blue feet, the pinkie-size claws making considerable scars in the dirt.

I took a breath and cast Mist. A ten-by-ten area of thick fog appeared around me, with the basan in the middle. The monstrous rooster clucked out a softball-size blue fireball but didn't run like I was worried it would. I slipped around the tree and blended into the mist.

I hadn't gotten any new abilities since I'd started cultivating fog every day, but my mist's range had grown from a couple feet wide to the size of a small room. Monsters that relied heavily on sight were strongly affected by the mist, and it made my sneak attacks more effective. But other monsters didn't seem fazed at all, and I was stuck in a tough fight. As for me, it always felt like my senses were dialed up to a ten when I was surrounded by the fog, so it didn't matter if it affected the monster or not—when I was against something new, I always preferred to activate it.

Rooster monster still in sight, I soundlessly advanced. It clucked. I halted. It looked right at me. Its mouth opened and blasted fire at me. I didn't even have time to react before it charged, wings flapping and claws leaving scratches in the ground. I dodged the fire shot, then sidestepped the basan. The rooster flapped its wings and changed directions midair, wafting the mist around us.

I grimaced and raised my left arm. The monster's feet clamped onto my arm bracer, the talons gouging the plated leather as they tried to sink in. The basan's head lunged down at mine, beak open to take out my eyes, so I blocked it with my kindjal and found myself in an awkward position. The basan wouldn't let go of my left arm, and my kindjal was wedged in its beak.

"Damn chicken," I muttered.

It lifted its left foot and clawed at my chest. Releasing my kindjal, I grabbed its leg then swung around and threw the monster into the tree with all I had. Its head smacked against the trunk with a thud, the kindjal falling out of its beak, and the grip on my arm loosened enough that I could wrench it off. Never mind the four blue gouges in the arm bracer;

that would mend overnight. The basan recovered, and at the same time, my short sword appeared back in my hand.

Five minutes later, that annoying bird was dead. I'd never been a country girl, but if collecting eggs was anything like that, I'd never leave the city.

I huffed a breath and touched the drop item orbs. A cluster of mangled feathers and a blue beak appeared in my Items Bag. I didn't know what they'd sell for, but I wasn't expecting much from their appearance. I might have stabbed the energy crystal harder than I needed to, but damn, that chicken had pissed me off.

I canceled Mist and sat back against the war-scarred tree to take a break. I'd barely taken a sip of water when the sound of voices reached my ears. Hm. Someone else was nearby. Were they friend or foe?

Okay, that was a stupid question. It seemed like everyone was my foe. But I really was curious about who could be close enough that I could hear them but not sense them. And did they know I was here? What if they'd seen my mist? Since I was still a melee Hunter on the records, it would cause a commotion if someone saw me use both magic and melee. It wouldn't be worth the trouble until I was strong enough to defend myself against haters. Not to mention, weak Hunters with unusual abilities often found themselves as research subjects for the Association's testing department. I'd heard the fatality rate was pretty high there.

I rolled to my feet and walked to where the voices were coming from. At first, it seemed there were two voices, a male and a female. But the closer I got, I could only hear a female talking. Nonstop.

I stepped around a bunch of trees and stopped, staring at a tree nearly as thick as I was tall that had fallen to the ground. From how the underbrush bent beneath it, it must have happened recently. I turned my head and saw the shredded trunk where the tree had broken from its stump. Part of it was a clean break, like it had been sliced with a very sharp blade. The other half was jagged, like it'd been hit hard with a lot of force, causing it to snap at the cut.

As for what might have hit it, I had a guess. And that guess was the monster lying on the ground on the other side of the stump. It looked like a giant white gorilla, but it had four arms. If it had been standing, it would have been at least ten feet tall, but luckily for me, it lay dead, slumped over like a huge ball of flesh and fur, its arms bent in odd angles and its blank eyes staring at me.

I couldn't help but compare this monster to the stupid chicken I'd just killed.

I let out a silent sigh. I had a long way to go, still.

"So, about that energy crystal," a coy female voice said from beyond the carcass. "I can have it, right?"

The carcass shifted. I nearly jumped out of my skin and took off running, but it just flopped over onto its back. Its head lolled, connected to the neck by a thread, revealing a man and woman. The man had his foot hovering in the air like he'd just kicked the monster over. I barely saw them before my System started flashing [**DO NOT PROVOKE!**] in my vision.

The man—what was his name again? Kesstel?—sighed. "Do what you want." He then looked up, and his pale blue eyes locked with mine. Unlike all the other Hunters who went into the Gate, his only protection was a steel breastplate and shoulder pads. Under that was a blue-and-white tunic with a black belt around his waist, his black pants tucked into black boots. With his straight posture and those fantasy clothes, he looked like a prince.

All I could think was, *just how strong is he?* I couldn't help but take a step backward.

The young blonde woman didn't seem to notice me as she leaned closer to Kesstel, her bust barely contained within her fancy maroon mage robes. Gold and magic stones gleamed against her neck, wrists, and fingers. Seriously, was she in the Gate or at a red-carpet party? She hugged his arm. "You're the best!"

Kesstel stepped forward, breaking away from her grip without a single glance at her.

I didn't wait to see if he'd greet me or attack. I swung around and took off as fast as I could. With Feather Step, I shot through the forest like a ghost. I was getting faster with each level I gained, but Kesstel was even faster.

I'd barely run fifty feet before my wrist was caught and I was towed to a stop. His hand clamped around mine, loose enough he wasn't squeezing me, but his grip was like a steel trap I couldn't get out of. I twisted around and pushed at his hand. It was like a cotton ball trying to move a hundred-pound weight.

"Don't touch me!"

Surprisingly, he let go.

I'd put so much force in pushing his unmovable hand that I fell back. I gasped and stumbled, but quickly crouched to run again. He stopped me with three words.

"Warrior of Mist," his voice broke through my panicked mind.

My eyes widened, and I looked up into his face. Where had he heard that? How did he know it applied to me? The System had said it'd frozen my stats and wouldn't reveal my true rankings to other people. He shouldn't be able to see my class. What did he want now that he knew it?

It was funny. His eyes were so piercingly blue, but there was a . . . detachment to his gaze. As if he were looking at me, but not *at* me. Like we were worlds apart. Was that how all S-ranking Hunters were? Oh, yes. He was an S. He was obviously suppressing his aura, but I could still feel it.

He folded his arms across his chest and stared at me. "Doesn't feel good to have your secret shouted out loud, does it?"

Like how I'd voiced his secret. So no one else knew about the Katharian thing? What did he know about the Warriors of Mist? I'd looked everywhere I could think of, but it was like the Warriors of Mist didn't even exist, except for me. Not even a story of them.

My chin lifted as I pretended I wasn't nervous. He might be an S, but I was done with people taking advantage of me. "Where did you hear that term?" Maybe I could go there and find out more.

"Where did you hear mine?" He jerked his chin, sending the ball back into my court.

" . . . I can't tell you." I actually *really* couldn't. I mean, I shouldn't be able to see the red title over his head. The monster red title.

God, it was still unnerving to see it over a human. It was something the normal Guide wouldn't show, and I wasn't allowed to talk about my System, nor did I want to give someone else that power over me.

His features were as blank as mine, just as on guard, as he bore holes through me with his gaze. It was clear he wasn't going to give up his information if I wasn't going to give up mine.

"Kesstel, what are you doing?" The young woman we'd left behind found us. She huffed for breath. "God, you just took off. You know I hate to run." She patted her chest and shot a smile at him. Then she blinked as she noticed me. "Oh, hello. I'm Bethany Wilks, A rank. And you are?" Her words and tone sounded nice, but her smile took on a sharpness as she stepped closer to Kesstel, obviously staking a claim.

I looked at her, completely unimpressed. I'd just gotten away from a psychotic bitch; there was no way I was jumping back into that cesspool, especially for a guy I didn't want anything to do with.

A System window opened up, telling me the government had finished reviewing the monsters I killed during the Gate Surge and the money had been deposited into my account. It took every ounce of will I had not to react to the number on the screen. Too bad I wouldn't be keeping any of it.

Another notice popped up right after, telling me a package had come in for me.

I glanced at Kesstel. He still hadn't taken his eyes off me. He knew what a Warrior of Mist was, but even if I could talk about it with him, I wouldn't do it with an audience.

I turned and started to walk away.

"I'm not done talking," he said, but he didn't grab me again.

"I am," I tossed over my shoulder and kept moving.

CHAPTER 27

Henry looked up when I knocked on his office door and gave me a surprised smile. "Jynn girl. What are you doing here? It's not even dark yet." His eyes narrowed to slits as he smiled at his own joke.

I smiled back.

Well, it's true. Since getting the System, I'd started to stay out later. Initially, because I needed to destroy three crystals. But then also because I'd had to take the drop items to the armorer and sell them. My Items Bag filled to the brim every day, and so I needed to hock the loot to fit in the next day's items. The daily task took so much time that it was always dark when I returned to the hostel.

I stepped into Henry's office and closed the glass door behind me. If someone walked up and looked in, they could see what I was doing, but I didn't want people to overhear. I didn't trust anyone in this building aside from the old man in front of me, and I wanted to keep him safe.

Henry frowned. "Is everything okay? Is Leticia acting up again?"

I laughed and rubbed my brows. "Nope, she's great." Couldn't be better. "I'm here because I owe you twenty-one crystals, and I want to pay some of it back. It's only about a third of what I owe you, but I'll get there." I pulled up my System menu and clicked on the bank account at the bottom left of the screen. After a couple more clicks, a money transfer window opened in front of Henry.

He was still blinking at me in confusion. Then he looked at the window, and his brows shot up on his wrinkled forehead. Did he forget how many I'd borrowed? I hadn't. I remembered every single one. Knowing the huge dollar amount I owed was daunting; seeing it displayed like that was intimidating. If anyone overheard the conversation about to happen, there was a real possibility they'd get greedy enough to hurt Henry.

He frowned and looked at me. For a minute, I thought he was going to actually refuse the transfer. "Jynn—" He stopped then sighed and nodded slowly. "Good, good." He reached out and accepted the transfer. "You aren't putting yourself in a tight spot with this, are you?"

I shook my head. "No. It's from the Gate Surge the other day. I'm okay. Promise." There were still two hundred dollars left in my account, and I needed a new Items Bag. Desperately. I just hoped I could find a big enough one for less than that.

"Ah." Henry gave an exaggerated sigh. "Little Jynn is growing up so fast and becoming a fine Hunter. What am I going to do when you're too mature to need old, fat Henry anymore?"

His praise warmed my heart. I laughed. "Oh, don't say that. Nothing could beat your amazing cooking."

After talking a little longer, I went up to my room. Once inside, I pulled a pair of needle-nose pliers and a bag of tiny silver links from my bag. Setting them on the desk, I went to the new safe in my closet and carefully pulled out my mother's broken bracelet. I should have fixed it a while ago, but it had been harder than I thought it would be to find a matching replacement link. In the end, I had to order them in from across the country.

I picked up the pliers and held the bracelet in my hand like it was glass. Slowly, I pried open the bent links, took them off, then replaced them with new ones. Each action seemed to take forever, but I didn't dare go any faster. Once the chain was fixed, I picked up the ruby rose that had broken off. Luckily, it wasn't the ruby itself which was broken but the link attaching it to the chain. With my pliers, I took off the damaged part and fitted a new one.

After I fastened it back on, I leaned back and held the bracelet up in the air. The light glinted off the red stone, making the sides of the rose flare in different shades of red. I lowered it and opened the clasp before draping the bracelet on my wrist.

As soon as it touched my skin, I froze. I couldn't help but stare at the jewelry against my skin. The longer I looked at it, the more I remembered how it had gleamed on Mom's wrist.

She'd quietly beamed the day Dad first gave it to her. I'd never forget how it jingled on her wrist as we'd walk hand in hand under the warm sun. And her sweet smile when she thought no one was looking just before she'd hug it to her chest—I knew then she was thinking of Dad inside the Gate.

But then Dad died. Mom's lips would curl with bittersweet emotion when she looked at the bracelet after that. In a fit of grief, one night she took it off, marched to the garbage, and stood there for ten minutes with it dangling over the trash can as she cried. Her tears didn't stop as she put it back on and sank to the floor, clutching it to her chest.

I couldn't wear it. I'd die a hundred deaths if it were damaged, lost, or stolen for good. I felt sick just thinking how Leticia had it for the short time she did.

I took it from my wrist and connected the clasp before placing it back in the safe. I gently arranged it on a cloth napkin and locked it inside. Touching the cold dial, I smiled as my heart swelled with bittersweet emotion. My small piece of Mom was finally safely tucked away again.

Now, it was time to call my sister.

I blinked away the sleep and rubbed the blur from my eyes. A System window appeared over me.

[Daily Task: Walk out and kill two Nixies.]

I sat up from my bed like caffeine ran through my veins. "What's a nixie?" I looked it up as I quickly dressed. When the monster's information popped up, I stopped with my shirt half on, staring at the screen. "What the . . . ?"

A nixie was a water fey that lived in Prine Lake. They were humanoid, but very slender and beautiful. They also had a habit of attacking sailors and drowning them—if the Hunter didn't die from the nixie's toothed spear first. And they were only found in the middle of the lake; they never neared the shore.

"Walk out?" I muttered as I finished getting ready.

An hour later, I stood on the shore of Prine Lake, staring across the water. A perpetual rainbow arched over the huge lake, the colors vivid against the bright blue sky. Under it hung a thin layer of mist which gleamed pale gold in the sun, the moisture lazily rising and swirling across the surface of the pale teal water. I'd heard there were lakes in Canada with water this color. Glacier water, or something like that. Like everything else in Gate Vale, there wasn't a good explanation as to why the water was this color, but it was an absolutely stunning view with the golden mist, rainbow, and mountains in the background.

But as much as I appreciated the view, I was perplexed by it. I crouched and frowned at the water gently lapping against the rocky shore inches from my feet. *Walk out? Walk out on what?* Was the System seriously telling me to walk on water? I wasn't a water mage, and even if I were, there were only a handful worldwide who could actually walk on water.

I opened the Tasks page again and read the short directive. Why would it say walk? Not sail or swim but walk? And to where—the middle of the lake? If I didn't follow the task exactly like it said, would it not count as completed? Would I have to start over? That would suck. I mean, not only would it take a lot of time but it sounded like nixies weren't the easiest to deal with. Never mind the fact they lived underwater.

My mouth pursed to the side, and I stood up. The System wouldn't do anything to harm me. In theory. It wanted something from me, but I hadn't done anything for it yet. And I seriously doubted it would go through all the trouble of training me just to kill a few monsters a day. Until it got what it wanted, I could only assume it wouldn't purposely harm me. If it wanted me to kill the nixies, there was a reason. Just like cultivating had a reason—to improve my abilities.

I took a deep breath and lifted my foot. *Walk on water, right?* Since I was told to do it, that meant I could . . . right?

I lowered my foot.

My boot skimmed the surface and sank right down. Since I expected there to be something to step on, my balance was thrown off, and I pitched forward. My feet seeped into the mud under the water and stuck. With a shocked squawk, I landed on my hands and knees, the force of my fall splashing water all over my face and body.

I gasped and shook the water off my face.

Loud laughter exploded behind me.

Climbing up to my feet, I looked over my shoulder. Two men in full armor stood at the forest line not too far off from Prine Lake's shore. They were laughing so hard that one was bent over, slapping his thigh.

"Oh god, I don't think I've seen anything that funny in ages! Hey, girl, there's a lake there, in case you missed it." The man with a red tunic beneath his armor wiped under his eye with the back of his armor-plated hand.

"What did you think would happen?" the Hunter in a green tunic and black armor asked. "That you would just walk right out there?" He gasped, still slapping his thigh with a metallic *thunk*.

I moaned and retreated from the lake, trying to repress the heat searing my face. That was exactly what I thought I would do. And I had an audience for my amazing fail. *Awesome.* "Can I help you with something?" I asked, trying to salvage any scrap of dignity I could.

The Hunter in green and black hunched over, laughing all over again.

The red Hunter smiled at me. "You know, there's a boat rental shop on the north end of Gate Square. If you wanna go out on the lake, that's the way to do it. You'd get a lot farther than . . . whatever that was. But I don't think a little E like you should go. All the monsters there are over your head." By the time he stopped talking, most of the ridicule had left his face.

I nodded slowly. "Thanks for the info." Still, I didn't think I should get a boat. I turned around and looked at the lake again.

Behind me, the Hunter who'd actually been helpful was talking to his partner. "Come on, dude. Let's go."

"Nah, nah, man. Look at her. She's going to do it again. I wanna see her do it." Apparently, he was still laughing at me.

I huffed a breath and ignored what they were saying.

If I was told to walk out there, then the System thought I already had the ability to accomplish the task. No official new ability had appeared in my menu, so it had to be one I already had and just needed to activate. Already had . . . *Ah!*

I activated Feather Step and leapt out onto the water. I felt the rippling of waves against my toes but moved to my next step before my weight had a chance to sink beneath the surface.

Two exclamations of shock faded behind me, which I barely heard anyway over the cheering in my head.

I was walking on water. Seriously, I was walking on water! "This is so awesome!"

Laughing like an idiot, I sprinted across the glassy surface, rising and falling with each rippling swell. I twisted around and looked back at the shrinking shoreline. I didn't think the mist was that thick, but soon, the shore and the two Hunters on it were barely visible. The fog wasn't gold right against me, but within a couple feet, the sunlight refracting on it lit it up. Smiling, I reached out to the vapor. Instead of sifting through my spread fingers, the mist drew into my hand.

"Cool," I whispered, rubbing my fingers together.

But it wasn't just my hand the mist reacted to. The whole area around me seemed to spiral around me, drawing closer until it was absorbed into my body. I didn't even have to cultivate to activate the effect, which was a good thing because I was still running. I couldn't help but notice that as soon as the mist was drawn into me, thin wisps rose from the surface of the water to replace what was taken away, as if the lake were trying to regenerate what went missing.

I was so focused on it that my pace slowed. Instantly, my foot sank into the water. Jumping, I took another quick step so I was on top of the surface again. The water on the bottom of my boot shook off with my movement and immediately dissipated into the air, adding to the fog.

It was cool and all, but it also brought up a problem I hadn't thought of before I set out. What was I going to do when I ran out of MP and had to stop running? And where was my destination? I assumed the middle of the lake, but I wasn't even halfway there yet. It would be impossible to reach the middle of the lake, fight two monsters, and get back to shore Feather Stepping the entire way. Maybe I should have rented a boat after all. That way, I could at least stand on it while I fought the nixies.

I huffed a breath. "If only I could walk on mist."

I mean, there were water and fire users who could walk on their element. Granted, their level was higher than my own; I didn't even really know what all I could do with my Mist ability—the System still hadn't given me any clear guidelines or limitations. To what extent could I control the mist?

I rolled my eyes. What the hell? If it didn't tell me not to, then why couldn't I?

I glanced at my MP as it clicked down one more point. I guess now was as good a time to find out as any. What's the worst that could happen?

Ah, well, I guess the worst would be that I'd fall into the water and get caught up with nixies and drown. I wasn't the best swimmer, so I'd be in trouble even if I didn't meet a monster.

A jolt of alarm shot from my skull down to my toes as my sixth sense went off. A split second later, the water exploded where my foot had been. A red fish the size of a large cat soared out of the water, its oversized jaws closing in the air with an audible snap, four-inch fangs protruding out of the sides of its mouth. It flailed in the air for a second while its round, green eyes focused on me with purpose. Above its head read: [**Fanged Snapper Lv9**].

I twisted around and slashed out with my kindjal. The fish split in half and dropped to the water with two plops. A drop item orb appeared, bobbing up and down on the water, but I didn't have time to do anything about it or bother with the sinking energy crystal. With every single step I took, another fanged snapper leapt through the air. I twisted and turned, slicing and stabbing as I went, but there seemed to be no end to them.

CHAPTER 28

A fanged snapper jumped out of the water and clamped its oversized jaws on my calf. My leather pants and toughened skin kept the huge fangs from sinking into my skin too much, but it still knocked off eight points and hurt like hell.

I gasped and slashed down, cutting its disproportionately large head off. The two pieces fell into the water and another orb appeared in its place, joining the dozens already floating on the surface.

[You have Leveled Up!]

I didn't have time to celebrate or tend to my cut—or any of the dozen other injuries I now sported—because more fanged snappers jumped from the water at me.

I sidestepped another fish, Feather Step allowing me to tiptoe across the water like a fairy. But every time I touched the surface, more fish were alerted. It didn't matter where I ran, I couldn't elude the monster fish. Was there ever going to be an end? I couldn't keep going on. I was at 70/90 MP and 121/190 HP already, and I hadn't even found any nixies yet.

"What the hell was this System thinking? Walk out to the middle of the lake—it'll be fun!" I yelled as I shish-kabobbed another snapper, this time actually hitting the energy crystal. It exploded into little lights, and an item orb dropped to float on the water. Without pausing, I flicked my kindjal right into the next fish that soared through the air. "Come on, Jynn, think!" What could I use to help me?

I could activate Mist even though it would use up more MP. But my stats did improve when I was in it, so I'd be able to dodge the snappers more easily. I leaned to the side, and a high-flying fish sailed past my head.

"To hell with it," I muttered as I twisted and sliced two monsters in half. "Mist!"

My usual ten-foot cloud appeared, but then, the mist hovering above the lake drew into it. My ability and the lake's magic merged until every inch within a twenty-foot radius of me filled with the water particles. But I couldn't revel in just how cool it was; my focus remained on running across the water as monsters continued jumping at me. A small glimmer inside me hoped I could escape them within the mist, but that wasn't the case. I mean, they were responding to me touching the surface of the water.

I killed another few fish. "Just stop already!"

Instantly, I felt something change in the mist around me. I couldn't describe the feeling; it was just a sudden awareness that something was different. In that moment of awareness, five fish stopped midjump, jaws gaping and glassy eyes focused on me. Frozen. Beneath the surface of the pale teal water, I could see the shapes of red fanged snappers still swimming. One shot upward and jumped out of the water. Its flaring nares hit the mist like it was a solid barrier, and then the fanged snapper plummeted back into the water.

"What?" I whispered, looking at a fish hanging midair at my hip. My brows pulled together as I reached out and poked at it. Or I meant to—my finger stopped an inch from its shiny red scales. The mist around its body was solid, like tinted glass. Inside, the monster's eyes moved around, but apparently, it couldn't move the rest of its body.

I was so shocked, my feet stalled. A leaping fish latched onto my boot as I started to sink into the water, jerking at me, trying to pull me deeper. I gasped and grabbed onto the closest thing—the fanged snapper at my hip. My fingers closed around the force surrounding it, and I pulled myself up, jerking my boot from the snapper's mouth. It wasn't until I was on top of the suspended fish that I realized I was literally squatting on it. Well, the solidified mist surrounding it.

"Okay, this is weird. And cool." I wriggled my wet toes inside my boot and watched as the water droplets that fell from my sole turned into more mist. "So I can make Mist solid." I had hoped that would be the case before the fish monsters attacked, but I didn't think it would actually work.

I frowned at the fanged snappers suspended around me, lifting my kindjal. With a flick of my wrist, I slashed out at the closest one, the blade slicing through the barrier and severing the monster's head. The body fell, leaving a glowing orb in the air.

This might be too much of a cheat, I thought, and killed the rest of the fish until the only one left was the one I stood on.

I looked at my captive perch then at the open air around me. Could I only make the mist solid around an object, or could it solidify anywhere? My lips pursed to the side. *How do I do it?* The first time had been mostly a fluke.

Thinking of an ability activated it; what if imagining different ways to use it amplified its range of applications? What if I thought of a box?

Picturing one to my left, again I felt like something was different around me—a change in the pressure, a sense of awareness. This time, I knew that the mist beside me had altered—gathered, even—but I couldn't see it with my eyes.

Tentatively, I stretched out my leg and rested my foot where I imagined a box to be—my boot hit a solid force. Tapping at it a couple times, I slowly shifted my weight onto it. Luckily, I didn't plop into the lake. I let out a relieved breath and then felt around, trying to figure out how big it was. The area was about three feet by two, just like I'd hoped. Big enough to comfortably sit in.

Once settled, I checked my MP. Apart from the initial casting, it hadn't changed. Good. That meant I could rest on this solid mist.

My lips curled up, and I cut the last fanged snapper in half. Carefully, I reached down and touched the orbs still floating on the water, beautifully illuminating the golden mist from below. A couple fish snapped at my fingers, but I was quicker than them. One by one, fanged snapper scales appeared in my Items Bag.

Very quickly, I ran into a problem—my Items Bag was full, but there were still orbs to collect. I frowned and pulled out the scales, staring at the small red discs. It was pretty how they shimmered in my hand as the sunlight reflected off them, giving them a deep pink sheen. I had no idea what they'd sell for, but in case it was anything decent, I didn't want to just leave without them. In the end, I started slipping them into the pocket of my pants. The thin scales were cool on my skin, but they didn't obstruct my movements at all because they weren't bulky. Hopefully, they wouldn't be broken by the end of the day.

When I was done, I took a deep breath then jumped down to the water. I activated Feather Step and released the block over the surface at the same time. Instantly, ten fanged snappers jumped into the air.

"Let's play," I whispered and swung my kindjal.

* * *

On and on, I killed the monster fish; I didn't even stop when I leveled up again. When my HP dropped into the red and I was too tired to lift my kindjal anymore, I jumped up onto the mist and blocked the fish from reaching me. Lying down on my stomach, I watched the water below as the fish wiggled while I waited for Regen to heal my HP and MP. I was usually asleep when this happened, so it was cool to watch my numbers increase and feel the fatigue fade away.

After fifteen minutes or so, the fanged snappers finally gave up and disappeared into the depths of the lake. I continued to watch the smooth surface. What else was in it?

I'd never been to a lake before. In fact, there were very few humans who traveled beyond the city walls. Why would they? On the other side of the walls was only a wilderness full of monsters and death. Nearly all of Earth's native animals were killed by the monsters when the Gates first appeared. Human populations were very scarce and hidden behind huge walls for protection. There were some recreational activities available, but those were heavily guarded by special Hunters and usually pretty expensive. So it was safe to say that I—and most of the Garden City inhabitants—had never left the protection of the city.

For the most part, I was bored as I waited for my HP and MP to regenerate. I watched several boats appear in the distance, but they always turned back before the mist got too thick—before they got close to me.

There was only one instance which freaked me out. I had been staring at the water when I noticed a shadow moving beneath me. It was huge, at least the length of two buses put together, and too far under the water for me to discern exactly what it was. Suddenly, a navy-blue bony fin as tall as me broke the surface of the water just feet from me—even though the mist should have blocked anything from emerging.

I froze and watched the fin slice through the surface as I prayed that the monster wouldn't notice me. How could there even be something that big in this lake? And what level could something that large be? I wasn't stupid enough to find out. I was getting stronger, yes, but there was still a long way from level fifteen to level one hundred. After a couple nerve-wracking minutes, the fin lowered back into the water, and the shadow disappeared.

It was gone now, but it'd left me with a lot to think about. Clearly, my making mist solid cheat wasn't as all-powerful as I thought it was; there were limitations to it. The fanged snappers were about two feet long and a lower level than me. Was that why I could catch them? This monster had so easily broken through my barrier.

Unfortunately, there wasn't a clear answer in my Guide.

An hour later, I stood up and stretched my muscles. God, pretending to be a human statue was painful. I was stiff, but so full of energy. I bit my lips and looked around. I could use Feather Step to keep going and find the nixies, but I wanted to try something else instead.

Determined, I walked to the edge of my solid platform . . . and kept going. I simply believed that I wouldn't fall; I somehow just knew I could walk on the mist. And I was right. The platform didn't extend or anything; in fact, it disappeared as soon as I left it because I didn't need it anymore, but the mist solidified directly under my feet as I stepped down and disappeared as soon as my foot was up.

I had a feeling this was the kind of walking the System meant when it gave me the task.

Of course, I didn't stay walking for long—there wasn't enough time for that, but it was nice to know the mist would support me even after I started to run.

By the time I got to the middle of the lake, I was breathing heavily. I took a couple minutes to calm my breathing down as I thought of my next problem. How would I get the nixies to come to me?

Even if I knew how to fish, I doubted that would work. What should I do?

Looking down at the water, my attention was drawn to my own legs. I had healed, the cuts were gone, but the dried blood still crusted on my legs and torn pants. Really, I was going through way too many clothes lately. Unlike my arm bracers and leather breastplate, my pants didn't magically repair every night. This pair had finally gotten to the point where I wouldn't be able to stitch them back together anymore. But that wasn't what I was actually concentrating on.

I needed to get the nixies' attention. I just hoped I wasn't biting off more than I could chew. Reaching down into the lake, I cupped water in my hands then paused for a second.

"This is stupid."

I splashed the water on my lower leg. The cold liquid hit my skin and ran down, taking most of the dried blood with it. Some of the reddened water evaporated, but most fell back into the lake. The blood spread across the water like an oil spill before it faded.

I hoped the right monster would get my calling card.

Jynn Devhro

Rank D

Level 15

EXP to Next Level 345

HP 211/211

MP 100/100

Stat Points 0

Strength 39 (+10)

Agility 30

Magic 26

Perception 30

Constitution 30 (+10)

Intelligence 25

Skills

Throw

Critical Hit

Quick Hit

Abilities

Mist (10 ft)

Feather Step

Regen (Limited)

CHAPTER 29

I stared down at the water, waiting for something bad to happen. My whole body tensed as if energy were piling into my muscles, ready to release in an instant. My fingers tightened on the handle of my kindjal, its weight soothing my nerves.

But nothing happened.

"Hmm . . ." I leaned down, peering into the teal liquid.

Slowly, a face appeared beneath the surface. A human face—an extremely gorgeous human face. Was it male or female? Its large, calm eyes captivated me, numbing my curiosity and drawing me in. The longer I looked into them, the prettier they became. A yard of thick blue hair danced in the current around the face, a flawless ebb and flow that revealed flashes of fin-like ears.

My eyes widened.

It moved closer to me, until mere surface water separated us.

I couldn't take my eyes off its enigmatic gaze. It was so beautiful. How the navy-blue lashes contrasted against the creamy, flawless skin. The deep blue irises were flecked with bright green which seemed to shift and move like a peaceful stream. No, there wasn't just green in those soothing depths. There were purples, teals, and violets, all swirling together in a fascinating splash of color.

A slow hum whispered in my mind, the words indiscernible, and yet I loved the sound. It soothed my once-racing pulse like I'd found a haven in the middle of a storm. Slowly, the remaining pent-up energy in my body drained away.

The face smiled at me, focused only on me as if I were the most important person in the world. A slender, pale hand appeared and reached from the water toward me. Delicate white nails tipped the fingers between which a fine webbing stretched up almost to the first knuckle.

The webbed hand neared my face. Yes, I wanted to be touched by this gentle, gorgeous creature. Maybe this would be the person whom I'd never have to guard against. Whom I knew would have my back, always. I'd struggled alone for so long; I just wanted someone to trust. Someone who—

My hand flicked up, the kindjal severing delicate fingertips from their webbing.

The creature screamed a high-pitched wail which permeated the water. Its fingers plopped into the lake, staining the surface blackish green. Instantly, the gentle aura vanished, replaced with vicious fury.

"Someone like that doesn't exist," I whispered and thrust down at the nixie. Anger raged in my chest, choked my heart, and sent a shock of energy through my lax muscles. I didn't know if I was angry at the nixie for tricking me into thinking I could trust it . . . or at myself for still wanting someone at my side.

You'd think that after being beaten down and thrown away so many times, I would get a hint. From the moment I tested as the weakest Hunter, my fate was sealed. I was meant to be alone. I'd always been alone, and I always would be—this System made that all too clear. I was different now; a kind of different no one else could match or know about.

So any more thoughts of wanting a partner, someone I could trust, should just die.

The water fey jerked back, and I got my first look at its body. Its bare chest was flat like a man's, but the shape of its shoulders, torso, and slender waist was decidedly feminine. Its hips flared to two pale legs. At its knees, pale blue webbed fins flowed down over long, webbed feet—like the graceful fins of a goldfish.

My kindjal missed. I didn't know if it was because the nixie moved faster than me or if it was because of refraction. I reached out to grab the bleeding hand to keep it from fleeing, but my sixth sense went off.

I dodged to the left just as something pierced the air to my right, and a spear tipped with a giant shark-like tooth embedded in my misty platform. I kicked out, sending it skittering across the water while I turned and saw another nixie baring pointed teeth at me. Now that they were mad, their eyes were murderous rather than mesmerizing, as the first nixie's had been. The beautiful blue rainbow had changed to a flat, almost lifeless black hole. It lunged up at me, aiming to grab my legs.

If it got me in the water, I was screwed. I jumped up and felt its sharp nails leave deep gouges in my calves. The water fey's fingers trailed to my boots, where its nails hooked into their rims. It jerked me down just as I created a ledge of solid mist above me to grab onto. I shouted as I hung on, struggling to kick out of the grip.

"Let go!" I yelled, kicking my free leg.

The nixie's hold slackened, and I slipped free. Flipping up on the mist, I stared at the two fey ten feet below. They circled the water and stared up at me, black rage in their flat eyes. Blood dripped from my boot into the water below, the red fading into purple for a second before it disappeared in the gentle tide.

"Well, I found a couple nixies," I muttered to myself. "Go me. Now, to figure out how to kill them while they're underwater. Yay."

I launched to the side, behind the first water fey, my boots skittering just an inch off the lake. The nixies rushed me, nails elongating to sharp claws. I thrust out my left hand, palm out and fingers spread, and a mist barrier appeared between us. They hit the wall, which only slowed their momentum for a second before they crashed right through.

So there really was a limitation to my ability. Hm. That's fine. That second of slowing them down was all I needed.

I dodged to the right and slipped behind the first nixie. Since it was already hurt, might as well keep at it, right?

I stabbed at its back. Its tail slashed out and hit my chest. My blade left a long cut as I was thrown five feet back. Desperately, I focused my ability to make sure there'd be solid mist where I landed on my back and rolled to my feet.

I had barely stopped when I had to dodge out of the way of another spear attack. I hissed as the pointed tooth sliced across my side. It had missed my vitals, but it still hurt. Flicking my kindjal and knocking the spear away, I landed a hard kick on the pretty face of the second nixie, who let out a sharp wail and sank into the water. Not too far, I hoped. I still needed to kill it.

The first water fey was back. It kicked its webbed feet hard and sent a large splash of water in my direction. I gasped and created another mist barrier. The water slapped against the shield and dripped down, most of it becoming new mist. Meanwhile, the nixie burst out of the water right under me. One slender arm clamped around my waist in a suffocating, bruising hold which slowly chipped away at my HP.

Its long left hand reached up to my neck. I grabbed its wrist, and it became a test of strength.

The nixie flailed, trying to push and pull me off balance. I only had the two solid platforms under my feet—they held my weight plus the weight of the nixie, but if I slipped off them, it would spell trouble.

Its right hand gripped my back, nails painfully digging through my leather armor as it tried to climb up. Its mouth opened wide as it screeched, sending a briny puff of air as it revealed sharp teeth which obviously wanted to bite me.

I gritted my teeth and tried to use my grip on its wrist to force it away. I twisted and bent my right arm in an awkwardly painful position, then activated Critical Hit and Quick Hit at the same time. My right hand shot forward as if guided by the kindjal. Since it knew what to do, I let it happen. My blade sank into the tender flesh in the nixie's armpit and angled down, then I felt the blade hit something hard—the nixie's energy crystal. There was a slight resistance before it shattered.

The water fey didn't even have time to react in shock or pain before it exploded into small lights. I reached out and caught the two drop item orbs before they could hit the water.

Several dings echoed in my head.

[Daily Task: Kill two Nixies. (1/2)]

[Mist has been upgraded. Mist Creation is now possible.]

Waves of water exploded around me, ten-foot swells rising up on all sides. I gasped and threw my hands out, creating a bubble shield. The waves crashed into the barrier and fizzled into more mist.

The water churned, no longer a glistening teal. From those frothing waves, a dozen nixies appeared above the surface, surrounding me. They each held a spear and were level sixteen or higher.

To my right, a nixie hissed and glared at me with hatred. Its perfect features were marred by a crooked nose, black blood slowly dripping from a nostril. Judging by it, I could only assume it was the second nixie I'd booted in the face. Apparently, it'd cried to mommy and came back with reinforcements.

A small part of me was glad that it came back. I still needed to kill it—or any nixie, really. I just needed a second one for today. But now I was in a jam.

I glanced at my half-empty HP bar. Mentally, I checked over my aching leg that was still drip-dripping blood into the water, then my bleeding side and back, and lastly my aching ribs. All this had happened while killing one nixie. Did I really think I could take on a dozen at once?

No, I didn't. Even so, I took a deep breath and gripped my kindjal tighter.

Funny. I thought I'd be more scared than this. But my mind was calm and focused on one thing: survival.

The level twenty-five monster in front of me raised its hands in the air and glared at me with dead, black eyes. Unlike the other nixies, there was a bulky red coral necklace circling its neck, and a bracelet made out of what looked like fanged snapper scales on its wrist. As its hands rose, two waves of water swelled into the air behind it. *Shit.* It had water powers? Was this what crashed into me a second ago?

I held my hand out, concentrating hard on holding my protective bubble steady.

The nixie hissed and jerked its hands, ready to throw the water at me.

Suddenly, it froze. The rest of the nixies jerked in shock and looked down into the water. An odd song full of disjointed pitches and clicks echoed from their throats. Were they . . . nervous?

My brows pulled together as I tried to see the cause of their sudden change while still monitoring the unnerved creatures.

A giant shadow rose up from the depths of the lake right beneath us. A second later, a huge fin broke through the surface of the water right outside the circle of nixies.

CHAPTER 30

The nixies hissed and screamed.

"Oh, my . . . " My voice failed as I stared at the giant sailfin that towered over me. Just how massive was the body supporting it?

The nixies dove to the side, attempting to escape.

Water exploded around us without warning, and an enormous pectoral fin erupted through the surface. It struck my bubble before hitting the nixies with a bone-crushing force. My shield shattered, and I was thrown high into the air, spinning and gasping. My HP dropped seventy percent more, leaving the bar in the red. I flailed in the air until I was finally able to control my body, then once I was upright, I controlled the mist around me. Landing on a solid surface, I took a deep breath, trying to make the world stop spinning. From thirty feet up, I stared down at the huge shape becoming more and more clear as the enormous fin splashed back into the water.

The water fey fared a little worse than me. They were also launched into the air, but there was nothing graceful about them as they flailed, screaming. Some were thrown to the sides, clearing the shadow under the water before they slapped back onto the water and sank down, disappearing from view while leaving black stains in their wake.

The second nixie with the broken nose and the leader were pitched straight up into the sky. The leader clawed at the air, its eyes wide with fear; I couldn't help but wonder if this was the first time it was ever out of the water. The accompanying nixie looked just as frightened.

There was another water explosion which sent the nixies back up into the air. Even though I hovered to the side, I was drenched again.

From the water, a dinosaur appeared. Seriously, a seventy-foot dinosaur! It was covered in navy blue scales, each probably the size of my hands. Its head alone was twice as long as I was tall, then there was its long neck and the smooth oval body; the stubby tail lashed about as the enormous flippers agitated the water. Above its head read: [**Plesiosaurus Lv68**].

I gaped at it. Why didn't I know there was a Loch Ness monster in the Gate? Like for reals; I had no idea!

The leader screamed as its rise ended and it began to plummet. The plesiosaurus opened its mouth wide and jerked its head up. The nixie's scream was cut off as the plesiosaurus snapped its jaws shut with a sharp thud, the whole nixie gone in one bite.

A chill went through my body.

When its leader was eaten, the second nixie squealed in terror. It continued to fall past the plesiosaurus's head, belly-flopping right on its back, just barely missing being skewered on the bony dorsal fin which ran the whole length. The nixie groaned and wiggled around, trying to claw off the monster, but it was obviously disoriented.

The plesiosaurus swallowed, the bulge sinking from its head down its neck to its body before disappearing. Satisfied, it turned its head and looked at the nixie on its back.

My eyes widened, and I stood up.

That was my nixie! My kill! All the rest of them were gone, and I just knew that with the arrival of the plesiosaurus, I'd never find another one today. If ever.

The dinosaur opened its mouth and angled down.

"That's mine!" I hissed, thrusting out my hand. I cast Mist at the same time the plesiosaurus lowered its head. Simultaneously, I kicked off my platform and cast Feather Step. In the corner of my vision, my MP bar flashed yellow, letting me know I was getting low.

A thick fog appeared around the frightened nixie. The plesiosaurus roared as if confused, the low sound vibrating through my chest. My heart jumped out of rhythm, but my mind was clear as I closed in. I just had to kill the nixie before the dinosaur did. I didn't even need to destroy the energy crystal, just kill the damn monster.

The plesiosaurus paused only for a moment before it lunged down. Its teeth sank into the nixie's legs, whether or not it meant to. The water fey screamed and slapped at the plesiosaurus's lips around its legs, but nothing happened.

I landed on the monster's back just as it lifted its head into the air, dragging the screaming nixie with it. Black blood trailed along the dinosaur's lip line, making the navy-blue scales gleam multicolored in the sun. A pretty color, but gruesome. I tsked in anger and looked up at the nixie dangling fifteen feet above my head. Its scream weakened, and the beautiful humanoid body dangled limp as blood covered it—ghastly to look at.

I lunged forward, Feather Stepping on the mist that rippled around the monster just as the plesiosaurus tossed the water fey another five feet into the air and opened its mouth for the nixie to fall into. I arched my arm back and activated Critical Hit and Throw at the same time. The kindjal shot through the air like a long bullet.

A foot from the open mouth, the kindjal pierced the nixie's chest. The blade went straight through until the guard hit its torso with enough force that the nixie shook. The monster exploded into shimmering sparkles just as the plesiosaurus's mouth clamped shut.

Ding! [**Daily Task: (Kill two Nixies) Completed. +25 EXP**]

Ding! [**Would you like to accept your reward? Y/N?**]

Ding! [**You have Leveled Up!**]

I didn't have time to respond to the System; I was too busy panicking.

My sword! My kindjal! It was right there when the plesiosaurus shut its mouth! Oh, please! Please tell me I didn't just lose it!

The plesiosaurus roared and shook its mouth like it was confused that it was empty. It turned its head and focused a round, sea-green eye on me. After all, I was currently hanging out right at eye level. Its orb narrowed with bloodlust.

A shudder went down my spine as all thoughts for my kindjal disappeared along with my courage. Oops, it was time to go.

I turned and ran as fast as I could, Feather Stepping on the mist like my life depended on it. 'Cause it did.

The plesiosaurus lunged at me. Its huge maw clamped shut, missing my hair by inches, so close that I could smell the bloody fish stench on its breath and hear its pointed teeth rubbing against each other. When it missed again, the dinosaur roared in anger, nearly erupting my eardrums.

It chased after me. It was large and fast, but it also seemed to need to swim under the water. Since I was running on the topmost layer of golden mist hanging over the lake, it meant that I had a little bit of time to react when it reached me. Every time it lunged, there was always a water explosion first, helping me keep out of the way of its huge jaws.

It didn't seem discouraged when it couldn't catch me. In fact, I'd say the repeated failures seemed to egg the plesiosaurus on, making it lunge faster. It tried to splash me with waves of water, obviously try-ing to knock me down, roaring in anger and snapping at the air just behind me.

All the while, I ran like hell was at my heels. Because it was. If I stopped—or even slowed down—for one second, I was dead. On and on it went, continually dodging the latest attacks while I watched my MP tick down a point every five minutes.

In the distance, I could see boats full of Hunters about-face when they saw the plesiosaurus charging through the water like . . . well, an enraged monster. Mages used magic to speed the boats out of the way, aiming for the shoreline opposite me and my Loch Ness monster. A small part of me hoped the plesiosaurus would get distracted by the boats, since they were causing such a disturbance on the lake—there had to be someone who could actually take on the dinosaur in one of them. But no. The monster stayed on me, dogging my every move.

Finally, I neared the shore. I could see the individual trees off the rocky beach, and there was a small crowd gathering along the water to my right; they pointed at the plesiosaurus, a lot more excited than I was.

There was a huge thump, then the monster let out a roar which rum-bled in my chest and nearly deafened me. I glanced over my shoulder but didn't slow down.

For the first time, the plesiosaurus struggled in the water. It slapped its flippers around, trying to drag itself forward as it snapped at the air in my direction. But its speed had been considerably reduced. It took me a sec-ond to realize what was happening—the lake was becoming too shallow for the dinosaur. Still, it struggled on as if it hated losing its prey.

I kept going, though. I was running out of MP and still had a distance to clear on the lake. Since I wasn't desperate anymore, I changed direc-tions and Feather Stepped away from the crowd of people.

A wet explosion sounded behind me, followed by furious roars. At least the sounds weren't so close this time.

Looking over my shoulder again, I saw the plesiosaurus throwing water in the air and roaring at the top of its lungs. But it didn't get any closer. The waterline only reached about halfway up its body—apparently not enough to let it go any farther. With one last display of anger, it turned around and started to work its way back to deeper water.

I sighed in relief as I passed over the waves crashing against the shore and kept running toward the forest on the other side of the rocky beach, creating solid mist steps to keep myself up in the air. The crowd was coming my way, and I didn't really have an explanation as to why I was being chased by a dinosaur. Or why I was running on air.

I started to angle down, aiming toward a break in the tree canopy. Or at least that's what I wanted to do until my MP hit zero.

Feather Step and Mist ended simultaneously, and I dropped through the air right into the tree branches below. Gasping, I lifted my arms to protect my face as I crashed through the canopy, barely missing thick branches as smaller ones caught and snagged at my clothing. They left little cuts and tears on my clothes, but they also helped slow my descent. Finally, I reached out and grabbed a branch, the bark burning my fingers. My careening weight rebounded, and my arm felt like it was almost pulled from its socket, but I kept my grip and swayed to a stop.

I looked down and blinked. The ground was just ten inches below my toes. With a tired smile, I let go of the branch. I wanted to lie down right then and there, but I forced myself to run a small distance longer. Any thoughts of escaping the crowd of Hunters I could hear in the distance flew away when I came across a patch of green grass under a pink flowering tree. It looked so lovely, I staggered over and flopped down right there.

I puffed out huge breaths, so tired and sore that I didn't want to move. I could literally close my eyes and sleep right there and then on the solid ground, with the smell of grass and sweet flowers in the air. Which was stupid. I was in the Gate—sleeping would be a death sentence. But god, would it feel nice.

I rolled over and looked up at the blue sky on the other side of the leaves. The events of today played through my mind. I did everything the task required, but . . .

"My sword!" I moaned, covering my face with my battered hands. I loved that thing, and I'd thrown it into a monster's mouth. I didn't even think about what I was doing when it happened. I just wanted my kill, and I threw away my awesome, pretty sword to get it.

I was distracted from my thoughts when the System dinged in my ear once more. I spread my fingers and saw that the same notification from earlier appeared again; the one I never had a chance to address before the plesiosaurus started chasing me.

[Would you like to accept your reward? Y/N?]

I looked at it. *Oh, yeah, I think I leveled up, too, right?* "Yes," I whispered out loud, accepting the reward.

[Gained Ability: Mirror.]

Mirror? What was that? Man, this System really liked to use weird names and give unusual abilities.

I opened my menu and paused as I remembered something. When I fought the drake, I also lost my kindjal. That was actually the moment I found out that it would always return. Well, it had always returned to my hand, and it's not like the drake actually ate my kindjal like the plesiosaurus.

Holding out my hand, I tried to summon my kindjal from my Items Bag. The familiar warm handle appeared in my palm, and I gaped at the steel-and-crystal blade, thinking it was the most beautiful thing in the world. Not just because it was pretty to look at but because it was back.

I whooped and threw my hands in the air, freezing midmotion when I sensed strong forces getting closer.

A Hunter in studded leather armor pushed aside a bush next to me. Her eyes landed on my form, and she yelled in excitement, "Hey, I found her!" before she got a good look at me, and the light in her eyes dimmed until she just stared at me blankly.

I blinked back at her. Who was she trying to find? "Um, hi?"

"Did you find her, Jules?" Another Hunter pushed past the bush into my little spot. He stared down at me, his eyes flicking from just above my head where my title bar would be down to my face. Then he just stared too.

I frowned at them. I knew I was ragged looking—I mean, come on, after what I went through, who wouldn't be? But did they have to stare like that? It wasn't like I was indecent.

"Oh, I wanna see!" Yet another Hunter appeared, a healer in a purple robe. She also blinked down at me.

Now I was really starting to feel like an animal on exhibit. "Can I help you?" Someone had to break this odd atmosphere.

"Ah." The first girl glanced at her companions. "We're looking for some-one. A woman who can walk on air. She landed around here somewhere." She glanced at my title bar again. "Have you seen anyone like that?"

Ah, so that's what was going on. After all, walking on air was a novelty; no one could do it. Well, they found her, but she didn't want to talk to them. All I wanted was some dry clothes and a warm bed. Even though the weather was great in this forest, the slight breeze was sending goose bumps all over my damp skin.

I shook my head. "I haven't seen anyone else. Just you." Which was true.

The man tsked under his breath. "Where did she go? I wanna know more about that dinosaur."

The healer gaped at him. "Hang on, you aren't thinking about fighting it, are you?"

I glanced at him. He shouldn't even try. The plesiosaurus was level sixty-eight and he was only level fifty-nine. It might be manageable, I guessed, but the monster had a major field advantage. My benefit was that I was high above the water, making the monster come to me. And I wasn't trying to kill it, just run away.

But I couldn't tell the Hunter this. According to the System, my title bar was frozen, forever showing I was an E rank. So someone like me wouldn't know what ranks the Hunters in front of me were.

I gasped and played along. "What dinosaur?" Hopefully, my acting was good enough. It's not like I'd ever taken theater before.

"There's a dinosaur in Prine Lake!" the female Hunter burst out. "I had no idea! It must be new." Her eyes lit up like a Christmas tree.

I widened my eyes. "No way! Man, I'd stay away from that!"

The man hummed under his breath. "Anyway, we gotta go." He glanced at his companions. "Let's go find her."

He and the female Hunter ran off; the healer hung around a second longer. Since I was so beat up, she kindly healed me quickly before hurrying after the other two.

I watched them disappear, feeling flabbergasted and amused at the same time. I must have made a big splash on the lake if people were trying to find me. Luckily, it seemed like they didn't get a good look at my face. My false title bar helped, too. Fame was never something I wanted. There was good fame and bad fame. I wanted neither.

I started the long trek back home. As soon as I stepped through the barrier, a warning shot down my spine, and I looked across Gate Square. I totally didn't expect to see the human monster Kesstel standing idly nearby, a red warning sign still flashing over his head. Before he could turn my way, I activated Feather Step and ran for all I was worth. Just as I turned the corner of a building, I glanced over my shoulder.

He stood in the same place, facing me. Even from this distance, I could feel his piercing gaze as he watched me turn and run again.

CHAPTER 31

The next day, I did something I always swore I wouldn't—I easily picked off three E-ranked monsters early in the morning then
booked it out of the Gate once my daily task was completed. The reason
would be worth it.

Back at the E Hostel, I locked myself in my bedroom with the fanged
snapper scales, a pair of needle-nose pliers, the leftover links from repair-
ing Mom's bracelet, and my kindjal for the next two hours.

By noon, I was showered and dressed in my best clothes—jeans and
a rarely worn forest green shirt—and standing at the southern entrance
to Eden. I shifted from side to side, anxiously awaiting my little sis. I
lost count of how many times I glanced at the walkway gate every time
it opened and let someone in. It always led to disappointment, but that
didn't keep my heart from jumping every time the iron fence swung
open.

I glanced at the clock on my menu screen. I *had* said noon, right? I
hadn't given her the wrong time, had I?

The iron gate swung open again, and I looked up.

"Jynn!" Aliya squealed as she caught sight of me. She ran over and
threw herself into my arms. "I missed you," she whispered, squeezing
tighter.

I smiled and let her hold me as tight as she wanted. "I missed you, too."

All Hunters could bring one human family member into Eden once
every six months, but this was the first time I'd taken advantage of it. I
didn't have the confidence to let Aliya know what was going on before.
Now, things were different. I might not be in a great place yet, but I wasn't
dregs in the bottom anymore.

After a second, I stepped back and motioned with my arms. "Welcome to Eden."

She looked around, her hazel eyes bright as she took in the paved road, the red-bricked buildings, and the trees lining the streets. She smiled and gave a small laugh. "It's a lot more normal than I thought it would be. When I hear stories about Eden, it sounds like a fantasy land."

I laughed and nodded to the side. "Yeah, it's pretty normal." On the surface, at least.

I understood what she meant, what with how humans romanticized Hunters and what they did in the Gate. Growing up, I'd even heard tales about how little magical lights danced in the air in Eden, and how you could see cute little monster pets running around the streets, playing with each other in adorable ways. It would be cool if it were real, but it wasn't.

"So it's your first time here. What do you want to see first?"

She smiled and pointed straight ahead to the black arch looming over the buildings. "I want to see the Gate."

I nodded slowly, not too surprised. "Okay." Looping an arm around her shoulders, we started to walk. She was tall enough now that our heights were almost the same.

I pulled her to a stop almost immediately as a thought came to me. "Ah, I need to warn you, Aliya." I looked down into her eyes. "We can go over there, but sometimes, the people coming out of the Gate are bloody. It's not really a pretty sight."

The curl of her lips flattened a bit, and she sighed. "I know, Jynn. I wanna see it anyway."

Since Aliya was a human, she couldn't actually step into Gate Square, so we stood at the border of the circular space and watched Hunters coming and going from the huge black arch.

My sister tilted her head back and gaped up at it. "It's so . . . big." Her face screwed up in a puzzled frown. "I feel a little weird standing so close. Like a force is pressing against me." She pressed a hand to her chest.

I frowned at her. Odd. I'd never felt that before. "Are you okay? We should go."

She laughed and shook her head. "Nope, I'm good. It's just . . . new."

Her gaze dropped to the Hunters entering and exiting the Gate. She oohed and awed at them, pointing out individuals in fancy armor. "Oh my gosh, Jynn! Look at her!" Aliya gasped at a woman with long brunette hair. The woman's mage robes seemed to float around her with every step she took. "Wow, all she's missing are the pointed ears. I thought she was an elven princess at first."

The A-ranked Hunter in bright white-and-silver armor beside the mage glanced over at Aliya and smirked in amusement, then kept walking like it was nothing. The "elven princess" didn't look over, but she lifted a hand to conceal a small laugh.

I sighed and slapped a hand over my face. "My dear sister, Hunters have good hearing. If you're going to talk about someone, keep it down." Then again, my loud mouth had caught me the unwanted attention of an S-ranked human monster. Did I really have any room to complain?

Aliya gasped, her face burning red. She peeked a glance at the mage's back before hiding her face in her hands. "Oh, right."

I laughed and patted her back. "Well, Hunters also like their egos stroked. Just don't say anything bad out loud, okay?"

She gave a nervous laugh and dropped her hands. "Okay." She looked back at the Gate, her eyes full of light.

I stared at her. How long had it been since I looked at the Gate like that? As if it were a treasure map I couldn't wait to explore. Did I ever get a chance to? I was so scared my first time going in with a group of Es from the hostel—the first and last time I entered the Gate in a party. That one hunt marked me as useless, and I was left scared and alone in the Gate. I wasn't scared anymore, though I was still alone. But I'd never looked at the Gate in wonder like this beloved girl at my side. I doubted I ever would.

Aliya jolted, her eyes widening.

I turned my head and followed her gaze to the base of the Gate.

A couple Hunters were walking out of the black arch, their bodies huddled together. It took a second to realize the two of them were supporting a third unconscious man between them. The unconscious man was bloody head to toe and missing half of his left leg. From this distance, I couldn't tell if the blood on the other Hunters was from the third man or if it was from their own injuries. The one on the right had to be injured, too, by the way he limped.

Aliya's face paled as she watched them hobble toward the hospital. "Will they be okay?"

"As long as they can live long enough to get to the hospital, they'll be okay. Some of the best healers are in there. Regrowing a leg is nothing to them." Especially to Jonovan.

Her head bobbed in thought. "I wish healing magic like that worked on normal humans, too. That would save a lot of trouble, huh?" Her eyes wandered the square. She didn't look at the Hunters but focused on the buildings in the process of being rebuilt and the ground which had been power washed to get all the blood out. "This is where the Gate Surge happened, huh?" Her voice was quiet and solemn.

I nodded. It happened only last week, but it felt like such a long time ago.

She looked up at me, her eyes wide and frightened. "Did you get hurt?" Her breath hitched. "I was so scared when I heard the alarm. Then Uncle Carl was pushing me and Aunt Mina into the bathroom, but all I could think about was that you were in Eden, fighting those monsters. Risking your life while I just hid in a bathtub." She reached out and hugged me tight. "You kept dancing around the question when I asked earlier on the phone. Tell me, really, did you get hurt?"

I sighed and patted her back. What could I say to make her feel better without outright lying? "It's normal for Hunters to get hurt in a situation like that. But healers were there to help and patch up all the Hunters. Now things are great." I smiled, trying to make her feel at ease.

Her lips quivered into a smile, but her eyes remained dark. "I know you aren't in a guild. I'm worried you don't have someone watching your back. Just wait a little longer for me to graduate, then we can be a team. I'll be strong enough to make sure neither one of us ever gets hurt again."

Oh, this girl. I hugged her tight and resisted ruffling her hair, but only because it looked like she actually put in the effort to curl it nicely. "Nope, it's the big sister's job to protect the younger one. How can I hold my head high if I'm hiding behind you all day?" I laughed and stepped back.

No, by the time she graduated, I'd be strong enough to ensure the light of wonder never died in her eyes. But that did bring up a new idea. The rooms in the hostel weren't meant for two people, and I'd never want her to live in that place, anyway. Maybe I needed to start saving up a down payment for a two-bedroom place once I finished paying Henry back.

I nodded to the side. "Let's grab a bite to eat really fast, then there's a place I want to go to for dessert. Deal?"

She nodded, brightening up like the sun again. "Deal! You also said you wanted to go shopping for something?"

I led her over to a small café on South Exit Main Street. Since it was so close to the exit, it was a no-man's-land where Hunters of all ranks ate, mostly while visiting with humans. My turkey bacon avocado panini was good, but it wasn't what I really wanted to eat, so as soon as we were done, I dragged Aliya over to A District. From there, I followed my nose to the pastry shop I'd found last week.

"Wow." Aliya looked in through the front window. "They look so yummy! And cute! Look, that one looks like a mouse!" She pointed to a chocolate cake bite that was pulled to a point with a pink dot. Two chocolate circles were popped up like ears behind two white-icing eyes.

I smiled and pulled her in. "Come on. Today is a day to splurge and have fun. That's what sister dates are for, right?"

We were immediately hugged with the smell of sweet sugar, chocolate, and baking pastries. The walls were painted in thick off-white and rose-pink stripes. Aliya's shoes tapped on the dark wooden floors as she stepped in. Delicate white metal tables and chairs dotted the sides of the showroom, opening the way to the display of goodies lit up behind a glass shield.

Aliya took a deep breath and hummed in thought. "It's a shame that we just ate somewhere else. I mean, we could have just had lunch here." She smiled at the display window filled with nothing but sweets. "That might have filled our stomachs."

I smirked and tapped the back of her head. "Hey, I am a responsible older sister. And you're too old to fill up on just sugar." Go me. I was actually able to spew that with a straight face.

All my efforts were wasted when Aliya laughed in my face. "Yeah, you tell yourself that. And pretend like you didn't consider it at least once already."

I somehow managed to keep the guilty blush from my face. To distract her, I walked up to the counter where a middle-aged woman stood.

The woman smiled at Aliya and was tactful enough to hide the disapproving glance she sent at me. "Afternoon. What can I get for you?"

After an agonizing couple of minutes, we finally whittled the choices down to a chocolate tres leches cake in a clear cup, a large éclair, and a lemon bar. Armed with utensils and glasses of milk, we sat down to divide and conquer our spoils with delight. Aliya chose a table right by the window so she could people watch while we ate, then she talked away, telling me about her classes at school and how she'd joined the after-school art club. I listened to her with a nostalgic smile.

"Oh, did you hear?" Aliya took a bite of the lemon bar and hummed in appreciation. "Aunt Mina got a job. Telemarketing, part-time." She gave a bland smile. "Aunt Mina doesn't love it; I can tell. She always looks so worn out when she comes home. But she doesn't complain about it, and they didn't throw a fit when she had to call in yesterday because of a migraine."

I nodded slowly. "That's good. I'm glad to hear that."

With her working, it would lessen the load on me. But I wasn't going to rely on it too much. I'd heard that telemarketing had a high turnover rate, and it was only part-time. Knowing Aunt Mina, she would probably try turning it to full-time, but we'd see how that went. At the same time, I didn't want her to ruin her health, especially now that I was finally starting to make enough to support them.

Speaking of health . . .

"How is Uncle Carl doing?" I asked quietly, poking at my half of the éclair with a silver fork.

Aliya took a deep breath and looked out the window. "I don't know. He . . . I don't think he's trying to find a job anymore. He stays locked up in his room most of the time, or he'll suddenly just disappear. Once he didn't even come home for almost twenty-four hours. The police finally brought him back after fishing him out of the water fountain in the city park."

My eyes widened, and my heart nearly stopped. "What? Why did he do that? And why didn't you tell me?"

Aliya looked to the side and tapped her fork on her half-empty cup. "We didn't want to worry you. The Gate is already dangerous enough; we didn't want you to be distracted and get hurt," she whispered softly.

I sighed, covering my face with my hands. God, what a family we were. Each of us was broken, but so desperate to hide it from the others so they didn't worry.

Well, I guess not all of us were messed up. Aliya seemed normal, at least.

"It's just hard, you know." I looked up at her when her voice cracked. Aliya took a sip of milk then cleared her throat. "Uncle Carl is the only father figure I've ever known. I don't remember Dad—he only lived with us on the weekends, and I was five when he died. I think my clearest memory of him is at his funeral. And it was a closed casket because of . . . you know."

I nodded. I did know. All too often, deaths in the Gate led to closed-casket funerals. If they found the body at all.

"Uncle Carl has been there for me basically my whole life. But now, it's like I don't even recognize him. I know that depression is hard on him; I understand that, and I don't blame him for it. I just wish he'd think about our feelings a little before he hurt himself. How much we'd miss him. Sometimes when he leaves, I don't even know if he's going to come back alive." Aliya's voice got quieter and quieter as she talked, until her words were barely louder than a whisper.

My heart broke, hearing the pain in my sister's voice and thinking about what was happening to my uncle. It hurt even more knowing there was nothing I could do about it. It wasn't like Uncle Carl's depression was a physical monster I could kill. If it were, I would go through heaven and hell to get rid of his demon, but all I could do was listen about it from the other side of the Wall as my family struggled with it.

I walked around and hugged Aliya tight, but couldn't think of anything to say.

Her hand shook as she gripped my shirt, pressing her face into my stomach and taking a few gasping breaths. After a minute, she pulled away and gave me a big smile, even though her eyes were still red. "I'm okay. Really. I'm not that weak. Besides, it's a shame to ruin these awesome sweets with salty tears."

I smiled at her. "Right."

She laughed and glanced outside. Suddenly, her eyes widened, and she gasped.

A jolt of awareness crashed through my bones. I turned and looked out the window.

And met a pair of electric blue eyes.

CHAPTER 32

On the other side of the street, Kesstel was looking over Bethany Wilks's head and staring straight at me.

Man, even in street clothes—a simple black shirt and jeans—he looked like a prince. Was it the way he carried himself? The straight line of his back and relaxed shoulders spoke volumes. He knew he was on top of the world—even while lugging three shopping bags from designer stores in each hand. Did he want to flaunt it that badly? Why didn't he just put them in his Items Bag?

Beside him, Bethany was dressed to kill in her flower-print summer dress and flowing curls. She was talking endlessly at him, not noticing he wasn't even paying attention. Then her thick lashes lowered coquettishly and she peeked up at him, her red lips curling in a smile.

He blinked and looked down at her, finally reacting to whatever she'd just said.

Released from his gaze, I sighed. The power in his stare was so heavy it was hard to breathe.

"Wow," Aliya whispered. "They look like movie stars."

I hummed under my breath and sat back down. "Yep."

My sister tapped her finger against her chin, thinking. "I know that woman. What was her name? Bethany Wilks, the daughter of the Hunter Council's treasurer, right? Isn't she the new face of the Hunters?"

I turned my head and watched their backs get farther away. So she had money, talent, and prestige. What a good catch. What a good pair. What a—

I frowned, killing the thought before it could go any further. I took a huge bite of the chocolate tres leches cake and savored the creamy goodness, letting it lift my mood.

"She's the one who announced the results of the Gate Surge here. I'm glad that Eden handled it better than other countries did." Aliya popped the last of her éclair in her mouth.

I froze, my cup half raised to my lips. "What do you mean, *other countries*?"

Aliya blinked at me. "The Gate Surges from last week," she prompted. When I continued to stare at her with wide eyes, she frowned. "How can you *not* know?"

My mouth wrinkled in a frown as I tried to come up with something to say while shock crashed through my mind. "I don't watch the news, and I spend a lot of time in the Gate."

The news was never on when I ate at the hostel, and I didn't have a phone or laptop to view stuff like that. Every second of my day was spent either trying to level up or sleeping, and since I avoided people, it wasn't like I had the chance to learn about anything newsworthy from them.

"The Gate Surge last week didn't just happen in Eden. *Every single* Gate in the whole world had a Surge—simultaneously. Last I heard, nearly a million people died. And there are some Gates, like the one in France, that aren't even under control yet. I heard they just reached out to the German United Union for help." Aliya took a little sip of her milk. "There might be more deaths, but it's hard to get information out of the rebel areas, like in the North Mexican No-Man's-Land or the Montana Wilds."

When the Gates appeared twenty years ago and governments collapsed, some cities and countries were taken over by strong Hunters. Northern Mexico was like that. A gang of Hunters took over the area and even stole part of the southern states which belonged to the US, and the US simply didn't have the resources to get their land back. They were struggling, like all the other countries, just to rebuild their government and control the Gate situation. Even now, reclaiming the southern territories was low on the priority list.

Some places were just too hard to get to, like the two Gates in the Siberian tundra. There simply weren't enough Hunters in the area to handle them. Everyone was either killed by the monsters or fled, never going back. It posed quite the setback on surrounding territories, since they had to deal with the monsters from their own Gates, plus the ones that came down from the north.

I sat there, shocked at Aliya's words. "The whole world had a Gate Surge?" Something like that could actually happen? I mean, it happened when the Gates first appeared, but that was the only time. It hadn't happened since. So why now?

I frowned, thinking of the portal that collapsed. Could that be a reason? But why? There were over a hundred Gates, each with more than a dozen portals in them. How could a single collapsed portal affect them all? And it was a person here in Eden who'd caused it.

"At least Eden's Gate had a warning. None of the other Gates did; they just burst open, and people were overtaken." She glanced at me and frowned. "I heard the monsters were really hyped up and violent." Her voice shrank.

I didn't have to ask to know she was thinking about me being in the middle of the Gate Surge again. It must really be bothering her for her to keep bringing it up. I sighed and stabbed my last bite of lemon bar before holding it out to her. "But that's in the past. And I'm okay."

Her lips curled up as she took the last bite. "Right."

I paused, looking at how she was trying to hide her unease with a smile again. Yep, we were definitely sisters. A thought came to mind, and I smiled big. "Hey, I made something for you."

She blinked, completely distracted. "What?"

I held out my hand, and a bracelet appeared in my palm. The light streaming in the window reflected off the red fanged snapper scales, causing them to shimmer rosy pink. Silver links connected the half-inch scales, and it was all secured together with a hook-like clasp I rigged from a couple links.

Aliya gasped and slowly reached out to pick it up. "You made this? It's beautiful." She moved it around in the light, watching with amazement as the scales changed color.

I'd planned to give it to her as a goodbye present, but it seemed I'd made the right choice to give it to her now. "Yep. They're fanged snapper scales. I got them yesterday. Believe me, the fish they came from weren't nearly as pretty as their scales. And they ended up being just enough." An identical matching bracelet appeared in my hand. Reaching out, I showed her how to work the clasp before putting my own on.

She grinned and moved her arm around, admiring it. "I can't believe you made this."

I laughed. "Well, one of us was paying attention when Mom used to make jewelry." I'd never tell her how many scales I shattered in the process. The only thing I had to punch out holes for the links was my kindjal, and it took a couple tries to figure out how and where to press before I got it down. There were actually several mistakes on my bracelet, since it was the tester, while Aliya's was almost perfect, but she'd never know that.

I downed the rest of my milk and stood up. "Are you ready? Let's go shopping." Although we wouldn't go anywhere near the shops that the perfect couple had just come from, I had faith we'd still have fun.

Aliya jumped to her feet and helped me collect our plastic dishes. "Right!"

Twenty minutes later, we stepped into the Exquisite Equipment shop. Unlike the armorer shops I frequented every night, this store was simply for small trinkets like magic or strength-enhancing necklaces and rings. They were cool to look at—as long as you didn't look at the price tags. Aliya gawked at them but, just like me, didn't dare get too close. She hugged her arms to her chest and stroked the red bracelet with her fingers, a happy glow on her face.

What I wanted was in the back of the store. As soon as I got there, a woman around thirty with short brown hair and wearing a black apron stamped with the store's logo appeared. She glanced at my title bar and then at Aliya, who was obviously not old enough, before giving us a professionally warm smile. "Looking for a new Items Bag?"

I nodded and looked around.

I knew they could look like a lot of things, but I didn't know there'd be so many choices. The cheapest were simple red velvet bags like the one I already had, but these held fifteen items; mine only held ten. The most expensive ones were rings which held five hundred items. They were so cool looking—some were twisted designer bands, while others were encrusted with jewels.

My eyes landed on the Items Bags shaped like satchels and purses. They were bulkier compared to the rings and velvet bags, but to make up for that, they weren't as expensive and held a decent amount of items. Another bonus was that I could put things in the actual pack, too, instead of only in the virtual Items Bag repository. Not very big things because of their size, but it was still an option I liked. I couldn't help but be attracted to the hip satchels on mannequins along the wood back walls.

The shop employee smiled, as if relieved I wasn't paying more attention to the rings. It didn't take a rocket science degree to know it would be a miracle for an E to afford something like that. "Our designers just released a new batch of hip satchels, all the latest fashion. Suitable for all types of Hunters and their needs."

I nodded and walked up to the first one. I liked the leather play on the belt and thigh strap. The pack itself was a little plain, but that wasn't important. A tag hanging from a hemp string said this hip satchel held fifty items . . . and it cost one hundred and ten dollars.

I swallowed hard before I could choke on the price. I knew they were expensive, but god! And this was the simplest model here. The price was a kick in the pants.

I stared at the tag, thinking hard. On a normal day, holding fifty items would be enough. But there were some instances, like during the Gate Surge and on Prine Lake, that it wasn't. And that was now. Who knew what would happen in the future when I became stronger and needed to take out more monsters to level up?

"Oh, Jynn, look at this one!" Aliya broke through my thoughts.

I looked over to see her holding out a red leather hip satchel, very glitzy and feminine. It must have been effective because it was being sold, but it was so full of studs, belt buckles, and thin leather ruffles that I didn't know how anyone would fight while wearing it. Wouldn't it be so bulky that it would get caught on stuff? I guess a mage wouldn't have that problem, since they rarely did hand-to-hand combat, but most melee Hunters wouldn't touch that with a ten-foot pole . . . maybe?

The shopkeeper beamed and went to Aliya. "You have a good eye. I love that one! It's our newest release; came out just yesterday. Every time I walk by, I have to remind myself that I have enough Items Bags already."

I smiled and mentally shook my head. Well, some women did view Items Bags as purses. They held the same function—to carry stuff—just had a different name and appearance.

I glanced at the rack of purses to my left.

Well, sometimes, different appearances. The main difference was, since Items Bags were tied to the Hunter through magic, stealing them was useless to thieves. The Hunter lost their stuff, but the thief couldn't extract the items inside no matter what they did.

A black leather hip satchel just to Aliya's right caught my attention, and I walked over.

"Ah, your bracelet is so cute," the shopkeeper gushed, pointing at my sister's wrist. I could almost see her thinking, *Oh, what a cute little under-aged girl! And a potential future customer.* Then she glanced at me and grinned. "Oh, matching bracelets. That's so cute. You two must be good sisters."

I nodded in acknowledgement as I checked out the black Items Bag. A smooth, thin gray braid decorated the double belt which wrapped around the hips twice. The bag itself was about ten by five inches, with the top half held closed by a slim buckle. The bottom half was decorated lightly with gray stitching without a distinct pattern, but it looked nice anyway.

"It's made with fanged snapper scales, right?" the woman kept talking to my sister.

Aliya beamed, completely sold on her flattering words. "Yep! My sister made it for me."

I smiled and picked up the satchel, running my hands over the buckle. It didn't feel that catchy. It should be alright fighting with it on. I mean, Hunters wore bulkier gear all the time; it's just that my style was turning out to be more *sleek and stealthy*, and I needed gear that could conform to that.

"May I?" The shopkeeper pointed to Aliya's wrist. When she got a positive response, the woman lifted Aliya's wrist carefully and looked closer at the bracelet. "Wow, you did a good job," she complimented me. "This type of scale can be hard to handle. And look, you even managed to get some scales that have magic." She pointed to a few of them. "I am amazed they didn't break when you made this. Fanged snapper scales with magic in them are very delicate—most jewelers won't deal with them because they shatter too easily."

I blinked, completely thrown out of any thoughts involving the Items Bag, and focused on her. "Magic?"

"What? Where?" Aliya gasped, peering closer at the scales.

The woman smiled. "You must be a melee Hunter," she guessed, her tone turning kind. "I'm not surprised you can't see it, then." She pointed at two of the scales. "Do you see how this one and this one shimmer just a little bit more than the rest? These two scales have a trace of magic inside them. Not a lot, mind you. Just enough that I can tell."

Ironically, the two she was pointing to were also the two with lopsided holes in them. But if they were delicate, that would explain why they gave me so much trouble. And why last night Maveric had given me such a lowball offer for them. Since I thought the nixie leader's bracelet looked cool and I had all the scales, I had wanted to make one for my sister.

I paused, remembering all the scales I broke this morning while making the bracelets. How many of those had magic inside them? It was spilled milk, since I already threw the pieces away, but I couldn't help but wonder.

I lifted my own wrist and turned my hand around, watching the scales shimmer in the light.

The woman looked over and smiled. "Hey, it looks like you have three magic scales on yours."

As soon as she said it, I could tell which ones she meant. The longer I looked at them, the more I could tell they were different. They seemed to . . . glow? Just a tiny bit.

"Wow," Aliya whispered. "My first piece of equipment." She grinned and hugged the bracelet to her chest.

The woman laughed. "Oh, so you want to be a Hunter?"

My sister nodded and started to gush about our future together.

Leaving her to talk the shopkeeper's ear off, I tried on the hip satchel. It didn't feel constricting nor bulky. In fact, it felt made for me. I noticed a full-length mirror and walked over to do a visual check, turning this way and that, even doing a butt check.

"What do you think?" I asked Aliya.

She stopped midsentence and looked at me. "I love it! It looks just like you."

I nodded and finally checked the tag. Honestly, I almost didn't want to look at it.

Inwardly, I grimaced. It held a hundred items, which was great—just what I was looking for. But it cost two hundred and twenty-five dollars. After paying for lunch and the pastries today, this satchel was going to completely wipe out my remaining funds.

"It does look good on you," the saleswoman complimented. "Is that the one you want?"

I hesitated. I really did like it, but was it worth being completely broke again? "Um, I haven't decided yet."

To give myself more time, I started to do some stretches and simple moves just to see how it felt, hoping that would give me a reason not to want it anymore. But I was disappointed and pleased at the same time. It shifted with my every movement as if it were a part of me, the leather bending and moving as if it were actually nylon mesh, each motion performed flawlessly.

While Aliya watched me, the shopkeeper looked at my sister.

"You know, they say that there's no way to determine if you're going to be a Hunter or not in the future," she spoke like she was spilling a secret. Her tone instantly got Aliya's attention. "But I have a close friend who swears that the reason why she's a high-ranking mage now is because she always wore a magic necklace that her father gave her."

"Really?" My sister gasped and looked at her bracelet.

"But it's not a guarantee," I added.

The woman laughed. "That's true. There is no way to know until you're tested. Just study hard and keep practicing in your Hunter course." She patted Aliya on the shoulder before turning to me. "Did you want to try on another one?"

I took a deep breath and shook my head. "No, I want this one."

"Wonderful!" The woman led us to the cash register at the front of the store. "Could you take out your current Items Bag? I'll transfer everything over for you then help you attach your new bag."

I set the little red velvet bag and the hip satchel on the counter.

She blinked down. "Oh, is this your original Items Bag?"

I nodded while Aliya stared down at it, starstruck. It was easy to tell she was dying to pick it up and play with it.

The shopkeeper smiled. "Well, Hunters get a ten percent discount when they trade in their original Items Bag. Do you want to keep looking?"

Really? I couldn't feel more relieved. It was only a twenty-two-dollar difference, but at least my bank account wasn't going to be a zero. It made me want it even more. "No, this is the one."

The woman nodded. A blue System window appeared in front of her, and she pushed on the screen like it was a touch tablet. "Okay, then—"

"Wait," Aliya broke in. "I wanna help pay, too."

I blinked down at her. "What?"

She shook her head and gave me a determined look. "I wanted to buy you something today, but before I could, you kept paying for everything. So I wanna help you pay for this. It's not much, but I want to." She took out three twenties and put them on the counter.

I frowned at the bills, my heart squeezing tight. "Aliya—"

"It's no big deal," she said, like money fell off trees. "Half of the money is from Aunt Mina, and I've been doing odd jobs around the apartment complex, saving up for something like this." She pushed the money at the shopkeeper then glared at me. "Now say thank you."

I sighed but couldn't resist smiling tenderly at her. I looped an arm around her shoulders and squeezed. "Thank you."

She smiled and hugged back.

The shopkeeper took the bills and adjusted the total before showing me my portion. I accepted the transaction and watched as the woman placed one hand on the red velvet bag and the other on the hip satchel. The two Items Bags under her hands started to glow red. Slowly, a wispy red tentacle sprouted out from each red glow. The tentacles drifted in the air as they reached out to each other until a red arch was formed. A moment later, the magic ceased, and the woman lifted her hands.

A System notice popped up. [**Your Items Bag has been upgraded.**]

"All done." The shopkeeper held out my new hip satchel. "It was a pleasure working with you. Come again."

We thanked her and left.

I spent the next couple hours showing Aliya around the city and goofing off, but all good things must come to an end, and once 5:00 p.m. hit, visiting hours ended.

I stood at the south exit and waved until my sister disappeared.

How great would it be if she didn't have to leave to go home? Maybe I *did* want her to be a Hunter, after all. By the time she got tested, I'd be strong enough that Aliya wouldn't ever have to be in danger, and I should know by then what it was the System wanted from me.

Should.

For now, since I'd been in too much of a hurry this morning preparing to see my sis, it was time to go to the hostel gym and get in the workout I'd missed. It was time to figure out how to use my upgraded Mist ability and whatever Mirror was.

CHAPTER 33

I stood at the entrance of Glenn Holt and stared down the path, thumping my fist against my thigh in agitation. The green aspen-like leaves swayed lazily in the gentle breeze, and flashes of sunlight breached the canopy. Green-and-gold bushes grew around the off-white trunks and framed the dirt path which cut through the woods. Red and pink flowers dotted the landscape, adding just the right amount of color to the peaceful scene.

God, I hated this forest. It'd now been nearly two months since I was abducted by red orcs in this forest. My life had drastically changed since then, but I still hadn't been able to take a step inside the damn place.

My fist thumped harder against my thigh until it started to hurt. Taking a deep breath, I pulled up my daily tasks. I swear the list was getting longer every day.

[Cultivate in Fogmire for thirty minutes—Completed.] There were two left: **[Destroy five Energy Crystals.]** and **[Collect five Pearl Duku.]**.

I'd checked and checked again. The only pearl duku trees were in Glenn Holt. For the first time, I was seriously debating on intentionally not completing a daily task. While I wasn't the kind of person who willingly looked for punishment, at the moment, it didn't seem like it would be so bad, no matter what it was, as long as I never had to go into this forest again. All for some super poisonous fruit the size of a quarter.

Somewhere in the middle of the forest was a cave I needed to find. I didn't know where it was, but that wasn't the hardest part. No, the hardest part was taking the first step.

I scowled and closed out my menu. I sucked in a deep breath and took a step down the path . . . or I meant to. Before my boot landed, my muscles seized up. I couldn't put my foot down on that dirt path. Images of red orcs flashed through my mind, and I could almost feel Blake's hands gripping my limbs as he lifted me and tossed me to my death.

I jumped back. My shoulder hit someone right behind me, and my heart rate soared. I whipped around, expecting to see Blake and his group behind me.

A woman a couple years older than me in red armor blinked in surprise. "Excuse me."

Beside her, a similarly aged man in black robes frowned at me.

I swallowed my heart back into place. "Oh, sorry." Stepping off the dirt path into the bush so they could pass, I watched as the pair of D-ranked Hunters disappeared down the forest trail.

I let out a frustrated moan and scrubbed my face with my hands. What was I doing, getting so worked up just because of a bunch of trees? I wasn't that weak anymore, and I refused to be a victim still. I lowered my hand to my side and fisted my fingers as I glared at the path. Head held high, I entered the forest.

I should be looking for the caves in the middle of Glenn Holt, but I couldn't stop my memory from guiding my feet through the woods. It had only been a couple of minutes of terror, being tied and marched through these trees, but I'd never forget the route we took, the feel of the coarse rope against my skin, or the smell of the bloody red orcs pressing us faster.

I stopped in front of two trees bowing together to form an arch. They looked different from the last time I was here, but I knew it was the place. The biggest difference was the fact that there wasn't a black portal shimmering under the arch. To make sure, I stepped closer and passed my hand between the trunks. It was normal air, as if there had never been a portal to hell there to begin with.

"So it was a Portal Burst," I whispered.

That would explain why I'd never heard there was a portal in Glenn Holt. It just showed up, let a bunch of red orcs out, then stayed open long enough for them to kidnap a group of Hunters and return. I didn't know if it was still open after the others came back. Since I wasn't conscious until four days later, I doubted I'd ever find out. But that didn't matter anymore. As long as it didn't open ever again—or at least not until after I left this forest—it could do whatever it wanted.

Still, I couldn't help but sigh in relief as a heavy weight lifted off my shoulders. Glenn Holt didn't feel so secretively sinister anymore. I could do this.

It was time to find a cave.

Since I didn't know where to go, I figured the best thing would be to follow the path which led through the forest. An hour's walk later and I had destroyed four energy crystals from one E- and three D-ranked monsters. I was glad to have my new Items Bag because it was filling fast, what with each monster dropping one to two items.

"Hah!" I yelled, thrusting my kindjal into the chest of a D-ranked werecat and shattering the energy crystal. The monster exploded into little glowing lights.

[+56 EXP]

The System dinged. [**Daily Task: (Destroy five Energy Crystals) Completed. +25 EXP**]

[**You have Leveled Up!**]

"Sweet!" I hummed as I scooped up the drop items then adjusted my stats. Hmm, I was level seventeen now, but still a D rank. How many more levels would it take to get an S rank?

With that on my mind, I moved farther into the woods.

The forest path opened up in front of me, revealing a pond. Its surface was so smooth it looked like faintly glowing silver glass, and the trees around it grew thick and tall, bending over the water and spreading their branches out, blocking out the sunlight as if someone had purposefully woven the branches together. The dim light made the pond glow even more.

In the middle was an island just big enough to fit a stone arch about fifteen feet in diameter. Within that arch was a tree which looked like a weeping willow—only, it glowed. Faintly glowing pink leaves drifted lazily from thin branches on a nonexistent breeze. Between the leaves, clusters of bright white fruit twinkled in the faint light. Even the bark had ribbons of white neon webbing up and down its trunk and branches. All of this was under a huge cloche-like rock arch.

This had to be a pearl duku tree. It had to be one of the most beautiful scenes I'd ever seen in Gate Vale . . . so what was the catch?

I looked around but didn't spot anything which could be a threat. I frowned at the pond and kicked a rock into the smooth surface. The splash was barely more than a ripple, and the rock vanished after a couple feet. I waited another couple of minutes, but nothing happened.

"Alright then," I said, activating Feather Step. I stepped onto the pond.

Instantly, the pearl duku tree exploded into thousands of pink glowing lights. I paused, shocked.

No, it wasn't that the tree exploded—every single leaf had soared into the air to form a glowing mass of lights. It took another second for me to realize they weren't leaves at all—they were butterflies. According to their title bars, thousands of bloodsucking level ten gem butterflies. And they were coming at me like a swarm of angry bees.

"What the—?"

I threw up my hands and cast Mist—only, this time, I didn't pull from the power I had stored inside me; I used Mist Creation. The still water beneath my feet evaporated and blended with the air, creating a thick mist that I could control. I couldn't control the water or the air separately, but I could blend the two together and use them to my advantage, concentrating the two elements together as thickly as I could. The butterflies entered my mist and immediately slowed down. After a short while, some even fell into the water, their wings weighed down with dew.

My kindjal appeared in my right hand, and I put my left against the short sword's handle. As I pulled my hands apart, I cast Mirror. A second kindjal, a replica of the one in my right, appeared in my left. God, I loved this new skill.

I Feather Stepped forward and slashed at the butterflies with both weapons. No matter where I aimed, I hit several at once. But my task wasn't to kill these monsters—it was to get the pearl duku. Swinging my kindjals around and holding my mist thick, I ran to the tree.

The butterflies kept coming at me, and while I was able to keep most of them at bay, a few landed on me. I knew the instant they did because of the intense bee-stinging bite they inflicted. Slashing them away from my body, I couldn't help but notice that the longer they were on me, the longer they sucked on my blood, the redder their wings became. *Ugh.* I fought my way across the pond until I finally reached my target.

Panting, I inspected the pearl duku tree. Now that I was closer, it was obvious why they were called what they were. The fruit dangling from the thin branches really did look like huge white pearls glowing in the dim light.

The kindjal disappeared from my left hand, and I reached out to grab a handful of the fruit hanging on the nearly bare branch. My grip was too hard, and the fruit exploded in my hand. A milky gelatin squished between my fingers while opalescent juice dripped down my wrist into my arm bracer.

"Crud!" I gasped, shaking my hand out. The skins of the pearl duku flung to the ground several feet from me.

The gem butterflies stirred. Some were thrown into a whole new kind of frenzy, aiming at my hand as if it'd mortally offended them, while another portion flew to the broken pieces of pearl duku on the ground. They landed on it, each little bug trying to push others out of the way.

I swung my remaining sword even faster while pulling another fistful of fruit off the tree. This time, I quickly slotted them into my Items Bag before I could crush them.

[Daily Task: (Collect five Pearl Duku) Completed. +25 EXP]

I huffed a breath of relief then turned and ran back across the pond, a small swarm of butterflies chasing after me and my left hand. I swung at them while trying to collect as many drop items as I could. Since their energy crystals were so small and most of them sank into the water, it was nearly impossible for me to destroy them and collect orbs at the same time. My mist slowed the buggy monsters, and they weren't so hard for me to evade, but I could see how a melee Hunter or a mage without an area spell could have trouble with them.

Even so, I was still breathing hard by the time I made it to shore and ran into the woods. The butterflies still hounded after me until, suddenly, they stopped.

I slowed down and turned, blinking at the mass of pink lights that shifted and swirled in the distance. Their wings made an angry *sha-sha* sound, but they didn't come any closer. They didn't move one inch from under the dim shadow the overhead trees cast. I blinked again and looked at the sunlight hitting the ground around me. It clicked.

Oh, they couldn't go in the sun.

"Maybe they should have been called vampire butterflies," I muttered.

My kindjal disappeared, and I lifted my left hand, trying to think of what to do about the fruit juice on it. Then I paused. My hand was completely dry, as if it had never gotten wet to begin with.

"Hmm." I had a feeling the System wanted the pearl fruit for something, just like it had wanted the Essence of Nothing. Curious, I opened my menu. There were sixty pairs of gem wings in there. They were pretty to look at, as if someone really did carve delicate wings out of pink quartz. In the midst of them were two pearl duku.

"Two?" I muttered to myself. I knew for sure I'd grabbed five. The System even marked it off as five. So where did the other three go? Or . . . ?

I glanced at my left hand and wiggled my fingers around. Was it really like the Essence of Nothing that had vanished from my Items Bag? The System wanted it for something, and since there was some on my hand, it took that first and the remaining from my Items Bag? That's why there was some left over? It seemed far-fetched, but was it really?

With that still on my mind, I turned around and walked back toward the trail. Just as I stepped onto the compressed dirt, I heard the sounds of people talking.

"You've got to be kidding me, Miles. That's an idiotic idea." A woman sighed in exasperation.

Hm. Was her voice familiar? I turned around and saw a man and a woman standing off the side of the trail, the same couple I'd bumped into earlier today just outside of Glenn Holt.

The man, Miles, stared at her with avid eyes. "No, I'm serious, baby." He held up his gloved hands. In his fingers was a small glowing energy crystal, shining like a little star. "Haven't you ever wondered about it? These crystals are full of energy. What if Hunters could absorb that energy into their bodies and use it to become stronger?"

CHAPTER 34

The woman gave Miles a look which expressed exactly what I was thinking.

"Huh?" she asked in a flat, are-you-stupid? voice.

"Just hear me out, honey," the mage rushed on. "I really do think that a person could extract and use the energy in a crystal."

The woman tapped her forehead and gave him a patient smile. "Miles, that was proved impossible over fifteen years ago."

It was true. When crystals became the main source of energy, extensive experiments were done on them to make sure there weren't any negative side effects. Some of those experiments involved Hunters and humans trying to extract the energy so that a person could use it and become physically or magically stronger. Every single test had been a failure. No matter what they did, a person couldn't absorb a crystal's power.

I rolled my eyes and turned away, not interested in their conversation anymore. If he wanted to play with crystals like that, that was on his time.

But the man's voice still carried in the wind. "I know. But I think they were doing it wrong. I've been reading a lot, and I think the right way is through cultivation."

My eyes widened, and I froze midstep. That was a word I didn't hear from other people's mouths. Slowly, I turned around and walked back. They still hadn't noticed me. To keep it that way, I jumped into a nearby tree and perched on a branch to watch. Spying might be rude, but the man had finally gotten my attention.

The woman still didn't look convinced. "Reading? Babe, those are fiction books. Fiction—as in fantasy! They aren't real. If a process like that were possible, it would have been discovered years ago."

"But all fiction is based on some sort of real event. Even Moby Dick was based on a real whale," Miles argued back, nodding his head in self-righteousness.

"Yet there has never been a person who's gone forty thousand leagues under the sea in a submarine," she replied in the same blunt tone. "And there sure as hell isn't a prehistoric land in the middle of the Earth. Most fiction is the product of someone with an overactive imagination and too much time on their hands."

He opened his mouth then paused. "But there have been people in submarines who've reached the bottom of the ocean." He threw his hands in the air and hurried on. "I really want to try this, honey. I can't accept that we'll be stuck in the same place in the Hunter hierarchy our whole lives. You deserve so much better than that, and I'm going to give it to you."

The girlfriend sighed. "Miles, I'm happy right now. Don't get caught up trying to change something you can't and drive yourself crazy over it." Her words were smart, but her tone had softened.

He gave her a tight hug and rubbed his cheek against her brunette hair. "I won't. But I still want to try this." He stood back, holding up the crystal. "All the books I read had a specific way to cultivate. I just want to try it and see if it's possible. If it is, it could change our lives forever. If not, oh well, it was a nice dream. What do you say?"

The woman stared at Miles for a second then slowly nodded. "Alright. But don't come crying to me when it doesn't work." She gave him a quick kiss before turning around. "I'll watch your back for one hour. Just one hour, you hear me?" She stabbed a finger at him.

He grinned like an idiot. "I love you."

She smiled as she grumbled under her breath.

I watched their play, smiling to myself. The man sat down cross-legged on the ground. He held his hands differently than what I did, but all in all, it actually looked like a real cultivation position—not that I was a pro. I had to be a toddler at best, but I was getting better every day. Since my eyes were closed when I cultivated, I'd never actually seen the whole process. I couldn't resist leaning over so I could pay close attention.

A minute passed. Five minutes passed. The woman noticed a dire rat and ran off to kill it. She didn't notice the second dire rat sneaking up on the man while she was gone, but I killed it by pairing Throw and Critical Hit. My kindjal exploded the energy crystal, so by the time the woman returned, the rat carcass had disappeared and my kindjal was back in my hand. The drop orb stayed on the ground just six feet from him for a couple minutes, completely invisible to the woman, until it disappeared by itself.

Twenty minutes of nothing else passed by. I lounged on the branch, swinging a leg back and forth under me. I wasn't in that much of a hurry. My first time cultivating wasn't successful, even though I had a manual in front of me. This guy was going off books he'd read in the past. Who knew how much he remembered?

Miles hadn't moved a muscle, but I could tell he was concentrating hard from the thin layer of sweat building on his forehead. His girlfriend kept looking at him, but she bit her lip and looked away without disturbing him.

Another forty minutes passed by with only minor monster interruptions—that the girlfriend knew about. Some of them I took care of before she even knew they were there. The girlfriend checked her Guide menu for the tenth time, probably checking the time, and silently sighed. She turned to Miles and opened her mouth before pausing and closing it again. Finally, she gripped her hands together and walked up to him. She opened her mouth. "Mi—"

Suddenly, the energy crystal resting in Miles's hands lit up like a mini blue sun.

The woman gasped and stumbled back, holding a hand up to block her eyes. I gasped and leaned closer.

Energy, strong and bright, pulsed from the crystal. It swirled around the stone for a second then slowly drifted toward the man's chest. As soon as it touched him, the energy rushed into his body.

His eyes popped open. "I can feel it!" he gasped. "I can feel the power. Oh my god, it's so strong. I can feel it in my heart, in my arms, my hands." He laughed in delight. "It works, honey! It works!"

I stared at him, wide-eyed, seeing what they couldn't. The title bar over his head was changing. Before, it said he was level seventeen, the same as me. The same as his girlfriend. The number had now increased to eighteen.

It worked? He really was absorbing the energy from a crystal and becoming stronger. Even though I was waiting for it, the thought still blew my mind—and all the contradicting theories I grew up with. If Hunters really could absorb the power in energy crystals, why hadn't they done that from the beginning? For as long as I could remember, crystals were used as an energy source to power the world. Batteries full of clean energy with no effect on humans or Hunters.

The mage's level rose to nineteen, the light of the crystal still strong.

If Hunters really could absorb the power, why was there such a heavy caste system in this bloodthirsty society? Why did Es and Ds still exist if they could just cultivate a crystal and become stronger?

A flash of anger boiled in me as the helplessness of my past came to mind. Did I really go through all that shit for nothing? Could I really have avoided the pain of being stuck at the bottom of society's food chain if it weren't for believing the words of the government? But why would they lie to us? Wouldn't it be better for them if Hunters were stronger? Then we could more easily handle the threats inside the Gates.

The woman stepped closer to Miles then back a couple feet. "Are you okay? How do you feel?" Her voice trembled, like she was excited and scared at the same time.

"I feel invincible!" the mage yelled in elation. His level rose to twenty.

"Oh my god," the woman whispered in awe. "This is amazing."

His laughter slowly died, and he looked down at the crystal in his hands. His brows pulled together. At first, he looked confused . . . then concerned.

"What's going on?" The woman stepped closer.

"I don't . . . " Suddenly, he threw his head back and screamed. His voice was raw and brutal, obviously in intense pain, but there was no visible problem.

Shocked, I jumped to my feet.

"Miles!" the woman screamed, running to him. She grabbed his shoulder with one hand and gripped the crystal in his fingers with the other. No matter how hard she pulled, neither the crystal nor his position changed. It was like they were frozen in place as he screamed in agony. "Miles! What's wrong? Miles!"

He didn't move—no, he *was* moving. Without shifting position, his body was moving. It was *changing*. Under his black robes, his arms thickened and twisted in odd shapes. His torso elongated and thinned as his neck widened. His legs twisted around, and the boots slid off his feet. The fingers holding the dim crystal grew broader and sharpened at their tips until they were claws.

The woman screamed in horror and stumbled back, her hands covering her mouth as she gasped for air, staring at the man as he changed into a monster.

His human scream morphed into a reptilian roar. Red scales replaced his skin, spreading into place as his clothes slid off his narrow shoulders and pooled in his lap. His hair fell out as his face lengthened and flattened until it was more lizard-like than human. A four-foot tail shot out of the folds of his clothes.

The monster's level hit twenty-one. The crystal in its claws flashed bright before it vanished as the monster the Hunter became opened its mouth wide and roared into the air. A blast of fire shot from its mouth and dissipated in the air above.

"Miles?" the woman whispered, like she couldn't understand what was happening. Her legs shook as she edged back.

I could barely process what I was seeing. Oh my god, what just happened? Did I really just watch a human turn into a monster?

The huge, red lizard lunged for the woman, crawling on all fours and leaving the pile of clothing behind.

She blocked his first attack with her long sword. "Miles! Miles! It's me! Come on, wake up!" she begged, her whole body shaking with her sobs.

Fast as lightning, the lizard whipped at her with its tail. While she blocked that, the monster's head shot forward in a blur of movement, and its wide mouth clamped shut on her throat and shoulder. The force of the attack knocked the woman backward, the monster on top of her. It all happened in seconds.

I flung my kindjal at the lizard as I jumped from the tree. The monster dodged back from the woman, and my kindjal sank into the ground between them. It looked up at me and hissed low, pulling its lips away from red gums. I closed the distance between us with Feather Step as the lizard whipped out its tail. I deflected it with the newly returned kindjal and twisted in the air, kicking the monster hard in the chest. It stumbled back five feet.

I glanced over my shoulder at the quiet woman on the ground; her eyes were wide with horror, mouth slack, face white as a sheet. Blood continued to flow from the holes in her throat, the blood puddling around her growing wider. It could only mean one thing.

The lizard monster hissed as I faced it, and I quickly cast Mirror with my kindjal.

God, I hate this forest.

If I survived the next ten minutes, I would *never* step foot in here again.

CHAPTER 35

The lizard shot at me like a blur. I gasped and mirrored his movements, blocking his attacks where I predicted he'd be. The monster's long claws clashed against my kindjal with a force that sent the soles of my boots skidding back across the dirt. My heel hit the woman's body, and I jumped back before I lost my balance.

The monster stepped right on the corpse's chest and kept coming.

I knew it was a monster now, but two minutes ago, the lizard had been a man. A man who'd wanted to make his girlfriend's life better. Then he'd turned into a monster and killed her.

I knew what I had to do—I had to kill the monster, but my heart hurt. Only, two minutes ago, he was just like me—struggling under an oppressive caste system as he desperately tried to improve his loved one's life.

I cast Mist and dodged away from the monster's tail as it slapped against the ground, creating a divot. Empowered by the mist, I slashed out, slicing left and right with my twin blades. The lizard swiped back, its claws slamming into my swords. The collision threw me off balance again and sent a stinging shock up my arms. Stumbling back, I grimaced at the four deep cuts on one of my upper arms.

The lizard hissed and inspected its hand. Black blood leaked from two deep cuts spanning its digits, while more gushed from a small stub where a pinkie should have been.

Why? I thought. How could a man turn into a monster? I'd never once heard of anything like this happening. I mean, it should be impossible! If this could happen, why wasn't the knowledge available to the public?

The monster roared at me, and from the black depths of its open maw, a light sparked. A second later, a stream of fire erupted from its mouth. I dodged, but wasn't fast enough to escape the blast as heat seared my left shoulder. Gasping, I quickly patted at the hot material, trying to cool it with mist.

More alarming than the pain was watching my mist evaporate with the monster's fire. This fog was part of the reserve I kept inside my body, the reward for hours of cultivating. Everything that evaporated would take precious time to replace.

"Damn," I muttered. So my mist was fine against water, but weak against fire. Good to know.

I rushed at the monster, two kindjals ready. The lizard spit a fireball at me, but I created a solid mist shield over my left kindjal and used it to deflect the blast. The shield started evaporating as soon as it came into contact with the fire, but it was strong enough to accomplish what I wanted it to.

The lizard lunged at me, but as soon as its injured claws hit the ground, it shrieked in pain and flinched back. I took advantage of its hesitation and double slashed. My left kindjal hit its left shoulder, blade slicing through the red scales. The right kindjal hit that same spot a split second later, deepening the cut into a solid gash which leaked black blood.

The monster shrieked, snapping at my head. I leaned away as its lips brushed my cheek, jaws clamping shut, just barely missing my face. Hot lizard breath blasted my hair back, and a chill went down my spine. Its mouth gaped open, and I got a close view of the fire sparking inside its throat. God, if that hit me at this range . . .

"Ha!" I yelled, thrusting my kindjal down its throat. My arm drove into its open mouth up to my elbow, and I could feel the moist heat of its fleshy throat through my gloves and arm bracer.

The monster's green reptilian eyes widened as it flailed. Its injured claws gripped my leather breastplate and dug in, leaving cuts on my chest. Its mouth clamped shut over my arm, and I cried out as teeth sank into my skin.

But the more it thrashed, the more my sword swam in its insides. Despite the pain, I twisted and thrust my left kindjal into its underbelly before jerking down, trying to gut it. The monster stiffened then collapsed to the ground. Strength left its jaw, and I pulled my bleeding arm free from its mouth.

I stared down at the conquered lizard. I didn't want to kill it . . . kill him. Really, I didn't. But reflex and survival instincts kicked in. It was him or me.

A System message appeared over the reptilian corpse. [+85 EXP]

I stared at the message, almost sick to my stomach. That was originally a human. And I got EXP from the kill. An orb appeared on the ground next to the lizard monster's head. I couldn't seem to move.

[**Take the Drop Item orb and destroy the Energy Crystal.**] The System prompted.

My eyes widened. "What? Energy crystal?" There was no way there was an energy crystal in this monster. Humans didn't have crystals inside them.

Or did they? I wanted—needed—to know, but I still found myself hesitating.

The System flashed the same message again, urging me forward. Swallowing, I reached out a trembling hand to the drop orb. My finger brushed against it. Instantly, a glossy red lizard hide appeared in my Items Bag. Lizard hide which used to be human skin.

The carcass vanished, leaving a glowing energy crystal on the ground where the monster had just been.

I stumbled back until my shaking knees gave out and I collapsed, unable to take my eyes off of it. "Oh my god," I whispered. "How? How the hell did that get in there? *What is going on?*"

The System flashed a third message urging me to destroy the crystal. Slowly, I climbed to my feet and approached it, numbly lifting my kindjal and stabbing down. The crystal shattered and dissolved into light.

I barely remember rummaging through the female corpse's clothes and the empty mage robes. Try as I might, I couldn't find any identification cards. That was one of the drawbacks about Items Bags; when the person died, everything inside the bags vanished—including identification cards. Her Guide pearl would have her information, but I couldn't bring myself to dig it out of her temple or carry her dead body with me out of the Gate. As for the mage who'd turned into a monster, there wasn't even a pearl left behind. And seeing the lizard skin made me nauseous.

I pulled it out and left it next to the woman on the ground.

As I ran back to Eden, the surroundings blurred together. People died in Gate Vale all the time, but I'd never been part of it before. I didn't really know what to do. It wasn't really that I was upset the woman was dead. Rather, I was horrified that the man had become a monster—a real monster with an energy crystal.

People had to know about this. People needed to know there was something wrong with the energy crystals. Those stones powered our entire world—houses, cars, cell phones, hospitals, streetlamps. Energy crystals were *everywhere*. And thousands more came out of the Gates every day. So why didn't people know they were so dangerous if a person absorbed their energy?

Was this the reason why the System had me destroy the energy crystals? In fact, I hadn't even touched one since the System bonded with me.

I ran through the Gate and came out into Eden. After taking a dozen steps away from the Gate, I stopped, staring at the city. Hunters entered and exited the Gate completely unaware that I was there.

The back of my neck prickled. Maybe someone *had* taken notice of me.

Looking across Gate Square, I met Kesstel's piercing gaze.

His long stride ate up the distance between us. Unlike the rest of the people here, he was in casual wear even though it was still in the afternoon.

I usually ran as soon as I saw him, but not this time. Instead, I looked down at the ground and scowled.

He stopped next to me and inspected me, taking in the dried blood on my body. "Are—"

"Not today," I interrupted. "I . . . " My voice drifted, and I turned to my right, away from him. Away from the E Hostel.

A part of me wanted to go back to my room and forget everything that just happened. Pretend like it never did, like I hadn't watched a Hunter transform before my eyes. But I couldn't. People had to know.

While my mind replayed the events over and over again, trying to make sense of them all, my feet carried me across Gate Square until I was a block north from it. Kesstel followed me the whole way, always five feet behind. His gaze was locked on me, never leaving, just like the faint frown on his face.

I completely ignored him. Right now, I just couldn't deal with him. No matter what he wanted, it would have to wait.

I stopped outside a grandiose cream marble building. The same person who'd designed the library must have designed the Hunter's Association building, giving it a Roman and Renaissance flare. It was mostly square shaped, with columns and a shallow-stepped staircase spanning the front of the structure. In the middle was a towering dome full of intricate details.

If I were part of the Hunter Council, I'd march up to the large wooden doors at the center of the building and enter from there. Instead, I circled around to a small wing on the right side of the structure where a metal plaque above a door read: Hunter's Incidents Office. I imagined the inside of the main building was as grand as the outside, but when I opened the heavy metal door to this small annex, I was greeted with something normal.

Tan tile spread across the floor leading to a long, off-white counter divided by fiberglass panes. Incident associates worked on computers between each section, some assisting people while others tapped away on their computers.

The door shut behind me. I was getting so used to Kesstel's presence I didn't even have to look over my shoulder to know he'd followed me inside. I should be irritated that he was tailing me, but I didn't have it in me to spare him a glance. Besides, if he overheard my concerns, that just meant one more person would know.

I walked between the rope dividers which cut through the middle of the tiled waiting area. Two receptionists were available to choose from. Between the bored-looking man glaring at his computer and the nice-looking woman staring at me expectantly, my choice was obvious.

Approaching her counter, I relaxed a little when Kesstel didn't follow but simply leaned against the wall next to the door.

She smiled at me. "What can I do for you today?"

I took a breath, suddenly nervous. How much of this could I even tell her? Would any of it be restricted by the System's rules? "I want to report two deaths. And make the Council aware of a problem with the energy crystals."

The receptionist's brown eyes widened with surprise, and she sat up straighter. "Alright." She put her hands on the keyboard. "First, let's start with your name." She took down my general information then glanced at me. "Can you tell me what happened?"

I nodded slowly. As I spoke, the woman tapped on her keyboard. "When I was in Glenn Holt, I came across a couple. The man tried to—" My voice cut off before I could say *cultivate*. I frowned and changed my wording, hoping it would work. "Ah, he absorbed the power inside an energy crystal."

She paused and looked up. "You mean, the energy actually went inside his body?"

I nodded. "Yes."

She frowned. "That's impossible. When the Gates first opened and we started using the crystals as an energy source, hundreds of tests were performed on them. It's impossible for them to affect Hunters and humans."

I bobbed my head. "I know. That's what I thought, too. But I watched this guy absorb the energy before he turned into a monster."

Her hands lifted off the keyboard. "He turned into a monster?"

"Yes. A fire-breathing lizard bigger than I am. The Guide didn't have a name for it, so it must be a new type." God, this really did sound crazy. "Look, I know it's hard to accept, but I really did see it with my own eyes. The energy crystals are dangerous. I think more testing should be done on them, to make sure this doesn't happen again." I paused. "I mean, there has to be other records like this. Someone else must have seen someone turn into a monster in the last twenty years."

Slowly, her head shook side to side. "I've never seen a report about someone absorbing an energy crystal and then turning." She took a breath and tapped on the keyboard in silence for a moment. "You said you had two deaths to report?" She glanced at me, obviously wanting to move on to a new subject.

My hands fisted, and I took a deep breath to calm my nerves. "Yes. After the man turned into a lizard, he killed his partner. I don't know if they were married or dating or what, but the monster killed her. Then I killed the monster."

She slowly looked down at her keyboard and tapped on it. "And their names?"

I shook my head. "I don't know. His name was Miles, but I never found out hers. Or their last names."

"And where are their bodies now?"

I paused, shifting my weight to lean on my hip. I could tell by her tone that she didn't believe a word I was saying. "Her body is in Glenn Holt still. I didn't know if I should move it or not, because it's a crime scene, right? His, Miles, well . . . his body disappeared." I almost didn't want to say the last part. If she didn't believe me before, it would be all that much harder now.

The incident associate stared at me, her hands still on the keyboard. "So you say that you saw a man absorb an energy crystal and turn into a lizard. You killed him, and then he . . . disappeared?"

I stared at her incredulous face, my hand fisting on the counter. Maybe I should have talked to the bored man instead. "Look, his body might be gone, but hers is still there. You just need to send someone to check it, and it'll prove what I'm telling you." But even I didn't believe my own words. Any number of monsters could kill a Hunter. I'd left the hide there, but how was that supposed to prove anything either?

Maybe I should have carried her body and the lizard skin out, but it was too late to regret that now. Even then, what would it prove? The monster Miles turned into wasn't named, so the Guide wouldn't recognize it. How would they be able to prove the woman was killed by that monster? A monster that didn't even exist anymore.

The receptionist took a breath and looked at me long and hard. Her incredulous look softened into a gentle smile. "Miss, there are some plants inside the Gate that can release strong pollen which can cause hallucinations or delusions." Her words were slow, as if she were talking to somebody who wasn't right in the head. "Why don't you go get an exam at the hospital first, and then we'll talk again?"

I stared at her. This really wasn't going anywhere, was it? She actually thought I was crazy. "No, I'm serious." I thumped my fists on the wooden counter, just hard enough to cause the people next to me to look over, but not enough to damage anything. "Energy crystals are dangerous. They can turn Hunters into monsters. And people need to know about it." If they weren't dangerous, the System wouldn't have warned me against them.

The woman leaned back away from the computer and took her hands off the keyboard.

With a frustrated sound, I shoved away and strode out of the building. What should I do now? Was there anyone who would actually believe me?

I kept my head down and didn't even look at the S-ranked Hunter who followed me outside. The door had barely shut before he spoke, his voice low and smooth. "You're not wrong."

My eyes widened, and I turned. "You know what I'm talking about?"

Kesstel frowned at me for a moment, as if debating on something. He then sighed and nodded his head to the right, toward a small green park. "Why don't we go sit down?"

CHAPTER 36

I followed Kesstel to the small, wooded area. Walking to a bench surrounded by some trees and a tall yellow rose bush on the right side, Kesstel sat down and looked up at me expectantly.

I stared down at him and tried not to fidget. That warning still hung over his head, but it wasn't like I was trying to provoke him, right? I just wanted to know what was going on. If the System wasn't going to tell me, then I had to use other means. If Kesstel tried anything or began acting provoked, I could always just run away, right?

I perched on the far side of the bench, my butt barely on the cold stone, and looked up at him.

Kesstel's mouth relaxed into almost a smile, but not quite. Was he amused that I was still on guard? A rosy-pink cardboard box appeared in his hand, and he set it on the bench between us.

I blinked at it, surprised. The label on the box looked familiar, but I still asked, "What is that?"

"Bribery," he bluntly stated. He glanced at me, the corner of his mouth still hooked up in a half smile. "You think I haven't noticed you run like a bat out of hell whenever you see me? I'm not so uncouth that I'd force my attention on a young woman." He opened the pastry box. From inside, a waft of sweet heaven drifted into the air. "I thought I'd try a gentler approach to get your attention."

I stared at him, completely shocked at how shameless and blunt he was. The smell of baked goods coiled around me, and I couldn't resist glancing down. Inside was an éclair and a chocolate tres leches cake. Just like the ones my sister and I had shared. He'd noticed . . .

"I don't care for sweets, so if you don't eat them, they're going in the trash," he commented, a slight warning edge in his tone.

My mouth nearly fell open, and one more negative point was tacked on his scoreboard in my mind. It was a sin to waste food—especially dessert!

Still, I couldn't bring myself to reach into the box.

"What did you mean when you said I'm not wrong?" I looked into his eyes.

Instinctively, I wanted to shy away. God, just meeting his gaze felt like he could see into my soul. Feeling the residue of his suppressed power sent a cold shiver through my whole body. But I refused to let it show.

My hands fisted in my lap, and I lifted my chin. "Have you seen someone turn into a monster, too?"

His eyes narrowed, and a frown flashed on his face, so fast I would have missed it if I wasn't staring at him so intently. "Yes. But first . . . " He waved his hand. A chill went down my spine as a magical dome about ten feet wide appeared over us. It was clear, with the barest sheen of light radiating from it.

The sounds of the city were instantly cut off, like we were in our own little world in the corner of the green park. It was obvious I'd be stuck in here until Kesstel took away the barrier. Oddly, I didn't feel threatened by being penned up with him; I was only on edge from the pressure that Kesstel, as an S, released.

"The receptionist a minute ago"—his words broke through my thoughts—"said the government did some testing when the Gates were first opened? If they did, they must have done it on Earth, where there wasn't enough magic in the air. It's unfortunate, really. It's probably never occurred to them that half the Hunters that go missing might actually be in the Gate still. Then again, even if they knew, it wouldn't matter."

It took me a second to realize what he was saying. My heart nearly stopped, and I jumped to my feet. "Hang on! Are you telling me some of the monsters in the Gate are actually people?" I thrust a finger toward the black arch looming in the sky. "The monsters that we kill every day?"

Kesstel's chin tipped up until his eyes locked with mine. "Not some. All."

I couldn't seem to get enough air in my lungs. Shock ricocheted around my head, turning my mind to mush. My knees gave out, and I sank back down to the bench, unable to take my wide eyes off him.

He hummed low and rubbed his chin as if he'd just thought of something. "Hm, maybe not all. Animals and plants can transform into monsters, too, though it's rarer. But at least ninety percent of the monsters in Gate Vale were once people—although not all of them looked exactly like you and me."

I gaped at him, trying to digest what he'd just said while hundreds of questions came to my mind.

He didn't give me the chance to ask one before he spoke again. "Now that I've answered two of your questions, you have to answer some of mine."

I swallowed and nodded. That was only fair. Unfortunately, I might not actually be able to.

He lifted a finger, signaling the first one. "Where did you hear the name *Katharian*?"

I glanced at the title bar above his head. It had changed a bit from the first time I saw it. It now read:

Kesstel Noblé

Katharian

Lv: ???

I opened my mouth. I didn't know if the System would let me answer, but it was only fair to pay him back for his information, even if his answers just caused more questions. "My Guide System told me."

His eyes narrowed. "Is that so?" He frowned at me.

It took everything I had not to squirm under his piercing stare, but I didn't volunteer any more information. He'd asked a question and that was the answer. Really, anyone's System could tell them the same thing. Only, I had a feeling that Kesstel was a bit like me and other Hunters couldn't see his real title; there wasn't any other reason I could think of which would make him care so much about why I could see it. Then again, it didn't make me very comfortable knowing he could see my real title bar, either. Could he even see my level?

He held up another finger. "Second question. How did a nearly normal human become a fledgling Warrior of Mist?"

My eyes widened. "So you really know what they are?"

"Answer the question first." His lips thinned.

I bit my lips, wondering how much I could say. "I don't really know," I admitted honestly, looking down at my fingers twisting in my lap. A sense of uncertainty built up in me, questioning everything I was. What if I was a mistake? What if it was an accident that the System attached to me? "I got pulled into a Portal Burst. Just when I was about to die, I heard a voice, then I woke up in the Hunter hospital after being unconscious for four days. And I was different. It was only recently that I found out I'm being trained as a Warrior of Mist."

"How recent?"

"A couple months ago." I looked up at him. "I don't even really know what a Warrior of Mist is. But you do?"

"Somewhat." He ran a hand through his hair and sighed. "Well, that explains a couple things," he muttered.

I scowled at him. "Well, what about you? What is a Katharian?"

For a moment, he didn't move. "Are you sure you want to know? Knowledge is a one-way door."

I paused. I couldn't deny a part of me wanted to run away and forget everything I'd just seen in the Gate and learned since—the part of me that was a scared little girl groping in the dark for someone to hold on to. That weakness inside of me that I wanted to kill so badly it hurt. But for once, the rational side of me agreed with her. Instinctively, I knew that whatever was happening was completely over my head, and I wasn't strong enough to survive if I got sucked into it. I'd worked so hard to have a nice, easy life. And I could still choose to cover my ears and have that.

Only . . .

I glanced at the title over Kesstel's head and remembered watching that Hunter turn into a monster. "What's a Katharian?" I asked again.

He was quiet for a couple seconds before he softly answered, "Me. The world I'm from was called Kathar."

I gaped at him. "*What?*"

He reached out to the bush beside him and broke off a twig like he was picking a flower. "You know how the Gates are on Earth." He leaned over and drew a circle in the dirt at our feet, writing *Earth* inside it. "Every Gate leads to its own individual Gate Vale wherein the Hunters kill monsters, yes?" He drew an oval next to the circle and labeled it *Vales*. Then he drew several arches, connecting the circle to the oval. "And each Gate Vale has portals around it which open every night and refill the Vale with monsters. You know all this, correct?" He drew little circles around the oval to represent the portals. He looked up and waited for my response.

I nodded. This was something everyone knew.

He looked back at his picture. "What Earthians don't understand is that there is a spherical being on the other side of the Vales." He drew a big circle nearly twice the size of the Earth. Then he started to draw arches attaching the portals to the new circle. "This being, this interdimensional planet, is a parasite which swallows other planets. It consumes other worlds in order to survive." He sat back and faced me. "My world was devoured several planets ago."

It took me a second to wrap my mind around what he said. My hands clenched and unclenched. "Wait, what?"

"These Gates are its 'mouth.'" He wiggled two fingers in quotation marks. "They attach to a planet and fill it with parasitic magic. When the planet's soul weakens enough, it gets swallowed up by the parasite. Any remaining land is turned into a portal, and the inhabitants who survive transform into monsters to be set loose on the next planet." His foot swiped across the ground, erasing the picture. His gaze bore into mine. "Do you believe me?"

I gaped at him. This was crazy. What he was saying was crazy. He was crazy. There was no way something like that was happening. There was no giant parasite monster planet on the other side of the Gate waiting to eat our planet and then turn people into . . .

"Why did that Hunter turn into a monster just now?" My voice was weak.

"Energy crystals are the main way this parasite pollutes a planet. Monsters carry the crystals out of the Gates, and they get spread all over the world. The crystals are a part of the parasite, like scales it sheds, so when a Hunter is infected with that magic, they change into monsters. But it only works when there's enough magic around them to prompt the change. There's not enough magic in the air on Earth yet, but it has to be getting close. Especially with the effective method you Earthians have created to assist the parasite in spreading the crystals."

Oh my god. My gut twisted painfully as I thought about the thousands, if not millions of crystals that were taken out of the Gates every day. "Why haven't you told anyone?" I jumped to my feet. "People—we—need to know."

Kesstel shrugged and looked in the direction of the Hunter's Association building. "I did. They didn't believe me." He paused. "They never do," he said softly before looking back at me. "And it's not like I could lead them to where the parasite is. It's on the other side of a portal, but I don't know which one. If I did, I wouldn't be here right now."

How could he be so . . . so nonchalant?! This was a huge problem. If he was right, then Earth was going to collapse! It was going to get eaten by a huge parasitic planet, and any survivors would be turned into monsters. "You could have shown them how people change . . . " My voice died out as I realized what a horrible thing I was suggesting.

"Who would volunteer?" He smirked. "Once you turn into a monster, there's no turning back. It's either a death sentence or a life as a mindless eating machine. The crystals inside them drive them to attack the current intelligent species which rules the current infected planet."

Current intelligent species. I'd heard that before. A chill went down my spine as I remembered a huge, red orc laughing as it slowly sliced me to death. My left hand crossed over my chest, and I gripped my right arm, trying to keep my body from shivering.

"The Warriors of Mist"—Kesstel's voice broke through my thoughts— "are an elite group from a world the parasite has already devoured."

My eyes widened, and I slowly turned my head toward him.

He opened his mouth, then paused and looked away, his smile taking on a bitter feel. Suddenly, his expression dropped, his posture straightened. With a quick glance, he checked the watch on his wrist and sighed. "I have a prior engagement I'm needed at. Any more questions will have to wait. I'll leave first."

He'd quickly drawn me in with that tantalizing detail of where Warriors of Mist came from, and now he was leaving. My head was spinning with information as I watched him walk away with a lazy, predatory gait. The magic dome around us popped as he exited it, and the sounds of the city came rushing back to my ears.

I gaped after him. Kesstel didn't even look back as he disappeared from my sight.

I sank back against the bench, the pastry box inches from my thigh. I felt like a statue, frozen in place, my mind a shocked block of rock.

Why didn't I know this before? My System had to know already, especially if it had already seen the parasite swallow other worlds. Its own world. Why was I learning this from Kesstel, a man the System kept warning me away from, and not from the System itself?

A System window popped open. [**I am limited. Too much interaction will reveal you to it. You are simply not strong enough to protect yourself yet.**]

I stared at the message. "It" had to be the parasitic planet. But something else caught my attention. This was the first time the System had used the word *I*. I kind of suspected already that unlike the Guide Hunters used, there was a person behind my System. But this was the first time it admitted to it.

Who are you? I thought to the System. *What do you want me to do?*

[**Get stronger.**]

After that, the System didn't respond to any of my questions.

Jynn Devhro

Rank	D	**Level**	17
		EXP to Next Level	462
HP	98/259	**Stat Points**	0
MP	45/121		
Strength	41 (+10)	**Agility**	34
Magic	30	**Perception**	32
Constitution	34 (+10)	**Intelligence**	27

Skills	**Abilities**
Throw	Mist (Improved) (20 ft)
Critical Hit	Feather Step
Quick Hit	Regen (Limited)
Mirror	

CHAPTER 37

My mind was still a mess, but my feet were steady as I marched up to the Hunter's Association building. This time, I didn't go around the side but walked right up to the front door and pushed it open.

It was as quiet as a museum inside. The interior was gorgeous, the floor and ceiling made of white and gray marble. Banners with the symbols of the major guilds hung from soft, muted gray walls, and ferns and small trees were placed artistically throughout the entrance.

I reached a high-ceilinged room. In the middle of it was a large circle of uniform marble pillars which supported a tall dome that rose in awing glory. Light beamed down from artistically arched windows on the spire and illuminated a man-size energy crystal at the center of the pillars. Blue opalescent rainbows refracted off, casting a dazzling display all over the room.

This was hands down the most gorgeous building I'd ever been in, but a cold, oppressive feeling marred the room as if there was a weight crushing my chest, making it hard to breathe. All I wanted to do was leave—and most of it had to do with the energy crystal in the middle of the room. That thing was dangerous, not only to Hunters but to all inhabitants of Earth. Yet here it was, boastingly on display.

A woman cleared her throat, drawing my attention to the side. A C-ranked Hunter sat behind a large dark wood desk. Her black hair was pinned back just as smooth and smart as the gray suit she wore. A bronze plaque on the table read Secretary Mae. The barest hint of a smile graced her lips. "Can I help you?" Her words were barely more than a whisper, but even that sounded too loud for this room.

Now that I wasn't so distracted by the energy crystal, I finally noticed the A-ranked Hunters flanking the doors I was standing in front of;

another A rank stood next to the secretary. All of them wore black suits, looking neat and orderly. Their cold eyes bore into my body before slightly shifting away. Apparently, I was deemed nonthreatening.

I glanced at them before walking to Secretary Mae. It was my second time talking to a government official today; I just prayed it went better than last time, but I didn't even really know where to start.

Stopping in front of her desk, I took a deep breath. "I'd like to see the Hunter's Council president, please." My words were polite, but my tone was strong. If I wanted to get my point across, I couldn't show any weakness. In a place like this, it was just asking to be eaten alive.

The woman's eyes swept over my figure. Suddenly, I was very aware of how rumpled I still looked, since I hadn't taken any time to clean up after going into the Gate. I was covered in dried blood, with scabs showing through several tears in my clothing. My hair probably looked like a knotted mess. Then her eyes flicked up to the title over my head.

"Do you have an appointment?" Secretary Mae asked in a cool, professional tone.

"No." I swallowed. "But this is urgent. There's a huge threat to everyone—Hunters, humans, the whole of the Earth. The Council needs to know."

Just like that, I had the attention of all the Hunters around me. The man standing next to the desk released his pressure; it washed over me like a tidal wave, sucking the air out of my lungs.

I gritted my teeth and refused to bow to his power.

"What do you mean?" the secretary demanded.

I focused on her as if the man at her side didn't exist. "Energy crystals are dangerous. We need to get rid of all of them." Obviously, there was more to it than that, but I wanted to tell that directly to the Council. The pressure immediately let up, and I finally took a full breath. God, did he have to do that? Did he think I was going to lie or something?

Secretary Mae stared at me incredulously, just like the Hunter at her side. I was sure the man and woman behind me were using the same expression.

"Every single country on Earth," the receptionist said slowly, "uses energy crystals as a power source. They literally enable us to live. And you're saying they are dangerous?"

Just like that, any thoughts of succeeding withered and died. Even so, I wasn't going to give up just yet. "Yes. I need to see the Council and tell them about it."

Secretary Mae hummed low. "Electricity is dangerous. So is coal and nuclear energy, yet they've been used. Are still being used in some cases. Since there is power in energy crystals, it's obvious they would be dangerous if not properly handled. But that isn't a reason to stop using them. Unlike coal and nuclear energy, they don't damage the environment."

"No, they are worse. They're dangerous to people and the world." I started to step forward but stopped when the A-ranked Hunter at her side narrowed his eyes in warning. I wasn't going to do anything to her; I just felt like I was yelling in this quiet place, so I wanted to get closer so I could speak lower. "Like, really, *really* dangerous. I need to tell the Council. We need to stop collecting energy crystals and put all the ones we have back inside the Gates."

The female Hunter behind me coughed, holding back a laugh from the sound of it.

Secretary Mae frowned at me and tilted her head to the side. "Your job, as a Hunter, is to kill the monsters that threaten the lives of everyone on Earth. Your other job is to collect energy crystals from the Gate and bring them out for the betterment of our society. Hunters who refuse to abide by this task without special permission to make other contributions to society are sent to a safe location to make sure they aren't a danger to the global population."

God, she was actually able to make Hunter prison—the Holding Place—sound pleasant. This *safe location* was a holding facility where traitorous and dangerous Hunters were kept separated from everyone and everything, doing menial chores for the rest of their days. Behind unbreakable bars and under the watch of unforgiving guards.

Her eyes narrowed. "Are you saying you want to stop being a Hunter, stop collecting crystals, and are willing to take on this punishment?"

My eyes widened. "No, no, that's not what I meant." Dying would be better than being sent to the Holding Place. My family would suffer without me no matter what, but at least they wouldn't be shamed for having a defector in their family tree. But neither of those options were something I could do.

I sighed and rapped my knuckles on my thigh. "I know it sounds crazy, but the energy crystals can turn people into monsters." Now the woman behind me flat-out laughed. What was the use of talking to these people? "I just need to see the Council president."

The secretary tapped on her computer screen. "The earliest appointment available is in four and a half months." She glanced at me. "Do you want me to put your name down?"

Four months? My stomach sank like a rock in a black pit. So many things could happen by then. Even so, I gave her my information and left, ignoring the ridicule on the faces of the guards.

I knew what I said sounded crazy. I didn't even want to admit it, but I also couldn't deny that I'd watched a man turn into a monster either. Between that and the System's communication, I knew Kesstel's words were true. And there had to be more to it than that.

At the top of the stairs, I heard a peal of laughter and looked over.

Speak of the devil, I thought. Kesstel and the glamorous Bethany Wilks walked around the corner of the Hunter's Association building. She looked up at him, her red lips in a bright smile. So she's what he had to run off to.

I stared at him and the red title bar over his head. I kind of understood now why it was red. If Kesstel wasn't from Earth, then my System must have assumed he was a monster. I imagined that if I met other people who were from other worlds, their titles would be red, too.

But if that was something which could happen easily, wouldn't the population know about it?

I couldn't help but glance around at the city from atop the steps. How many people were like Kesstel?

I felt a pressure settle on me and knew he was staring at me. I couldn't resist looking down at him. When we were talking, his posture had been relaxed, and there was even a bit of emotion on his face. But now he was a timeless robot, his face nothing but a blank slate.

There was nothing about him which revealed he wasn't from Earth. From his looks to his mannerisms to the way he dressed, there was nothing that said he was different.

Just like m— I forcibly cut off that train of thought.

Why didn't he try harder to convince them? He was an S. Though I didn't know which one he was, the words of someone like him would be taken a hell of a lot more seriously than those of an "E" like me. I bet if he walked up to Secretary Mae, she'd bend over backward to help him see the Council immediately.

I couldn't help but scowl at the thought.

Kesstel's steps slowed down until he was behind Bethany. He still hadn't taken his eyes off me. His brows pulled together, and he frowned in response to my glare.

The mage next to him stopped and turned back to Kesstel before following his gaze to me. For a second, she froze, obviously recognizing me from the other day. Then her eyes narrowed, and she glared at me, shifting a little in front of Kesstel.

She turned around and grabbed his arm.

I rolled my eyes and turned the opposite direction. It was nearly dinnertime, and there was loot I needed to sell. Plus, I still had to figure out what to do with the pastries in my Items Bag. I couldn't just throw them away . . . but it also pained me to give them to someone else. I knew how good they were, and I wanted them. Could I really bring myself to eat something from the enemy?

I moaned and scrubbed my hands through my hair, making my ponytail even worse. Ah, I really should try to make myself look a little better if I was going to walk around Eden.

Pulling the elastic out of my hair, I used my hands to straighten my hair as much as I could without a mirror.

"Oh my god! Jynn!"

I turned toward the sound, the elastic hanging from my mouth and my hands in my hair.

A second later, a young woman glommed on to me. Her arms locked around my waist while we staggered back, effectively imprisoning me. "Jynn! Jynn! They said you were dead!" Then she promptly burst into tears.

CHAPTER 38

What just happened? I wiggled around until I finally got a glimpse of her face. "Ah, Emma?" I mumbled around the elastic in my mouth and her long brown hair in my face.

She stepped back and shoved at the tears streaming down her cheeks as she continued to sob. "Blake said the red orcs killed you before you could get through. He . . . lied! Why would he lie? But you're alive!" Her words were broken up between sobs and gasps for air. "I'm so glad you're alive." She flung her arms around me again.

This time, I was ready to catch her. I gave up on my hair and looped one arm around her while I took the elastic out of my mouth. "I'm glad I'm not dead, too." I pushed all thoughts about dangerous crystals to the back of my mind and patted her back gently as she slowly stopped crying.

"The portal collapsed as soon as Blake stepped out." Emma let go for real this time and took a couple steps away. "How did you get back?"

I sighed. "Ah, I don't really know. I blacked out and woke up in the hospital."

Emma's dark eyes widened. "A miracle."

She'd changed a lot since the last time I saw her. My last picture of Emma was of a timid girl in misshaped armor. It was a far cry from now—outside of the tears that clung to her lashes. Her light armor was fitted to her figure, the pattern welded on the reddish-pink metal shaped like obscure triangles, or maybe arrowheads pressed together. Her once long brown hair had been trimmed and was now tied back in a high ponytail. But the biggest difference was the battle-ready and confident way she carried herself.

I smiled at her, remembering the way this girl had literally carried me on her back to save my life. "Something like that." I glanced over her shoulder at the B-ranked young man in navy-blue heavy armor standing there. Since he hadn't moved away yet, I could only assume he was with her.

"Oh, right." Emma blinked and motioned to him. "Jynn, this is Mason. He's part of the team I'm on. Mason, this is Jynn. I've told you about her, remember?"

That was the second time she'd introduced me like that. Did I really make that much of an impression on her? I nodded a greeting to him. I couldn't say I was the best at names and faces, but I knew for sure he wasn't part of Blake's group when we went into the portal.

If Mason and his group were responsible for the healthy glow of this girl, they couldn't be bad people.

Mason nodded back politely, the sun shining almost blond on his light brown hair. "Nice to meet you."

"You too." I turned back to Emma. "Are you still with the Stone Mace guild?"

She nodded. "Yeah. I'm contracted with them for another four years. But I did drop out of Blake's team." She paused and shook her head. "Goodness' sake, Jynn, your hair is a mess." She stepped forward and took the elastic from my hand.

I blinked at her.

A comb appeared in Emma's hand, and she started to work the knots out of my hair. "But yeah, I quit Blake's team. You could say our time in the portal and watching how he handled things was educating. A lot of people said I was stupid for leaving. Apparently, it's hard to get in with him, but I didn't want to partner up with a group of people I couldn't trust." She twisted the elastic in my hair and stepped back. "Done!" She returned to Mason and beamed up at him. "But then I met Mason, and he invited me to join his group. It's been great since."

He smiled down at her. "We're glad to have you."

I looked back and forth between them. I could practically see the little hearts floating in the air around them. *Ooh. Must be nice to be young.* I was so happy to see she'd had a happy ending. "I'm glad you found someone you could trust."

"Hey, Jynn." Emma turned her grin to me. "How about you join us for a couple days? I know you are a lower rank and not in the guild, but you're trustworthy. I'm sure my group wouldn't mind, right?" She looked up and nearly killed Mason with her hopeful smile.

He stiffened, panic setting in his cute brown eyes as he obviously tried to think of a way to handle this. He glanced just over my head, obviously noting my rank again. "Um, sure. A couple days won't hurt." He looked like he'd just swallowed a fly. Painfully.

Okay, she still had some learning to do. Poor guy. Luckily for him, I was the one Emma invited. "Ah, thanks, but I'll pass." There were just too many things I had to hide to ever want to work with a partner. Besides, I appreciated Emma, but I wasn't going to let my life rest in the hands of another person ever again.

Mason looked down, trying to hide his relief.

Emma frowned, obviously hurt. She wore all her thoughts on her sleeve still, didn't she?

"I could take a couple days off from my group and spend them with you. It could be just the two of us, and we don't have to do anything dangerous. I just wanna hang out. For the longest time, I thought that if I just ran a little faster, held on a little tighter so we didn't separate, that you wouldn't have died. And I . . . " Her voice died out.

I frowned as guilt weighed on my heart. I didn't know she would beat herself up like this. Wasn't it supposed to be easy to forget about a little E like me? I glanced away then sighed. "I don't partner up," I said, giving her a small smile. "But we could exchange contact info, and you can message me whenever you want. We could hang out after the workday is over."

I almost couldn't believe these words were coming out of my mouth. I'd never asked for someone else's number or thought there would be someone I wouldn't mind seeing in my contact list.

Emma's face shone like the sun, and she quickly pulled out her Guide like she was scared I would change my mind if she wasn't fast enough.

Swallowing a laugh, I opened my own System window to accept her information. Moments later, my contact list had its first friend contact.

"Are you done hunting for the day?" Emma asked, glancing at my rumpled appearance.

I nodded. "Just heading home." After the crappy day I had, all I wanted to do was take a hot bath and lay in bed. But first I had to sell my stuff. Only, I didn't want Emma following me. I'd told the armorer, Maveric, I was in charge of selling the loot for my group, which was why I was bringing in better and better stuff. But I couldn't get away with that excuse if Emma and Mason were there. "What about you?"

"Kind of." Emma smiled up at Mason. "The Stone Mace guild is going to be in charge of a large operation in Feng Jungle in a couple days, and we need to pick up some supplies for it."

So I was crashing their date.

Mason hummed low and tapped on the back of her head softly with his knuckle. "Hey."

She gasped and covered her mouth. "Oh, right." She laughed and dropped her hands. "But I trust Jynn a hundred percent."

What a weighty sentence. I didn't know if I should laugh or cry as the pressure set in. It looked like I wasn't just crashing their date but was also learning about things I shouldn't. Sometimes, there were missions that guilds took on inside the Gate, big ones which usually involved a lot of money where that guild had exclusive access to a certain location in Gate Vale for a period of time. Missions like that were usually kept hush-hush.

It was time to go, before Emma got us both into trouble.

I quickly bid them goodbye and promised to respond whenever Emma contacted me. So many shocking things had happened today, I was grateful for the distraction. I was emotionally exhausted, but I couldn't help the small smile that curled my lips as I walked away.

CHAPTER 39

The System's timer dinged. I opened my eyes and read the message. **[Cultivate for thirty minutes—Completed.]**

Instead of jumping to my feet, I stayed on the branch with my legs crossed and my fingers pressed together. My gaze swept over the thick mist drifting through the semibarren trees of Fogmire. That mist swirled around me, some of it even floating to and disappearing inside my chest, even though I'd finished cultivating—a trick that just activated a couple days ago.

When I'd first started using Mist, I had to put effort into cultivating and drawing the moist particles *into* me. Now, the mist was drawn *to* me, ever-flowing as long as I stood in it. It wasn't nearly as effective as cultivating, like a barely there sip on my palate instead of a flowing stream, but I still enjoyed the feeling.

However, my mind right now wasn't on my own cultivation but on Miles's from yesterday. And what it meant. I just couldn't get rid of the uneasy feeling.

Sighing, I bent over to rub my palms on my forehead. I should be uneasy. My planet was in danger, and my own people were happily helping it along.

I hadn't completely given up on telling everyone about it. Last night, I'd borrowed Henry's computer and made an anonymous post on the Hunter's forums about the dangers of the energy crystals. Within an hour, hundreds of people had responded negatively to it, and the administrators pulled the post down. So I made another one, only to end with the same results. Only, that time, my account got blocked for a month.

I was starting to understand what Kesstel said about how no one ever believed him. It made sense—I mean, the very livelihood of billions of people depended on energy crystals.

So what should I do now?

A monster entered my range of awareness. My eyes narrowed, and I turned my head to the right. Even though the mist was thick, it didn't impede my vision. If anything, it helped me see things, as if the dew particles created a 3D image in my mind.

Forty feet away, a large lizard covered in white opalescent scales hopped onto the branch of a dark tree. Thick black claws gripped the bark as the large dog-size monster walked headfirst down the trunk, a bright blue tongue slipping in and out of its mouth.

A lizard. Just like what Miles had turned into.

Its title bar popped open: [**Frost Anole Lv19**].

The lizard monster reached the ground and slowly moved toward me. It paused and raised its nose in the air, its blue tongue flicking in and out again, before creeping toward me once more. Its feet, with toes and claws twice the length of my fingers, moved silently over the moist ground. Honestly, if I didn't have an advantage with the fog, I'd have no idea it was there.

I slowly stood up and pulled out my kindjal. A second later, I held a short sword in each hand. Taking aim, I threw one of them at it, but just before the tip pierced its neck, the frost anole dodged to the side; the blade sank through the monster's shoulder, pinning it to the ground.

The lizard hissed and screeched in pain while its scaled body writhed, curling against the weapon. The blade lifted out of the ground as the anole twisted, and as soon as its white belly was revealed, I lunged down. Just like before, it dodged out of the way at the last second, evading my attack. I cleanly missed, leaving a gouge in the soft soil.

The monster lashed out with its front claws. I blocked with my blade, only to be smacked in the chest with its tail. I grunted, all the air beaten out of my body as I stumbled back, but I kept my eyes on the lizard. It lunged forward, mouth wide open and angling for my head, its pointed white teeth bright against its black gums.

I froze as yesterday's scene replayed in my mind. I'd watched a man turn into a lizard, then shoved my kindjal down its throat. And Kesstel's words—God, did this monster use to be a human, too?

I Feather Stepped back and brought my kindjal up to block. The frost anole bit down on the blade, ice forming around its mouth and spreading across the crystalized metal. Twisting, I wrenched the kindjal free and kicked the monster right in the skull. It fell back a couple feet and shook its head, as if confused.

But I didn't try to get closer. I couldn't help but stare at it. I swore to myself when I started this journey that I wouldn't get stronger on the blood of a human. But if all the monsters in the Gate used to be human, wasn't I doing just that?

My foot shifted back; I wasn't even aware of it until the ball of my foot landed on the ground. My eyes widened in shock. I was . . . hesitating.

The frost anole instantly caught the scent of my weakness, and in a flash, it jumped at me.

I swung around and leaped into the tree, paused for a second, then fled as fast as I could through the mist.

An hour later, I sat on top of a red-bricked building overlooking Gate Square and watched the activity below. When I first had the impulse to Feather Step up here, I thought I was being silly, but I'd needed to get away from the bustle and noise below—maybe then I could think clearly. The black Gate loomed ahead, just as intimidating at this height as it was when I was on the ground next to it. I'd rarely associated it with anything good, but right now, it seemed more sinister than ever before.

If I was to believe Kesstel's words, there was a parasitic planet on the other side of the Gate. One that could turn people into monsters—no, *it was* turning people into monsters with energy crystals. And according to my daily tasks, I still needed to destroy five of those.

I sighed and shoved my hands through my hair, messing up my pony-tail. It had all been good and fine when I didn't know the monsters used to be human.

Kesstel had said that after someone turned into a monster, there was no way to turn them back. But was that really true? If a Hunter could trans-form one way, why not transform back? What if every monster I killed was someone who had a family waiting for them at home? A brother or sister, a mom or dad desperate for news of their missing loved one?

My sigh turned into a moan of frustration as guilt tore at me. I knew what I needed to do—the System's daily tasks were very clear on that mat-ter—but I . . .

Slowly, I stood up and—

Ding! [**For failing to comply with the Daily Task, a 24-hour Punish-ment Period is now in effect.**]

* * *

My eyes cracked open. I slowly focused on the off-white ceiling above me. It was the same ceiling I'd stared at every morning for the last year, so why did the act of staring at it feel different?

No, I was what felt different. My body felt . . . heavy. Sluggish.

I slowly sat up and dropped my face into my hands. What was going on? I wasn't poisoned yesterday, and all my injuries had been healed by my Limited Regen ability.

The System dinged. I dropped my hands and looked up.

[**Daily Task: Cultivate for thirty minutes.**]

[**Daily Task: Destroy five Energy Crystals. Upon completion, stats will be returned.**]

[**Task: Prevent the Energy Crystal in Feng Jungle from crossing into Earth.**]

I gasped. "What?" *Stats will be returned?* What did that mean?

My stomach sank and twisted painfully as I pulled up my Stats window. Oh my god. I was still level seventeen, but my stats had been reduced to what they were before I had started to level up.

I stared at the single-digit stats and dinky little 12 HP bar, feeling numb.

The bottom of the screen read: [**Failure to complete yesterday's Daily Task has incurred a Punishment Period. All stats have been reduced to their original value until the next Daily Task is completed or after twenty-four hours, whichever ends first. Abilities and Skills are still available.**]

That's why I felt so odd. I'd gotten used to the feeling of being stronger. Of the feeling of power coursing through every muscle as I moved. Of my radius of awareness being wide enough to feel any threat within forty feet of me. Now, suddenly, I was back to where I'd started: a weakling with no awareness, just waiting to be picked off. It was horrible, seeing all my hard work suddenly disappear.

I stared at the message at the bottom of the screen, fully understanding what it meant. If I wasn't going to do what the System wanted, I didn't deserve the benefits it gave me. If I didn't complete today's task, the punishment period would start all over again. It allowed me to keep my abilities and skills, but if I didn't complete the next daily task, those were probably going to be taken away next. How long would it be before I lost the System all together?

My insides froze. No. *No!* I couldn't lose the System. I had just gotten my life together; I was finally making enough money that I wasn't losing sleep and nourishment trying to figure out how to help my family. I was finally becoming confident in myself, thinking that maybe I was worth being alive.

If I lost the System, I'd be a nothing again. I couldn't go back to that. I didn't want to be weak anymore.

My hands fisted together until my palms ached. Closing my eyes and taking a deep breath, I slowly let the air out, forcing my panicked emotions to calm down. I'd gotten comfortable with the System and its seemingly lax rules. I took for granted it not punishing me the last time I didn't fulfill the daily task, when the Gate Surge happened. But there was a line, and I'd crossed it yesterday. Blatant disobedience.

I wasn't mad at the System for my punishment. I was horrified at knowing I was a nothing again, but at the same time, it felt like a heavy weight was taken off my shoulders.

I'd been stressing about how to figure out which monsters used to be humans. About thinking that I was tearing apart someone's family, and if I should really do it or not. I was under the illusion I actually had a choice in the matter.

But I didn't.

Even if they used to be human, if the System told me to destroy the energy crystal, that's what I was going to do. There was a giant monster on the other side of the Gate Vale waiting to absorb my planet. Every crystal I destroyed kept it at bay. It was a drop in the ocean, but that was my task. Prevent the crystals from getting into Earth.

I finally looked at the last task that had popped up.

[**Task: Prevent the Energy Crystal in Feng Jungle from crossing into Earth.**]

It didn't say *Daily* on it. So did that mean I could take as much time as I needed on it?

I frowned. I'd heard about Feng Jungle recently, but where?

As I thought, I got up and walked to my closet. My hand paused just before I touched a shirt hanging in there. *Ah*, wasn't that where Emma said the Stone Mace guild was going to go tomorrow, or the next day?

Slowly, I pulled the shirt from the hanger and put it on. The Feng Jungle was a long way away from the Gate's entrance. Since cars didn't work in the Gate and horses were moving targets, in order to get to the farther away places, magic was required. It was something I'd never done, since I'd never been paired with a mage.

The Stone Mace guild was going there for a special mission. While I changed into some pants, my mind raced over past events. Wasn't it just last year that another guild carried out a special mission which brought a car-size crystal out of the Gate? Was that what the Stone Mace guild was doing? Bringing a huge crystal out? That would probably be the energy crystal I was supposed to keep from getting to Earth.

I opened my contacts and looked at Emma's number. It was time to phone a friend.

Since I didn't have my own cell phone yet, I went to Henry's office to use the phone there. I glanced at the clock. Habit made me a morning person, but I didn't know if Emma was too. I hoped I wasn't waking her up too early.

"Hello?" her soft voice carried through the speaker.

"Hey, Emma, it's Jynn." I paused and tapped on the desk, trying to think of how to word what I wanted.

"Jynn! Good morning!" Instantly, Emma's voice was amped up to a thousand watts. "Oh my goodness, I didn't think you'd call me so soon."

"Yeah, about that." I paused. "I want to ask a favor from you."

"Of course, anything for you," she said without hesitating.

I blinked, completely taken aback.

Emma, I thought, aching inside. *You really shouldn't be so fast at promising things. You don't even know what I'm going to say!*

I took a deep breath and focused on what was important. "You said a couple days ago that you were going to Feng Jungle with your guild? I, ah, I've always wanted to see it. It's not a place I can get to by myself, you know? So I hoped that you'd let me go with you?" I tried to keep my voice as longing and sweet as I could, selling *cute* with all my guts to get what I wanted.

A disgusted shiver shook my body. God, I couldn't believe I was acting like that, but I had to get to Feng Jungle somehow. For the first time, I actually felt like a leech. Other Es attached to groups and guilds all the time, doing petty work so they could brag about the places they'd been and showing off the "free" energy crystals they'd earned to other Es. It was something I swore I'd never do, but here I was, leeching off my only friend.

I dropped my head to the desk and started bonking my forehead on the wood.

"Oh!" Emma sounded surprised, then she hummed in thought. "Ah, well, I'd have to ask. I'm sure that Mason wouldn't mind me bringing a friend. Other Hunters bring people all the time." I had a feeling that Mason wouldn't say no to anything she asked. Sadly for him, I doubted Emma had figured that out yet. "I'm glad you called now. We're leaving in an hour."

My eyes widened, and I froze, head flat on the desk. They'd leave in an hour . . . and I was on probation. I might be going to one of the toughest locations in Gate Vale, where I needed to kill five monsters to fill my daily quota, and only with my beginner stats.

Jynn Devhro

Rank	D	**Level**	17
		EXP to Next Level	462
HP	12/12	**Stat Points**	0
MP	5/5		
Strength	8 (+10)	**Agility**	10
Magic	8	**Perception**	12
Constitution	8 (+10)	**Intelligence**	8

Skills	**Abilities**
Throw	Mist (Improved) (20 ft)
Critical Hit	Feather Step
Quick Hit	Regen (Limited)
Mirror	

CHAPTER 40

I remember when I was a child, sitting on my mom's lap and watching a celebration on TV. The Hunter's Association Headquarters building had just been completed, marking the ten-year anniversary since the Gates opened and humanity had clawed its way back from extinction. It looked like a palace made out of smooth white granite, with pillars and a spire in the middle. Hunters dressed in fancy armor and mage robes filled the square in front of the new building, and colorful magical displays filled the air like fireworks as everyone celebrated.

I had craned my neck and wiggled around the couch, thinking that if I looked at the TV screen from a different angle, I would see my dad in the crowd. I never did, but I wasn't too disappointed. After all, my dad was one of the Hunter heroes who fought real monsters and kept the world safe. Just like the heroes in my picture books.

A couple months later, my dad died, and the sparkly rose-tinted glasses I saw the world through cracked and peeled like a cheap dollar store trick.

I never thought that one day—and so many unexpected twists and turns in my life later—I'd be standing here, surrounded by powerful Hunters and listening to the president of the Stone Mace guild talking.

"Is everyone ready?" President Price asked. He surveyed the crowd of Hunters waiting at the bottom of the steps of the guild. As an A-ranked tank, his stature was impressive. Bold black-and-red armor amplified the bulk of his muscular body, making him appear larger than life. His squared features were handsome in a strong, mature way, with full lips and narrow eyes.

His dark gaze landed on me for a second. He frowned briefly, obviously wondering why there was an E-ranked Hunter mixed in with his elites, before looking away.

I let out a silent breath and shifted, trying to ease the tension in my body. I used to struggle under the oppressive auras of strong Hunters daily. It felt like a boulder pressing on my chest, making it hard to breathe. Because of the System, that edge had dulled. But now, in my weakened state—a direct result of my own rebellious actions—the crushing predatory threat I felt from other Hunters was back in full force. Especially during the brief moment the guild leader had sent his displeasure at me.

"Are you nervous, Jynn?" Emma whispered as she shifted closer to me. Her dark eyes were bright, and the excited flush on her cheeks was the same reddish pink as the light armor she wore. The white Guide pearl half embedded in her right temple winked and flashed in the sun as she shifted.

I smiled at her to hide how much I was dying inside and shook my head, my pale brown hair swaying in its ponytail. The whole mission had been laid out in the confidential agreement I signed fifteen minutes ago—we were going to Feng Jungle, where we'd find a giant energy crystal which had been sighted there, and we'd bring it back to Eden.

And I was taking advantage of my closest friendship so I could secretly screw up the entire mission. Such a jerk move.

Emma beamed at me, completely ignorant to how she'd been scammed. "Don't worry about a thing. Just keep close to me, and nothing bad will happen."

The gazes of six surrounding Hunters zeroed in on me, five of which were hostile and one patiently neutral. Mason, the neutral one, was the only name I remembered from everyone Emma had introduced me to. All the rest of Mason's group had clearly already labeled me as deadweight, but they were nice enough not to show it in front of Emma.

President Price cleared his throat, drawing everyone's attention back to him. "On the other side of the Gate, mages have already set up a travel route. Each group leader is responsible for handing out the route tokens to their squad. Don't lose them," he warned. "If you do, you'll have to walk back to the Gate." He didn't have to add that only an S could survive the long perilous journey back to the Gate before nightfall. "Once at Feng Jungle, teams will go to their assigned areas and search for our target. This will probably be a multiple day quest, and it won't end until we are successful. Expect the unexpected; Hunters of all ranks disappear in Feng

Jungle all the time for unknown reasons. If you come across a tough situation, call for help—losing a bit of pride is better than losing your life."

He said that, but it was obvious from the scattered expressions of smirking lips, determined brows, and a few eye rolls on Hunters around me that no one agreed with their president. The fight for hierarchy in a guild was brutal, a constant bloodbath which drove Hunters to abuse themselves just to get a cut above the person next to them. As someone who'd inherited a cushy position, I was sure Wardyn Price had never had to deal with that kind of competition, though I bet he knew it went on—and let it happen anyway. When he looked at the group, did he see the faces of the people or the dollars the guild spent in developing the Hunters he commanded?

"Let's move out!" Price motioned with his hand toward the Gate.

The Stone Mace guild cheered as one. I glanced at Emma—she threw her hands in the air and hollered with her guild. The echo of their voices ricocheted off surrounding buildings. "I'm so excited!" she squealed. "It's my first large operation."

"Mine too." I smiled weakly.

I counted heads around me. There were about a hundred Hunters, give or take. Despite today's technology, they were all dressed in armor and mage robes right out of the movies; the difference was their gear was legit. Since these people were also the best of the Stone Mace guild, their gear was high quality.

Every Hunter also had an emblem on their shoulder signifying which squad they belonged to. Whether it was a leather patch or a metal patch depended on what kind of armor he or she wore, but all patches had the Stone Mace symbol at their center from which multicolored stripes spiraled to the edges. Emma and her squad's patches were trimmed with maroon.

I, of course, had no patch at all. Nor was my armor, called Her Resistance, as glamorous. My black leather breastplate was simple, just like the matching black arm bracers and leg armor. Perfect for hiding their amazing benefits in plain sight. If someone looked closely, they could tell that my black leg bracers didn't exactly match, since they were gear I owned before I got the System.

"How often does your guild do big operations like this?" I asked as I fell in step with the rest of the crowd behind President Price.

"Ones this size?" Mason spoke up from the other side of Emma. "Not often. Our guild takes on quite a few quests, but normally, only the top five teams are involved. This is the third time in the last four years since I've been in the guild that they actually included the top eight teams." He paused and answered my silent question. "We're number seven right now."

I considered the size of the group I'd just counted. If there were only eight teams here, and Emma's team only had seven in it, she was in a considerably small team. They had five Bs and two Cs, one of which was Emma. I didn't know how many teams the guild had, but I had a feeling the reason why Emma's squad was ranked so high without an A ranker was because of their synergistic teamwork.

I could see the way they moved around each other, always shifting and pivoting, automatically keeping the healer, the mage, and the archer—Emma—at the center of the group. It was a subconscious defense formation which would maximize their potential. I couldn't be more aware of this—because I was also being shuffled into the middle of the group.

Other teams seemed to move in similar ways, always aware of where their teammates were in relation to their position. But there were other groups who strutted forward, ready to plow through no matter if they were pushing aside another team or their own teammate. I wasn't too surprised to see most groups like that consisted mostly of As. Power and pride went hand in hand; they had since the beginning of humanity and would continue until the end of the world.

The road opened up to the very wide Gate Square.

President Price led us to the Gate and motioned for us to stop.

I shifted until I could look through a gap to see what he was doing.

He walked over to clap hands then lock fists with a man standing at the head of a squad waiting at the Gate entrance.

My eyes widened as I recognized the Hunter being so buddy-buddy with the Stone Mace guild president. I could still feel his painful grip on me—the ghost of a memory—as he lifted me in the air, feel the helplessness as I was thrown to my death. For no apparent reason, that man had decided to end my life. And in doing so, he changed it forever.

Blake.

He smiled wide and clapped the president on the shoulder, his gauntlets clanging against Price's black leather pauldron. They exchanged words, and President Price laughed.

"I forgot to tell you he was coming," Emma whispered low in my ear. She knew half the story, since she was present for it. Thankfully, she missed the part where Blake tried to murder me. If not, she might have already been silenced by him. Good people didn't normally live long in

Eden. "Sorry, Jynn. Blake leads the top team in the guild. He goes on every important expedition."

Mason glanced at us and frowned.

I took a breath and forced my heart rate to slow. The top team, even though he's only a B. In fact, every single person in his team was an A, *except* for Blake. I recognized several faces standing behind him, like his right-hand man Mark and the lockpick Penny. They made such a deep impression on me that I'd never forget them, even with my lousy facial memory. But it seemed like at least half of Blake's teammates were new.

"It's fine," I muttered. It didn't matter if he was there or not. I just needed to get to Feng Jungle.

"What's up?" Mason asked, trying to be discreet though others in their group glanced at me, obviously listening in, too.

I pressed a smile to my lips. "Nothing. Really." I watched as the president walked into the Gate with Blake and his group a half a step behind. I just needed to make sure I didn't see them again.

"If it's going to complicate our teamwork, we need to know," a melee Hunter pressed. What was her name again? Lita? No, it was Reina, a versatile melee fighter from the looks of her light steel armor, and the only frontline female in the group. She frowned at me, dislike heavy in her dark blue eyes.

"It won't. I promise," Emma piped up.

Reina glanced at Emma, her face softening. She was obviously trying to be nice to Emma, but like the other people in the team, she didn't like that I was there.

The force of the crowd thinned as they filtered around us toward the Gate. I was a pebble caught in a current of power.

Pressure settled on my body, the threat coming from somewhere to my right. I glanced over, wary and a little shocked. Who knew me in this crowd enough to specifically threaten me? I mean, I was a hermit. I went out of my way to avoid people.

Two men a couple years older than me flat-out glared at me as they walked by. Their eyes stayed on my face all the way until they vanished into the Gate; an impressive feat, if I did say so myself. But what the hell? Who were they? I sucked at faces and names, but I knew for a fact that I'd never seen those men before in my entire life. They were both C ranked. Were they upset an E was going on the quest?

I glanced at where the hostile men disappeared into the Gate, then at my unfriendly temporary team members around me. This was why I avoided people.

Seriously, what did I do wrong? Breathe?

"Okay, okay." Mason drew my attention. "That's enough. I need to give you all this." He held out his hands. Eight purple stones cut into nautilus spirals appeared on his palms. "There's one for everyone. It has to be on you—in your hand or Items Bag, it doesn't matter—when you step on the magic circle; it'll take you to the one paired in Feng Jungle. Don't lose it—there aren't any extras."

I waited until everyone else took one, then I pulled a cloth napkin from my Items Bag and used it as a buffer between my skin and the crystal. I didn't know if it was okay to touch this stone; all I knew was that the System wouldn't let me touch an energy crystal. And from my experience a couple days ago, I didn't want to. I'd never forget the horror of watching a man get turned into a monster by one. Or the hopelessness when no one believed me.

I got more odd looks as I wrapped up the token in the napkin and buckled it into the pocket of my hip satchel.

I ignored them and looked at Mason, waiting for his order. Until the mission was over, I was part of their team by contract. Even though I was more comfortable as a loner, it was time to take orders like a good little Hunter.

Mason took a breath. "Here we go." He turned and led the team to the Gate.

Inside Gate Vale, four mages with Stone Mace badges on their robes were positioned fifty feet beyond the entrance. They stood around a glowing purple circle lying on the grass. A thin group of Hunters hovered around them, waiting for their turn to be transported.

I'd seen hundreds of transportation circles, but I'd never been in one. Most of them were done by mages in guilds, and no one else could use them. The Hunter's Association had some available for nonguild Hunters to use to get to the far corners of Gate Vale, but they were crazy expensive to use. Then again, I'd heard that kind of magic was also crazy hard to do, even for an A-ranked mage. Since mages specialized in a specific type of magic, wind and space mages who could cast the wind-based transportation spell were scarce. An Ability Stone could teach a mage a new type of magic—but only if they were compatible, compounded on how hard it was to find an Ability Stone at all.

We were the last group to use the transportation circle. I watched as Emma's squad stepped into the purple glow one at a time. One by one, they turned into a blur of movement that arched up and aimed for the northern corner of Gate Vale.

Mason glanced at Emma and smiled. "See you on the other side. Be careful when landing—it can be rough."

She grinned back. "Thanks for the reminder."

He stepped forward into the circle. The magic wasn't flat; it was more like a self-contained pool of light which wafted from the ground just high enough to conceal Mason's ankles. He gave Emma one last smile. The next second, the magic flashed bright, and he was nothing but a blur.

How often did people get motion sick during transport? And if they did, what happened to their bile until they arrived at their destination?

I shuddered and watched as Emma hurried forward.

"Don't worry. I'll be waiting on the other side," she promised very seriously.

I smiled. What was this, acting like my nanny? "Sure thing. I'll see you in a couple minutes."

She stepped in the magic and disappeared.

My turn. A smile pulled at my lips, and I almost felt giddy. I'd heard this was the closest a person could get to flying.

The magic cooled my feet through my boots, like I was walking in invisible snow, but I only felt it for a second before my body became weightless. It wasn't quite like Feather Stepping. When I used that ability, I felt weightless—more so with every level I gained—but I remained in control of my body.

That wasn't the case here. My body lifted up into the air. Then suddenly, the world turned in a mesh of colors around me.

CHAPTER 41

Air blasted my face, and I flinched at the force of sudden acceleration, but I didn't let my eyes close all the way; I wanted to see what was going on. From the outside, I'd seen the Hunters turn into blurs of movement. Now that I was using the transportation magic myself, I could see the thin pale-purple membrane over my body. The magic was like a cocoon on a barely visible string which arched from the Gate's location to where Feng Jungle was, which both protected and accelerated my movement at the same time.

My speed seemed to stabilize, and the g-force on my body lessened. I finally relaxed enough to notice that Emma was traveling just forty feet in front of me, also tied to that same purple magic string.

I looked down at the world below me. "Amazing." My whisper echoed back at me. I'd never been this high before with a bird's-eye view. Like a giant 3D map, Gate Vale spread out below me with vivid colors and clear borders between different locations.

Even the forests had distinctly different shades of green which clearly separated them. There wasn't any rhyme or reason to where each location was arranged, like how the sandy Sun Desert was right beside the pale green Feng Jungle, with no physical barrier between. It was just sand one step, jungle the next. Or the grayish Skull Bog on the other side of Feng Jungle, sandwiched between the rim of the golden Prine Lake, the jungle, and the mountains that encompassed Gate Vale.

I sailed right over the rainbow hovering above Prine Lake. I couldn't help but stare down at the thick golden mist which blocked the water. Right, I still needed to find time to cultivate today. Ugh, that might be hard, but I didn't dare mess up another daily task. I doubted there was any benefit in cultivating in Feng Jungle—I didn't know if there was even any mist there—but as long as I spent thirty minutes doing it, even if it proved fruitless, it would still check off the task. Lame, but it might work, right? Hopefully.

I passed over the corner of the bog and began to arch down toward the jungle. As I approached the ground, my speed decreased. I glanced at Emma ahead of me. With the speeds we were going, I would catch up to her right after we landed. If I wasn't careful, I might land right on her.

She flipped around in the air until her feet were first. Through the purple magic cocoon, she looked up and mouthed something to me. I had no idea what she said, but apparently, she was fine because she looked down at the approaching ground and the purple magic circle she was aiming at.

Following her lead, I flipped around, too. The mere thought was all I needed to cause the magic to automatically support my movement.

Emma landed on the circle and staggered forward toward Mason, who stood at the front of the team. He lifted his arms to steady her . . . but didn't need to. Emma planted her feet then spun around. She braced herself and reached out in my direction.

I landed, the momentum that had kept me airborne suddenly propelling me forward. I couldn't help stumbling from its strength. Before I could duck around her, Emma steadied me.

I blinked at her.

"Oh, thanks." I was weak, yeah, but my agility was good enough I would have been fine if she hadn't grabbed me. Ah, well, she was sweet.

She beamed at me and patted my shoulder. "You're welcome." When she turned around, I met Mason's eyes.

"Sorry," I mouthed.

He blinked as if surprised, then gave a gloomy nod; he jerked his head to indicate that I should join the rest of the team. When I was grouped with them, Mason stood in front and opened a Guide window. Flipping it around, the image on the transparent blue screen became visible to us all. The Guide detailed the Feng Jungle terrain, marked with natural paths, a tunnel-like cliff structure on the northeast side, and a river which snaked around the west side of the jungle.

Mason pointed to a purple dot at the bottom of the map. "This is where we are. The jungle has been divided into eight sections." He motioned to the dotted lines breaking up the map. "Each team is in charge of a section. Our job is to get to ours and thoroughly search it for the energy crystal. Rumor has it this crystal is as big as a car and will be divided between

Eden's and Garden City's hospitals to replace their old crystals. It's gonna improve a lot of lives. We've gotta find it."

My eyes widened. Suddenly, I felt like a jerk. I mean, this was going to power hospitals where injured and sick people were being treated. Where my own mother was lying in a coma. But I couldn't let that crystal out of Gate Vale.

The human population didn't know that energy crystals were poisoning Earth with their magic. I didn't even know about it until just a couple days ago. Unfortunately, energy crystals were also the main power source throughout the entire globe. They were such a big deal that no one believed me when I tried to warn them.

Thankfully, or maybe because it knew, the System assigned me daily tasks which involved destroying energy crystals. But task or not, a crystal the size of the one in Feng Jungle would cause a lot of damage to Earth. It was common knowledge that the bigger the crystal, the more energy it had. I didn't want to think how much magic that one had. Or how much closer the parasite planet the energy crystals came from would be to swallowing Earth if it left the Gate.

"It's for the people," Mason went on, "but there's a bonus for whoever finds it first." Mason nodded to the side. "That would be great, yeah? I don't know about you, but I'd love to upgrade my gear with all that cash." He grinned as a light of competition lit in his eyes. "Let's hope it's in our section."

Mason pointed to the upper northeast corner of the Guide map. "This is our spot. We can take this trail up until it bends." His finger slid across the screen from our location along a thick line. "Then we have to trek the rest of the way up." His finger continued to slide up through the tunneled cliffs to the space on the other side. "Keep your eyes peeled. Not just for monsters but for our target. We know it's huge, but we don't know if it's above the surface or buried in the ground like the one the Fire Bird guild dealt with last time."

Mason took a breath and looked at everyone. "We good? You all understand?" He was asking the group, but his eyes lingered on me and Emma, since it was our first time on a guild task. "Glory is great, but being alive is better," Mason said. Unlike the guild leader, there was a deep truth in Mason's words. "I hate burying my friends; let's not do that today. Work as a team, and everything will be fine. Deal?"

I nodded with the rest of the group. As of right now, I was part of their team. And until my contract was over once the mission ended, I was going to try my best to help.

Mason smiled. "Okay, let's get going."

I was shifted to the middle of the formation as I turned and finally took my first good look at Feng Jungle. It was beautiful. When I'd first walked over to join the team, I saw the random rainbow colors between the trees and thought they were flowers. I was wrong.

Between the tall trees, nestled against smooth, silvery bark, were clusters of rainbow crystals. Some of the spires were as small as my pinky nail, while others would reach up to my knee if I were standing by them. And they were everywhere—on the ground, on the branches, hiding up in huge, deep green leaves. I even saw a cluster hanging from a vine which looped two trees together. Silvery green bushes and tall grass collected on the ground, and the shrubbery naturally parted to create a path across the rich brown soil.

"It's beautiful," Emma whispered next to me. "Like a fairy tale."

The corner of my mouth kicked up. "Yeah, well, the prettier it is, the more it wants to kill you, right?"

The melee tank on the other side of me snorted. "Hell yeah. That applies to Gate Vale and women, am I right?" He smiled, his brown eyes light with humor.

I paused, surprised. Then I bobbed my head. "Right."

Reina whacked the melee tank on the back of his steel helmet. "Shut it, Billy."

"Abuse! Abuse!" he moaned, making a show of dancing down the trail in pain.

"Knock it off," Mason scolded from the lead position without pausing to see if Billy was being real or not.

A quiet settled over us. Feng Jungle's foliage began to thicken, and everyone's weapons appeared in their hands.

The forest was quiet—beautiful, but eerily quiet. There were no sounds of leaves rustling in the wind, *because* there was no wind. It made the air stagnant and stale, even though we were surrounded by visual signs of rich resources. Even the random puddles of water which reflected the rainbow crystals were perfectly still, without a ripple of disturbance. There were no sounds, no movement whatsoever.

Was it because the rest of the guild had already taken care of the monsters on the path? I could only wonder as we walked for twenty minutes before Mason suddenly stopped.

At the same time, Emma notched a silver-and-maroon arrow in her glistening silver recurve bow. She twisted to the right and drew back just as Mason motioned to the bushes on the right. She let loose her arrow as the rest of the team lowered into position; Billy didn't even flinch as it sailed right over his shoulder.

A monster leapt out of the bushes. It looked like a huge wolf, but instead of fur, it was covered in long grass. Its face and paws were silvery white, but the rest of its body was green and covered in vines. The red title above its head read: [**Verdure Wolf Lv36**].

It wasn't even all the way through the bush when Emma's arrow sank into its chest. It yelped and landed on the ground, but it kept coming at Billy, whose heavy two-handed claymore was up and ready to attack.

"Reina, Emma, left," Mason commanded just as another verdure wolf appeared on that side. "Kip with me, ahead." He raised his own sword and met a third wolf.

Billy worked together with an axe-wielding Hunter against one wolf, their heavy movements slow but flawless. As soon as Billy lifted his sword, the other man's huge, double-sided axe smashed down at the monster. When the monster attacked, one blocked while the other countered.

On the other side, Reina's lightning-quick movements and Emma's endless string of arrows kept the wolf in the defense while its HP steadily dropped. Ahead, Mason went at the final monster with his shining bastard swords while the mage, Kip, backed him up with fireballs that caused the monster to lose clumps of grass at a time.

All the while, I stood there like a plant next to the healer. At least she was waiting to help someone if they needed it. With my current strength, I literally had nothing I could contribute to the fight. I couldn't even hold the bags because everything was kept in people's Items Bags.

Just a delicate little flower who needed to be protected. So useless. So frustrating. I couldn't believe they'd agreed to let me come along.

In minutes, the monsters were dead. The healer stepped in and took care of some scratches on Reina and Mason while I helped retrieve and clean Emma's arrows. Billy and the Axe Guy dug out the energy crystals, but Mason stopped the Axe Guy when he pulled out a skinning knife and squatted in front of one of the wolves.

"Leave it. We don't have the time." Mason jerked his head down the trail.

The guy nodded slowly and stood up.

"Damn," Billy moaned and sighed down at the dead monster. "That grass fur is so cool, too. Do you think it would grow if you planted it in a garden?"

I gaped at him while Emma cringed in disgust. She grabbed me and dragged me over to Mason like she was scared my ears would get tainted if I kept listening to him.

"That is so gross, I don't even want to know the answer to that question." Kip gagged and walked over to Mason.

"Ditto." Reina caught up with us.

"What?" Billy asked when suddenly he was left behind. He hurried over and fell into place. "I mean, if you think about it, we're wearing and fighting with pieces of monsters already. What's so weird about planting—"

"I think that's enough, Billy," Reina cut in. "You're going to make Morgan sick." She glanced at the healer by me, whose cute face was starting to look as green as the carcasses we were leaving behind.

I glanced back at the dead monsters. I didn't get any EXP or drop items from them. Was that because I didn't take part in the fight even though I was in the team? Did I have to personally kill the monsters to get it? I also couldn't help but think of the energy crystals that were dug out of the monsters—the carcasses didn't disappear when they were taken away, so there was something different, either about my System or my sword, which exploded the remains when I destroyed a crystal.

But more pressing were the crystals that Mason, the leader of the group, had in his Items Bag. Now that I knew how dangerous they were, the idea that they were in Emma's friend's hands bothered me.

Emma glanced at me. "Are you okay?"

I blinked out of my thoughts and looked at her. My lips parted, ready to ask them to leave the crystals, but I found myself pausing. I was here because they let me come. I was already going to purposefully screw up their mission to the best of my abilities. Should I really try to convince them to drop hundreds of dollars' worth of crystals, too?

The violent reactions Hunters had to my online posts came to my mind. Did I really want to deal with that right now, when I was so weak? I'd never be able to survive if they abandoned me here. True, I didn't think they'd purposefully do it—for Emma's sake, at least—but they didn't have to make sure I was safe in the circle, either.

I forced a small smile on my face. "Ah, I was just thinking how impressive your guys' teamwork is. I can only think of a couple of times I've seen such flawless coordination like that."

Coward, I thought to myself. But what if Emma and her blind adoration for me believed me and no one else did? I didn't want to cause a rift between Emma and yet another team. Especially when she was in such a good group of people who obviously cared for her.

My compliment distracted Emma, and she started to whisper, telling me all about the hours they'd spent working on formations and tactical moves, and all the other things she'd learned since she'd joined the group.

Instead of shushing her, the team kept a better look out and let her ramble under her breath as much as she wanted.

CHAPTER 42

"Would you look at that?" Billy muttered under his breath.

"Why is something like this in the middle of the jungle?" Reina whispered.

Thirty minutes ago, we'd branched off the path and trekked through the jungle underbrush. Since then, we'd added six more energy crystals to the list and finally made it to the landmark that signaled the entrance to our designated search location—a dark brown plateau which towered over the trees.

In front of us was a gap between two stone slabs at least twenty feet wide. There was plenty of room to walk through the tunnel . . . if not for the thick white webs which clung to the rock walls and covered the few short trees within. The tunnel wasn't even that long, maybe fifty or sixty feet; I could see the valley on the other side. But the thought of walking through that webbing sent chills down my spine. Not even the beautiful rainbow crystals dotting the glossy white fibers could ease my agitation.

"I'm gonna burn it," Kip announced to no one. "Yep, it's gotta burn. I don't—I don't do spiders. Not their creepy legs. And their gross eyes. And their disgusting everything else." Fire spread from her fingers and pooled in her palm.

"Hold up." Mason motioned for her to stop and took a couple steps forward. With his sword at the ready, he peered into the tunnel. "I don't see or sense anything. Emma?"

She notched an arrow to her bow and stepped beside him; she must have the highest Perception stat, perfect for a natural archer. She looked around, checking every visible and nonvisible nook and cranny. "I can't sense anything, either."

"Anyone else vote that we just climb over and take the top route?" Billy wondered. "I mean, that's a trap no matter how I look at it." He motioned to the webbing, his expression just as reluctant as Kip's. "Has anyone else watched that old movie with the possessed ring and the big, evil fire eye? I hate the spider part."

"There's a barrier along the top of the plateau. No one and nothing can cross it—not even monsters." Mason backed away from the tunnel, using his body as a shield for Emma until they returned to formation. He scowled, his eyes full of bitter confusion. "There wasn't any mention about this tunnel in the information I received."

I finally spoke up. "So, either it's new or they didn't give you all the information? Does that happen a lot?"

Emma shook her head while everyone's features tightened. "No. Our guild spent a lot of money to outbid the other guilds for this task, and President Price expects to make it all back—and a lot more. With so much money on the line, why would they shortchange us?"

"So this is new since they made the maps?" I shifted so I could get a good look at it around Mason's shoulder.

"Since last night," Mason added.

"Does anyone feel anything?" Axe Guy asked.

Everyone shook their heads.

Mason took a deep breath. "We've walked into traps before. Keep on your guard. Just because we can't see or feel the monsters, it doesn't mean they aren't there. Let's go." He led us forward.

Slowly, we entered the tunnel; there was enough space that we could easily walk in formation without touching the webbing. Everyone was on edge, waiting to attack at the slightest movement. Billy kept shifting the grip on his sword, and fire pooled around Kip's hands. Emma kept her arrow half drawn and ready to shoot at a moment's notice.

I gripped my kindjal. I was dying to Mirror it so I had a weapon in each hand, but with my depleted stats, I only had 5 MP right now; I had to be very careful about what I used it on.

I was just like the rest of the team—I couldn't sense or see any threat, but aside from the fact that we were walking through the middle of a huge spiderweb, something just *felt* wrong. I couldn't place what. It just . . . was.

"Halfway there," Mason whispered. "Remain vigilant."

Billy's knees buckled, and he dropped. He hit the ground with a clank, his armor clattering against itself. He lay facedown and motionless.

"Billy!" Reina gasped.

"What the—?" The words were barely out of Morgan's mouth before she, too, collapsed.

A teal System window popped up in front of my face, nearly scaring me out of my skin.

[Anomaly detected. Autoimmunity activated.]

What anomaly? I twisted this way and that, searching, but I couldn't see anything which would cause them to collapse. What was going on?

"Morgan!" Emma wailed before she slumped, unconscious.

Mason caught her as he also went down.

Within seconds, Emma's entire team lay motionless on the ground.

My breathing increased as my heartbeat quickened. *What the hell is going on?*

Still vigilant, I rushed to Emma and pulled her off Mason, pressing my fingers to her neck to count her pulse. It was strong and steady. Sighing, I checked her over for injuries. Luckily, I didn't find any.

Just then, I noticed the air that Emma exhaled. It was misted, as if she were in the dead of winter, not the middle of a hot, humid jungle. I put my hand over her mouth and tried to manipulate the fog. It didn't respond to me. I didn't know what it was, but there was one thing I knew for sure—it wasn't mist that she was breathing out. So what was it? The *anomaly*?

I checked the others. They were just like Emma. Their pulses were fine, and they appeared uninjured, but they were unconscious and exhaling faint smoke with every breath.

Scowling, I stood up and looked around. I still couldn't detect a monster or living plant. What had caused this? How did I fix this? My System had reduced my stats, leaving my abilities impaired and my body weak, so I couldn't possibly protect anyone from anything in this jungle. But I couldn't just leave them here while I went to look for help. Even if I could make it out alive, I wouldn't leave Emma, and I doubted she'd forgive me if I just grabbed her and left her team behind.

I glanced at Mason. He should have an emergency signal, but if I used it, we'd be forced to leave Feng Jungle. Not only did I not want that—I had a task to complete here—but what if the team woke up and were just fine before the search party got here?

I dropped next to Billy and banged on his helmet with my kindjal. "Hey, wake up."

He didn't move.

I scowled down at my guinea pig and pulled out a bottle of water, splashing some on his face. "Wake up!"

Nothing.

In frustration, I nudged his arm harder than I meant to. His arm flopped at a funny angle. Just as I was about to give up and return to Emma, something bright flashed on his gauntlet. Frowning, I looked back. I didn't think Billy was wearing any rings, and he didn't have any jewels on his armor. So where did that flash come from?

I crouched down and leaned in close to his gloved hand. Something colorful wiggled between the steel plates of his gauntlet. Quickly, I pulled his claymore out of his slack grip and jerked the gauntlet off his hand. From inside, an inch-long colorful *thing* fell to the ground, flopping on the dirt at my feet and curling into a ball.

What the hell? I leaned down. Was it a caterpillar? Its fat, fluffy body was nearly transparent except for two thin rainbow strips which ran from head to tail. The stripes shimmered in the low light as it wriggled about. I leaned in closer. There was something tiny and solid inside it, about where the head or brain should be. Was it an energy crystal? They came that small?

This minuscule creature had to be new to Gate Vale, since its title bar read: [**??? Lv8**].

There were really monsters this weak in this jungle? I lifted my kindjal to crush it.

The caterpillar sprang into the air and landed on Billy's bare hand. In a flash, it burrowed its head into his skin. A large drop of blood rolled down his hand as the caterpillar pushed its way inside and slipped right under, burrowing through his flesh.

Billy's brows tightened in pain, but he didn't wake up.

"No!" I gasped, lashing out at the caterpillar with my kindjal. I left a long scrape on the back of Billy's hand, but I flicked the tiny monster off him. As soon as it landed on the ground, I slashed down and cut it in half lengthwise, just to make sure I got the crystal.

[**EXP +20**]

I glanced around at the white webbing. I had thought, just like everyone else, that this was a spider's nest. Had we been wrong? I looked around the ground, trying to spot more rainbow flashes.

My eyes widened when I saw one on Emma's left arm. A second later, she winced.

I jumped over Billy and grabbed her arm. I twisted it around but couldn't see the shiny caterpillar. Had it already burrowed into her? Quickly pulling at the buckles on her arm bracer, I jerked the armor off.

Just above her wrist was a bloody hole, and on the other side was an inch-long bump under her skin. I could see two rainbow lines glimmering beneath her taut flesh as the caterpillar slowly wiggled and slid its way farther up her arm.

I hissed as nausea and fear twisted in my stomach; I'd never seen nor heard of anything like this before. My left hand clamped down on her arm, cutting off the monster's progression, while I carefully pressed my kindjal to Emma's flesh and cut along the raised, wriggling lump. The bloody thing wiggled and twisted as if the sudden air on it was confusing, then it turned and tried to burrow in farther, pushing at my grip. Trying not to cause any more damage to Emma or damage the caterpillar so it didn't leave a piece in her, I slid my blade under the monster and twisted my wrist.

It popped out of Emma's arm and landed on the ground. With another flick of my wrist, I received another 20 EXP, and the monster vanished, leaving a bloody smear on the ground. Just like the other one, there was no drop orb, but that wasn't important right now.

Emma sighed and relaxed, yet she continued to lay there, unconscious.

The slightest movement on Mason's face drew my attention to him. That's when I noticed that everyone in Emma's team, except for her and Billy, had pained expressions on their faces.

"Oh no," I whispered, reaching for Mason.

Where was it? Had the monster entered his arm, too? I examined his forearm. Nothing. Maybe elsewhere? There wasn't time to strip him down and search—everyone needed help! What if it had gone inside Mason through his torso or thigh? I doubted I'd be able to get it out. And what would happen if it stayed inside him? Inside everyone?

I narrowed my gaze, looking for any traces of blood. A tiny glow appeared on Mason's right calf. It was just like the faint glow from the magic scales on the matching fanged snapper bracelets I'd made for my sister, or the glow I saw when I used Critical Hit on a monster to stab their energy crystal. And that glow was slowly moving up Mason's leg.

I took a second to look at Mason's armor to figure out how it worked, then unbuckled his cuisse so I could remove his greave. With quick movements, I cut open his maroon pants from his knee to his ankle. I could tell it was quality material, but I was sure he'd forgive me someday. Right where the faint magic glow was, I could see two rainbow lines as a bulge slithered its way up his leg. Using the same method as with Emma, I cut it out and killed it.

When his tight expression relaxed, I went to Morgan and looked for a faintly glowing spot on her body. Her mage robes were easier to handle—I just had to slide the sleeves up to bare her upper arms before I cut the caterpillar out. Kip's were just as easy, except there were two caterpillars on her—one in each leg.

As soon as I killed the second one on Kip, a System window popped up.

[Daily Task: (Destroy five Energy Crystals) Completed. +45 EXP. The Punishment Period has ended. All stats have been returned.]

I could feel my body getting lighter as my stats returned, but I didn't have time to revel in the buoyant feeling. Instead, I immediately turned to the next body beside me.

The Axe Guy also had two on him, but his heavy armor was harder to deal with. By the time I got the monsters out of his thigh and near his armpit, I was breathing hard. My fingers ached from all the buckles and straps that I unfastened as fast as I could.

Still, I jumped to my feet and ran to Reina's side. Dropping down, I looked her over for a faint glow—there it was, right on her shoulder.

I quickly unbuckled her chest plate and pulled it to the side. Right as I reached for the wriggling little monster, its faint light flickered. Suddenly, the small rainbow light expanded and spread until it covered her entire body.

CHAPTER 43

Reina's eyes snapped open. Her pupils were extremely dilated, gaze unfocused, as her mouth gaped open in a silent painful scream. Her body bowed off the ground, limbs taut, as the title bar over her head changed, her level increasing from fifty-three to fifty-four.

My eyes widened as horror set in. *Please, no. Someone tell me I'm not seeing this.*

I'd seen a similar thing happen once before; it still made me sick to my stomach. But I didn't know what to do for Reina. I couldn't see the shimmer where the caterpillar monster was inside her. How did I get it out of her chest?

Reina's arms started to shrink, as if something was sucking out all the fat and muscle from inside, leaving only narrow bones covered in skin. No, not really skin. Her flesh was darkening to an opalescent black color. Thick, bristly hair grew on her arms. Her wide eyes kept expanding and expanding until her ballooning eyes took up half of her blackened face. A red, matted film covered her eyes as two antennae popped out of her forehead. Her mouth shrank in size as mandibles grew over the hole.

She was turning into a bug.

Reina convulsed and arched higher into the air, almost defying gravity. Two large bumps grew on her back, then with a loud *rip*, huge white moth wings exploded out from her shoulders. They twitched against the dirt but stayed unnaturally clean while two more bumps grew on the sides of her withered yet morphing body. Her level increased to fifty-five.

I gritted my teeth. I had to do something. There was no way I could handle a level fifty-five monster that was fully conscious. I could just run away—I had my stats back and there was time before Reina finished changing. But I'd never forgive myself if I just left Emma to die. And if she lived, how would I explain it to her that I'd abandoned her team to face this?

I didn't know if it was because Reina's transformation wasn't complete, but I couldn't see the location of her monster energy crystal. I needed to find a different way to kill her. Grabbing Billy's huge-ass claymore and lifting it with both hands as high over my head as I could, I took a deep breath and thrust downward, plunging the blade into her chest. Instead of the soft *shh* of sharpened steel piercing skin, there was a loud crack as it broke through the newly formed exoskeleton to nail her to the ground.

No, not *her*. Reina wasn't human anymore.

Monster Reina's face contorted as its body started to wiggle and wither against the sword. The hands, which were a disgusting mix of insect and human, clawed at the blade but didn't seem to be aware enough to remove it. A second pair of arms popped out of its sides and grabbed at the claymore as black blood leaked from the fresh wounds. The bulbous head thrashed back and forth as clumps of hair fell from its lumpy skull. A small scream came from its mouth.

I ground my teeth against the guilt and disgust curling together in my stomach and took out my kindjal. I dropped down to one knee and tried to cut off the head. I desperately needed a quick kill move, and this was the only one which I knew would absolutely kill the monster without destroying the energy crystal. The problem was, I couldn't push my blade through the blackened exoskeleton. It was the first time I'd encountered something it couldn't pierce.

A flailing arm grabbed my leg, its pincer-like fingers latching onto my greave and pulling, trying to dig its claws into my skin. I winced at the sudden pain as 17 HP dropped from my bar. God, and it wasn't even fully conscious yet. I had to end this now.

Propping my left foot on the back of my blade, I jumped. Coming down, I put all my weight against the crystalized steel. There was a loud crack, then Monster Reina's head popped off and my kindjal sank into the ground. The hand clinging to my leg spasmed before flopping to the ground with the rest of its six limbs.

[+720 EXP]
[**You have Leveled Up!**]
[**You have Leveled Up!**]

I staggered away from Reina's body and shifted my weight off my aching right leg. Even though I'd just gained two levels at once, I wasn't jumping for joy. I stared down at the half-transformed body, then lifted my kindjal and looked at the black blood slowly dripping off the beautiful blade. I had sworn I wouldn't become strong off the blood of humans, yet this was the second time I'd killed someone who I knew was a person. I knew their faces. In Reina's case, I'd even exchanged words with her.

I didn't want to kill her—*it*. But I needed to protect myself and Emma. Was it guilt that weighed my shoulders down? No, just disappointment. In myself, mostly. If I hadn't lost my head yesterday and willfully disobeyed the System, I wouldn't have been so weak today. And if I'd been stronger, faster, maybe I would have gotten to Reina in time.

Was there a silver lining here? *Could* there be a silver lining with death? I now had evidence that energy crystals could transform Hunters into monsters. When President Price saw this, he'd surely back me up, and I wouldn't have to wait four months to talk to the Council.

I snorted and sighed. God, how callous was I? All I could think was how to use the mangled body of a person, half transformed into a monster, for my own agenda before its warmth had even cooled.

As I stewed, the System prompted me. [**Destroy the Energy Crystal. I won't be able to warn you again.**]

"What?" I stuttered. Didn't I stop it before an energy crystal was formed? Besides, *I need this body! It's my evidence!*

Of course, the System didn't respond.

What do you want from me? I mentally screamed at the System. *I'm just one weak girl. What do you expect me to do?*

The thought barely left my mind when I remembered the message it'd left me the other day: *Get stronger.*

Mentally growling with frustration, I marched up to Monster Reina's carcass and glared at it. Slowly, my instant anger morphed into bitter sadness. Maybe it was better this way. When I died, I'd rather my body vanish than be treated like a science experiment.

I looked around at the webbing which clung to the cliff walls and scattered trees, forming the white tunnel. At least this mess was still here; it could serve just as well, I supposed. It would be better if I could find and catch another caterpillar, but I couldn't feel any monsters close right now. Although that didn't mean I let my guard down.

Now that everything was still, I could finally make out a faintly glowing circle hovering over the ill-formed thorax. It was just like the faint glow the monster caterpillars gave off. Instinctively, I knew that was where a newly formed energy crystal was. Pulling out the claymore, I stabbed through that hole at the energy crystal. Her body exploded into tiny little lights that vanished into thin air, taking all the black blood on me, the claymore, and the ground with it.

On the ground, where she used to be, was a thumb-size red agate stone. I stared at it for a second before my System identified it.

[Skill Stone]

Really? I didn't think I'd ever get one of those. Skill Stones were super rare.

Carefully, I reached down. I could touch it, right? It was different from an energy crystal, so it shouldn't be a problem, I think?

The System didn't warn me away, but I poked it just to double-check. When I wasn't warned to stop prodding it, I picked it up and held the cold stone in my hand. Looking at it made me think about something I should have done as soon as the team collapsed.

I put the Skill Stone into my Items Bag then walked over to Mason, kneeling beside him. "Sorry," I muttered and started to leaf through the small sack tied to his belt until I found a token like a smooth, circular disc the same size as a large button with the Stone Mace symbol on it. At least I didn't have to take off anymore of his armor to find it.

I sat back and examined the object. My System autolabeled it.

[Distress Signal. Press the symbol and throw it into the air.]

I did as instructed and threw it straight up. It soared thirty feet overhead before it suddenly exploded into a glowing image of the Stone Mace guild symbol spread out at least ten feet in diameter. I guessed that meant someone was notified? So, all I had to do was wait now, right?

I looked around at Emma's team still crumpled in various positions on the ground, some of them still bleeding. Maybe I should do something about that? I began to drag them closer together, positioning them in a row. It sounded like a good idea to begin with. Until I got to the last man in full armor.

"This was a stupid idea," I muttered to myself, scowling at the divots his armor made on the ground.

Wiping the sweat from my forehead, I rested my hands on my belt. God, I needed water. My tongue lined my teeth, feeling out every bone-dry crevice for a lick of moisture. I stopped, breath stuck in my throat.

Something shifted against the white webbing next to the drag mark I was scowling at. My kindjal instantly appeared in my hand as I focused on it. There was steam coming from the webbing. I frowned and looked around. No, it wasn't just in that one spot. All the webbing in the whole tunnel was smoking.

My eyes widened. I didn't know what it was, but it couldn't be good.

A spare shirt from my Items Bag appeared in my hand, and I pressed it over my nose and mouth before I looked down at the people at my feet—and the smoky film that was starting to form around them. *Crud.*

With quick movements, I cut my shirt into pieces. First, I tied one around my face, then I bent down and tied the strips of cloth around the other's faces. In the end, I crouched next to Emma with one hand pressing the cloth over her mouth and nose while I held the kindjal in my free hand.

I watched the smoking webbing. Were more of those caterpillar monsters going to come?

It took me a second to realize the webs weren't actually smoking—they were evaporating. I gaped as they shrank and thinned until sticky clumps fell to the ground and disappeared in puffs of smoke. In minutes, the whole white tunnel had vanished, leaving nothing behind except for the dead trees and the jagged canyon sides.

"No!" I jumped to my feet and looked around. It was all gone. All of it.

As if the parasites didn't want Hunters to know they existed.

I hacked at brittle dead trees with my kindjal, sweating hard, frustration boiling over.

Goddammit! It was all that thing's—that damn parasite planet's—fault! Everything! The Gates and monsters. How the world fell apart twenty years ago. The deaths of billions of people. The reason why the human population still steadily declined. Even my father's death and how it spearheaded the crumbling of my family. The trauma that I couldn't escape and would keep going through. All of it.

And it won't end until the parasitic planet eats Earth.

With a final heave, I struck the tree trunk. The brittle wood cracked and splintered in half then fell to the side, barely missing Axe Guy. I stood there, breathing heavily but listening carefully. I shouldn't have lost my head like that. Who knew what monster would be attracted to that much noise?

My breathing evened out as my senses grew more alert, but nothing came. I glanced up at the guild symbol still flashing overhead. Someone would come, right? I walked over to Emma, crouched beside her, then smoothed the cloth over her face. I guessed it was fine to take it off, since the smoking was gone, but it wouldn't hurt her to keep it on her, either.

In that silent moment, my stomach grumbled. I sighed. Crud. I'd been in such a hurry to get to Emma before the guild left on their mission that

I'd forgotten to grab a lunch from Henry. My face scrunched up in a scowl as I checked my surroundings again.

A thought popped into my head, and I paused. I did actually have something to eat in my Items Bag.

I extended my hand, and a pink pastry box appeared in my palm. Even though it'd been a couple days since I got it, the smell of fresh baked goods immediately filled my nose like a breath of heaven. My Items Bag couldn't keep cold things cold or hot things hot, but any food in it was preserved at its freshest state. If I put a bowl of ice cream in my Items Bag, I'd end with a bowl of flavored cream. But if I put ice cream in a thermal then put that in my bag, it would stay an ice-creamy cold perfection until I took it out.

The thought of something cold and quenching further parched my tongue, but this éclair and a bottle of water would have to do.

Slowly, I opened the pastry box and pulled the éclair out. I closed the box and put it away, then looked at the puffed pastry. Honestly, I never actually meant to eat anything from Kesstel; I just couldn't bring myself to throw perfectly good food away. But right now wasn't the time to drag my feet. I needed the calories, even if they were empty ones.

Still vigilant of my surroundings, I took a small bite. Instantly, my mouth was blasted with a sweet, creamy custard. I let out a slow sigh as I savored the bite.

"So good," I mouthed the words. It was just a—*ridiculously* yummy— pastry, but for some reason, the weight of failing to keep all of Emma's teammates alive seemed to lessen enough that I could finally breathe.

Man, I'm too easy to please, I thought as I glanced around for any more rainbow caterpillars.

As much as I mocked myself in my head, I still savored every single bite until the éclair was gone. Once it was, I pulled up my stats and adjusted my extra stat points.

I was so close to level twenty. *So close!* It was such a relief to see these numbers instead of the crappy single digits from this morning.

System? I said in my head. *Why didn't I pass out like Emma and her team? I'm so much weaker than them, why were they the ones affected?*

There was a long enough pause that I didn't think the System was going to respond at all. Then a teal message popped up. [**Your power comes from the System, not the parasitic planet. Therefore, you have a buffer between you and the parasite's influences.**]

Shock reverberated through my mind. Before I could come up with more questions, a shiver of alarm went down my spine.

The rustling of branches and underbrush from outside the canyon entrance cut through my thoughts. *Please let it be a rescue team that spotted my distress signal.*

Jynn Devhro

Rank D		**Level** 19	
		EXP to Next Level 322	
HP 246/315		**Stat Points** 0	
MP 146/146			
Strength 43 (+10)		**Agility** 38	
Magic 33		**Perception** 35	
Constitution 36 (+10)		**Intelligence** 31	

Skills	**Abilities**
Throw	Mist (Improved) (20 ft)
Critical Hit	Feather Step
Quick Hit	Regen (Limited)
Mirror	

CHAPTER 44

The familiar panting and growls of verdure wolves reached my ears.

My eyes widened in alarm. At the center of Emma's team, I crouched low and cast Mist. The thick moist particles spread to the walls of the canyon and filled up the entire space. I didn't know how well it masked our scent, but it should have been thick enough to visually hide us. As for myself, I could see perfectly through the fog—and if I actually needed to fight the monsters, I was going to need all the extra boost I could get.

A moment later, four verdure wolves stepped out of the jungle, stopping where the mist began at the entrance of the canyon. The largest of the wolves, a level forty alpha, sniffed at the fog. A low growl rumbled from its throat as it took a step forward and narrowed its bright green eyes at our location. Its line of sight seemed slightly over my head—it must not have been able to actually tell where we were. But it obviously wasn't going to back off because of the fog.

Damn. I Mirrored my kindjal and gripped the handles tight in both hands. Emma's team was still comatose, but at least they were alive. I'd like to keep them that way. These wolves weren't going to be what finished us all off.

The alpha took another step into the mist. Pale vapor wafted around its legs, kind of pretty against the green and white of its grassy fur.

A pale flash of blue struck from somewhere beyond the rock wall on the right and pierced the verdure alpha. It yelped as the force knocked it off its feet and smashed it to the ground. The monster stopped moving, and the tip of a huge ice arrow sticking out of the wolf's motionless chest came into focus.

Before the other wolves could properly react, three Hunters appeared from the direction the arrow had come from. With quick movements, they hacked at the monsters.

I blinked, just as shocked as the wolves. I didn't even know there were Hunters in the area. Quickly, I looked up at the guild symbol overhead. Was this the rescue team? Either way, it should be safe now that they were here.

I quickly drew the mist back into my body. Hopefully, they didn't notice it.

The last of the wolves dropped dead. A Hunter stood over the fallen body with a satisfied smile on his face. He laughed a little and rested his dripping sword against his shoulder. My eyes widened—I knew him.

"That was a nice little warm-up," Mark joked to the Hunter beside him.

No. I had to be wrong. This couldn't possibly be true.

But I couldn't deny it when Blake walked up to a carcass and kicked it. "One of our guild teams really fell to something as weak as this?" Unlike the other Hunters on his team, there wasn't a scratch or spot on his armor. Blinking, he turned his head toward me. "What the hell?" He glanced at the Hunters laid out in a row at my side. With long, confident steps, he strutted up to me. "What the hell happened here, you E insect?" He was staring down at me, his lip curled in disgust.

All I could do was stare at him as the scenes of my trauma played in my head. Then his words finally clicked in my ears, and I stopped breathing. Did he . . . did he seriously not recognize me? Didn't he know I was the one he threw to her death? Or was it that he didn't care enough to bother remembering my face?

Fury and loathing built up in my chest. My hands fisted around my kindjals so tight my fingers ached. I needed the pain. It was the only thing keeping me from lunging at him; a tiny sliver of awareness which kept me from wasting everything I'd done so far. To hell with morals—I wanted him dead so badly, I could see it in my mind. I wanted him to know what it felt like to be thrown to murderous red orcs. To feel the hopelessness of knowing you were going to die painfully and there was nothing you could do about it. And I wanted to see that realization on his face as it happened.

But that moment wouldn't happen right now. I was too weak. But that wouldn't always be the case. I just needed to be patient.

Blake's gaze rested on my shoulder where there wasn't a badge. "You aren't even in my guild. What are you doing here?" he sneered.

I cleared my throat to force the knot down. "I'm here as a contracted guest." That was all he needed to know. "Are you here to help?"

Mark approached and leaned around Blake. He peered down at Mason in delight. "Oh, it really is that arrogant little shit's team." His eyes landed on Emma, and he scowled ugly. "Hmm, they needed to be knocked down a peg." Mark kicked Mason in the chest hard enough to move his inert body a couple inches.

"Stop it!" I yelled, hating the fact that I wasn't stronger.

Mark finally looked at me. His brow wrinkled in confusion as his head tilted to the side.

Blake looked up as if bored that he didn't get a better reaction. "Send them away." He jerked his chin in the direction of his fellow guild members on the ground.

Several Hunters entered the canyon and walked up to us. They stooped down, inspecting Emma's team, looking at them like they were looking at dolls.

A gorgeous woman in red robes looked at Blake. "They're injured."

He clicked his tongue. "It's not life-threatening. Leave it. It'll just be a waste of MP."

Why was he a part of a rescue team? I mean, seriously?

"And their armor and weapons?" She gestured at the scattered gear on the ground.

Before he could say anything, I piped up. "I'll take them." I reached out and collected the gear into my Items Bag.

"Stealing?" A Hunter kicked out and swept my legs out from under me.

I twisted to avoid falling on Kip and landed awkwardly and hard on the ground. I glared at them. "No. Do you really want me to take precious time putting them back on right now?"

Blake huffed impatiently. "Come on, already. Don't have time to chitchat."

The red-robed mage reached out and touched Billy's shoulder. She whispered something, a soft chant. A moment later, Billy levitated. She moved to the rest of Emma's team until all the unconscious Hunters were floating five feet off the ground. Then she walked up to me and tapped my shoulder.

I gasped as a chill wrapped around my body, freezing me into place, before I rose up and joined the rest of the team. I wanted to scream and curse, tell them I could walk just fine, but I couldn't even move my mouth enough to tell her off. Did she really have to treat me like I was a lifeless doll, too?

With a pleased smile, she signaled to Blake. "Ready!"

He looked at me and the rest of Mason's levitated teammates. "Perfect. Let's go." He turned around and started to run.

When Mason's team moved through the brush, we were careful and kept in formation to ensure we were always ready for anything. Blake's large team charged right through at a full sprint. Anything in their way was cut down as fast as possible, whether it was a plant, monster, or rainbow crystal. Even small trees toppled needlessly to the ground. There was almost no defense against their aggressive trampling.

All the while, Mason's team and I soared behind them like balloons on a string. The magic which kept us up and immobile also acted like a barrier, so we weren't hurt as we were pulled through the jungle at such a reckless rate of speed, but still, humiliation burned in me as endless as my worrisome thoughts. Where were they taking us?

We finally came out of the jungle, the purple transportation circle coming into view.

The mage swished her finger, and the force which kept me and the others afloat now carried us to the circle. We started to lower to the ground. Once we were about a foot up, the magic around us suddenly disappeared, and we dropped the rest of the way to the ground in a pile of people.

Billy's leg landed right on my stomach, and I gasped. Scowling, I pushed him off me.

The mage raised her red-tipped fingers over her mouth and giggled, her eyes just as delighted as the rest of Blake's group.

God, they were all a bunch of vicious people. I guessed Blake's special aura just drew them to him.

Blake jerked his chin toward the transportation circle. "Throw them in there," he ordered me. "A medical staff is waiting for them on the other side. Mason's team is done for the day. If he's lucky, you all might have another chance tomorrow, but I don't plan on letting that happen." He smirked and signaled for his group to follow him back into the jungle.

Mark followed Blake, but his attention remained on me. Just before they were out of sight, he tapped on a teammate's shoulder. The female Hunter glanced over her shoulder at me, just long enough for me to see it was Penny he talked to as they both shot me a parting glance. Then just like that, Blake's team disappeared into the depths of the Feng Jungle.

Weird. What was that look about? I tsked.

And what a gracious, magnanimous savior Blake was. He seemed even worse than during my last encounter with him. Was it because he wasn't trying to save face in front of a newbie like Emma had been?

I knelt down beside her team. I was sure Blake was telling the truth when he said that medical staff were waiting on the other side. This was a guild-run operation; he wouldn't try anything sneaky under the nose of President Price. At least, I hoped not.

Even so, I couldn't go first to protect them on the other side because then who would send them over? But then who, exactly, would be prepared to catch them when they got to the other side? Damn him; Blake could have spent just a moment longer to actually help me get the team inside the transportation circle.

I huffed and tapped my fingers on my aching forehead. *Emma and her people are high leveled,* I told myself. *The inertia coming out of the circle isn't enough to kill them.*

Right. I just had to keep telling myself that. And I had all their weapons, so it wasn't like Emma was going to accidentally land on Billy's unreasonably huge claymore.

I walked over and grabbed Axe Guy. This silent giant was the biggest, so I should send him through first. It would be awful if he landed on petite Morgan.

I already knew it was a pain, but damn, I hated dragging a man in full armor. How many times had I done this today? Still, I gritted my teeth and brought him to the purple magic circle. It took me a second to figure out how to position him so he entered it without me touching it too, but then I gave a small sigh of relief when he turned into a blur and shot up the thin purple arch back to the Gate.

From there, I grabbed the next biggest person, Billy. One by one, I placed the team into the magic circle and watched them go. Morgan was the last. She wasn't the largest, but my arms trembled as I exerted the last of my strength to push her into place.

Letting out a puff of air, I turned back to regard Feng Jungle. The day wasn't a total loss. I had my stats back, but there was no way I could take on this jungle by myself.

My shoulders fell. Ugh. How would I explain how Emma's team got injured and where Reina was?

If the Stone Mace guild didn't find the crystal today, they would look for it again tomorrow. And the next day. And the next. It would just keep going. I was contracted to stay with the team until the crystal was found; I just hoped it wasn't found before I had a chance to come back.

With one last look at the silvery green jungle, I stepped into the transportation circle. Immediately, I became weightless and shot through the sky on the magical cord, aiming for the entrance. I wasn't in the same mood to look around—I still did, but the sight of Gate Vale spreading out before me had lost its wonder.

How many caterpillar nests like the one we encountered were out there? Did they always knock out the Hunters and transform them so fast? Then, did the webs vanish like that every time? No wonder no one knew what was going on. I knew that a parasitic planet was causing all this, but I didn't know it was intelligent enough to set traps. Did it also prevent people from changing in front of crowds on purpose, just to stay under the radar? Goose bumps spread over my body. Just how smart was that thing?

The exit circle came into sight. A group of people were around it, holding Emma's teammates and moving them out of the way. I flipped around and got ready to land. Once my feet touched the ground, I hopped forward a couple steps until I came to a stop next to a healer. Instead of a Stone Mace patch on their shoulders, there was an Eden Hospital symbol on the breast of every healer's white robe. What strings did the guild have to pull to get hospital healers to wait here?

A healer bent over Mason and touched her faintly glowing hand to his shoulder. A second later, his face tightened, and he slowly opened his eyes. One by one, the team woke up.

"Mason?" Emma whispered, trying to sit up. I hurried over to her and put an arm around her back to brace her up before she collapsed back to the ground. She blinked at me in confusion then grabbed my arm in a weak grip. "Jynn, you're okay."

"Steady now," a female healer told Mason as he tried to sit up, too. Her soothing voice was like a drug. "I don't know what knocked you out. You might be dizzy still." She looked at me and frowned faintly. "Do you know?"

I hesitated then shook my head. "I don't." It wasn't a total lie. I didn't know exactly what those caterpillar things were, just that they were an anomaly—but saying that wouldn't explain anything.

She bobbed her head and looked at Mason. "You have a small cut on your arm. Would you like me to heal that?"

Other healers were muttering to the team in quiet voices.

"Where's Reina?" Billy's raised voice silenced every soothing word and gentle chant the healers were muttering. He struggled to his feet and almost fell down, but locked his legs and stayed upright. "*Where's Reina?*"

CHAPTER 45

The healers looked at each other at a loss. After all, everyone who had come through the circle was present and accounted for.

I let out a silent breath. "I'm sorry." My voice drew everyone's attention.

The healers looked at each other, then tactfully walked a distance away. They grouped together, some of them looking away to give us privacy and others staring intently with curiosity.

Billy glared at me. "What do you mean?"

I stood up and met his glare with a steady gaze. "I tried; I really did. You all fell unconscious. While I was helping you, she . . . " My voice died out as I took in how his expression turned darker and darker.

Did I really want to tell them what happened? How she turned into a monster and I killed her? Would they really believe me or write me off as a quack like the online forum did? I needed to complete my task and destroy that crystal. If my admission got me kicked off the team right now, I wouldn't be able to do that.

My silence was met with shocked faces which slowly changed to grief and denial. I didn't have to say anymore. If a Hunter didn't make it out of somewhere in Gate Vale, it meant only one thing.

Death.

Emma grabbed my hand and pulled herself up. "You . . . " Her voice cracked, and she blinked at the tears in her eyes. "You did . . . your best. I'm sure of it."

"Did your best?" Billy half screamed. His face turned red, the thick veins on his forehead bulging. "*Did your best?* Like hell! This is why Es aren't supposed to go on missions like this! They are nothing but baggage—weak, useless, and unable to protect anyone! How do we know you didn't purposefully k-kill Reina so you could take her spot!" His B-ranked aura spread out, heavy with anger, trying to smother me. He took a step toward me.

Mason stood up and pressed a shaking hand against Billy's chest to stop him from getting any closer. His own presence flared out like a shield, forcing Billy's back. "That's inappropriate and you know it." His voice lowered, threatening.

My teeth gritted together, and I forced my legs to stay strong even though it felt like a giant invisible hand was pressing down on me. I wasn't as affected by their higher-ranking pressure as I had been this morning; if my stats hadn't returned, I would have been on the ground right now, barely conscious, succumbing to the pressure of the two Hunters facing off. That's not to say I wasn't feeling it—I was. I just wouldn't show it.

I did kill Reina. I didn't regret it. And I'd do it again if it meant I could keep myself and Emma alive.

But with Billy's actions, any lingering guilt I had over it vanished. I lifted my chin and glared at him, then swept my gaze across the rest of the team. A mix of emotions were displayed, from condemnation to the denial on Emma's face.

I grabbed Emma's arm and pulled at her sleeve, spreading the tear on the material so they all could clearly see the scab on her arm. "Do you see this?" I demanded. "This right here!" I pointed at it. "This is where a monster burrowed under her skin, digging its way up to her chest. Trying to get to her heart, I'm sure." It was a guess, but it wouldn't surprise me if the change was sparked when the caterpillar reached the human heart.

Emma's face went white as a sheet, and she wobbled. I put a hand on her shoulder and gently set her on the ground before she fell over.

The rest of the team looked just as unsettled. Billy and Mason's power struggle dissipated as they focused on me.

By now, all the healers were staring at us. Even random Hunters that were entering or exiting the Gate entrance a short way away stopped to watch.

But I wasn't done yet. I glared at Billy's red face. "Take a look at your right hand. Do it. The same cut is on your hand, where I had to dig a monster out of you. That's why your gauntlet is missing, if you haven't noticed yet. There was only one on you and you." I pointed to Mason and Morgan. "And there were two on each of you." I motioned to Axe Guy and Kip. "I *tried*. While you were all unconscious on the ground, I was going as fast as I could to find those weird little monsters. But I could only go so fast. And it's not like I'm a pro at taking off armor." I waved my hand, and their missing gear appeared on the ground at my feet. It clanged together, metal bumping against metal. "By the time I finished with all of you, it was too late for Reina."

Their faces changed to horror as they checked the wounds on their bodies. I guess one thing I had going for me was that the healers hadn't been that quick to take care of such small wounds yet.

"So don't say I didn't try." I gritted my teeth and glared at Billy's wide eyes. "If I hadn't, you wouldn't be here."

Several emotions flashed over Billy's face, too fast for me to catch, before he settled on a scowl. "Why didn't you pass out? Did the monsters attack you, too?" He flung the words at me. "How do we know you didn't make these cuts as a cover?"

"Billy!" Emma gasped at him.

"Hey," Mason warned.

"How ungrateful can you be?" I demanded. "I don't know why I wasn't attacked. Maybe it's because I was too *weak and useless*. The monsters just overlooked me entirely and went for the greater threats." It had to be because I didn't pass out. The monsters were probably drawn to unconscious people only. Honestly, it was a fluke I even noticed them when I did. If I hadn't, I would have been killed when everyone turned into monsters. "The reason *why* doesn't matter. What matters is that I kept as many people as I could alive. I would rather have Reina here, too."

Billy opened his mouth but was cut off by Morgan. "Billy? I think you should stop now." She bowed her head, tears streaming down her cheeks.

Axe Guy rested an arm around her trembling shoulders.

"Yeah." Morgan hugged herself tight, her fingers brushing her arm near her armpit. Where a scab was, so close to her torso.

Mason leveled Billy with a look. "Fighting about this isn't going to change anything."

Billy looked at everyone with incredulity. "Are you seriously going to just leave it like this?"

"I don't think there's anything else that can be said or done," Mason said simply.

Billy growled low in frustration then glared at me. Without another word, he grabbed his gear from the pile on the ground and marched away. Moments later, he disappeared through the archway of the Gate.

The rest of the team took their stuff and walked away. Even the watching crowd lost interest and dissipated. That left me with just Mason and Emma.

Emma took a breath and stood up. "I'm sorry about Billy. He's not a bad guy, really. He just wears his emotions on his sleeve, you know?" Tears pooled her pretty eyes.

Just like someone else who looks guilty as hell, I thought, looking at Emma's face.

Mason reached out and put an arm around Emma's shoulder. "Billy and Reina." He swallowed hard, his voice thick. "They've been best friends since childhood. They were both raised in the Hope Program and were orphaned by ten. So you could say they were all each other had for most of their lives. They were each other's most important person." He looked down, and Emma rubbed her arm as she swallowed a sob.

I huffed a breath and looked to the side, still angry, but at least I understood now.

It was hard for Hunters to bear children. Even when they got pregnant, most female Hunters often miscarried before their second trimester. But humans and Hunters were separated for a reason. A Hunter's strong presence was too much for a normal or Unawakened human to handle for a long period. If a Hunter couple had a child, that child would go to the Hope building in Garden City. The mother had a four-month maternity leave, and the father had six weeks where they could stay with the baby as long as their Hunter aura didn't affect the baby's health. Then they would go back to Eden, and the baby would be raised by the caregivers in the Hope Program.

The parents had visitation rights on the weekends, but for the most part, the children were raised in an orphanage-like environment. Because of the high casualty rate of Hunters, there were more orphans than not in the Hope Program. It was also just as likely to come across an abandoned child whose parents were too busy to bother visiting. It was originally called the Hope Program because everyone thought that if two Hunters had a baby, it was guaranteed to be another Hunter—they were the hope of the future. But everyone had been wrong. Children from two Hunter parents had the same odds of becoming a Hunter as any other kid off the street who had one or no Hunter parent at all.

"I get it," I muttered. "But I still don't appreciate him attacking me like that."

Mason nodded. "I understand. I'll talk to him."

I looked up at the couple and took in the way Emma relied on him as she grieved. Then I remembered how his name was the first thing she'd said when she woke up. How devastated would she be if Mason was the one I killed? What if Emma was the one I couldn't get to in time? A chill went down my spine, and I banished the thought.

God, I was getting too attached, wasn't I?

"See you tomorrow," I muttered, turning to leave.

"Wait, are you coming tomorrow?" Emma asked hopefully.

I gave her a wan smile over my shoulder. "Yeah. I'm still under contract, right? There's a couple things I have to do, so I'm going to go for now." My lashes lowered as I muttered, "I'm sure there's a couple things you have to do, too." Handling grief was hard. "I'll go to the Incidents Office and fill out a report later."

With that, I headed to Fogmire to cultivate for thirty minutes.

An hour later, I slowly closed the door to the Incidents Office behind me. This was my second time closing that metal door in less than a week. It didn't feel good. This time I was at least able to make a full report. The receptionist wrote every word I said about the events which led to Reina's death. Of course, that's because I lied. But it was easier to believe than the truth.

I didn't say anything about her turning into a monster and me killing her. As far as the records would show, she disappeared while I dealt with the rest of the team. She was there one second and gone the next. No one would question that because some monsters really were that fast and silent, especially compared to the abilities of an E—they just didn't have the stats to keep up with the really fast ones.

I shouldn't have lied, but I felt like it was only fair that something was recorded about Reina's death. She—and the people who knew her—needed some sort of closure. Not to mention, I bet I'd get into trouble if I kept coming to make reports about the monster-humans I kept killing. The System wanted me to stay under the radar; I couldn't have the Hunter police tailing me to see if I was a psycho killer.

A bitter smile quirked my lips. As if they had any reason to look at me. But if they wanted someone to check out, I would gladly point them in the right direction.

At the top of the stairs in front of the building, I paused with my foot hanging out over the next step. A familiar presence emanated from down below. I blinked out of my thoughts and focused on him—Kesstel.

He looked up at me, his hands in the pockets of his jeans and his white-blond hair brushed back from his forehead with a casual flare. It was obvious he was waiting for me.

Why is it that I always see him here?

"How did you know I was here?" I slowly started down the stairs.

"You became actually pretty easy to track as soon as I knew what to look for. At least for me," he commented casually. "Like a white dot in a sea of black; although I'm sure you're nearly invisible to other Hunters—but I get the impression that's what you want, huh?"

He wasn't wrong. I stopped with only a couple stairs to go so that we were the same height, glancing at the red title over his head. Right now, I didn't want to see his face. Everything I'd learned and seen seemed to pile up around me, hammering cracks into the calm shell that I'd forged around my mind.

I didn't have anything else to hang the blame on except for him, even if it was unfair.

I turned away. "I'll see you later."

"Oh, I thought you might want these, Jynn."

I paused. He knew my name? When did I ever tell him? I looked over my shoulder.

In the one second I glanced away, Kesstel had moved to the trash bin at the corner of the stairs, next to the wooded area where he crushed my world days ago. A pink pastry box hung in his hand, ready to drop down into the garbage. "I guess you didn't like them after all."

"Gah!" I ran over and grabbed the box out of his hand before he could commit a horrible sin. "Seriously, you can't just throw stuff like this away!"

A sweet smell filled my nose. Intoxicated, I took a deep breath. It smelled so good, and I'd only eaten a single pastry all day. Ah, that's right, I still had that chocolate tres leches cake. I should eat that tonight. And everything inside this box. Tonight was a night where I could use some sweets therapy.

Kesstel breathed a small laugh. "Okay. I won't anymore; I promise." Then he sobered up. "You look upset."

The sides of the box bent as my fingers tightened on its edges. I stared down at the pink cardboard. My head and my heart screamed to run away; I didn't want to learn more about him, and I didn't want him to learn more about me. The best thing for me would be to keep a firm wall between us. But he was literally the only person I could talk to about what was going on.

I glanced up into his face then back down at the pastry box. "How can you stand seeing your teammates turn into monsters? And how do you handle killing them after they transform?" I held the box with one hand and smoothed out the wrinkles on the cardboard with my other.

"I don't partner up."

I blinked in surprise and looked fully into his face.

He shrugged. "What's the use when they're all going to die, anyway? In the end, it's going to be just me walking away when this world collapses. So what's the use of getting attached in the first place?" He was so casual, so sure, as he spoke.

I looked at Kesstel's vibrant blue eyes. They were so piercing, so polarizing. Yet every time I talked with him, I could still feel a vacantness, as if he wasn't really here with me at all. He was looking at me, but he wasn't *seeing* me. He seemed so perfect, but he didn't really feel anything, did he? It was completely different from me, who felt more than I wanted to.

"How do you know you won't get caught in the destruction if Earth collapses?" I asked.

He looked over my shoulder at the few Hunters who strolled by in the distance. When they were farther away, he spoke. "Because I'm not a human from Earth. When it collapses, I'll appear in a portal and wait there until the parasite connects to the next world and I can go out again."

He paused, the pleasant emotion sliding off his face as if he were thinking about something. Then he looked down at me as if in realization.

My eyes widened as our gazes collided. For the first time, he was *looking* at me, his attention completely focused one hundred percent on me.

His lips parted as if to say something before he pressed them together in a thin line and his brows wrinkled in a semiscowl.

"What?" I asked. It took everything I had to prevent myself from stepping back.

"Kesstel!" a soft voice rang out.

I blinked, recognizing it.

Bethany walked up, just as gorgeous as ever in the hot sun. When she saw me, she stopped, her eyes flaring wide. "Y-You! What are you doing here?" Her eyes narrowed as she lifted her chin in the air. Multiple power-enhancing stones from her necklace winked in the light.

Kesstel looked at the furious woman and sighed. "Ah."

I glared at him. *Don't you dare make me the mistress here!* I thought, forcing a smile on my face, strained as it was.

"I'll pay you back later," I muttered as I stored the pastries in my Items Bag. I'd give them back, but I really didn't want to watch them get destroyed from that woman's fury. "Bye."

With that, I power walked past him, in the opposite direction as Bethany Wilks. As soon as I rounded the corner, I fled with all my guts.

Nope, never looking at him again. It's just not worth it.

CHAPTER 46

It was funny how a quiet, sunny morning could feel so wrong. The streets of Eden were slow and sparsely populated, mostly because all the Hunters who weren't in the Gate's morning cleanup crew were still sleeping. Since Hunters only needed to deliver one energy crystal a day to maintain their livelihood, the unambitious tended to sleep in late. I'd never had that luxury, so I was used to—and even preferred—the quiet streets.

It almost felt normal, feeling the gentle sun on my brown hair as I walked noiselessly into Gate Square. Well, as normal as it could get after getting your life turned upside down. Again.

A large group of Hunters were gathered under the towering, two-hundred-foot-tall black arch. Any other given day I would have given them a wide berth, but today, I walked up to the group, frowning.

Was it just me or were there fewer Hunters than yesterday? Did some teams fail so badly they didn't even come back? Feng Jungle, although it looked like a magical metallic fairytale, was still very dangerous.

"Jynn!" Emma waved at me from the left side of the mass, her reddish-pink light armor making it easy to spot her.

The corner of my mouth kicked up in a smile, and I trotted over to her. "Morning."

I glanced around her team. It had obviously been a hard night for all of them, from the dark circles and puffy red eyes on each team member's face. Even so, they were all here to finish the job—retrieving a giant energy crystal from Feng Jungle. And that's what it meant to be a Hunter. People died every day, but the world kept turning and monsters still needed to be killed.

Kip and Morgan attempted wan smiles at me, and Axe Guy jerked his chin in a sharp greeting. Billy didn't even acknowledge my presence, which was typical, and normally, I wouldn't be too bothered by it. But remembering his anguish from yesterday caused unwarranted guilt to flutter in my gut.

No. Not my fault. I did my best. I swallowed hard. It wasn't my fault that Reina turned into a monster. But it was my fault that I killed her after she did. If I hadn't, the monster she turned into would have killed me, Emma, and all of her unconscious teammates. I didn't regret saving them, even if I took the blame for it.

"Good morning!" Emma smiled brightly at me, although her dark eyes were bloodshot and puffy.

Mason stood close beside her. "Morning." He looked as tired as the rest of the team, but he was putting on obvious airs, as if he weren't mourning like the rest of them. "Now that we're all here, I want to introduce you to Trace." He motioned to a melee Hunter standing just to the left of the team. "He was part of the team that disappeared in Feng Jungle yesterday. Since we have an . . . " Mason's voice faded out as grief passed over his face.

Billy scowled at the ground, using the brim of his helmet to hide most of his angry expression, his fists opening and closing.

Mason cleared his throat and smoothed his features. "Anyway, Trace is gonna join us for the rest of the mission."

Trace turned toward us, and I finally got a look at his face. He wasn't handsome or ugly, just a normal face with brown hair barely visible under his steel helm. But there was something about him . . .

Oh. Wasn't he one of the two guys who had glared at me so obviously yesterday outside the Gate? Even now, he kept glancing at me, then away, only to glance back. What was his deal?

Mason went on, oblivious. "The energy crystal wasn't found yesterday. There were some sections in Feng Jungle which didn't even get touched, like our northeast area." Mason cleared his throat. "It's still ours to explore. Each team is charged with scouring their section over and over again until the crystal is found." He paused, then continued with a brave face. "A lot of unexpected things happened yesterday. But we have a job to do. Let's do it and show everyone that we deserve to be number seven in the guild."

Several teams separated from the milling, massive crowd and walked toward the Gate, vanishing in its black hole.

Mason lifted his hand, and a blue Guide screen appeared. He read what was on it before nodding, obviously satisfied. "Well, it's time. President

Price should already be at Feng Jungle, so let's go." He turned to Trace and started to talk to him in a low voice as they walked to the Gate.

I never had a chance to hear what they were talking about; strong fingers gripped my arm and pulled me around.

Billy's muscular tank-like body towered over me as he glared. "Don't even think for a second that you can take Reina's spot in the team," he hissed under his breath. "An E like you will never join our team. So don't get any ideas. As soon as this mission is over and your contract ends, you're gone. Understand?"

I met his glare with a steady gaze. "Believe me, I never once thought about joining your team." I jerked my arm from his grip. "I'm grateful for the care you've given Emma. When I first met her, I was worried that her sweetness would be smothered in Eden. I'm glad she found a good team. But I knew from the beginning this would never be a place for me."

He stared at me, his mouth opening and closing like he didn't know what to say. Did he think I was going to argue with him over joining? That my next move would be to use my connection to Emma to become a permanent member? I had no ulterior motive to become a part of them, only to destroy the crystal I hoped they'd find today.

I dismissed Billy and headed toward Emma, who was waiting at the entrance with a worried expression. Standing off to the side, Trace stared at me, eyes narrowed and mouth slanting down.

. . . Hang on, he didn't think I was competing for a spot on the team, did he? I'd avoided drama for years, and now suddenly, it was coming at me left and right like thick, rancid pies. I was so over this.

Inside Gate Vale, Emma took my arm and walked me a short distance away from the group. Unlike with Billy, I didn't feel repulsion at her soft touch. "Um, Jynn, I just wanted to apologize."

I blinked down at her. "Why?" Really, I was the one who needed to apologize to her.

She took a breath. "I promised that I would keep you safe, but in the end, you protected us." She took another breath then gave me a determined look. "This time, I promise I won't let anything happen to you."

Images of her nannying me yesterday came to mind. Please tell me she wasn't going to up her antics. "Really, Emma. I'm okay. I can hold my own."

She nodded. "I know. You're so awesome. But Feng Jungle is a lot more dangerous than I thought it would be . . . " she trailed off, tears in her eyes.

I smiled and tapped her on the forehead, trying to distract her from crying. "Hey, hey. It's all good. Come on, Mason is waiting for us." I jerked my chin and took a couple steps toward the group. "So, are you and Mason official yet?"

Emma gasped and caught up to me. "W-What?" Her face turned bright red. "What makes you think that we . . . " Her voice got smaller and smaller until she stopped talking entirely.

I grinned at her.

Aliya never talked about boys—she was too much like me in that way; too busy for romance. Who knew that teasing someone about it could be so fun?

I held my hand up and whispered in her ear. "Here's a suggestion. Why don't you just kiss him and see what happens?"

Her knees buckled, and she almost flopped right on the ground. "Jynn!" she wailed, her face the same shade as her armor.

I laughed. Okay, maybe I shouldn't tease her right now, but at least she didn't look like she was going to cry anymore.

Emma's expression cleared up as she peeked at Mason with a sad smile. "I've been wondering what I should do. It just seems like nothing is permanent, you know? Everyone dies so easily."

I took a deep breath and looked down at her, thinking about my life. How it was before I got the System, and how it's changed. The giant threat on the other side of Gate Vale.

"Life is so short. You never know what's going to happen. But don't die with regrets." My lashes lowered as I remembered my time with the red orcs, my desperate thoughts as I was dying, the gut-wrenching guilt toward my family. "You will never get anything in Eden if you don't fight for it, be it love or your life. Figure out what you want and go after it with everything you have." I didn't expect a happy ending for me, but it didn't have to be that way for Emma. I smiled at her. "That's my opinion."

She nodded slowly. "Yeah."

I tapped her shoulder, and we rejoined her team. By then, all the other teams had already gone through the magic circle. We quickly lined up and sailed across Gate Vale to the jungle, where Mason put us in the same formation as yesterday, with Trace in place of Reina.

I looked at him. "I can fight, too. You don't have to worry about me."

Behind me, Billy snorted in contempt.

Mason looked worried but took a breath. "Okay," he said slowly. "Jynn, today you'll work with Emma and Trace. Watch out for Emma's arrows;

they come in fast and hard." He glanced at Trace. "And you use daggers, right?"

Trace nodded.

I nodded, too. "That should be fine. I use short swords and I know what I'm doing." Working as a team was going to be new, but I had enough spatial awareness that I could keep out of the way. Not to mention, I wanted to know if I actually got EXP if I joined in their fights.

Emma tapped her chest. "It'll be okay."

Mason smiled at her and nodded. "Then let's go."

I ended up being placed in the corner position between Trace and Axe Guy, but still slightly in the middle. At least I wasn't squished between Emma and Morgan anymore, completely unable to move. I followed along, keeping as vigilant as the rest of the team while we moved down the path which cut through the middle of the jungle. Since we were the last team to enter, it was a quiet walk, with only a couple monsters that popped out on Billy's and Mason's side.

We branched off of the trail to head to the northeast corner, and I couldn't help but look around. Any damage Blake's team did had vanished, leaving the jungle in its silvery-green glory.

Suddenly, I became aware of something thirty feet to our left.

A split second later, Mason lifted his hand and looked to the left. The team stopped, Trace a step slower than everyone else. Emma notched an arrow at the ready and aimed where he directed.

While they weren't paying attention to me, I Mirrored my kindjal. Whatever was coming at us was big and strong.

Emma drew back her bow, ready to shoot.

Alarm shot down my back as I suddenly felt a threat on our right. How did it get so close without us noticing? "Right!" I gasped as Emma released her arrow.

The bush in front of Trace exploded as a huge silver-green snake's head, bigger than I was tall, emerged. Its red mouth was wide, long white fangs bigger than my arm gleaming in the light. Emma's arrow thudded right into its open maw, nailing its whip-like tongue to its lower jaw. It shrieked and jerked to the side, barely missing Trace. Forty feet of long, thick body coiled as the level forty-nine serpent arched back at us.

At the same time, a wide tree right by Billy cracked. With a groan, it tipped toward our party, ready to flatten us. Billy yelled and jumped, swinging his claymore. His blade hit the trunk, and he grunted, powering the tree to the side. Its branches smashed into the surrounding trees, raining down pieces of silvery wood until the heavy trunk thudded on the ground, several feet from Axe Guy.

From where the tree had been, a second serpent lunged at us. Unlike the first one, this one's skin was a solid green color.

Kip thrust out her arm and launched a fireball at the green serpent as it aimed for Billy, who was still in the air. It jerked to the side, avoiding the fireball and Billy at the same time. Smooth as butter, it slid across the ground, crossing behind the silvery serpent, their long tails blending until they almost looked like a two-headed Hydra.

"Billy, Nick, and Kip, you take the green serpent. Everyone else with me on the silver one," Mason commanded. He lunged forward with his long sword, trying to separate the two.

I couldn't help but pause. These monsters were thirty levels higher than me. How was I going to help? If I used Mist—which I didn't want to do in front of people yet—the rest of the team would be as blind as the monsters. Not helpful. It took me only a second to reject the idea before I gripped my kindjals and ran forward to join Mason and Trace.

Mason swung his sword and slashed at the silver serpent's neck, sparks flashing as the blade hit the scales. A cut was left, but it wasn't as deep as his attack should have been. The monster snapped at Mason, fast as lightning, apparently not caring about the arrow stub still in its mouth or the slight trail of black blood that was leaking from its jaw. Mason jumped back, and the serpent missed him by inches.

I lunged up, aiming for its large red eye. The snake jerked and smashed against my body with the side of its triangle head—half my HP evaporated just like that.

I groaned in pain as I was flung through the air. An alarm went off in my head, and I turned to look behind me. The green serpent turned its head and opened its mouth wide, ready to snatch me out of the air.

<h1 style="text-align:center">CHAPTER 47</h1>

The green serpent's huge white fangs and red mouth came closer to my soaring body. I gasped and twisted in the air, trying to get out of the way, even though I knew I would fail.

A gray blur streaked on my right. The blur took on the shape of Billy, who smashed his blade down on the green serpent's nose. The strength of the impact crushed the monster's jaw closed and bowed its head, allowing me to sail right over it and land on its back.

A strong grip clapped around my arm, and I was jerked to the side, off the monster's scaly green back. Axe Guy—Nick?—didn't wait for me to get my bearings before he tossed me aside. I was barely out of the way when the green serpent slashed out with its two-foot-thick tail, hitting Axe Guy Nick right in the chest, who staggered with a pained grunt.

Would he even have taken that hit if it weren't for me?

I landed hard on the ground and gasped for air, staring up at Morgan's face. She leaned down and touched me with gold, glowing fingers. Instantly, my HP increased.

I nodded in thanks to Morgan and rolled to my feet.

"You should stay with me," she said, her eyes on the fight.

I shook my head. "I'm not useless."

She frowned and glanced at me. "Okay. Here."

A book appeared in her left hand. It flipped open by itself, pages waving through the air as it started to glow. The pages stopped turning halfway through, and a bright light radiated from the page. She waved her hand at me.

A warm sensation started at the crown of my head and spread down my body until it reached the soles of my feet.

[Protection: +15 Defense. Time limit: 15 minutes]

My eyes widened.

Morgan nodded, apparently satisfied. "That should help for a little bit."

Mason grunted nearby, and she turned her head toward him. He flopped through the air and landed on his back a couple feet in front of us. She moved to attend him as Emma jumped forward and put herself between them and the silver monster, setting off one arrow after another. Each one hit, but just like with the sword, the attacks were too shallow to do any serious damage. Kip's fire attacks were just as ineffective; the scales were just too thick.

Morgan waved her hand; a golden ball of light appeared then left her palm and encompassed Mason. The golden glow spread over him, and he climbed to his feet. He nodded at Morgan and tapped Emma slightly on the shoulder as he ran to rejoin the fight.

I stared hard at the silver serpent, concentrating on it, looking for a critical-hit spot. It moved so fast it was hard to see anything but a blur of scales. Then, I finally found it—the light glow of an energy crystal, three feet below its jawline, on the left side of its body.

Running over to Emma, I pointed. "Shoot right there. That's its weak spot."

She immediately drew an arrow and let it loose, shooting through the air in a deadly blur. It hit the scales but was deflected, leaving a small scratch inches lower than where I'd pointed.

"There?" she panted.

"Wait for me," I said, activating Feather Step. I was trying to be conservative with my MP because I didn't know what else was going to happen today, but this was getting serious. I lunged right over Trace's head and landed on the silver serpent.

It flailed, trying to throw me off, but I held on as it angled its head and snapped at me. At the same time, Mason swung his sword at an existing cut and left a deeper gash in the monster, and Trace flanked it and stabbed at it with his hooked daggers. The serpent paused and lifted its head in the air, hissing in pain.

I shimmied up its body until I found the location of the energy crystal. Gripping my kindjal, I stabbed up, sliding the blade between the scales, and with a jerk, I popped the top palm-size scale right off its underbelly.

"There! Hit it there!" I yelled.

The words were barely out of my mouth before an arrow sank in the exposed muscle tissue. The arrow tip missed my hand by inches, but that wasn't what caused alarm to seize my breath. The snake withered, nearly shaking me off. It turned its head but couldn't bend enough to reach me. Why didn't it die? I knew the arrow had hit the right place. Had it not gone in deep enough?

Two more arrows sank into the exposed tissue, but the monster still wouldn't die.

My hands slipped on the scales, and I started to slide down. Determined, I wedged my kindjal between two scales on the snake's back and used it to hold myself in place. If Emma couldn't shoot through the monster's muscle, maybe a good kick might send the embedded arrow all the way home. I angled my body, getting ready to stomp.

Just then, the green serpent snapped at me. I gasped and jerked away, my legs flailing free, and I barely held onto the kindjal as I tried to slide around the silver serpent's body to put it between me and the attacking monster. The green monster's fangs dug into the silver serpent's neck right where I'd been clinging to a second ago. After a quick snap, it pulled back, jerking and hissing as Billy and Nick sheared off a chunk of its flesh and Kip roasted the exposed muscle.

The silver serpent I clung to twisted and jerked in the air. Gripping my kindjal tightly with my left hand, I tried to swing back to where I'd been positioned before the other monster got in the way.

"Let it go!" Mason warned.

Before I could decide whether or not to follow his order, the silver monster turned its head to the side and lunged, aiming for the thick brush around us.

It was fleeing! I gasped and let go of my kindjal.

Suddenly, a deep, piercing agony cut through the fleshy part of my left upper arm, so strong that my mind numbed and I could only scream. A hooked dagger stabbed through my arm all the way up to its guard, the tip of the dagger pinning me right into the silver serpent's wound left by the other monster. The dagger's gut hook latched on the exposed muscle and effectively nailed me to the monster.

Pain ricocheted through my numb mind. I didn't even have time to figure out what I should do before the serpent plunged into the forest, moving at a dizzying speed.

Through the wind rushing past my ears and the foliage slapping me, I could hear Emma and several others yelling for me between the sounds of continued fighting. Those sounds quickly disappeared.

I was like a rag doll on the back of an out-of-control wagon. The silvery-green serpent slithered over the uneven ground, through bushes, and around trees. With each move it made, the dagger in my arm jerked more and sent intense stabs of pain through my body. As if that torture wasn't enough, the monster kept shifting purposefully to scrape me against every tree and giant rainbow crystal it passed. I had to keep shifting and pivoting from one side of the snake to the other, causing all the more damage to my arm.

My red blood mixed with the monster's black one and ran down its scales, leaving multicolored splashes on the ground and random leaves as the serpent crashed through the jungle. Everything combined steadily chipped away at my HP, even with the protection spell Morgan had cast on me.

I gritted my teeth and tried to clear my mind enough to figure out what to do. Gripping the dagger's handle with my right hand, I tried to stabilize myself so it didn't tear at my left arm anymore. Each of my breaths hissed through my teeth as I looked at the next tree the snake was aiming at. I kicked my feet up, knees bent, and held onto the handle as tight as I could. The soles of my boots landed on the tree trunk, and I jumped backward with everything I had.

My mouth gaped open in a silent scream as the dagger thrashed in the muscle of my arm. With a gruesome, fleshy rip, the gut hook of the dagger cut through the monster's muscle it was embedded in. For a second I was airborne, finally loose from the serpent. Even if the dagger remained in my arm, it would be the least of my problems. I twisted in the air and landed on the ground, my feet sliding across moist dirt before I stopped. Wincing, I gripped my limp arm beneath the dagger to brace it.

The monster hissed and whipped around, its huge red eyes focused on me.

Oh shit! Mist exploded out of me, filling up the area between me and the high-level monster. I didn't know how it hunted—sight, heat, or smell—but I hoped that the Mist would conceal some of that. I then quickly activated the skill I'd received from the Skill Stone I'd picked up yesterday—Stealth (Limited).

My body, already concealed in the white fog, turned completely invisible. It would be a heavy cost—10 MP for ten minutes on top of my already depleted MP—but I couldn't fight this monster. The only thing I could hope to do was get away.

The monster froze, as if confused by what was happening in front of it. I gripped my arm even tighter, bracing my injury from shaking as I used the serpent's momentary distraction to climb the mist as though it were stairs, right into the tree. Reaching the treetop, I pivoted to a thick branch where I knelt down behind a large rainbow crystal growing out of the silvery bark. I cupped my hand under my elbow to catch the blood dripping from my limp arm; the last thing I needed was the monster reacting to the noise of it falling and finding me.

The serpent lunged forward and struck at the mist. It got nothing but an empty mouth. The monster whipped its head back and forth in the fog, causing it to waft and curl in the air, but no matter what it did, it couldn't find me because I wasn't on the ground anymore.

A couple minutes later, it finally gave up. Slowly, it turned and slithered into the depths of the jungle, leaving a bloody black trail in its wake.

I shifted and leaned back against the tree trunk, still invisible and in pain. *I didn't think that would actually work so easily.* I knew about Stealth, but to my knowledge, it came in several levels. Since I had Limited Stealth, I thought it wouldn't be that effective against a high-leveled monster. Was it because I paired it with Mist?

I frowned, remembering how the red orcs had used it to sneak up on me months ago. How they were literally invisible and silent, not even a hint of their smell or presence.

My ability wasn't at that level yet. My sounds weren't masked—I was just naturally silent—and I didn't know the full extent of how much my presence and smell were erased, but it *did* turn me invisible, which was a start.

The monster was gone, but I still had a dagger in my arm. First Aid 101 suggested I wrap it up so the impaled object didn't wiggle around, and go to the nearest hospital or healer. Only, I was in the middle of a jungle on the far side of the Gate, and I had no idea where Emma's team was. My bearings got jumbled up while I was pinned to the monster, but I knew enough to know I was a long way from where I started. I couldn't trek through this high-leveled jungle with this in my arm.

God, this *destroy the Feng Jungle crystal* task was a lot more dangerous than I thought it would be. So much for sneaking in with Emma's team, finding the giant crystal, and destroying it without implicating Emma in the process. Nothing had gone right since I stepped into the forest. Not even counting yesterday, today was such a screw up that I'd somehow gotten *in the way* of a teammate's attack right as I was trying to *get out of the way.*

That's right, I knew where the hooked dagger had come from. It belonged to Trace. Whether or not he'd pinned me on purpose, I'd have to go over that with him later. Right now, I had more immediate needs to take care of. Getting my blood pumping faster with agitation wasn't going to help me at all.

I squeezed my eyes shut tight and took a deep breath as I accepted that no matter what happened next, it was going to hurt. The bright side was that I had a Regen ability, and it would heal my arm back to perfect condition—once I got the dagger out. The drawback was that I was going to have to stay still for at least an hour for that to happen. Technically, I had enough MP to keep Stealth activated the whole time, but then I'd be completely out—and who knew what else I'd encounter before I found Emma. If I found Emma.

This sucks.

I hissed out a pained breath and looked down through the thick mist to the trail of blood on the ground. I should be able to find my way back if I followed that, given that the monster didn't make too many detours trying to get me off or I wasn't found by a high-ranked monster first. Knowing Emma, she was probably trying to drag her team through the forest after me. A smile twitched at my stiff mouth before I grimaced.

Gotta get this thing out first. I moved my right hand and looked at the blood pooled in my palm. Droplets of the serpent's black blood skimmed the surface of my red, like oil drips in water. I knew human and monster blood couldn't mix, but I didn't see it often.

I sighed and looked at the amount of bodily fluids I held. I supposed that was one benefit of being a Hunter—we could bleed like an old Japanese cartoon and keep going. Since I didn't sense a monster around me, I tipped my hand and let the blood dribble to the ground before I pulled out the fresh spare shirt I put in my Items Bag this morning and used it to wipe the blood off my right palm.

When my skin was dry enough, I unbuckled the double belt of my hip satchel and wrapped the extra length around two protruding rainbow crystals, carefully strapping myself against them. The last thing I needed was to get the dagger out, then pass out from blood loss and fall out of the tree. Once my back was pressed snuggly against the cold stones, I sagged into the harness I'd created and silently panted in pain. After a minute, I summoned my kindjal to my hand and my spare pants onto my lap.

I took a couple deep breaths to psych myself up, then raised the kindjal.

CHAPTER 48

Carefully, I touched the tip of my weapon to the end of my leather belt and slowly pressed down using my own stomach like a cutting board. The blade indented the black leather and broke through the shiny surface. I quickly thrust my wrist down, and the blade cut right through the belt. The kindjal tip struck my chest plate and instantly stopped, leaving me with a small strip of leather two inches long and a half an inch wide. I knew that my kindjal couldn't cut my armor or my body, but it was still a little unnerving to purposefully stab at myself.

The blade disappeared from my hand, and I grabbed the piece of leather. It looked just big enough to cover the gut hook. Gripping the handle of the hooked dagger embedded in my arm, I shifted it until I could wedge the wicked-looking tip against the two crystals behind me. I paused as another shot of pain jarred my whole body, shuddering. A bead of sweat rolled down my nose as I took a couple breaths to steady myself. Twisting to my side as much as I could, I wedged the leather piece over the gut hook, making an impromptu sheath for that little part.

If it didn't have the gut hook, I could just pull the dagger out while ignoring every first aid rule in the process, but that wicked little part created more problems. If I were to just pull it back, the hook would rip my arm in half. I had Limited Regen, but I wasn't ready to test its limits just yet.

But god, it hurt so bad working that little piece of leather over the tip of the hook. Each time I moved, another jolt of mind-numbing pain shot from my arm to my whole body. Tears pricked my eyes, and I furiously blinked them away. Not what I needed right now.

Finally, the leather bit was on enough that I was semiconfident it wouldn't come off as I pulled the dagger out. I eased the tip of the dagger off of the red-smeared crystals behind me and slumped back, breathing hard. Blood loss and overexertion chipped away at my mental clarity. A slightly gray hue ringed the rim of my vision. My body sagged, too heavy.

I closed my eyes. "Come on, Jynn," I whispered, my voice dry and cracked. *You can do this.* I forced my thoughts to focus and opened my eyes.

I used my hand and mouth to tie the ruined shirt as a tourniquet around my arm above the dagger. While I waited for the blood flow to slow down, I also loosely wrapped my spare pair of pants around my arm just below where the dagger was. As soon as I was set, I gripped the handle of the dagger. Blood squished between my fingers and trailed down my hand. After all the thrashing and movement I'd been through since this thing got stuck in my arm, the cut was a lot wider than the blade. Hopefully, the hole in my arm was big enough.

I took a deep breath and started to work the weapon out. My hand was coated in red. My arm was saturated with sticky red. All I could see was red. I clenched my jaw against the gut-wrenching, nauseating pain. The blade inched out.

The leather piece that capped the gut hook hit the back of my arm, where the exit wound was. I hissed out a breath to keep from screaming. Tears streamed down my cheeks, but I leaned forward and bit the handle to keep it in place, then I reached around and started to work the leather inside the cut to help push it through. I moaned and shuddered, but was able to get it in.

From there, I grabbed the handle and began pulling the dagger painfully, slowly out. Every second took an eternity until finally, the bloodied cap showed through the entrance wound. The rest of it slid out with a sickening pop. Trace's hooked dagger slipped from my fingers and dropped to the jungle floor below.

As fast as I could, I stuffed some of my pants in my mouth and gripped the other side before pulling the pants as tight as I could over the gaping hole in my arm. I spit out the material then jerked at the tourniquet and loosened the ruined shirt. Once that was done, I gripped the pants over my limp arm and leaned back on my bloody crystal backrest.

Five minutes, I thought. If I didn't die from blood loss in the next five minutes, I'd be fine. At least, that's what I told myself. Limply, I tilted my head back and watched as the gray ring around my vision thickened and distorted my view of the shimmering silvery-green leaves overhead.

* * *

Something rustled in the bushes below.

My eyes snapped open. *Oh god, did I pass out? Ah, wait, I'm awake. I'm not dead.* But I didn't have time to celebrate, because I felt the presence of a monster below me. Careful not to make any noise, I leaned to the side enough that I could see a fat, lumpy brown monster pawing at the ground. Honestly, it looked like a wad of mud on stubby legs with a smooshed rectangle head. The System labeled it as a level forty-five mudhog. It didn't look dangerous, really, but that didn't change the fact that it was twice my level.

It stumbled around the ground, sniffing loudly at the bloody dagger I'd dropped. Then it shifted around and followed the trail of my blood across the soil to the base of the tree.

I froze. Did it know how to climb? I didn't know anything about this monster, and since it was on scene, I didn't have time to look it up.

The mudhog paused and sniffed the serpent's black blood, which was splashed across the bark with my own browning one. The monster stiffened then snorted. A huge gush of liquid erupted out of its nose and splattered the tree. As soon as the mud hit, it bubbled and smoked, and what I thought was mud began to corrode bark and leaves.

The monster gave a snorty squeal then turned around. It ambled away on its short legs, waddling and dripping sizzling mud with every step it took.

I released a silent sigh and looked at my left arm. I wiggled my fingers and twisted my hand, lifting it up to chest height. It still hurt, but the pain had lessened to a strong ache instead of mind-numbing agony. More importantly, I could actually move it, and nothing felt wrong anymore.

I opened my main menu. *How long was I out?* Long enough for my HP to increase up to seventy percent. I even recovered some MP, which was good.

Nodding slowly to myself, I tugged at the blood-soaked pants around my arm until they loosened. Tenderly, I touched the stiff material until it parted enough to see my skin underneath. The gaping hole was gone, a week-old wound in its place, the skin red and rough but solid. I couldn't resist poking at it, sighing at the slight sting. Good. I'd take it. This was a million times better than losing my arm entirely.

Now it was time to get out of here. Who knew what other monsters would be drawn to the scent of my blood? And I couldn't trust the serpent's blood to scare them away like with the mudhog.

I unbuckled my belt from the crystal and secured it around my waist. Luckily, it wasn't too affected by the half inch I cut off. Honestly, I could barely tell, and I knew what it looked like before. Taking out two water bottles, I drank the first one, downing the whole thing in two big breaths. The other I poured on my clothes, watching the reddened liquid cascade to the ground. The water didn't wash all the blood out, but it did help with the stiffness, and hopefully, it lessened the bloody smell. Once that was done, I took out a protein bar and ate the wooden fake-chocolate chunk as quickly as I could.

Well, that was as good as it got for me right now. I surveyed the tree line, the ground cover, and listened intently for any sounds. I couldn't fight off high-leveled monsters, but I had to follow that trail of blood to find my way back to where I was separated from Emma. I didn't expect to find her there, but it was at least a starting point to getting the hell out of here.

After another check, I jumped out of the tree. I landed next to the dagger and couldn't help scowling at the offending chunk of metal. With a sneer, I dug the tip of my boot under the blade and flicked it against the tree. It hit the mud left by the monster and dropped to the ground, some of the mud clinging to it. Smoke drifted up from the pattern-weld blade as the sizzling snot eroded holes through the metal. With great satisfaction, I watched as the gut hook melted right off.

It was obviously an expensive weapon, but Trace was just going to have to get a new dagger. Sorry not sorry.

With one last glare, I started trekking through the jungle, following the bloody trail the serpent left. I'd barely walked for five minutes when I felt something approaching me. Quickly, I scrambled up the closest tree and pulled out my kindjal, ready to activate Stealth and Mist if needed. A moment later, a human figure ran toward me.

I frowned and slowly stood up, recognizing the person.

Trace glanced up and paused when he caught sight of me, his eyes wide. He stopped not far from me. "You're not dead." There wasn't an ounce of relief in his voice.

Ah, well that answered a lot of questions. "Nope. I'm not." I glared down at him. "You were the only survivor from your last team. Do you have a habit of killing off your teammates? Or am I just the lucky one?"

He actually laughed like I'd made a joke. "No, I don't. I honestly don't know how my team died yesterday. Me and my buddy got separated from them while looking for you. The rest went MIA, and my buddy died while we were trying to get back to the transportation circle." He smiled like it wasn't a big deal. "But you, yeah, you're the lucky one."

My eyes narrowed. "Why me? What did I ever do to you? I didn't even know you yesterday. And I barely even know you now."

His head tipped to the side, a pleasant smile on his face. It was so unlike the quiet man whom I'd spent the whole morning with that it freaked me out.

Oh, and the way his eyes were dissecting me didn't help, either.

"You don't have to know me, and I don't have to know you. All I need to know is that you upset Miss Bethany because you won't stay away from her man. That's all that matters."

I gaped at him.

Are you kidding me? That's *why he's trying to kill me?* I talked to a guy, and his girlfriend sent a hitman after me? Man, I would have never guessed she was crazy just by looking at her. Then again, Trace seemed like a normal guy this morning, too. Then again, I was paying so much attention to Billy and Emma that I barely even looked at the guy.

I wanted to bury my head in my hands and scream in frustration, but I didn't dare take my eyes off Trace. He'd already struck me with one dagger and put me through a world of hurt. Who knew what he'd do if I looked away again?

"So, how about you just tell her that we talked and that I will never go near her man again? And we call it good?" I waved a hand, trying to act confident as I negotiated. Seriously, though, Kesstel was on my no-way-in-hell list now. As if he wasn't on my blacklist before then.

Trace snorted. "Ah, no. It's taken so much work to kill you, I really need to see you dead now. Since Little Emma cares so much about you, I couldn't openly, accidentally kill you—I still have to hold my spot in the guild, mind you. And that serpent should have finished you off." He glanced at my arm as if confused that it was whole. "How is your arm still intact? Where's my dagger? I do want it back."

I sneered. "Last I saw, it was dissolving into an acid puddle."

He scowled and tsked before his emotions turned on a dime and he smiled like a saint. "Oh well. It was a pleasant chat, but I'm going to kill you now." Another dagger appeared in his hand, and he threw it at me in a blur of speed.

No way in hell!

I raised my kindjal and deflected the blade. I had just gotten one of these things out; I was not getting another one stuck in me again! The guard of the dagger hit my kindjal and spun off to the side, falling some-where below. I countered with a throw of my own weapon.

He jerked to the side, kindjal barely missing him. He snorted. "That's a sword, not a dagger. What are you throwing it for?"

To distract you, idiot! Before he was done talking, I had already activated Feather Step and leaped to the next tree. My kindjal appeared back in my hand as I sped from branch to branch, following the serpent's trail of blood from above.

Trace kept right on my heels below. He laughed, oddly delighted. "Do you really think that a little E can outrun a C?"

For now, I had confidence that I could keep ahead. At least until my MP ran out. Hopefully, I'd find Emma by then.

CHAPTER 49

No matter how fast I went, I couldn't shake Trace off my trail. He stayed below me on the ground, just a step behind. He didn't have enough time to climb up to my height in the trees, but I wasn't in any better position, since my MP was dropping steadily. And I didn't know how far I was from Emma.

"If you're looking for the rest of the team, you're going to be sorely disappointed," Trace mocked from below. His obnoxious words were breathy, and his face was wet with sweat. "Every Hunter knows it's pointless to go after lost people."

"Shut up!" I snarled.

"What? It's just survival of the fittest. And that doesn't include you." His hand flashed out.

I felt the threat coming and tilted my body. Another one of those damn daggers shot right past my shoulder. Good hell, how many of those did he have? I wanted to give him a taste of his own medicine so badly.

My foot slipped on the smooth silvery bark, and I tipped to the side. I swore, reaching for a thick green vine that stretched between the trees. My fingers latched onto the rough plant, and I used it to swing at a ninety-degree turn, then with a small kick, I landed on a thick branch.

Meanwhile, Trace turned midstep and skidded across the ground. As he regained his balance, I twisted and threw my kindjal at him. He dodged, but not well enough, and my short sword impaled his shoulder all the way to the hilt. He yelled and dropped to one knee. He tipped his head back until he could see me, murder in his eyes.

"Feels great, huh? Too bad it doesn't have a gut hook, right?" I sneered and kept jumping. Two trees later, the kindjal appeared back in my hand.

"The hell kinda sword is that?" Trace snarled behind me.

"It's not a dagger, that's for sure," I tossed over my shoulder and kept going. That sharp turn to take a shot at Trace had led me astray. I needed a quick route back to the bloody trail.

That's when I saw a tunnel made out of thick, white webbing hanging between a cluster of trees. I nearly paused, but momentum forced me onward.

My god, there were more of them. My insides tightened painfully at the sight of the caterpillar tunnel, instinct warning me to keep away. But I turned in the treetops and started heading toward it, shuddering in repulsion as I got closer.

What I felt didn't matter. It was either Trace or me—and it wasn't going to be me.

I kicked off the side of a branch and landed on the rich ground. By now, I was able to put a little distance between us, but he remained doggedly on my tail. I glanced at him over my shoulder then bolted into the white tunnel. I never thought I'd ever voluntarily go in one of these again, but since I couldn't beat him by myself, desperate times called for desperate measures.

The System went off as expected, the only indication that there was even a problem. [**Anomaly detected. Autoimmunity activated.**]

The tunnel was about sixty feet long, and just as eerie as the one yesterday. As I ran, I kept an eye out for any rainbow shimmers. There weren't any, nor could I feel any monsters in the white webbing, but I knew they were there. I skidded to a stop on the far end of the tunnel and turned back to Trace.

He'd stopped just outside of the webbing, eyeing it with distrust. Obviously, he'd been a Hunter long enough to know not to enter such a strange place. He looked at me and licked his lips, clearly debating. As it was, there was no way he could get to me unless he came after me.

I lifted my chin. "I don't recommend you come in here. I don't think you could handle it." There was a challenge in my tone, as if he would be a wimp if he didn't.

He glared at me. "You really like pissing people off, don't you? I'm surprised someone hasn't killed you already."

I couldn't help but laugh. Seriously, he had no idea. The saddest part was that I didn't think I'd done anything to deserve any of it. I mean, take right now for example. All I'd done was talk to a guy, and now I had my own personal hitman. Where was the logic in that?

"So, Bethany Wil—"

"You are not worthy to speak her name!" he screamed, his eyes suddenly manic. "You should be ground into dust for even attempting to tarnish her name with your lowly lips."

My eyebrows rose high on my forehead. *Well, that was a little extreme, but whatever floats his boat.* I opened my arms. "I'm waiting."

Waiting for him to come in and get himself turned into a monster. I almost hoped he'd walk away as my conscience chimed in. *How is this any different from premeditated murder?*

No. I couldn't think of it that way. This wasn't murder—this was survival. And he really could walk away.

"But you really should just leave," I warned.

He took a breath and glanced around the webbed tunnel again. He flipped the dagger in his hand around and around, obviously thinking. I was a little surprised he hadn't thrown it at me yet. Was it his last one?

He lunged forward, sprinting at me full speed.

My eyes narrowed, torn between disappointment at his stupidity and relief that he'd just made things a lot easier for me. Whether or not he died, I could use this to catch a rainbow caterpillar to show the Council. Then I could just run away while he wandered the Vale as a monster for the rest of his life.

Ten feet in, Trace dropped to the ground like a piece of lead and skidded facedown to a stop.

I bolted toward him. *Gotta get to him before he transforms.* If I could find the caterpillar, I could put it in my empty water bottle and take it back to the Hunter Council. It could be the solid proof I needed to show my previous reports weren't crazy rants. They wouldn't be able to turn me away again if they watched a human become a monster with their own eyes.

Mere feet from him, his whole body lit up, just like Reina's did right before she'd transformed. I skidded to a stop. My eyes widened.

No! That was too fast! Had the caterpillar started on his chest?

Suddenly, his level increased from forty-one to forty-two, and his whole body twitched uncontrollably.

Oh crud! I cursed and ran, closing the gap between us, my kindjal out. Forget catching the caterpillar now; I had to deal with him before he turned all the way into a monster. Once he woke up, I wouldn't have a chance.

His arms and legs shrunk as he began turning into a moth, just like Reina. Two huge bulges grew on his back as I lunged to his side, ready to stab down on his neck with all I had, but just then, wings erupted from his back. They smacked into me, hard as steel, and sent me flying back through the air. I gasped in pain and landed against the tunnel wall.

White webbing clung to me, holding me in place as I struggled. I thrashed and lashed at the strings, kindjal cutting through them like warm butter, but there were so many that it didn't feel as productive as it should.

A screech rang through the air, and I looked back at Trace.

He—*it* lifted its head, the movement causing the last of the hair which clung to the black, bulbous scalp to fall away. Its face was a grotesque mix of human and bug features, with huge red insect eyes and a tiny mouth full of mandibles and fangs. It focused on me and screeched again, its wings beating the air as it wobbled a little, slowly hovering off the ground.

My gut twisted, and I started to struggle more against the webbing. Not to climb out of it but to cut through it to the other side. With one final slash, a gap opened behind me, and I twisted and jerked myself through, ripping at the white tentacles still latching onto me. Just as the last string let go, Moth Trace landed on the other side. Its twin right arms reached through the opening and clawed at me, but it couldn't fit its body through the hole with its wings.

I jerked back, just out of reach.

Just then, two large magic explosions in the distance happened at the same time. The biggest one was the farthest away, somewhere maybe east? It was enough that the ground shook, and I stumbled over the rolling dirt before I caught my balance against a tree. The smaller explosion came from the opposite direction—west?—and it was a lot closer.

I didn't know what caused them, but I did know they were Hunter made. Which meant that somewhere close by, there was someone who could help me kill this moth monster.

I activated Stealth and watched my MP flash red in warning. I didn't want to use it, but I was desperate. Turning on my heel, I Feather Stepped to a sprint toward the smaller explosion.

Behind me, I could hear the moth monster shrieking, and the sounds of thrashing wings. I peeked over my shoulder just enough to see it breaking out of the tunnel. All at once, the white tunnel started to evaporate. Just like last time, it had turned someone into a monster—mission accomplished—then disappeared. So frustrating.

But not nearly as terrifying as seeing the moth rise into the air and fly after me. Even though I was using Stealth, its buggy eyes stayed locked on me.

I gasped, putting every bit of power I could into my legs. When was the running going to end today? First it was Trace, then it was Monster Trace. Was he trying to run me to death?

I could hear the moth's wafting wings getting closer, as if I were slowing down, not speeding up.

The sound of humans talking reached my ears, and I perked up; I was getting closer to a group of Hunters. I couldn't understand their words yet, but I knew that someone—anyone—was on the other side of the trees.

The bottom of my boots skidded on the ground as I made a sharp turn and ducked at the same time. The monster sailed right over me, close enough that I could feel the wind under its wings. Then I jumped through the bushes, diving for all I was worth.

The group of Hunters came into view.

I stumbled to a stop and gaped at them, horrified.

There were nearly a hundred Hunters in this jungle, and I had run into Blake and his team two days in a row. Seriously, it could have been anyone else, but no, it had to be that bastard. First my plan for Trace flopped, and now I had to deal with Blake. What kind of luck was that?

Most of his team was bunched together, laughing and talking like they were on vacation, while a few Hunters skinned a large monster on the other side of a violently formed—and obviously recently made—clearing. I bet the open space had something to do with the explosion I'd heard moments earlier, given the tree scraps all over the ground.

When I came out of the brush, Blake's crew turned and looked at the wildly shuttering leaves. Some scowled but didn't move, while a few others stood up with their weapons at the ready. But it was obvious they couldn't see through the invisibility of my Stealth.

I glanced over my shoulder at the moth monster circling through the air. It angled its body, dipped downward, and soared right for me.

What the hell! I sprinted right at the Hunters, Blake or not.

CHAPTER 50

As I neared Blake's team, Penny shifted and glanced around, the long dark brown hair of her high ponytail swaying with each turn. Her eyes flicked over me, then moved away, then back. But she was the only one who even came close to looking at me. A wakizashi appeared in her hand, and she shifted, ready, but couldn't seem to pin down my presence.

"Penny," Blake barked, his handsome face tight. "Do you see anything?" He glanced around wildly with the rest of the Hunters.

"Something . . . " she muttered, unsure.

Moth-Monster Trace burst out of the bushes with a screech. The instant it appeared, the Hunter's auras intensified. It was like the air suddenly turned into lead, making it thick and hard to breathe. My body became sluggish, but I didn't stop running toward them. I really didn't want to stand in the middle of a battlefield.

I skidded around Blake, who stood at the front.

For a second, the world seemed to slow down as I looked into his face. God, how I wanted to stab him. I could see it so vividly in my mind. Lifting my kindjal, the whisper of the blade slicing between the expensive magi-steel breastplates, and then a slight resistance as the blade hit his skin and pushed through.

But it was just a thought, and it was gone as I dodged behind him into the middle of his team. Right now was not a good time to give myself away. Plus, I needed his aura to conceal me. It was a risk, attempting to use one enemy to get rid of another, but both would tear me apart if they detected my presence.

From the center of his group, I looked around at Blake's party. There really was no rhyme or reason to their defensive positioning. It was like a group of individuals just standing next to each other and just somewhat working together.

The moth monster rose into the air, the antennas on its head twitching wildly. Then its focus shifted around until it stopped, aimed directly at me.

Was it targeting me? This was more than just attacking the closest Hunter—it was locked onto me. Because I was the first one it saw? Or was it because I saw it transform?

I couldn't help but think it might be the latter. It would also make sense why no one reported their teammates turning into monsters. If the monsters were programmed to attack whoever saw them transform, there would never be any witnesses.

Quietly, I moved a little farther into the group, putting most of the seven Hunters between me and the hovering moth. Since they were distracted by the monster, right now would be the best time to sneak away.

"What is that thing?" a girl in light armor at my side asked in disgust.

The monster dove, focus still locked onto me. From an outsider's view, it seemed like it was aiming at the party as a whole.

A level seventy Hunter in red mage robes raised his hand. "I don't know, but it's dead now."

An arc of lightning exploded from his palm, hitting the moth in the abdomen and spreading until the entire monster was lit up. It convulsed and writhed in the air, wings folding, before it dropped to the ground with a thud, smoke rising from its body and the smell of burnt . . . *rotten eggs* filling the air.

As soon as it was dead, the heavy air dissipated, and I could breathe again.

I gaped at the carcass, shocked that Monster Trace was dead just like that.

Glancing around, I looked at their levels. Blake, at sixty-seven, was the only one who was lower than level seventy. The rest of his team were between levels seventy-one and eighty-two, even Mark and the two men standing by the carcass at the edge of the clearing.

Did I really make the right move, jumping into the midst of this group? Still, they didn't seem to know I was there. But why not? They were so much higher leveled than me, so what was the difference?

Pondering right now was not the thing to do. My Stealth could run out any minute now, and I'd be revealed to a man who behaved worse than a monster.

I slowly started to back out of the group.

Just as I left their scattered circle, Penny turned her head and looked in my general direction. "I swear . . . " her voice trailed off as she started to weave through her team.

"What is it?" Blake glanced at her.

The curvy mage who'd dragged me and Emma's team through the jungle like a kite yesterday tsked and folded her arms across her chest. "Jumping at ghosts again?" she mocked.

Penny shot her a glare. "Shut it, Daniella."

Daniella glanced at Blake coquettishly and smiled.

The rest of the team shifted around Penny as they walked towards the fried monster while she walked in my direction, still holding her waki-zashi. I continued to move backward, keeping my eyes on Penny while I tried to get closer to a huge tree at the edge of the man-made clearing.

The Hunters grouped around the dead moth.

Blake nudged it with his foot, making the stiff carcass rock back and forth. "So no one knows what this is?"

The Huntress who'd first asked opened her Guide and started flipping through it. "It's not in the *Monster Manual.*"

Blake smiled. "Perfect. Take it apart carefully. We'll turn it over to the study geeks—it's not a bad thing to get credit for discovering a new monster." He glanced over at Mark, who stood over the two Hunters skinning the large carcass on the other side of the clearing. "Are they done yet?"

Mark shook his head. "In a minute. We don't want to ruin the hide, right?"

Blake jerked his shoulder. "Well, hurry. We still need to find that crystal." He glanced around at his teammates and pointed. "Start taking care of this monster." He motioned to the moth at his feet. "Don't ruin it."

"Seriously, why can't you just put a whole carcass in an Items Bag?" one of the Hunters complained as he crouched and pulled a knife out.

All of this was happening while I slowly continued to back up and Penny came closer and closer. Five more feet, then I could sneak around the closest tree. There were two more minutes left of my Stealth, and I only had 15 MP left. I didn't dare take my eyes off Penny. She couldn't seem to pinpoint me, but that made her more on edge, which put *me* more on edge.

The back of my boot hit thick tree roots.

A System window suddenly flashed in my face. [**Task: Prevent the Energy Crystal in Feng Jungle from crossing into Earth.**]

I was so tightly wound that I jumped back, my heart nearly stopping in shock. At that very instant, Penny swung her wakizashi, her blade slicing the air where I'd just stood and missing me by inches. My nerves had just saved me from being hit.

Landing softly, I stumbled back over the root, clinging to the tree trunk to support me.

Penny struck out once more, her blade severing the whole ten-inch-thick root from the tree. It flung to the side, and silvery sap began leaking from the gash.

From the hole created, a pale blue glow faintly radiated.

My eyes widened. I recognized the color.

Penny gaped, obviously at a better angle to see inside the hole. "Ah, boss?" she whispered, looking over her shoulder.

Blake didn't hear her; he was too busy talking to Daniella while supervising the Hunters taking apart the moth monster.

"Boss!" Penny yelled.

He frowned and looked at her. "What?"

She shifted to the side and pointed to the blue glow coming from under the tree. "I think I just found the crystal."

"What?!" Blake hurried over.

I scrambled around the tree, putting it between me and the running Hunters. Any noise I made was overshadowed by their excited whoops. Blake peered closer to the hole, the pale blue light illuminating his face.

He gave a short laugh. "Let's check it out." He stood up and motioned to Daniella. "Move the tree."

Memories of her levitating me in the air yesterday came to mind, and I leaped out of the way as fast as I could. I landed next to another tree and swung around it just in time to activate Stealth again. Behind the safety of my cover, I leaned around and watched.

Daniella held out her hands and muttered under her breath. A second later, the giant tree shuddered. Its branches rattled, striking the branches of surrounding trees and causing fat leaves, twigs, and pieces of silvery bark to rain down on my head. Several rainbow crystals fell from the quivering treetops, and the shards stabbed into the rich soil on my right.

Not concerned at all, Daniella lifted her hands higher in the air. The tree groaned and shuddered until it was vibrating, rising a few inches into the air, but it stopped once its roots were pulled taut. Dirt rained from the bottom of the tree, but that didn't subtract from the brilliant blue light which radiated from the gap underneath. It lit up the space like a second sun.

I gasped, the sound smothered by the excited noises of the rest of the Hunters. I could only see a little bit, but the whole top curve of the energy crystal covered nearly the whole width of the tree's roots. If it was circular and not oval, the crystal had to be at least fifteen feet in diameter.

"Damn," Mark muttered. "It's huge! And we can't even see the whole thing yet!"

Blake gave a short, gloating laugh. He tapped the shoulder of two big Hunters beside him. "Cut it loose."

The men stepped forward, their huge, full armor clanking as they moved. Oversized double-sided axes appeared in their hands as they moved closer to the tree. They raised their weapons, and with quick moves, cut all the roots loose.

With a jerk, the tree levitated higher in the air. More branches snapped, raining down debris on me. The trees around it swayed as their branches were caught and pulled at by their ripped-out kin, connecting vines whipping loose. Daniella flicked her hand, and the hovering tree was thrown to the far side of the clearing, landing with a crash like thunder, the trunk cracked in half.

Blake smiled as he stepped forward, getting a good look at the crystal. He leaned down and brushed dirt clods off it, his fingers caressing the stone, his focus intense as he stared at it. "Perfect. It's perfect," he breathed.

He stood and looked around his team. "Looks like that finding bonus is ours. I think this deserves a celebration." He waved his hand, and several cases of beer appeared. "Just don't overdo it. We're still technically on the job." He laughed at his own joke.

I frowned. Even if it was hard for a Hunter to get drunk, did he seriously think that it was impossible for his group to be attacked? Then again, they were such a high level—was there really something in this forest which could hurt them?

Mark picked up a bottle and walked over to Blake. "Do you really need this to get a bonus?" He nodded at the crystal. "I mean, doesn't President Price give you whatever you want, anyway?"

Blake took the bottle that Daniella handed to him. He scowled and took a swig.

"Wardyn has been such a tightwad lately. All he does is count money and talk about improving the guild. Yapping on and on about recruiting all the best new Hunters during the next graduation and whatnot. I get it. But shit, he could loosen up a little." His mouth kicked up at the side. "But now he can't say no to me anymore." Glancing over his shoulder at the energy crystal, he handed the bottle back to Daniella. "I gotta let him know the good news."

Blake walked a little farther away and held out his hand. A rose quartz oval appeared, nearly the size of his palm.

My eyes bugged out, shocked. Cell phones didn't work in the Gate. Hunters could message each other through their Guide menu, but it didn't work if you were just on each other's friends list; you had to be partnered together, which was why I hadn't messaged Emma yet. I wasn't officially on her team. There was a difference.

But for those who didn't want to deal with messages, for a small fortune, they could get communication stones. Apparently, they were hard to make, and a pair could run in the millions-of-dollars range.

"Hey, Ward," Blake said to the pink stone. "I found it."

A voice responded from the other side, but I couldn't make out the words.

"Yeah," Blake gloated. "And it's bigger than we thought. I bet after the hospitals take their cut, there will still be enough to make another fortune." He snorted. "Forget the White Wolf guild; we should be able to jump the Thundercat guild." He paused and laughed at something President Price said. "Just get your ass over here and help me dig it up." Then he put the communication stone away and walked back to Daniella.

I flicked a look between the Hunters and the energy crystal, gauging the distance, then I checked how much time I had left in Stealth. Cautiously, I slipped around from my hiding place and silently crept forward. The Hunters were too busy laughing and joking and drinking to feel my presence.

Well, everyone but Penny. Unlike the rest of the team, she didn't have a beer in her hand. She would glance in my direction, frown, and look away. Then glance at me again. Every time she turned her head, I'd freeze, my heart in my throat.

Finally, I reached the edge of the hole and looked down. The System must have known I was near the crystal when my heel hit the tree that was on top of it; that was probably why the message popped up right then. Luckily, it also saved me from getting cut in half by Penny.

It was time to destroy this thing, but now that I was here, I felt torn. The crystal was bad—it was going to help a parasite destroy my planet. But it was also going to be used to power two hospitals and save people's lives. My own mother was in one of those hospitals in Garden City.

I let out a silent breath and focused on the energy crystal.

Was there really a choice?

That was an easy answer. Still, it was so big, how would I destroy it?

I gripped my kindjal and dropped to one knee beside the hole. I glanced up to make sure no one detected me, then I looked right at Blake.

A sneer curled my lips as I lifted my hand and flipped him off. For a second, I wished that he could see me, but it was too risky.

Instead, I raised my kindjal and thrust down.

CHAPTER 51

The tip of the kindjal hit the energy crystal with a *chink* and sank a quarter of an inch into the stone.

Every Hunter froze and looked toward me.

Web-like cracks spread from my kindjal out across the crystal.

The bottle fell from Blake's hand. "What—?"

A blinding flash pulsed from the cracks. I winced, even though my eyes didn't hurt at all from the light. The Hunters around me were a different story, however; they covered their eyes, gasping in shock. But the light sent my heart racing. What if the magic emanating from the crystal caused Blake's team to change into monsters?

A second pulse of blinding light issued forth, but this time, it didn't bring just light but also a power strong enough to vibrate through my immobile body. The force rippled through me, then hit all that surrounded me, knocking damaged trees over. The shock wave threw Hunters off their feet, causing them to skid across the ground, groaning and gasping as they went.

With the sound of glass breaking, the cracks in the crystal continued to spread, releasing another shock wave. It washed over me, filling my body with power and flinging my hair back from my face. The kindjal sank into the crystal all the way up to the hilt. My body was frozen in place, holding the weapon inside the blinding light radiating from the energy crystal.

This power, this force field which stunned us all and held me in place, suddenly reversed directions. It retracted, shot back toward me, and circled the blade of my kindjal before vanishing. The crystal etched in the steel of my blade started to glow just as brightly as the power it absorbed.

I gasped. The power from the energy crystal had just merged with my blade?

The crystal in the blade grew brighter. It was bright enough that my eyes should burn, but there was no discomfort as I stared at it. In fact, I couldn't seem to look away. Slowly, my kindjal started to change. The crystal part began to expand, overtaking the metal, then in a flash, the blade transformed. What had once been three-quarters steel and a quarter crystal was now equally half steel and half crystal.

My kindjal finished its transformation, and the energy crystal I crouched over exploded into tiny little lights, just like when I'd destroy a monster's crystal. The lights faded then disappeared, leaving nothing behind but a crater at my feet. I stared into the dark pit, shocked at how big the crystal had been.

Ding! [**Task: (Destroy the Feng Jungle Energy Crystal) Completed! +2000 EXP**]

Ding! [**You have Leveled Up!**]

Ding! [**You have Leveled Up!**]

Ding! [**You have Leveled Up!**]

Ding! [**Her Will has Upgraded!**]

Ding! [**Her Resistance has Upgraded!**]

[**Would you like to apply changes? Y/N?**]

Notification after notification popped open before my eyes, almost making me dizzy.

All that just from breaking one crystal? Where is another one of these?!

I focused on the last notification and lifted my hand to accept. I paused. My hand was clean. I wiggled my fingers. All the blood and grime I'd picked up since I was separated from Emma was gone, leaving my skin perfectly clear. *Curious.* I accepted the upgrade for my armor.

Instantly, everything on my body changed. My undershirt and pants altered into a dark gray under armor which felt and looked like armor, but it was as flexible as cotton. It covered me from neck to ankle to wrist. My leather breastplate was replaced by a black leather cuirass with a whimsical, airy pattern imprinted along the sides and bright silver accents in just the right places. Matching black pauldrons and arm bracers matched the set.

Around my hips hung a slanted miniskirt which tucked under my hip satchel and went halfway down my left thigh, leaving my right thigh open for the strap on the satchel. The new greaves and the boots matched the style of the cuirass. The leather was just like my last set—firm enough to stop attacks but flexible enough that I could do a backflip in it.

I grinned. If I could handpick fantasy armor for myself, it would look just like this.

A horrified yell broke through my glee.

"Where'd it go?" Blake staggered to his feet, rubbing his watering eyes.

I silently stepped back. It took a second before I realized my Stealth was still working and no one was looking at me. Since I just leveled up, my MP increased, giving me a little bit more time.

The group of Hunters were pushing up to their feet, unsteady and rubbing their eyes, squinting and blinking like they could barely see. They staggered toward the hole, obviously confused and disoriented.

"Where is it?!" Blake screamed and looked at Penny, his eyes swollen and bloodshot.

She ducked away from his glare, still rubbing her own watering eyes. "I don't know, boss," she said, obviously taken aback.

"Find it!" he demanded.

"Blake," Mark started, his tone more reasonable.

Blake cut him off. "I just told Wardyn that we found it. He's on his way here, right now. Do you seriously expect me to look him in the eye and tell him that the crystal he spent millions on *vanished* right under my nose?" With each word, his face turned more and more red. He glared at his team.

A cold smile spread across my face as I watched him. *Look for it all you want, you son of a bitch. You'll never find it.* I wanted to see President Price lose it on Blake, but it wouldn't be smart to stay here. This wasn't as good as throwing him to a pack of red orcs, but it would have to do for now. While the Hunters were still distracted, I turned and Feather Stepped away as fast as I could.

Behind me, Blake's screaming echoed. "I don't care what you have to do. *Find that damn crystal!*"

With a breath, I climbed into the trees. I'd spent so much time in them that climbing and leaping from branches was becoming second nature. Like a female Tarzan, jumping around, eluding detection. Blake's team wouldn't spot me up here; not with their eyes glued to the ground searching for something they'd never find.

The sound of trees cracking and snapping filled the air, and the ground vibrated. Turning, I watched as Blake's team began ripping the earth apart, looking for the crystal. I breathed a sigh of relief and kept leaping, leaving the sounds of their destruction behind me.

It was time to finally get out of here—I'd had enough of Gate Vale today. I just needed to find Emma first, but I didn't even know where I was. I didn't have a map, and even if I did, I'd been turned around so many times that I couldn't be sure what my location would be on it.

I took a deep breath and thought for a moment. Instead of running around the jungle looking for her where she might or might not be, maybe it would be better to wait for her at the transportation circle. She had to use that no matter what to leave the jungle. That way, we wouldn't miss each other by accident.

But how to get there?

On Earth, moss grew on the north side of the trees. In Gate Vale, the moss grew on trees facing the Gate, although there were some locations where it didn't grow. The transportation circle was between my location and the Gate, so if my theory proved correct, if I followed the moss, it would lead me toward the Gate, and I'd find the magic circle on the way. But if I found the edge of Feng Jungle where it met another landscape, then I just needed to walk that border until I reached the southern part of the jungle where the circle was.

My Stealth flickered and wore off. I was far enough from Blake that I technically didn't need it, but now I had to watch out for monsters. I needed the rest of my MP to Feather Step, so I couldn't use it on Stealth anymore.

I paused and looked closely at the tree I was standing on. My hand smoothed over the branch, but I couldn't find any moss. Humming with disappointment in my mind, I jumped to the next tree and looked again. There had to be some somewhere. My search continued, and my stomach started growling.

Right, I'd spent a lot of energy—and bled a lot—recently. I really needed to refuel. And now that I had a moment of quiet, I should assign the extra stat points I'd received from leveling up.

I smiled as I sat down on the branch. I still couldn't believe I'd gone up three levels in one go! It almost made this whole venture worth it. I was still a D rank, but I felt so much stronger now—and not just because of the change in armor.

Grinning, I opened my Stats menu and gasped in surprise. I now had 200 MP! Granted, it was at 20 MP right now because it was already low before I leveled up, but to think that I had that much to play with now, it was like a dream come true. I didn't have to be so careful with my MP usage anymore.

The other changes were connected to the boosts that my armor and weapon gave me. Before, my gear gave ten additional points to my Strength and Constitution. Now, they gave a twenty-point bonus.

I bit my lips to keep from whooping. After so many crappy things happening the last few days, something finally swung my way!

Pulling my sandwich from my Items Bag, I took a happy bite.

A low growling sounded behind me. All the hair stood up on my body as my gut sank to the ground. God, I hadn't even noticed that a monster had come so close to me.

I slipped off my branch and dropped to the ground. The air whooshed behind me, and something landed on the branch where I'd just been.

Glancing up from where I was crouching, I took in the monster. It looked like a white tiger, but the stripes were pale gray, and instead of a full, muscular body, it was thin and stretched, like a cheetah without such a thick torso, with two long tails swishing from its hindquarters. [**Feng Cat Lv60**] hung over its head. It turned its head and glared at me with deep blue eyes before jumping down . . . along with three other white-and-gray shadows.

My eyes widened. It wasn't alone?

My sandwich was replaced with my kindjal, which I Mirrored, then I cast Mist. The thick, moist particles spread out forty feet around me. In the mist, the monsters' coats should have made them nearly invisible, but my ability made them easier to see than ever. Unfortunately, that didn't change the fact that they were three times my level.

This was the worst place to solo in. I swear, there wasn't anything I could kill in this jungle—outside of those horrible caterpillars.

The Feng cats paused, obviously wary of the fog, but that didn't stop them from focusing on me and getting ready to attack. Hopefully, the mist would be enough to hide me completely from them in combination with Stealth—just like with the serpent earlier.

The lead Feng cat's eyes widened as it focused on something over my shoulder. It crouched low and flashed its teeth, letting out a small hiss. The other large cats behind it shifted and began to back up.

I gasped, recognizing the actions from an old friend's house cat. Were . . . they scared?

The monsters whipped around and disappeared into the forest in a flash. A second later, an overwhelming threatening pressure swept across the ground, trying to pin me in place.

The hair on the back of my neck lifted as I slowly turned around, searching the foliage. What could scare off level sixty monsters like that? At this point, what was the point of being surprised anymore? I mean, everything that could have gone wrong *had* gone wrong in the last couple days. Did that mean it was about time to up the ante?

Something shifted around a tree, and a sunbeam flashed off a metallic surface. A second later, whatever it was walked right into the fog. Even though it was in my mist and so close to me, I couldn't tell what it was. It was like there was a block on my senses that shielded it, like a black hole, moving at a steady pace right toward me.

I gripped my kindjals tighter and took a small step back, aiming to hide behind a tree.

A man finally came into view. He held his head high and seemed completely nonchalant in his blue tunic, black pants, and simple steel breastplate in this dangerous jungle. His blond brows rose high on his forehead, and his Hunter aura vanished. "I thought it was you."

Interestingly enough, for the first time, a warning wasn't posted over his head next to his red title bar. Why?

I gasped, finally able to breathe again, and lowered the kindjal to my side but didn't put it away. "Kesstel? What are you doing here? I thought the Stone Mace guild had exclusive rights to Feng Jungle?"

He smirked. "And who's going to tell me no?"

I paused. He had a point. There were very few people who could make an S do anything they didn't want to. And I had a feeling Kesstel was a little harder to control than others. Not because he was willful but because he just didn't care.

"Besides, when I felt the disturbance in the Vale, I knew you had to be around here, so I thought I'd stop by," he said in an offhanded way.

I blinked at him. "How did you know it was me?"

"There are only two people on Earth who can affect the parasite enough to make it mad. Both are standing right here." He swept his eyes around then focused on the direction I came from. The direction where the giant crystal had been. "Ah," he said slowly, as if he knew what had just happened, and started walking toward me.

My eyes narrowed as all the pain that Trace put me through came to mind. I thrust up my hand. "Stop!" I ordered.

He paused and looked at me, completely taken aback.

"You"—I pointed at him as I glared—"are not allowed within fifteen feet of me until you square things off with your girlfriend. Not only do I absolutely refuse to, I *literally* don't think I can survive getting tangled up in a lovers quarrel."

He looked at me like I was crazy. "I don't have a girlfriend."

Jynn Devhro

Rank D   **Level** 22

EXP to Next Level 874

HP 234/415   **Stat Points** 0

MP 15/191

Strength 46 (+20)   **Agility** 43

Magic 40   **Perception** 39

Constitution 41 (+20)   **Intelligence** 34

Skills	Abilities
Throw	Mist (Improved) (40 ft)
Critical Hit	Feather Step
Quick Hit	Regen (Limited)
Mirror	Stealth (Limited)

CHAPTER 52

I gaped at him. "Um, hello? Bethany Wilks; blonde, gorgeous, loaded in a couple different ways." And crazy enough to send a hitman after a girl Kesstel had talked to a handful of times.

"Ah," he said again slowly, like he finally understood what I was talking about. "She's not my girlfriend."

I snorted. Yeah, just like she didn't always show up right after I saw him every single time.

"She's the daughter of my employer," Kesstel finished. "I'm her bodyguard—for another two weeks."

" . . . What?" I blinked at him. Okay, that explained why they were always together, but it brought up another issue. "You're an S. Why . . . ?" Based on the money he could rake in from the high-leveled monsters he killed, there was no way he'd ever be short on money. Why would he need a regular job?

Kesstel took a slow step forward, then paused like he was waiting for something. I stood still, too distracted by my thoughts to care why. The first few times I talked with him, I found the apathetic glint in his blue eyes unnerving. Now, when he looked at me with his full attention, it put me on edge. Not because I felt like I was in danger but because . . . I don't know.

After a second, Kesstel closed the space between us. It wasn't until he was right in front of me that I realized he was well within the fifteen-foot perimeter I literally just announced. And I stood there and watched him do it. I shifted, slightly annoyed—at him or me, that was debatable—but didn't kick him away.

"I don't come from Earth, remember?" Kesstel held out a snack-size bag of roasted almonds. "Do you have any allergies?"

I blinked at the nuts in his hand. The sight of the food made my starving stomach cramp painfully; I'd tried to eat just a minute ago but was interrupted. My hands twitched, dying to grab the bag. Still, I glanced at him. "No allergies. You don't have to keep giving me food, you know."

The right side of his mouth kicked up in amusement. "I know." When I didn't take the bag, he slowly reached out and took my left hand.

I jumped at the feeling of his skin on mine and pulled back, but didn't break out of his gentle grip. Despite all the times we'd interacted, he hadn't tried to touch me since the first time we spoke. I waited, but I didn't get the gut-wrenching rejection to his touch I had with most people. That only put me even more on edge.

He glanced at me. "I'm not going to hurt you." His words were just as offhanded as the laughter in his eyes. Turning my hand over, he dropped the almond bag onto my palm before he let go and stepped back.

I frowned and glanced away, breathing in the smell of the roasted almonds. "I'm just not used to being touched by people." There were only a few people with good intentions who did. I tapped the butt of my kindjal on my thigh as I debated. After a second, I couldn't take the smell anymore, so I put my weapon away and opened the bag.

"What does where you're from have to do with being a bodyguard?" I popped an almond in my mouth.

Kesstel nodded. "Well, since I don't come from Earth, I don't have any of the necessary numbers to register as a Hunter. Social Security Number and whatnot." He tapped on the white Guide pearl embedded in his temple, the lump barely concealed by his hairline. "I was found pretty quickly when I came out of the Gate seven years ago. I wasn't going to tell them where I was from, and I didn't know anything about this world. The Hunter Council assumed I was one of the unregistered inhabitants from the Montana Wilds area that accidentally wandered into Eden, and that's why I was so tight-lipped. While they were trying to figure out what to do with an S-ranked Hunter who fell in their lap, Miss Wilks came into the room without knocking."

Another bag of almonds appeared in Kesstel's hand. He opened it and started to eat. "She'd just tested as a Hunter. She looked at me and announced she wanted me as a bodyguard. By then, I recognized that I needed to be registered as a Hunter if I wanted to blend in, so we struck a deal. If I worked as her bodyguard for seven years, they'd register me without the necessary paperwork and keep my information confidential." He shrugged and shook his head, frowning. "They lucked out, if you ask me.

I could have been some crazy killer, and they would have never known until it was too late."

I reached into my bag and blinked when I noticed it was empty. Did I really eat that fast? I'd been so distracted by Kesstel I didn't even notice. Frowning, I pressed out all the air and started to fold it until it was a little, one-inch square wad of plastic.

His lips twitched, and he held out his hand. It took me a second to realize he wanted my garbage. Should I really give it to him? I mean, considering our ranks, I was the grunt. Still, I reached out and placed it in his hand.

It disappeared, along with the bag he was snacking from. Then he motioned with his hand and started to walk. "Come on."

I caught up with him but stayed a half-step behind. "Where are we going?"

He glanced down at me, a slight wrinkle in his brow. His stride slowed just enough for me to catch up, then we went on, side by side. "I don't know why you're here, but I bet you used to be with a party? You aren't strong enough to be here alone yet."

I nodded. "We . . . " I paused, thinking about everything that'd happened since this morning. Where did I even start? "Ah, it's a long story. But I got separated. I was just planning to meet up with them at the transportation circle on the south side of Feng Jungle. And then you showed up."

He lifted a brow but didn't change the direction we were heading. It was a little odd, walking through the jungle with him. The nervous tension that'd plagued me from the moment I'd stepped into these woods was gone. I didn't know if it was because of the nonchalant way he strolled, but it affected and relaxed me. I almost didn't care where we were headed. I finally had the time to notice the smell of the fresh, earthy air and think of how pretty the rainbow crystals actually were. And I couldn't feel a monster's presence at all. I guess that was the benefit of being with the biggest, baddest "monster" in the area.

Kesstel reached out and lifted a low-hanging vine so I could walk under it without breaking his stride. "What did you do with the energy crystal that vanished a couple minutes ago?"

I bit my lips. "How do you know I had anything to do with it vanishing?" I asked, a little defensively. I wanted the blame to sit squarely on Blake's shoulders. If word got out that it was my doing, it would cause a lot of trouble for me.

I frowned up at Kesstel. I didn't think he would tattletale, though.

"The same reason why I knew you were in the area."

Because we were the only ones who could affect Gate Vale? I frowned, wondering how much I could actually tell him. Still, he'd just told me a lot about himself. It might sound a little far-fetched, but instinctively, I felt like Kesstel wasn't a liar. He seemed more like the kind of guy who would simply ignore you or flat-out say *no* than make up a lie.

"Okay, fine. Yes, it was me. I destroyed the crystal," I admitted. Carefully, I negotiated a bush and shifted my shoulder so I didn't bump into his arm.

He looked down at me, surprised. "Destroyed it? That should be impossible. How?"

I opened my hand, and my kindjal appeared. "I just stabbed it." I blinked up at him. "Can't you destroy crystals?"

He shook his head. "I just kill the monster and leave the crystal . . . unless I'm hunting with Miss Wilks—then she takes the crystal. I tell her to leave it there but . . . " He shrugged. "It's her world. If she wants to destroy it, that's her choice."

I scowled, but he went on before I could comment.

"Can I hold it?" Kesstel leaned over and looked at my blade. I had a feeling that he was seeing more than I did when he examined the crystal.

I paused. Was that allowed? "Um, sure?" I offered it to him.

As soon as his fingers touched it, it disappeared. I knew without checking that it went back into my Items Bag—even though I didn't put it there.

"Ah," I blinked in surprise. "I didn't . . . I mean . . . " He'd just saved my life, and now I was unintentionally playing tricks on him?

He looked just as surprised but got over it in a flash. He didn't even seem offended. "It's fine. It's not a normal blade, is it? That might be the only blade I've ever seen that can break an energy crystal."

Kesstel held out his hand, and a gorgeous bastard sword appeared in his palm. He gripped it and twisted the blade in a stream of light, showing off a fascinating pattern weld of silvery steel blended with bluish metal that sparkled in the light. "Crystals can be cut, crushed, smelted, and absorbed. But no matter their new shape, their essence stays the same, and they never lose their power. That's why any sword made with a crystal like this one or made with a monster's byproducts like other swords can't destroy a crystal. I thought nothing could— until today."

I frowned, remembering how Emma had hit the serpent several times right where its energy crystal was, and how that didn't seem to affect it at all. That must be why the monster didn't die. So, if I had stabbed it, it would have died because my kindjal held a power unlike any other blade?

Kesstel casually flicked his wrist and broke a rainbow crystal in his way into dust, sending a shimmer of colorful glitter into the air.

I looked at the pretty effect, such a sharp contrast from this morning.

"You said . . . " I piped up, then paused and glanced at him. He looked down at me, waiting, so I went on. "You said that you only have another couple of weeks of being Bethany Wilks's bodyguard. What is she going to do when you're gone? Are you going to keep being her bodyguard?" Did he like it? I bet he got a lot of perks from hanging out with a Councilman's daughter.

Still, if he was just her bodyguard, then why did she send a hitman after me? And what if Trace was one of her other bodyguards? I frowned. No, Trace hadn't been a high enough level to be a bodyguard for someone like her.

Kesstel rolled his eyes. "She'll be just fine without me. There are nine other bodyguards around her at any given time of the day. None of them are an S, but there's no reason for me to be there." He shook his head and put his sword away. "I thought I'd be like the other guards, an invisible babysitter, but no. She wanted me right next to her, like a pretty prize to flaunt around."

I laughed before I could stop myself and peeked up at him. "You are very confident in your looks, aren't you?" I teased.

"Of course I am," he said like it was a fact. "I was bred to be handsome." I blinked at him. " . . . What?"

He paused and pressed his lips together. The emotion evaporated from his face, leaving behind a cold mask. We walked in silence for a while, long enough for me to understand that he hadn't meant to say that.

Then Kesstel slowly spoke. "My world, Kathar, differed greatly from Earth and was much smaller. The closest I can describe it is that it was similar to your English Victorian era. I am the heir of the Noblé Duchy, the strongest duchy in my world." He paused. "While my parents did fall in love, feelings were the last thing that were considered when they were engaged as children. What was important were assets—and that included looks. Everything to ensure the heir would have the best benefits to successfully continue the Noblé line." He looked at me, the severe lines on his face smoothing. "And it's been proven that handsome people tend to gain the upper hand when negotiating."

I couldn't help but notice that he said *I am*, not *I used to be* the heir. I looked at the ground, frowning, and kicked aside a small pebble. Even though his world was gone, he still hadn't let it go.

I met his gaze and found him watching me intently, a slight frown creasing his lips.

What did I do to draw his focus so often like this?

CHAPTER 53

I couldn't hold Kesstel's stare and looked back down at the ground, my fist on my thigh as I tried to come up with something to say. I bit my lips and forced a smile.

"So you grew up with a silver spoon, huh? I wouldn't know what that's like." Out of the corner of my eye, something white caught my attention. "Damn, there's another one of those things." I halted. Another caterpillar tunnel was spun between a cluster of trees.

Scowling, I walked over to it.

Kesstel trailed behind. "What is that?"

I blinked at him, surprised. "I thought you knew everything."

He looked at me, his lips thinned slightly. He leaned his weight on his right hip and crossed his arms, waiting.

It was petty, but I felt a little happy that I knew something he didn't. "There are these little caterpillars in these tunnels that turn people into monsters. I've seen it happen twice now." I pulled my kindjal out and poked at the thick, white webbing. No matter how much I tried, I couldn't feel any monsters. "Do you feel their presence?" I asked Kesstel. His Perception stats should be a hell of a lot better than mine. "They aren't strong, like E rank. At least they were the last time I encountered them."

He shook his head. "Weaker monsters tend to flee before I get too close."

I sighed in defeat. Well, that explained why we were able to walk so leisurely through this jungle that kept trying to kill me. "I'm starting to think that I'm not meant to show these caterpillars to anyone." I looked up at Kesstel. "I just thought that if I could capture one and show it to someone or have someone else see a Hunter change into a monster, then I could convince the Council that the energy crystals are dangerous." I huffed out a breath in frustration.

He looked at the webs. "I already told them, seven years ago. It's hard to convince someone that their way of living is wrong when so much seems to be going right for them."

He reached out and touched the tunnel. When I'd been caught in the webbing earlier, it clung to me as if it were holding on and was reluctant to let go. But right now, it was like a limp string in Kesstel's hands; not sticky at all. In fact, it was almost like it resisted his touch.

Was it broken? I reached out and touched it. In the hot jungle, the white strands were cold and damp against my fingers. Just like before, it clung to me, pulling taut when I tried to pull my hand back. "Ugh." I hated the feeling.

Kesstel let go of the bit he was playing with and grabbed my fingers where the webbing was stuck. The strands instantly released me, and the web vibrated as it snapped back into position.

I glared at it. "How much did you tell the Council? When you were trying to convince them, I mean?" I asked, continuing the conversation while I walked toward the opening of the tunnel. It was the first time I could look at it without having to worry about my own safety. I might as well take advantage of what I could.

He shrugged and fell into step with me. "What I could. How the energy crystals were dangerous and would lead to the destruction of this world. They decided that I was full of conspiracy theories from the Montana Wilds region and cut me off before I could explain about the parasite. Then Miss Wilks came in and derailed everything." He stopped when we reached the front of the tunnel and looked inside. "Of course, I didn't tell them where I was from. That's something they don't need to ever know."

"But a blood sample might be useful in proving that you aren't from Earth," I suggested. "Just one vial and everything would come to light. And then maybe they'd take your warning more seriously."

"No." His flat tone was final. "It would only bring up more problems."

I glanced at him, taken aback by how strongly he felt about it. He didn't seem to care about many things. "Okay, if you say so." I stepped into the tunnel.

Kesstel grabbed my arm and pulled me back, his grip like a gentle steel clamp. "Don't go in there if you know this thing could turn you into a monster."

I blinked and looked up into his face. It was so odd, working with people who actually cared what happened to me. First Emma—and sorta her team—and now Kesstel. It was . . . uncomfortable.

It was also temporary.

I tugged my arm out of his hand. "It's okay. I'm immune." A surprising perk of being the System's gofer. I paused. "But I don't want you to go in, either. If you turn into a monster, that would be bad. Like, end-of-the-world bad."

He looked at me, his expression unreadable. Then his lips wobbled. A second later, he chuckled. His chuckle turned into full-blown, bending-over-and-holding-his-stomach laughter.

I stared at him. *Jeez*, I didn't think I was *that* funny.

Leaving him still chuckling, I walked into the tunnel. My System warned me of the anomaly I was immune to as I peered into the webbing. If only I had a microscope. Kesstel said he scared away weaker monsters, but I still hoped that the caterpillars were here. The problem was, they weren't attracted to me, and I'd never been able to sense them until they were on a person.

As soon as I stepped inside, Kesstel stopped laughing and focused on me, watching as I moved through the tunnel. "Even if you found one of these caterpillars, I doubt it would do anything. The parasite can control when and how people change into monsters. If there are too many witnesses around, the change won't happen no matter how much you try to force it. The parasite also makes sure there are no witnesses left living after the change happens."

I glared at him. "You don't have to be so pessimistic." I had plenty of that all by myself. "And I thought you didn't know about these tunnels?"

He shrugged and countered with, "Realistic. And I might not know about the tunnels, but I know enough about how the parasite works." He paused and tilted his head back, as if he was listening to something. "It sounds like the Stone Mace guild is pulling out of here, since the crystal is gone. Do you want to go back now or wait?"

I frowned at him, confused. "How do you know that?" Then again, I had a feeling he didn't miss much when it came to his surroundings.

"I can feel the presence of all the Hunters moving toward the south side of the jungle. That's where you said the transportation circle was, correct? You were going to meet your party there." He walked into the tunnel. "I'll help you find a caterpillar. Who knows how long it will take for you to find one alone."

"Wait!" I gasped, rushing to push him out. Like, for reals, he was the *last* person I wanted turned into a monster.

The moment he stepped inside, the white webbing began to smoke.

I stumbled and skidded to a stop beside him, gaping at the evaporating tunnel. "No! No! Stop!" I gasped. "Why is it *disappearing*?"

Ten seconds later, it was all gone, as if the monster tunnel had never been there to begin with.

I sighed and dropped my face into my hands. "Dammit . . . " With another sigh, I spread my fingers enough to peek at Kesstel. Was he just too strong for the tunnel to handle? Just like how the webbing wouldn't stick to him, the tunnel couldn't handle his aura?

Kesstel looked around where the tunnel used to be, his stance vigilant. "Was that normal?"

Moaning internally, I dropped my hands to my side. "Kind of."

I guess it was better than Kesstel turning into a monster. I shuddered just thinking about the horror he'd turn into. I had a feeling it wouldn't be a measly moth. No, it would be scarier. Like Godzilla scary or something.

He looked down at me and tipped his head to the side. "Let's get you back to your party, then."

There really was nothing else to do, so I fell into step with him.

For the most part, our walk through the jungle was quiet—mostly because of me. We had some light conversation, but most of my thoughts were on everything that'd happened today.

Several times, I glanced at Kesstel, wanting to ask if he knew Bethany Wilks had sent a hitman after me. But I kept stopping after the first word, leaving Kesstel completely confused. I had a feeling he really had nothing to do with it. And since his job as her bodyguard was ending in a couple weeks, I really shouldn't pull him into whatever this hitman mess was. As soon as Kesstel left, Bethany Wilks would leave me alone. Hopefully.

Mentally, I crossed my fingers.

Especially since there was nothing going on between me and Kesstel to begin with.

After settling that matter in my mind, I started to think about how I was going to show the Hunter's Council the monster tunnels. From what I understood, they appeared randomly and disappeared very quickly. It wasn't like I could get the Council to run around Gate Vale with me until we found one. It was even more surprising that Kesstel had never seen one before. And since his aura had made it collapse, did that mean it would react the same way to all high-ranked Hunters? Never mind the information that Kesstel had shared about how the parasitic planet could choose when and if someone actually transformed. I was sure it was the same for where the tunnels appeared.

My mind spun in circles, trying to figure out a solution to the seemingly impossible problem.

Kesstel stopped walking.

I blinked out of my thoughts and looked up at him. "What's wrong?"

He glanced at me. "We're just about there."

Now that I wasn't lost in my thoughts, I could hear the sounds of chatter. Lots of it. "Oh, right."

Jeez, what was I doing, letting my guard drop while I was in the Gate? I knew better than that.

I peeked up at Kesstel. It was mostly because the whole time with him felt more like a laid-back hike through a fairy-tale jungle instead of a battle against Hunters and monsters. There hadn't been a single hint or peep from a monster during our entire walk.

We reached the dirt path that cut through the woods heading straight for the transportation circle on the southern end of Feng Jungle. Hunters had been as scarce as monsters while I was with Kesstel, and I discovered why when I looked ahead. Fifty feet ahead, the trail ended at a small clearing where the magic circle was. That clearing was full of Hunters from the Stone Mace guild. They were grouped together and talking in hurried, hushed voices, but so many of them were together that their sounds carried down the trail.

I glanced at Kesstel, expecting him to leave.

He surprised me by continuing down the path. When he was five feet ahead, he looked over his shoulder, his expression clearly telling me to catch up.

I hesitated for a moment. I didn't need to join the rest of the group. I was sure Emma was in there, and I wanted to let her know I was okay, but that was it. There was nothing else there for me. Still, I wasn't going to just walk away from Kesstel. He was the reason I was finally able to take a breath today, and I didn't want to be rude. I mean, there wasn't a lot I could do to repay him; I could at least be kind.

I fell into step with him and approached the crowd. As we grew nearer, they all hushed. One voice echoed above the Hunters.

" . . . we don't know where it went," President Price said from somewhere on the other side of the crowd. "But it has been confirmed that the crystal is no longer in Feng Jungle." His words were abrupt, his voice like a dull razor smashing down in frustration.

A couple Hunters noticed Kesstel and me approaching the fringe of the group. They glanced at our patchless shoulders and frowned, one puzzled, the other a little more hostile. If Kesstel let out his S aura, no one would have the guts to glare, but he was keeping it contained—for me, I bet. More and more Hunters started to notice us, and slowly, the crowd turned and shifted, giving me a glimpse of President Price standing next to the transportation circle. A red-faced and scowling Blake stood near him.

In the crowd, Emma shifted. Her eyes widened when she saw me, and she stepped forward to come to me, but Mason grabbed her elbow. When she looked at him in confusion, he frowned and shook his head. He muttered something and she calmed down, but she continued to look at me with big wet eyes.

I couldn't help but shift uncomfortably from the attention Kesstel and I were drawing. I'd heard that people were typically more scared of talking in front of a crowd than they were of jumping out of a plane. I'd definitely happily leap out of a plane if it meant I didn't have to be here. I hated all their looks, full of ridicule and judgment.

Kesstel didn't seem to be as fazed by it. He stood tall, his chin up and gazing back with an apathetic stare. For all they knew, he could be thinking about the weather—or thinking about wiping out the entire group with one hit.

Price's eyes landed on Kesstel and widened. "You . . . "

Blake focused on us. He saw me and gasped, his features contorting. Did he recognize me from yesterday? After all, he didn't remember me from our adventure with the red orcs.

Then Blake looked at Kesstel. Instantly, he transformed with offensive rage. "Who are you and what are you doing here?"

Kesstel's face slowly shifted to a frown as he narrowed his eyes.

Price gaped at Blake. "Shut up!"

Blake flinched but glared back and argued his case. "Ward, he's not from our guild. He shouldn't be here. He must have stolen the crystal!"

"Shut up, idiot!" Price yelled.

"Do I look like a thief?" Kesstel took a step forward, and the outer edge of Hunters stepped back.

Kesstel released the full weight of his S-ranked aura.

CHAPTER 54

Kesstel's aura spread out over the Stone Mace guild like an avalanche. Hunters below A rank dropped to their knees, grunting and gasping under Kesstel's angry oppression. Some of the weaker Hunters grabbed their heads, probably suffering from instant headaches, and gulped at air, unable to breathe. The A-ranked Hunters bent over, knees trembling. Horror spread across the faces of everyone as they realized that an S god stood before them, and they didn't even know.

And now he was mad.

President Price, at the head of the crowd, was hunched over. His body shook as he struggled under Kesstel's aura to stand up—he was the guild's leader, after all. "Mr. Noblé," he gasped out, sweat dripping from the helmet buckle under his chin. "It was a mistake."

Blake, at his side, was on his knees, panting with his head nearly touching the ground. He seemed to be affected more than most B-ranked Hunters.

Even though I was just a few steps behind Kesstel, I wasn't affected in the slightest by his aura. I was aware of the force ahead of me, but that was it. But I knew if I took two steps forward, I'd be on the ground, flatter than anyone else. Still, the realization didn't cause a sense of glee from where I was standing.

My eyes locked on Emma. She was crouching on the ground with the rest of her team, grabbing at the collar of her breastplate with one hand, trying to pull the metal down as she gasped for air. Her other hand gripped Mason's arm where it was half wrapped around her as he hunched over her, uselessly trying to protect her from the weight that crushed them all.

My lips parted, and a single word cracked out. "Wait." I raised my hand to touch Kesstel's arm. Inches away, I stopped and stared at his broad shoulders.

Who was I, a weak Hunter, to tell him what to do? When we were hiking through the jungle, everything was so relaxed that I kind of forgot my place. We were just two people, walking and talking. I mean, I'd always known he was super strong, but I'd never known to what extent. Seeing Kesstel's aura unleashed like this—and knowing it was probably not even his full ability—was like a wake-up slap across the face.

My fingers trembled in the air, just inches from his elbow. I knew that I didn't have any right to speak against him, but I hated seeing Emma and her team oppressed like that. I frowned while I stared at her, torn at what to do.

He glanced back at me, as if he knew my dilemma. Glancing between me and where I stared, he decreased the strength of his aura and shifted until he was half a step in front of me.

Was he shielding me?

The crowd of Hunters collapsed on the ground.

"Thank you," I whispered. Maybe it was arrogant to think that Kesstel let up because of me, but everything implied that he did. Even so, I was grateful. I'd heard stories about angry S Hunters, and none of them ended happily.

Kesstel tipped his head to the side, acknowledging my gratitude.

Resisting the urge to smile, I stepped to the side so I could see around his shoulder to where Emma and her team were.

Mason had dropped to his knees, and Emma held his shoulders steady. She whispered something to him, and he nodded slowly. Looking at the rest of her team, she checked on them as they regained their composure. Then Emma turned toward me, and our eyes locked from around Kesstel. Worry and anxiety were thick in her gaze.

"Mr. Noblé," President Price said. His back was ramrod straight, his face pale. He flicked a glance behind Kesstel, trying to get a better look at me, but Kesstel had practically cut off all visual access. "As I said, his accusation was a mistake. A lot has happened today, and tempers are high. On behalf of my guild, I want to apologize."

Kesstel hummed low. "Was it a mistake? Are you sure? If you'd like, you're welcome to check my Items Bag." His mellow voice sent shivers down the spine.

I let out a small breath, glad that he wasn't talking to me. Still, I couldn't help but think how cool Kesstel was right now. How easily he controlled everyone before him. It wasn't just his power but his very air that demanded respect. It was completely different from Blake's bullyish insistence or Price's I-am-the-Boss facade. All I could say was that Kesstel must have totally aced his lordly duke training.

I wonder if he'd teach me?

What little color remained in President Price's face drained away. "No! No." He cleared his throat and announced, "I know that Mr. Noblé is a man of honor. This was a clear *misunderstanding*." He shot a glare at Blake, who was still putty on the ground. "If there is anything I can do to clear up any hard feelings, please just ask." Just like that, Price slipped into well-connected presidential mode.

"Ho, anything, huh?" Kesstel's voice lowered as a cold smile hooked his lip.

Price's face blanched.

Kesstel turned his head and glanced at me. I looked back, confused at what he wanted. Was there something on my face?

He turned back. "I can't think of anything right now." Kesstel didn't even wait for the president to properly sigh in relief before he went on. "As for the theft of your energy crystal—good luck finding it." He dismissed the president and turned to me. "Let's go."

"Ah . . . " I paused and looked past his arm to where Emma knelt, watching me.

He glanced over his shoulder in her general direction. I didn't know if he knew exactly where I was looking, but he had to be close. He faced me again, the apathetic glaze in his eyes melting away. "So here is fine?"

It took me a second to realize he was talking about the drop-off spot. Had he really been planning on taking me all the way out of Gate Vale? Still, I had a couple more daily tasks to complete with the last remaining hours available in the Gate, and I needed to check in with Emma before she became any more traumatized. I promise it wasn't my intention to keep "dying" on her.

I looked up at him and slowly nodded. Really, I didn't need any more of the attention Kesstel naturally drew to himself and those around him. As soon as he was gone, I could just fade into the background. "Right here is fine. Thank you." There were too many people staring at me to manage a full smile, so my face ended up in an odd spasm.

He must have thought my face was funny because he softly smiled and gave a short laugh. "Okay. Till next time."

I nodded. "Goodbye."

It wasn't until he was gone that I realized I'd totally just promised to see him again. Before I could take it back, he'd already walked away, parting the crowd of Hunters like he was parting the Red Sea. Mentally, I wanted to scream and cover my face with my hands. But as soon as Kesstel left my side, every Hunter turned to stare at me. Under so many eyes, my muscles froze stiff. I had half a mind to call Kesstel back so I could hide behind him, but my pride wouldn't let me.

Kesstel walked right past President Price as if he wasn't there. When he reached the still shriveled Blake, Kesstel paused and looked down. Blake focused on the feet standing before him before looking up into Kesstel's face. I don't know what he saw, but he went white as a ghost and his knees gave out. He clunked back onto his butt, his armor rattling as he shivered and stared at Kesstel in horror.

Kesstel snorted and walked away without looking back.

He crossed the clear boundaries into the marshland southeast of Feng Jungle until his form faded from view. I blinked out of my daze when someone moved into my personal space. It took me a second to register the two thin arms wrapping around me.

Emma hugged me tight and buried her head in my shoulder, shivering. I didn't know if it was leftover nerves from Kesstel's aura or if it had to do with her thinking I was dead. Her hot tears wet my neck where her cheek brushed my skin. "Wher-where did you go?" she sobbed. "I promised that I'd protect you and just like that, you were gone! Again!"

A helpless smile pulled on my lips as I smoothed her back. "I'm sorry. I didn't mean to scare you." I shifted back enough to look at her face. "But I'm back. And I'm fine. See?" I spread my arms out wide.

She shook her head, anxiety, relief, and mock anger playing across her face. "Goodness' sake, I'm starting to think you're invincible." She huffed a laugh and stepped back, wiping at her tears. "I mean, this is the second time you've come back from the dead, right?" She took a breath and finally smiled. "I like your new armor. It looks cool, and almost a little sexy. Where'd you get it? Why didn't you wear it earlier?"

I paused. "Ah, it's . . . " *Completely new. Courtesy of screwing over your guild. But at least you weren't implicated, so that's a bonus, right?*

I was saved from answering when Mason and the rest of his team joined us. By now, the rest of the guild had made it back on their feet and were talking excitedly with each other. And most of them were still staring at me. On the other side of the crowd, President Price and Blake were having a highly animated conversation, but I couldn't hear what it was about through all the people in the way.

Mason smiled at me. "Glad to see you." The rest of the team echoed his sentiments.

Billy scowled and frowned at me. "You're not dead." Unlike when Trace said those words, there was a softer tone in Billy's voice. As if he was actually glad that I was still alive.

"Billy," Morgan gasped, whacking him on the shoulder. "You could be a little nicer, you know."

I waved a hand. "No, he's fine. It's true; I'm not dead."

"And that's a good thing," Emma piped up.

"Where's Trace?" Mason asked, looking around as if he was expecting to see that son of a bitch hiding in the bushes somewhere. "He disappeared at the same time you did, while we were killing off the other serpent. I thought you two might be together."

"Ah, he . . . " I paused, trying to figure out what to say. Should I really tell Mason that he'd brought a hitman into his group? I bet he'd hate knowing that. "We were together briefly, but then he"—*turned into a monster*—"was killed by a monster." *Actually, it was a Hunter, but sometimes, what's the difference? I mean, in the end, Trace finally became the monster he was inside.*

"Who was that guy?" Axe Guy Nick turned his head and looked in the direction Kesstel had gone. "How did you become friends with an S?"

My mind stalled. We'd interacted several times, but I didn't know that I'd call Kesstel a *friend*. Honestly, I didn't know how to classify him. Obviously not a friend—I wasn't that brave—and I couldn't even say we were on the same team, even though I got a lot of my information from him. He didn't give a damn about saving Earth, while I was trying to figure out how to do just that. But I couldn't deny that he'd helped me out more than a few times.

Ah, the appropriate answer was, *it's complicated.*

I bit my lips. "His name is Kesstel. He found me in the jungle after I was separated from Trace, and he brought me out."

Kip piped up. "God, he's gorgeous *and* powerful. Can you introduce me?"

Kesstel's story of being bred handsome popped into my mind, and I almost laughed. Then I remembered Trace and wanted to smack my forehead. I didn't think anyone else should deal with being hunted down over a guy. "I don't know him that well. And I got the impression that he's kinda a lone wolf."

As apathetic as he was, I doubted he was interested in romance. Especially when he had Bethany Wilks as an option. Not to mention, it was typically not a good thing for Hunters to have too big a gap in power with their lovers. The weaker Hunter's health would start to decline if they were together too much. Maybe a B Hunter wouldn't have that much trouble with an S, but that depended on how strong the S was. I had a feeling Kesstel was off the charts.

"Well, well." President Price came through the crowd and stopped beside me. Mason and his team naturally stepped back, making room. Price had taken off his helmet and combed his hair back from his handsome, square face. "I didn't know that a friend of Kesstel Noblé was in my guild. It's an honor. You should have said something earlier so I wouldn't have been so blindsided just now." He grinned with the air of a successful businessman, but no matter how suave his smile was, there was a cold glint in his eyes as if he was trying to figure out how to use me to his advantage already.

I frowned, not impressed at all. "I'm not in your guild. It's just a short-term contract."

He flicked a glance at my shoulder, completely devoid of his guild's patch. The smile almost slid off his face before it came back even brighter. "I see. Well, what do you think about joining the Stone Mace guild? I can assure you, you would be signed on with the highest contract and enjoy the best benefits we have to offer." His low voice was smooth as butter, making his deal sound like only a fool wouldn't accept.

CHAPTER 55

Emma and her team stiffened, obviously shocked. An offer like that was unheard of for someone with my rank. Just letting a grunt E join a guild with this level of prestige would be considered generous.

I continued to look at President Price, not letting my thoughts show. He wasn't interested in signing me; he was interested in signing an S-ranked Hunter's friend. Ss normally didn't join guilds—they didn't need to, since the government paid them a lot of money to get rid of the stronger monsters in the Gate, on top of whatever income they got from selling the monster's byproducts. But there were a couple S Hunters in guilds, like the Soul Fae guild and Frost guild, mostly because their friends were in there. And any guild with an S was automatically bumped to the top of the pyramid.

I looked into Price's face and shook my head. "No, thank you." There wasn't an ounce of negotiation in my tone.

True, a contract like that would solve all my financial needs, even without knowing the full number he was offering. But no amount of money would be worth all the trouble I'd get in exchange.

I could only imagine how ugly Price would turn when he found out that he'd offered a high contract to an E, thinking he got a cash cow, only to find out it was a pile of manure instead. I knew one hundred percent that signing me would not rope Kesstel in. Not to mention Blake was in this guild. Even with Emma to smooth it over, I refused to commit to a guild with that asshole in it. If we were in the same guild, who knew how often we'd run into each other? Since Price and Blake were obviously on good terms, and Price was interested in me, I'd probably see him more than I wanted.

Not to mention the guild requirements I'd have to fulfill while eyes watched for slipups from everywhere. It just wouldn't work with my System, which seemed determined to keep me solo.

President Price's eyes flared wide, and he froze like a statue, obviously not expecting a little E to reject his generous offer without even taking the time to think about it.

Emma and the rest of her crew gasped, just as surprised.

Price took a deep breath and found his smile again. "Miss—"

"Since the expedition is over, there are things I need to do. But it was nice to meet you, President Price." I bobbed my head at him, then smiled at Emma. "I guess this is goodbye for now." I looked at the rest of the team. "Thanks for letting me hang out with you all."

Emma blinked out of her shock and stepped forward. "I'll accompany you." She nodded a quick hello-goodbye at her guild president and followed me as I walked through the crowd.

The Hunters were still split, creating a clear pathway to the pale purple transportation circle. They all stared at me with mixed emotions, from ridicule for declining the president's generous offer to relief that a weak E wouldn't be joining their guild after all. I took a page out of Kesstel's book and walked with my chin up, as calm and steady on the outside as I didn't feel inside. Emma walked at my side and kept glancing at me, a question on her face. The rest of Emma's group caught up to us just as we reached the circle.

But my whole attention was drawn to Blake, just ten feet away.

Mark had a hold of his elbow, and he was pulling Blake up to his feet. The two men looked at me. Mark's face was uncertain and confused. There was also a strong note of recognition in his eyes; he remembered who I was—and the fact that I should be dead. Blake's features were more extreme. Anger and blame burned in his eyes as his brows knotted together, turning his handsome face almost ugly. Even though he didn't know I was involved in the energy crystal fiasco, he'd obviously credited me with the humiliation he'd just suffered under Kesstel's hand.

Blake threw Mark's hands off and stood up straight. He lifted his chin and sneered down his nose at me. "What do you think you're looking at?" he snarled.

An asshole. "Nothing," I said evenly. "I'm looking at absolutely nothing." Because he was nothing. Before he could come up with something else, I stepped into the circle. My body became weightless, and a second later, I was hurtling across the sky at a breathtaking rate toward the Gate at the middle of Gate Vale.

I landed on the other side and took a couple running steps to get rid of the momentum the magic circle had put on my body. The last time I'd come out of the circle on this side, it was with an injured crew, and there were healers waiting for us. That wasn't the case now. A couple Hunters exiting the Gate looked over at me before they disregarded me entirely and exited the Vale.

As soon as I was clear, Emma landed, followed by Mason, Billy, Morgan, Kip, and Nick. Ever the perfectly supportive team.

I couldn't help but look at them. If Blake's team had an ounce of the work ethic and diligence that these six lower-leveled Hunters had, his team would be frighteningly strong. I couldn't even think of all the things they'd be able to do. I mean, with the talent that Blake had in his team, they wouldn't even really need to rely on a giant crystal or new recruits to increase the ranking of the Stone Mace guild. I could tell that with a glance. But he was wasting their talent instead of setting them up to grow and be the best they could be. Sad, really. Didn't any of them realize Blake was holding them back?

Mentally, I shook my head. If only those Hunters were under Mason. He was too much of a goody-goody, but he was a good team leader.

Emma walked up to me. "Jynn, are you sure you don't want to join our guild? I mean, a top-tier contract is . . . amazing. Like seven-digits-a-year amazing."

I shook my head. "I'm not who Price thinks I am. I was just lucky that Kesstel was there to save me, that's all." I checked the time on my main menu then smiled at her. "But I do actually have to go. It's already 4:00 p.m., and there are things I have to do before sunset. We'll have to hang out sometime outside of the Gate." I still had to cultivate for thirty minutes and destroy five energy crystals. *Ah, I guess I only need to destroy four now.*

Mason held out his hand. "I have to say, you're a lot tougher than I thought. I can see why Emma idolizes you so much."

She blushed and looked down.

I shook his hand. "Thanks. Emma's in a good team." I nodded at all of them.

Mason let go. "We'll contact you in a couple days with your pay."

Technically, my pay was under contract, so I knew what I should be getting. But it wouldn't surprise me if I actually got less than contracted. After all, the Stone Mace guild wasn't going to be getting the huge paycheck they'd gambled for. It made me wonder how the teams were going to be paid—*if* they were going to be paid for the trouble they went through at all. The guild took a huge hit, and I was making out like a bandit. I felt bad for Emma and her team, but not for the guild as a whole.

What I felt most guilty over was the Eden and Garden City hospitals. Since that energy crystal was supposed to go to them, they were the true losers in this mess. But for Earth's sake, I'd destroy the crystal again in a heartbeat. Anything to hold off the parasite planet for a little longer until I could figure out a way to make it go away.

I waved at them and turned. "Goodbye."

"Wait!" Billy stepped forward, reaching for my arm.

I sidestepped his hand and turned to face him. "What?"

His fingers closed into a fist, and he scowled as he dropped his hand back to his side. "Is it my fault that you turned down the contract?" He rushed on before I could answer. "I know what I said this morning about joining the team, but turning down a chance like this is a dumbass move. I don't know what you mean by 'I'm not who President Price thinks I am,' but you're never going to get a deal better than this."

My lips pulled to the side, and I shook my head. "My decision had nothing to do with what you said this morning." Honestly, so much had happened since he threatened me, I'd forgotten about it until now. "I don't partner up. It's as simple as that."

Even though I knew they were a good team, I wasn't a part of them. I didn't *want* to be a part of them—I'd never get any EXP if I was.

And now that I'd made such a strong negative impression on Blake, I had a feeling that I was going to need to get stronger even faster.

With that in mind, I turned and made my way to Fogmire to cultivate.

KESSTEL

From a dark cave set in the mountains surrounding Gate Vale, a tall figure in full armor emerged. The sunlight glinting off the armor was a sharp contrast to the seemingly endless dark pit behind him. The black smoke that seeped across the bare rocky ground seemed to tremble, as if afraid of his very presence.

The figure paused, and his full armor disappeared, replaced by a simple metal breastplate, a blue tunic, and black pants. Kesstel turned his head and scowled down the tunnel behind him. Such a disappointing portal. He had half a mind to go back and collapse it still, just to vent his frustration on wasting his time.

A month ago, he would have. But now might not be the best time to start another worldwide Gate Surge.

He left the black smoke and walked down the mountainside path that sloped to the silvery jungle in front of him. Feng Jungle—or as he heard it when someone spoke the name: Phoenix Jungle. A place of transformation. Someone was feeling poetic when they were giving out names.

Kesstel turned, disinterested. In a world with so many different languages, he didn't know if it was a curse or a blessing that he could understand all of them. It was usually fine until multiple languages were used in the same sentence.

A sudden distortion rippled through the air, and he turned back, his eyes focused on the northern part of the jungle. A bright pulse of light mushroomed high into the air; it whipped at trees and shot loose leaves everywhere. A moment later, a second pulse was issued.

Kesstel's eyes widened as he felt the very air of Gate Vale tremble around him as if in anger. It wasn't as big a reaction as when a portal collapsed, but something big had happened.

Suddenly, he became aware of a small presence where the pulse had come from—and where the energy pulse was being sucked back into. He'd spent so much time learning how to pinpoint that presence, he knew who it was immediately. Kesstel sighed. He should have known if something happened in Gate Vale, it had to be related to her. That little enigma.

He vanished from where he stood, leaving nothing but a small wisp of dust in his wake.

Kesstel stopped running once he was surrounded by silvery green trees, looking around. She'd moved from her original spot, so where was she now? Somewhere close by, but where?

It was like he could feel her but not at the same time. Odd.

Suddenly, her presence seemed to appear out of nowhere, roughly a hundred feet south of him. Along with several monsters around her. Did she ever stop getting in trouble?

He turned, his long stride eating up the distance.

Thick mist seeped through the trees. So familiar. So nostalgic. He paused as a memory threatened to resurface, like a drill that dug at the thick wall he'd locked his past behind. No, he wouldn't think about it. Not right now. There was no telling what he'd do if he did. He'd already decided to let it go for now, so he would.

Jynn Devhro stood in the middle of the mist, her short sword pointed at him and glaring.

At that moment, Kesstel couldn't help but remember a stray white tabby kitten he'd found in his horse stall as an adolescent. It was so cute, how it puffed up and arched its back, hissing at him, threatening, even though he could kill it with a tiny pinch. It had glared at him with wide, pointed eyes, full of mistrust and desperation. And it followed through on its threat when he reached out to touch it, leaving four deep cuts on the back of his hand.

Unfortunately, his brother's hound dog got to the kitten before Kesstel had the chance to fully tame it. But he still remembered the first sweet time it let him touch its soft head.

This time, Kesstel wouldn't let this kitten disappear until he watched her turn into a tiger. It would be easy to simply take over and solve all her troubles—if she'd ever open up about them. But she'd never grow if he did. And he wanted to see just how strong she would get.

One day she might turn her claws on him, but for right now, he didn't regret not killing this young Warrior of Mist the moment he saw her.

ABOUT THE AUTHOR

M. L. Reid is a walking contradiction. She loves art as much as science, so her collection of random knowledge is as eclectic as all the fungi in the world. She's a Kingdom Hearts and Final Fantasy fanatic and spends too much time reading Asian webnovels. Although a peacemaker, her favorite scenes to write are fight scenes. After her kids get older, she's totally going to start a sword collection.

DISCOVER
STORIES UNBOUND

PodiumAudio.com

9 781039 430228